Ice Cream Man

VOLUME THREE

• HOPSCOTCH MÉLANGE •

WRITTEN BY **W. MAXWELL PRINCE**
ART BY **MARTÍN MORAZZO**
COLORS BY **CHRIS O'HALLORAN**
LETTERING BY **GOOD OLD NEON**
COVER DESIGN BY **SHANNA MATUSZAK**
INTERIOR DESIGN BY **GOOD OLD NEON**

IMAGE COMICS, INC.

Robert Kirkman: Chief Operating Officer
Erik Larsen: Chief Financial Officer
Todd McFarlane: President
Marc Silvestri: Chief Executive Officer
Jim Valentino: Vice President
Eric Stephenson: Publisher / Chief Creative Officer
Corey Hart: Director of Sales
Jeff Boison: Director of Publishing Planning & Book Trade Sales
Chris Ross: Director of Digital Sales
Jeff Stang: Director of Specialty Sales
Kat Salazar: Director of PR & Marketing
Drew Gill: Art Director
Heather Doornink: Production Director
Nicole Lapalme: Controller

IMAGECOMICS.COM

"If men and women began to live their ephemeral dreams, every phantom would become a person with whom to begin a story of pursuits, pretenses, misunderstandings, clashes, oppressions, and the carousel of fantasies would stop."
–**Italo Calvino,** *Invisible Cities*

Which way should we go?
Email wmaxwellprince@gmail.com

ICE CREAM MAN, VOL. 3: HOPSCOTCH MÉLANGE. First printing. June 2019. Published by Image Comics, Inc. Office of publication: 2701 NW Vaughn St., Suite 780, Portland, OR 97210. Copyright © 2019 W. Maxwell Prince, Martín Morazzo & Chris O'Halloran. All rights reserved. Contains material originally published in single magazine form as ICE CREAM MAN #9-12. "Ice Cream Man," its logos, and the likenesses of all characters herein are trademarks of W. Maxwell Prince, Martín Morazzo & Chris O'Halloran unless otherwise noted. "Image" and the Image Comics logos are registered trademarks of Image Comics, Inc. No part of this publication may be reproduced or transmitted, in any form or by any means (except for short excerpts for journalistic or review purposes), without the express written permission of W. Maxwell Prince, Martín Morazzo & Chris O'Halloran, or Image Comics, Inc. All names, characters, events, and locales in this publication are entirely fictional. Any resemblance to actual persons (living or dead), events, or places, without satiric intent, is coincidental. Printed in the USA. For information regarding the CPSIA on this printed material call: 203-595-3636. For international rights, contact: foreignlicensing@imagecomics.com. ISBN: 978-1-5343-1226-5

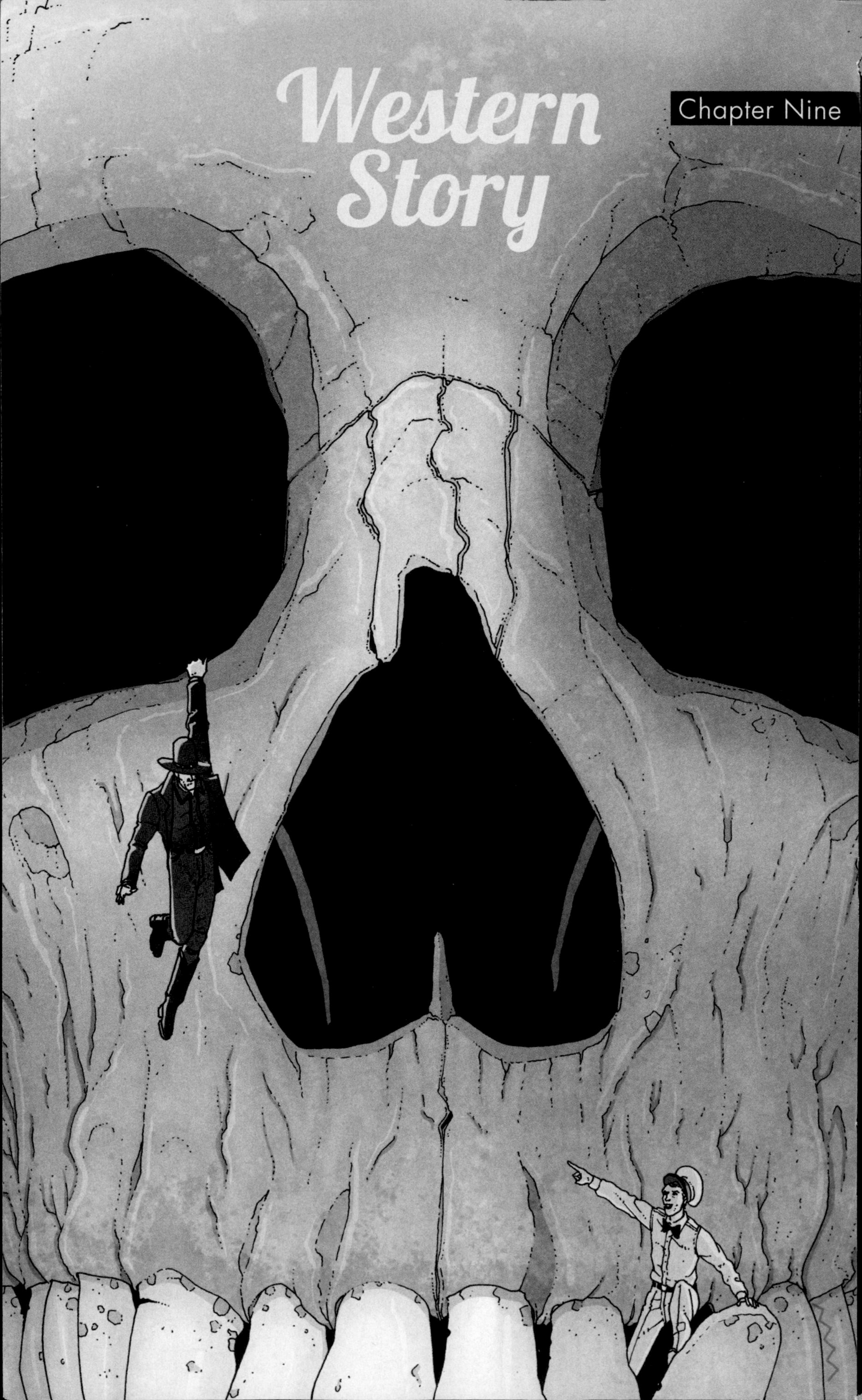
Western Story
Chapter Nine

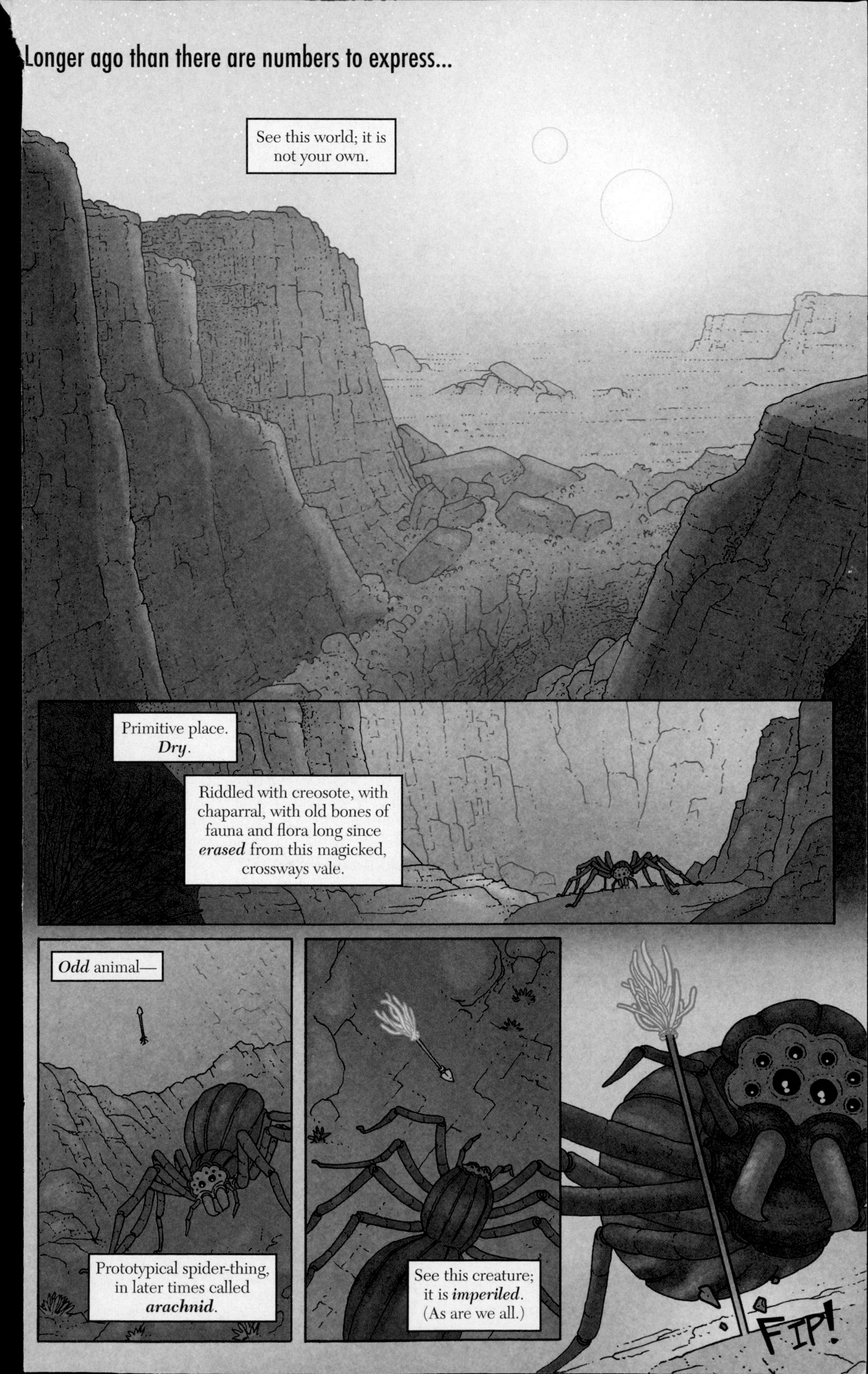
Longer ago than there are numbers to express...
See this world; it is not your own.
Primitive place. *Dry*.
Riddled with creosote, with chaparral, with old bones of fauna and flora long since *erased* from this magicked, crossways vale.
Odd animal—
Prototypical spider-thing, in later times called ***arachnid***.
See this creature; it is ***imperiled***. (As are we all.)
FIP!

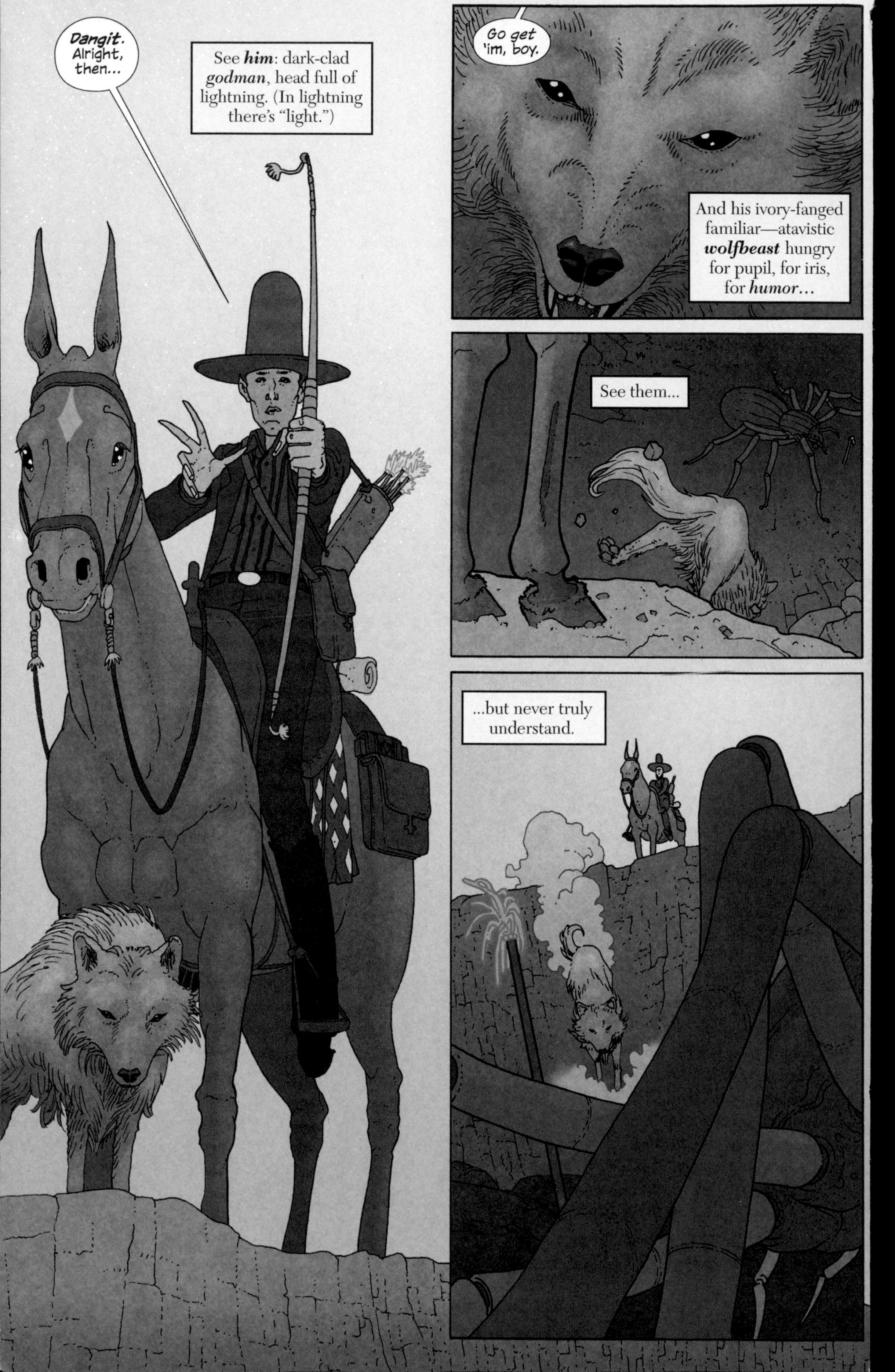
Dangit. Alright, then...
See him: dark-clad godman, head full of lightning. (In lightning there's "light.")
Go get 'im, boy.
And his ivory-fanged familiar—atavistic wolfbeast hungry for pupil, for iris, for humor...
See them...
...but never truly understand.

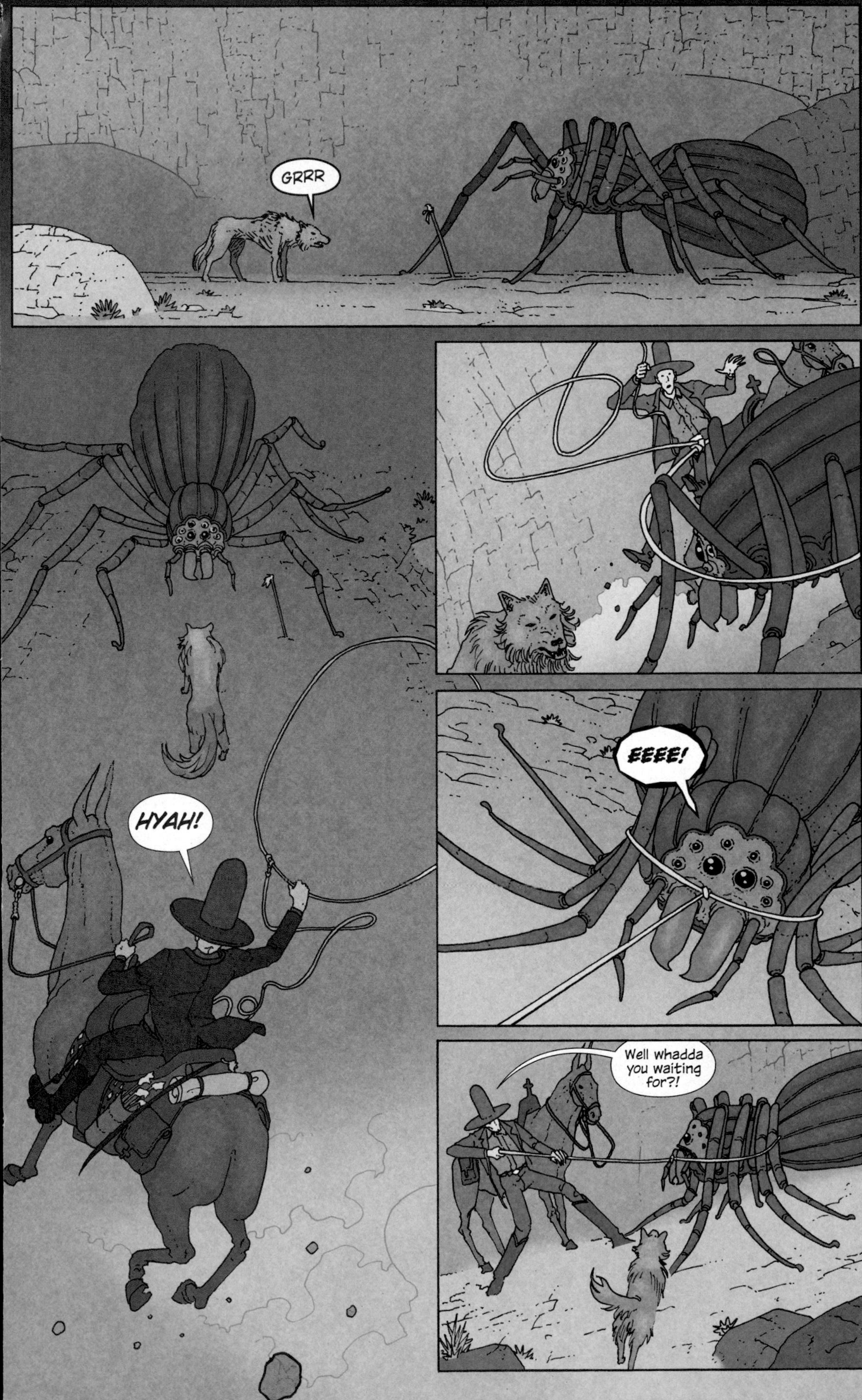
GRRR
HYAH!
EEEE!
Well whadda you waiting for?!

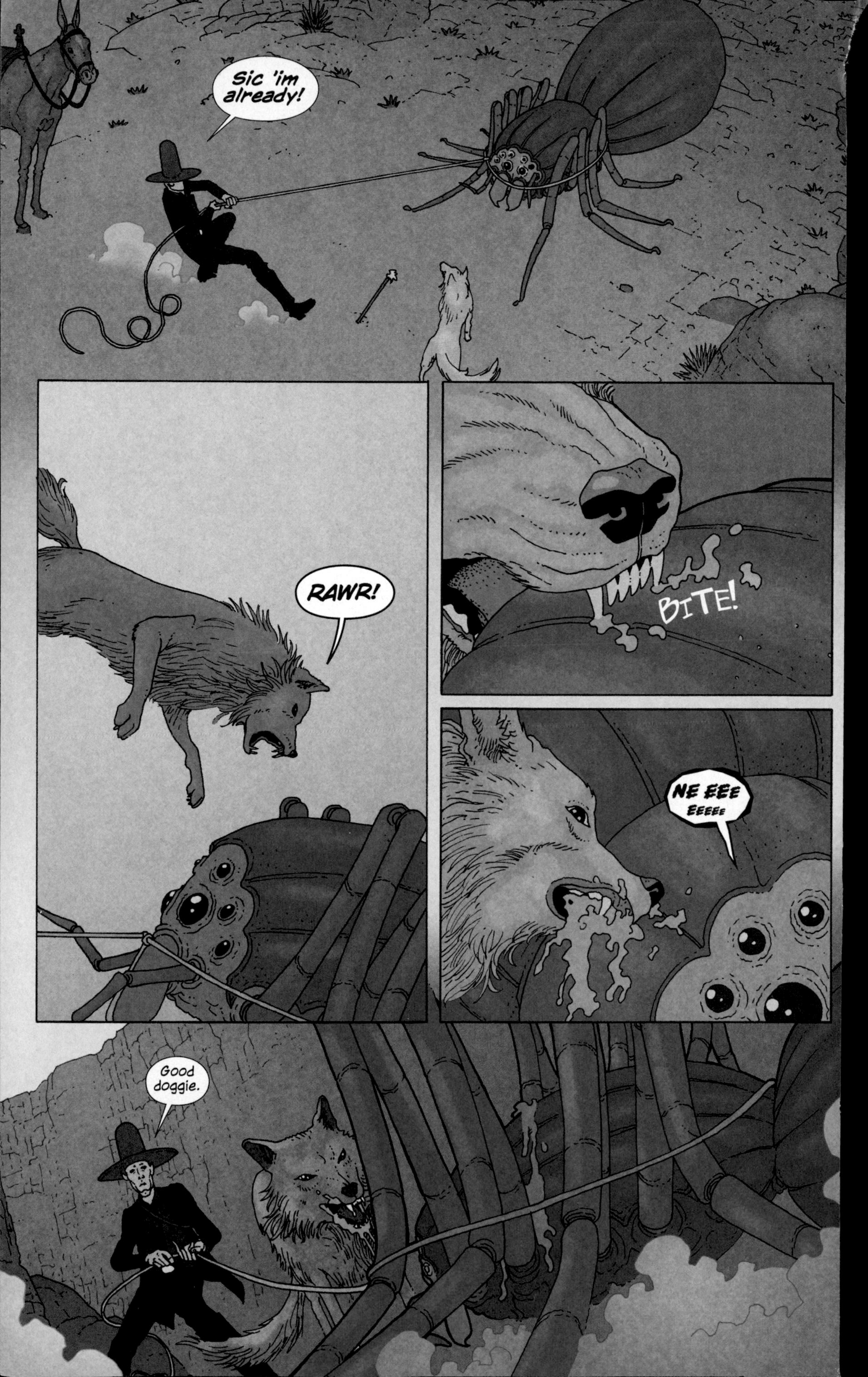
Sic 'im already!
RAWR!
BITE!
NE EEE
EEEEE
Good doggie.

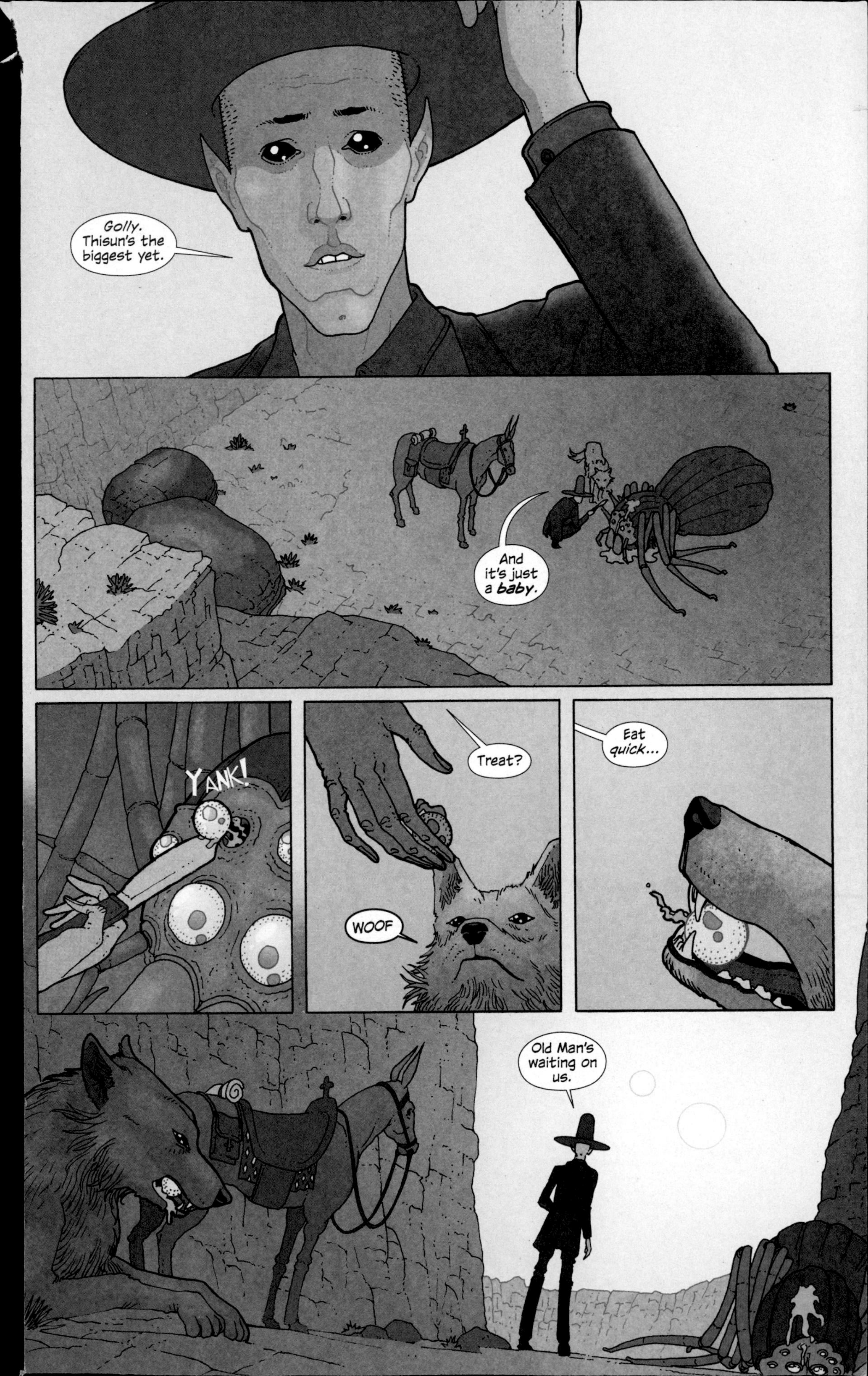
Golly. Thisun's the biggest yet.
And it's just a *baby*.
YANK!
Treat?
WOOF
Eat quick...
Old Man's waiting on us.

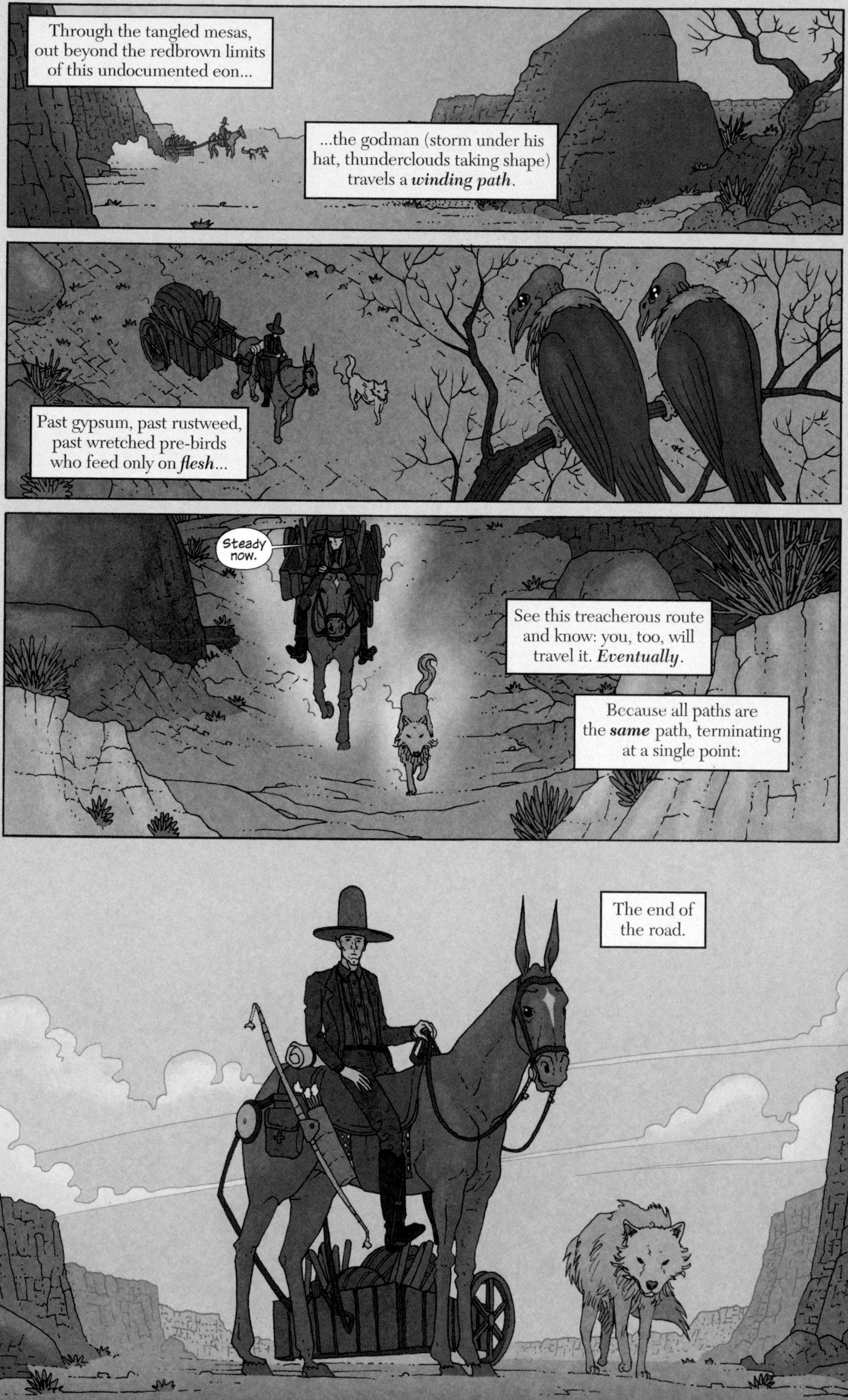

Through the tangled mesas, out beyond the redbrown limits of this undocumented eon...
...the godman (storm under his hat, thunderclouds taking shape) travels a *winding path*.
Past gypsum, past rustweed, past wretched pre-birds who feed only on *flesh*...
Steady now.
See this treacherous route and know: you, too, will travel it. *Eventually*.
Because all paths are the ***same*** path, terminating at a single point:
The end of the road.

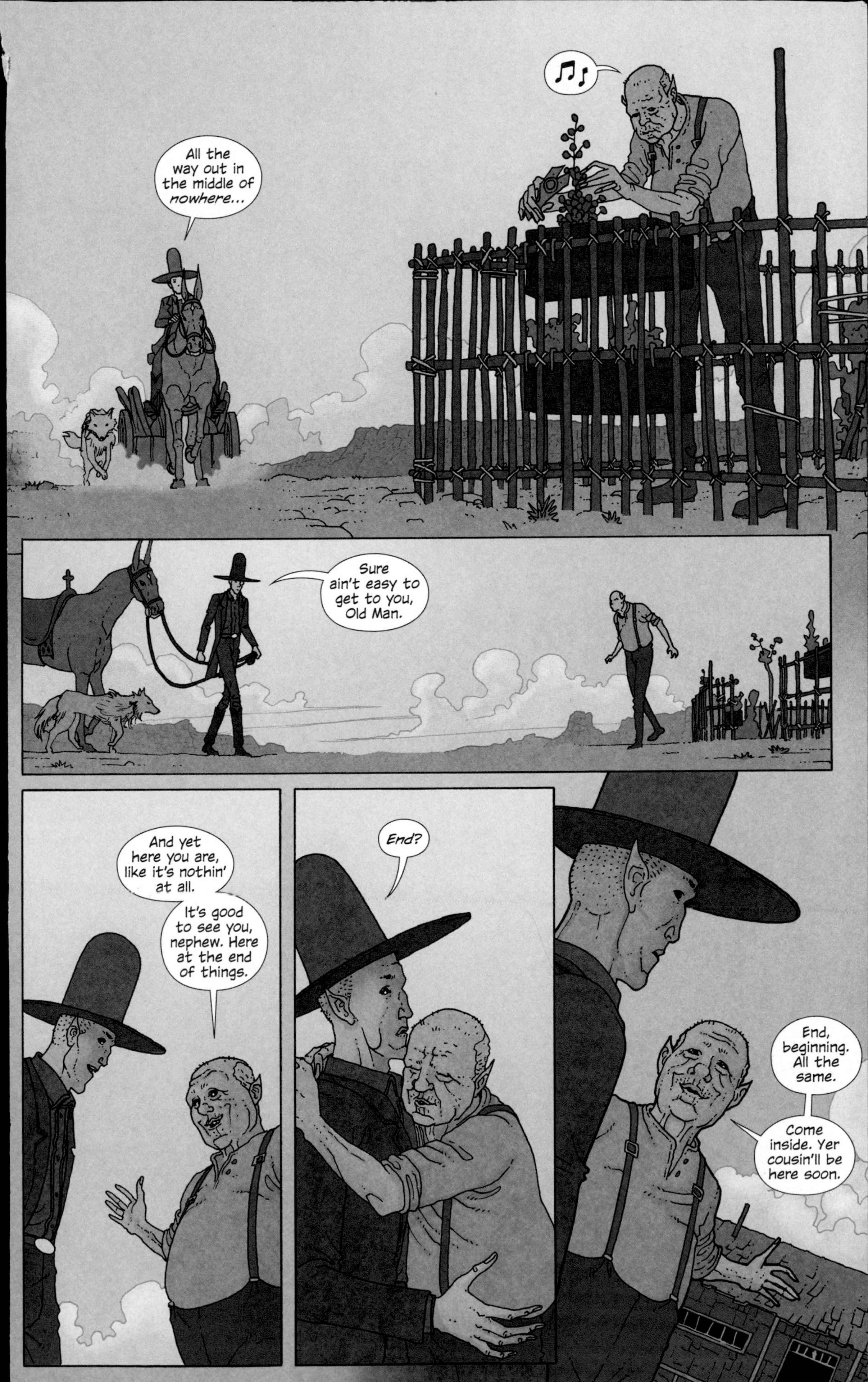
All the way out in the middle of *nowhere*...
♫♪
Sure ain't easy to get to you, Old Man.
And yet here you are, like it's nothin' at all.
It's good to see you, nephew. Here at the end of things.
End?
End, beginning. All the same.
Come inside. Yer cousin'll be here soon.

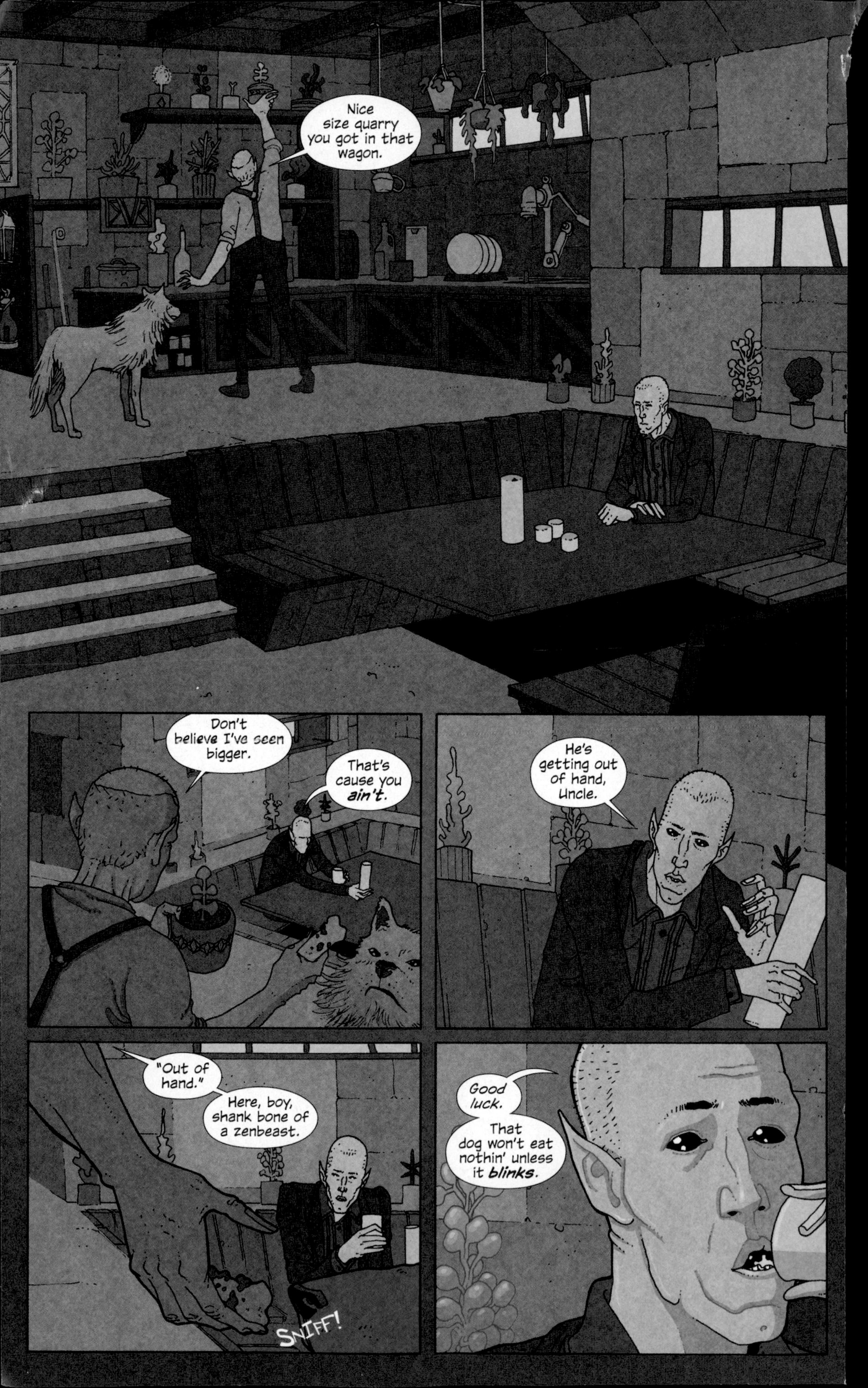
Nice size quarry you got in that wagon.
Don't believe I've seen bigger.
That's cause you *ain't*.
He's getting out of hand, Uncle.
"Out of hand."
Here, boy, shank bone of a zenbeast.
SNIFF!
Good luck.
That dog won't eat nothin' unless it *blinks*.

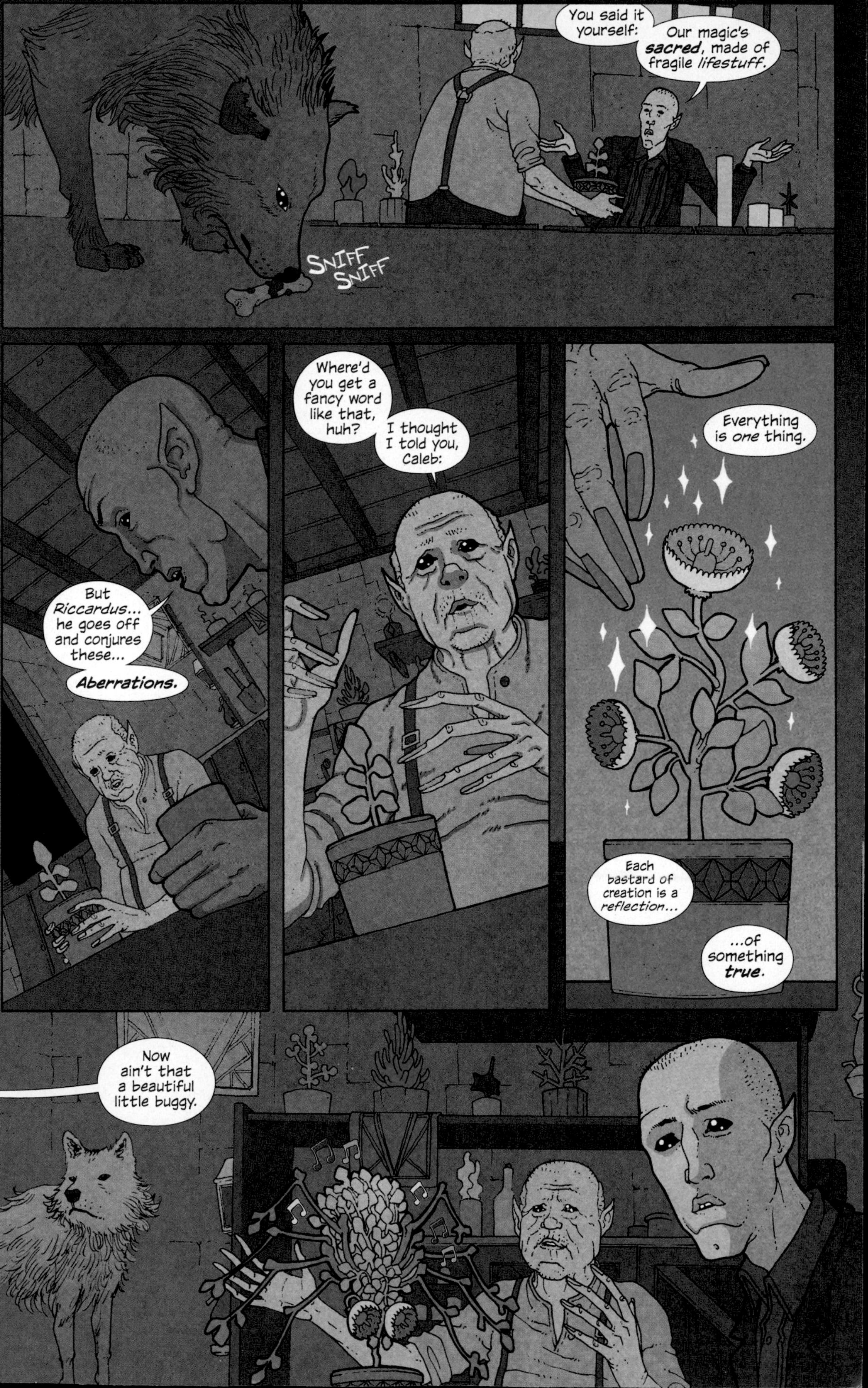
You said it yourself:
Our magic's **sacred**, made of fragile *lifestuff*.
SNIFF SNIFF
But *Riccardus*... he goes off and conjures these...
Aberrations.
Where'd you get a fancy word like that, huh?
I thought I told you, Caleb:
Everything is *one* thing.
Each bastard of creation is a *reflection*...
...of something ***true***.
Now ain't that a beautiful little buggy.

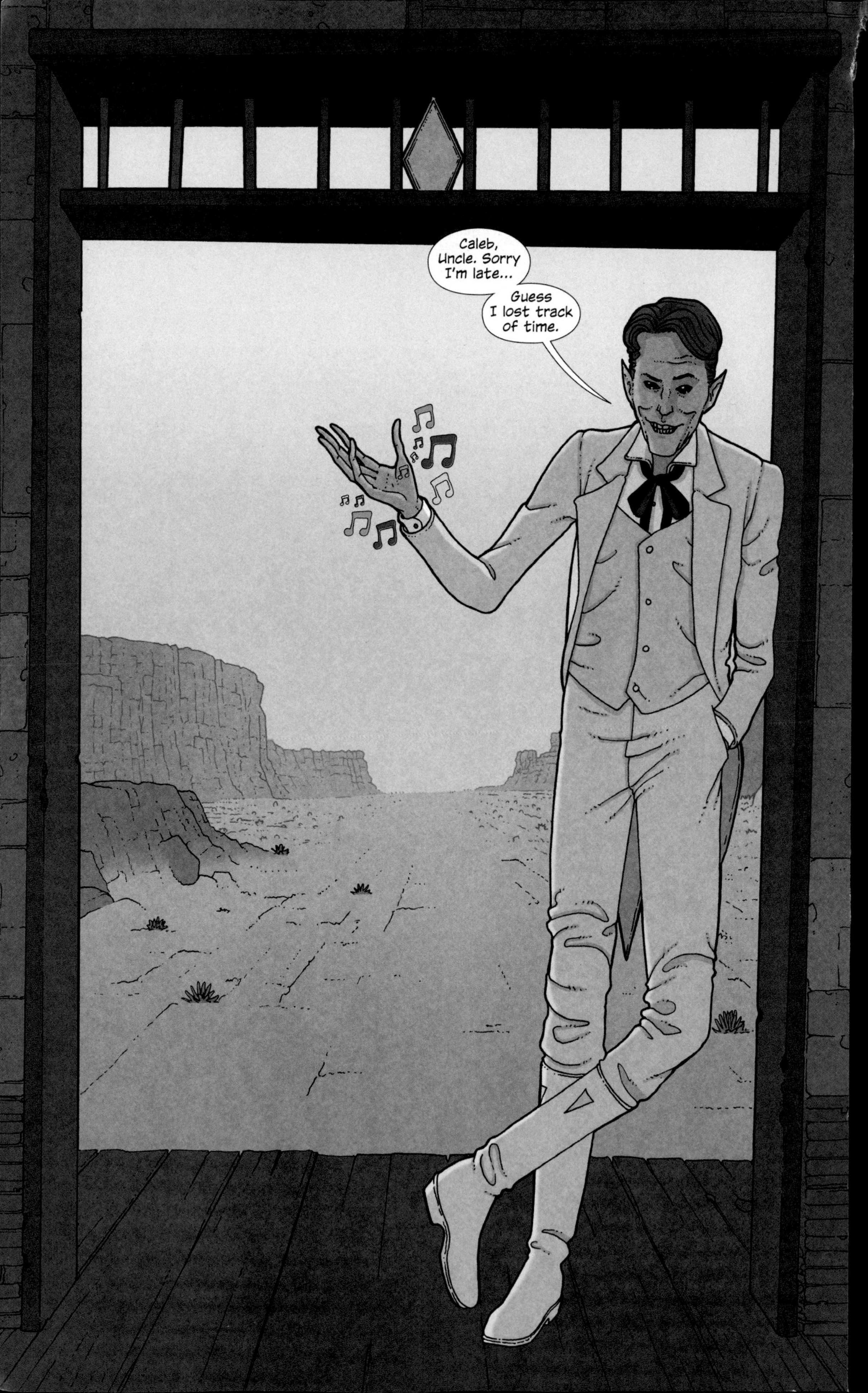

Caleb, Uncle. Sorry I'm late...
Guess I lost track of time.

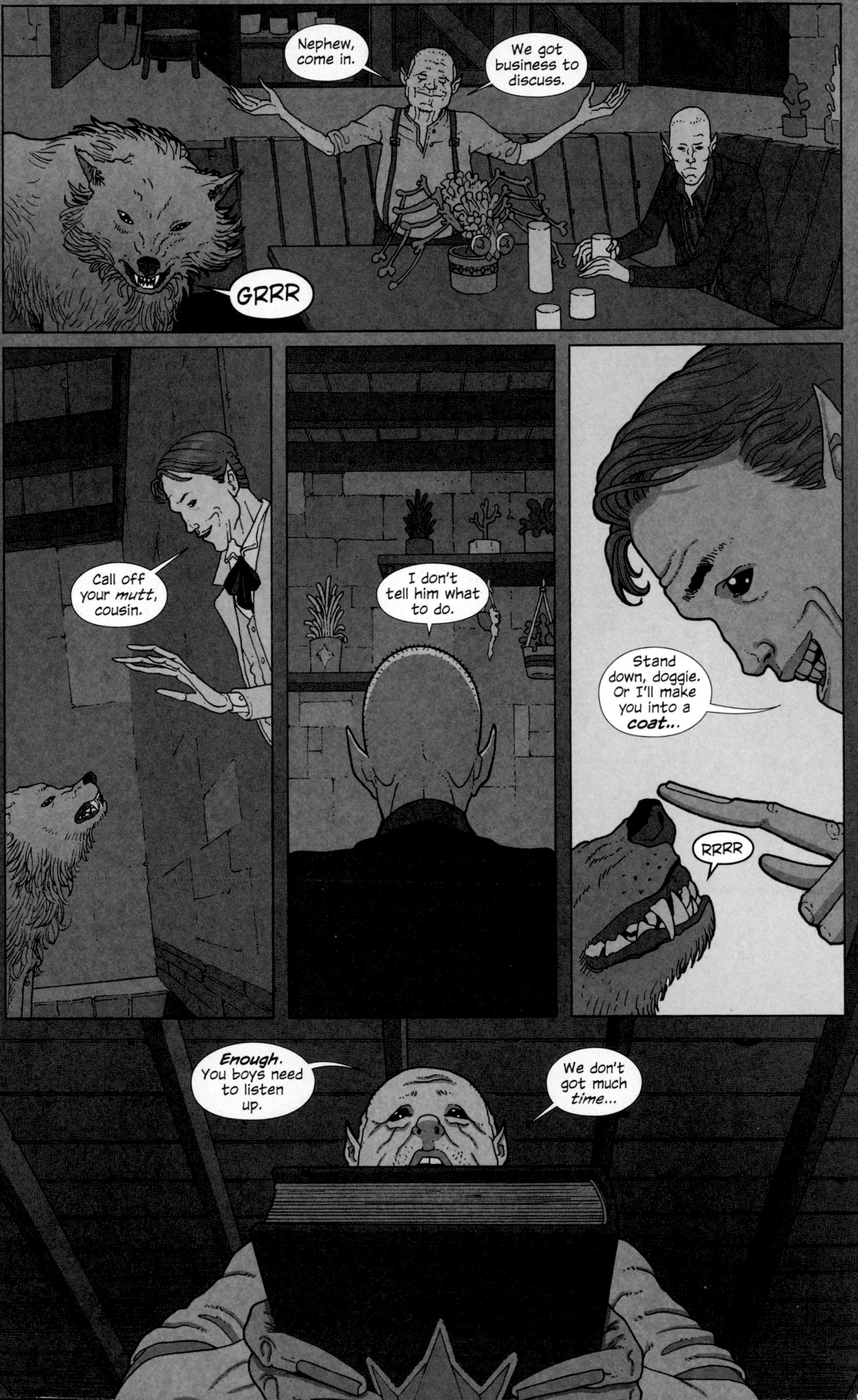
Nephew, come in.
We got business to discuss.
GRRR
Call off your *mutt*, cousin.
I don't tell him what to do.
Stand down, doggie. Or I'll make you into a *coat...*
RRRR
Enough. You boys need to listen up.
We don't got much *time...*

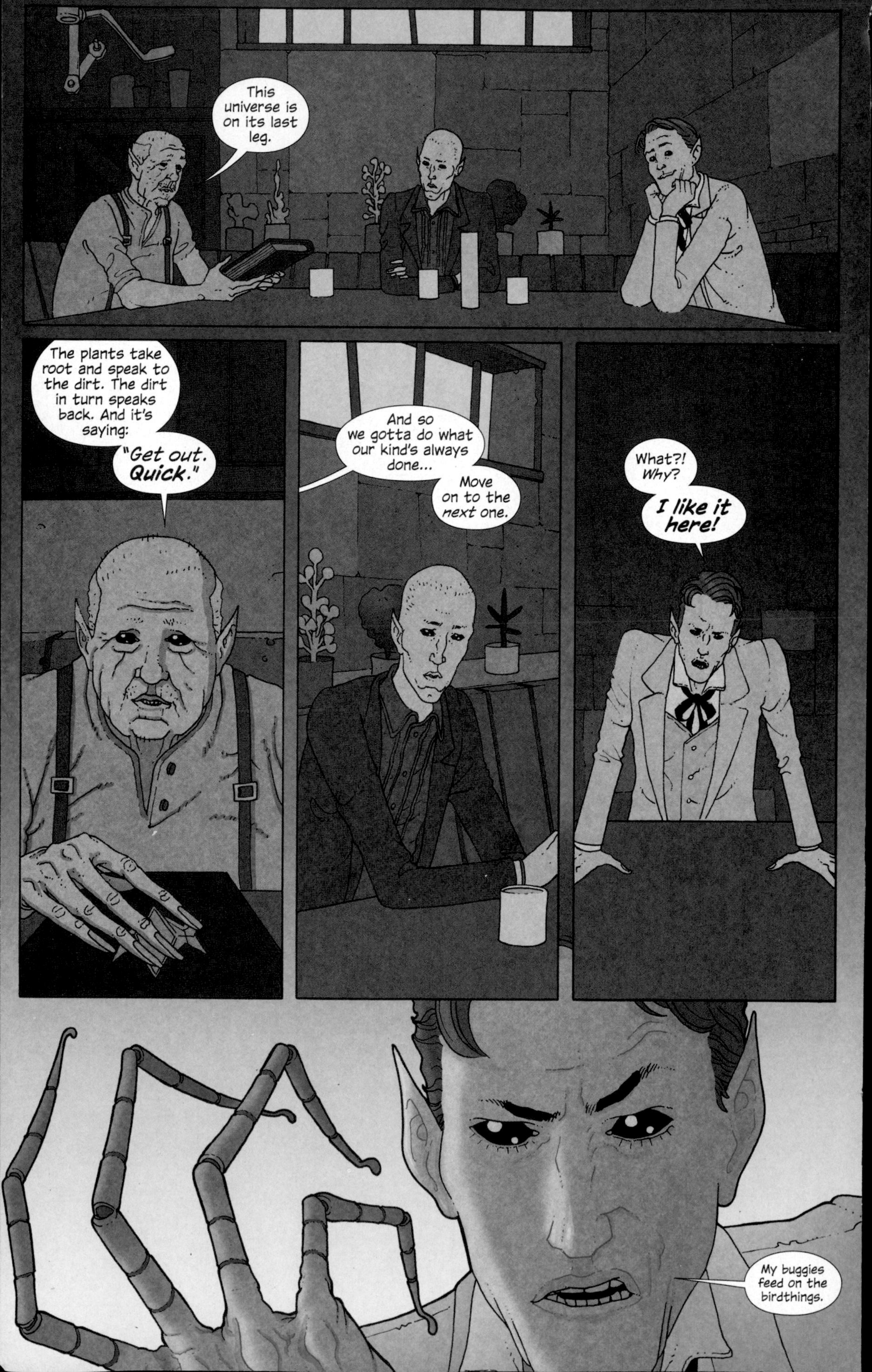
This universe is on its last leg.
The plants take root and speak to the dirt. The dirt in turn speaks back. And it's saying:
"Get out. Quick."
And so we gotta do what our kind's always done...
Move on to the next one.
What?! Why?
I like it here!
My buggies feed on the birdthings.

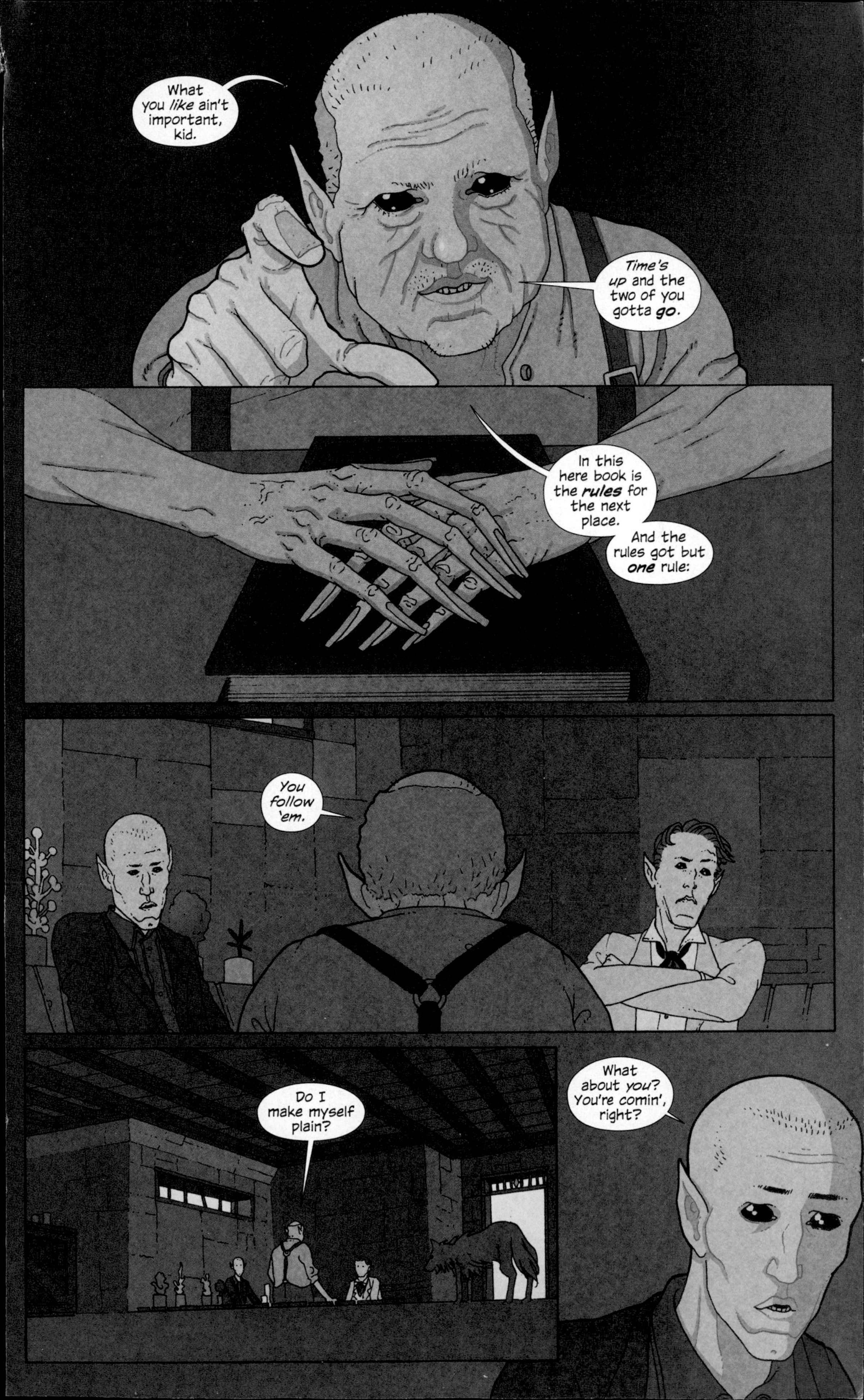
What you *like* ain't important, kid.
Time's up and the two of you gotta ***go***.
In this here book is the ***rules*** for the next place.
And the rules got but ***one*** rule:
You follow 'em.
Do I make myself plain?
What about *you*? You're comin', right?

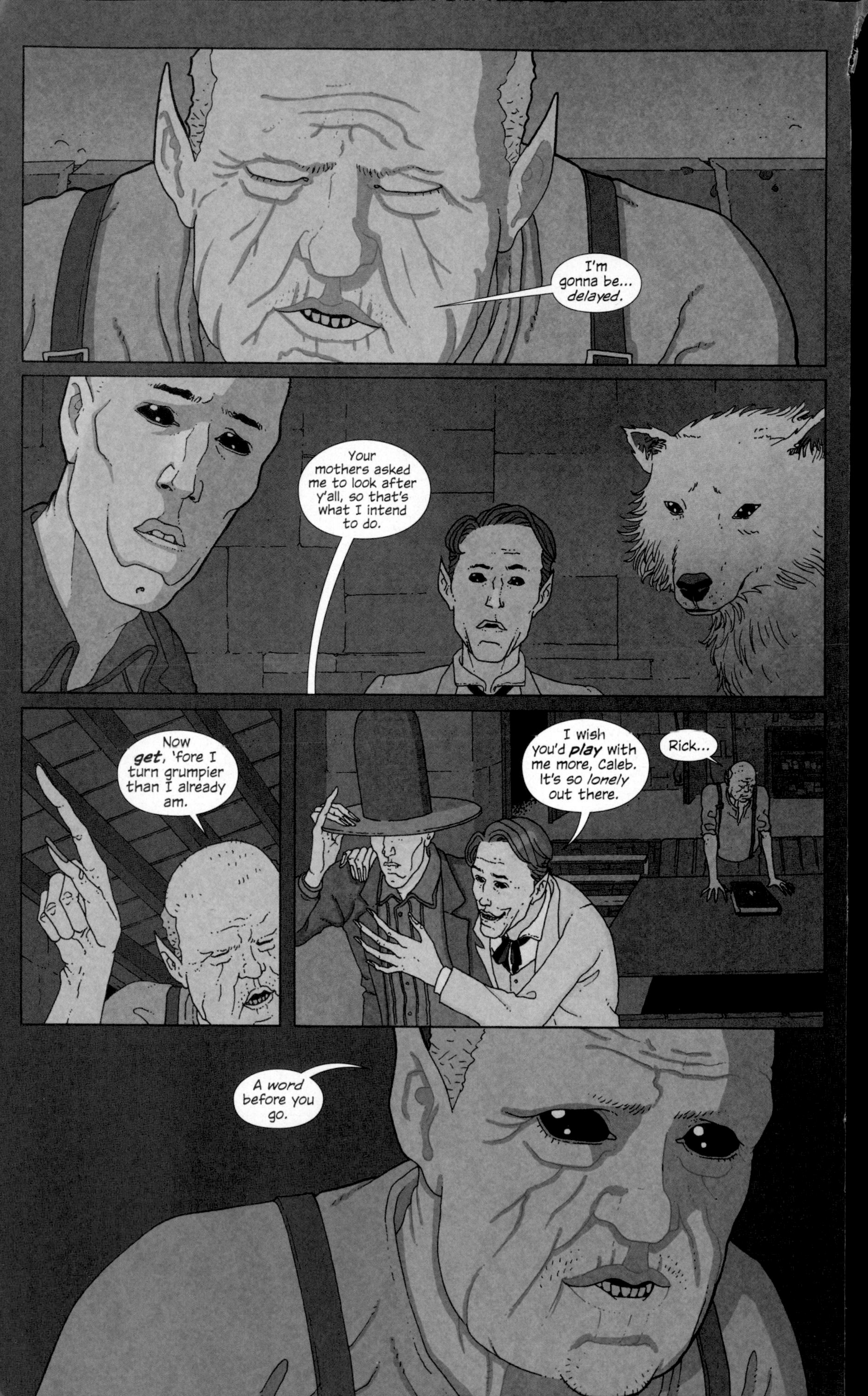
I'm gonna be... *delayed*.
Your mothers asked me to look after y'all, so that's what I intend to do.
Now **get**, 'fore I turn grumpier than I already am.
I wish you'd **play** with me more, Caleb. It's so *lonely* out there.
Rick...
A *word* before you go.

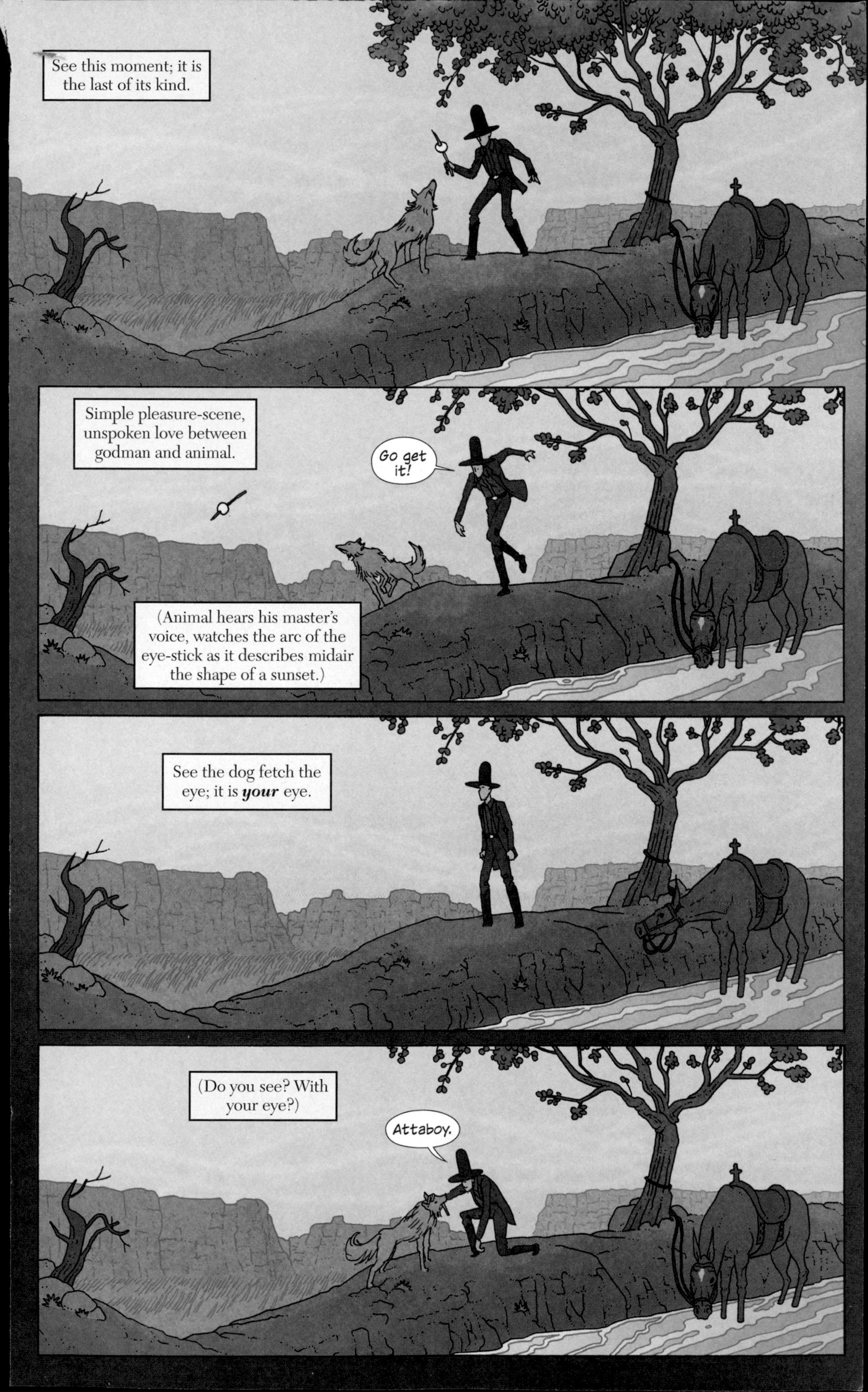
See this moment; it is the last of its kind.
Simple pleasure-scene, unspoken love between godman and animal.
Go get it!
(Animal hears his master's voice, watches the arc of the eye-stick as it describes midair the shape of a sunset.)
See the dog fetch the eye; it is ***your*** eye.
(Do you see? With your eye?)
Attaboy.

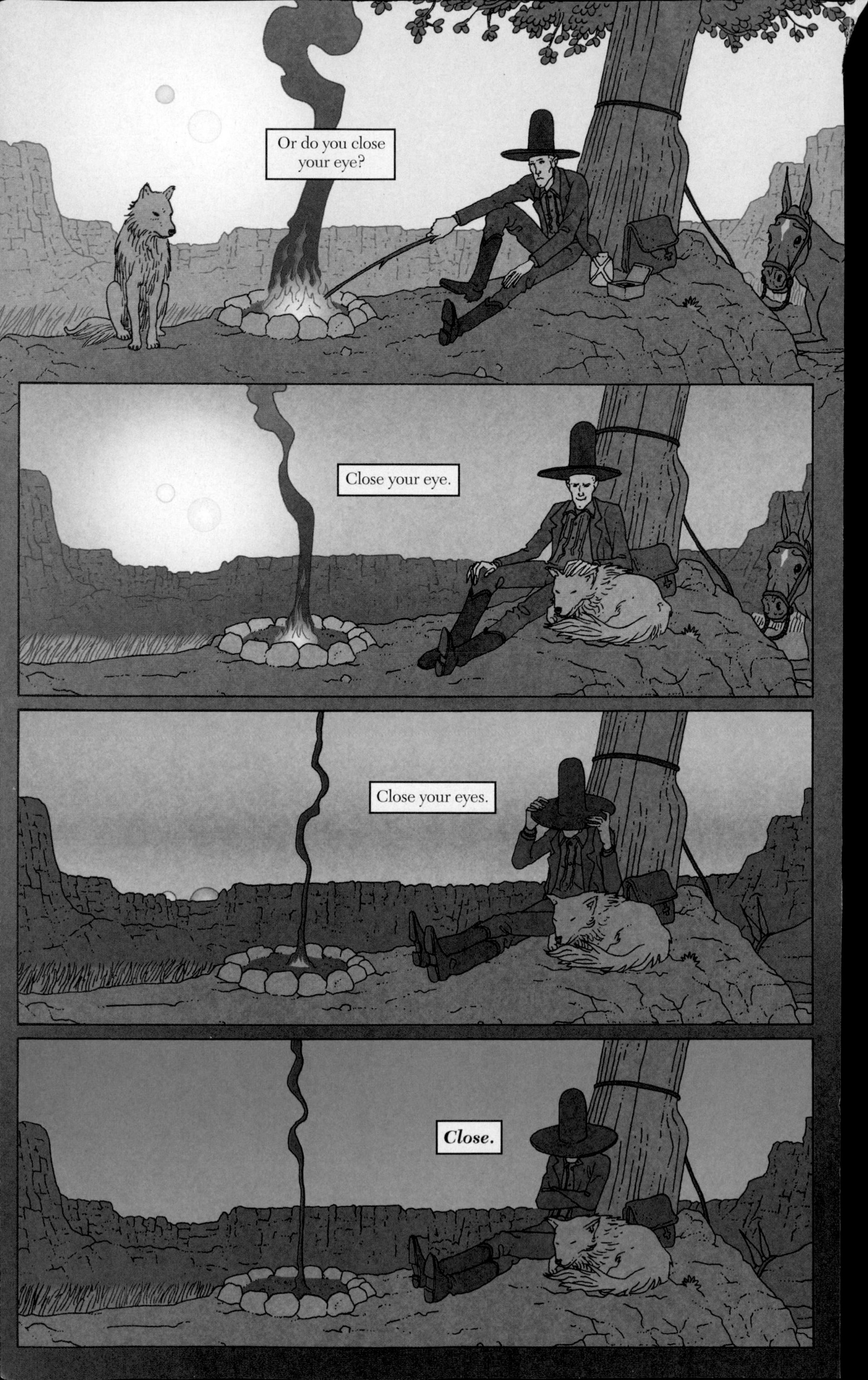
Or do you close your eye?
Close your eye.
Close your eyes.
Close.

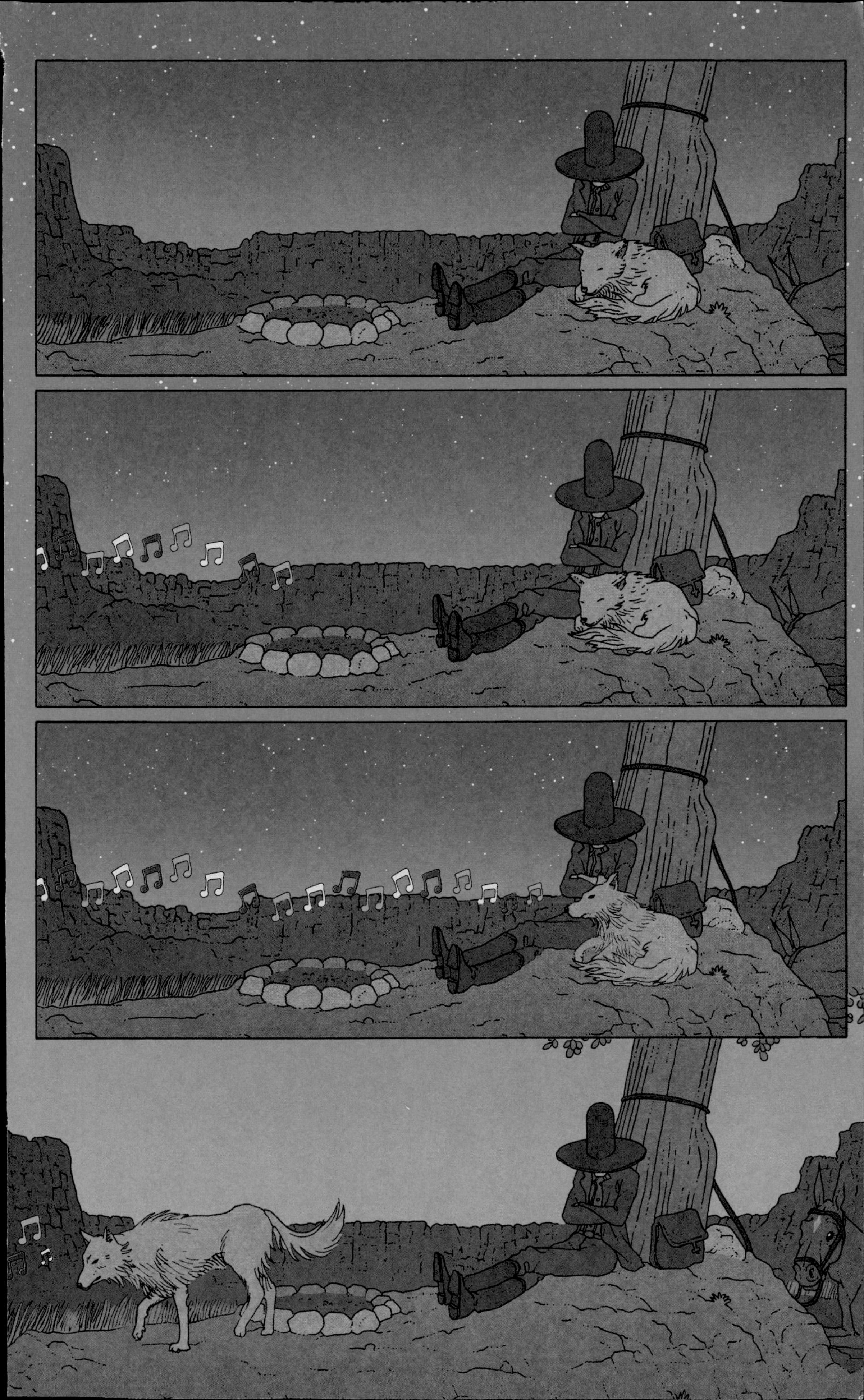

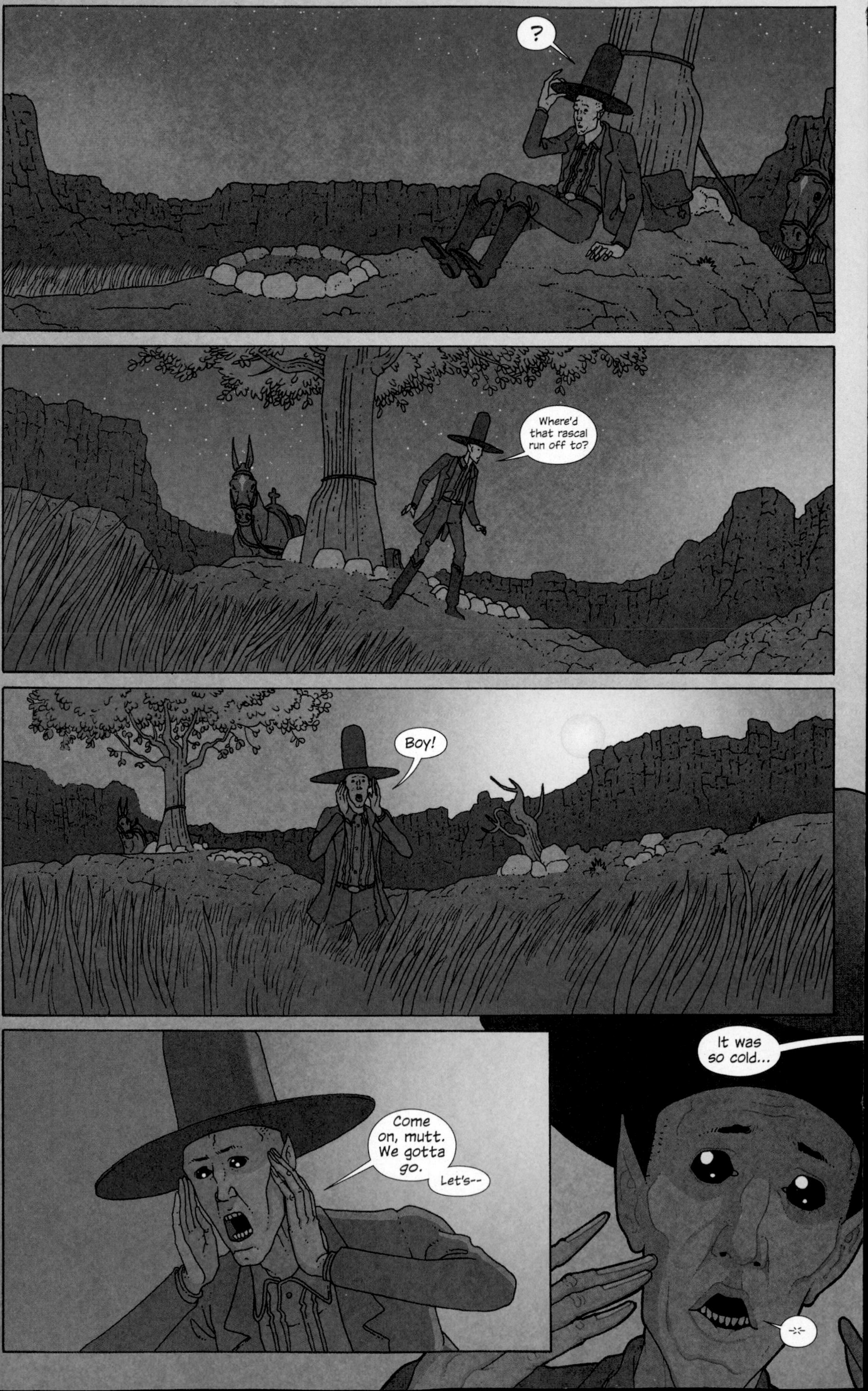
?
Where'd that rascal run off to?
Boy!
Come on, mutt. We gotta go.
Let's--
It was so cold...

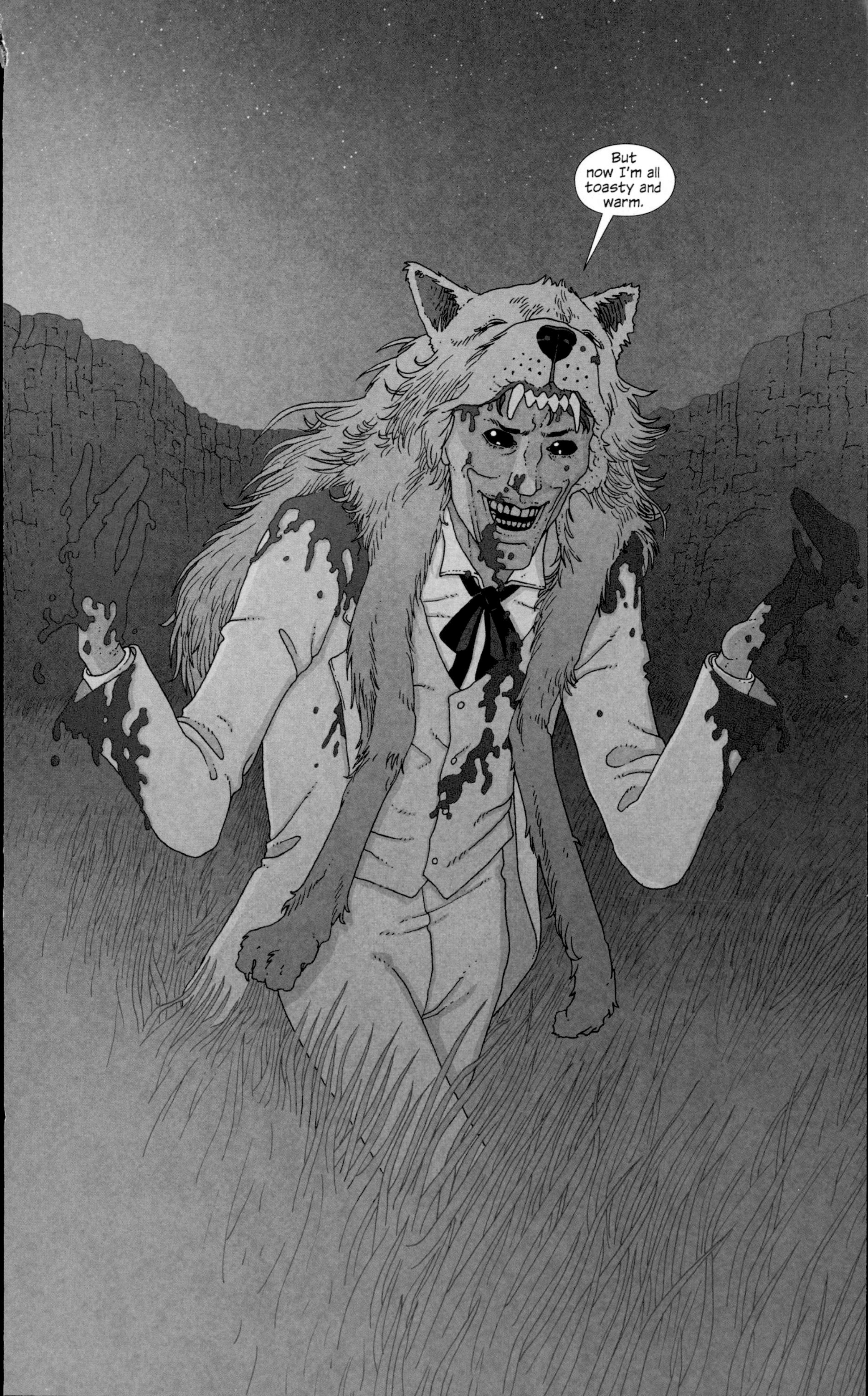
But now I'm all toasty and warm.

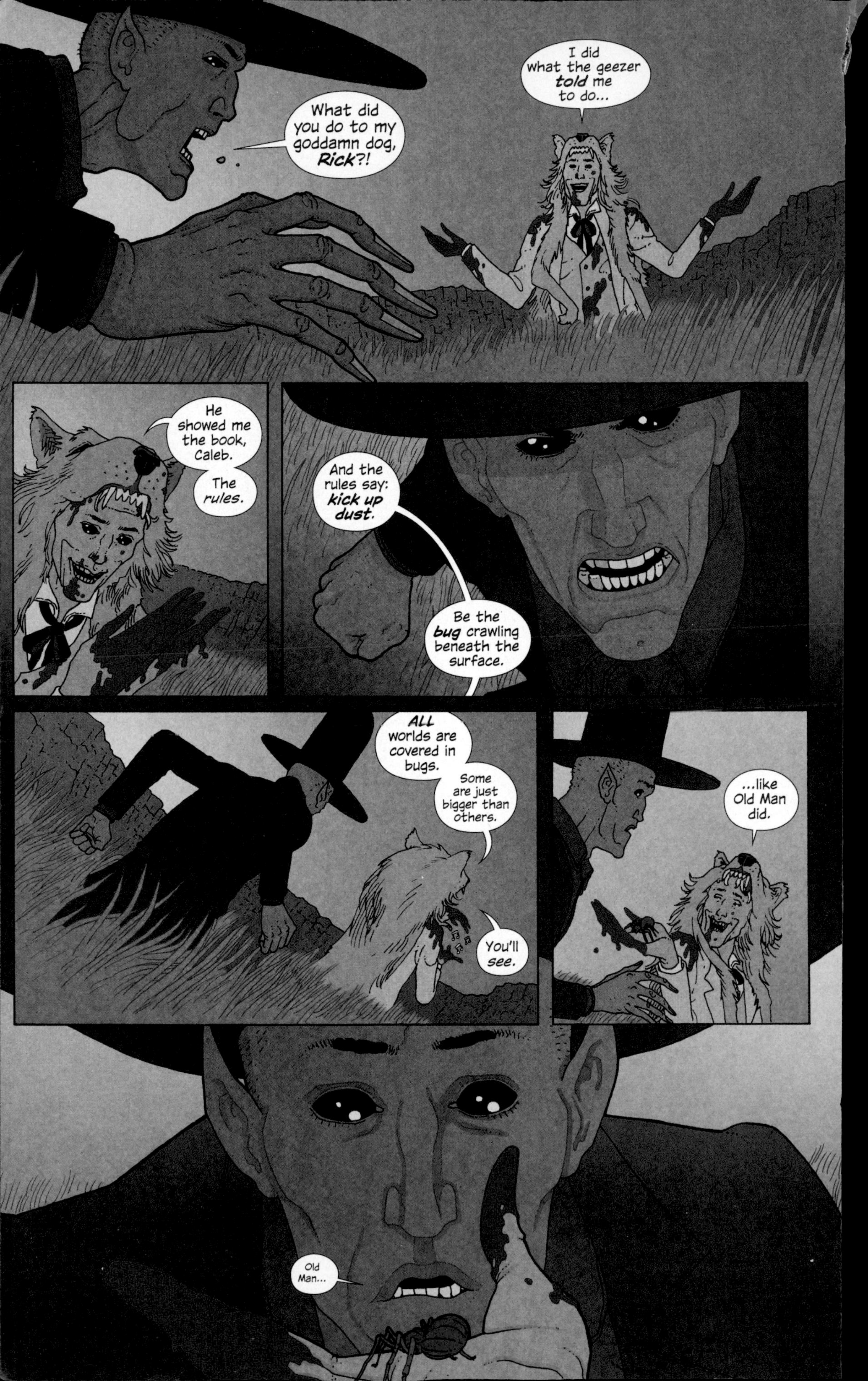
I did what the geezer *told* me to do...
What did you do to my goddamn dog, ***Rick***?!
He showed me the book, Caleb.
The *rules.*
And the rules say: ***kick up dust.***
Be the ***bug*** crawling beneath the surface.
ALL worlds are covered in bugs.
Some are just bigger than others.
You'll *see.*
...like Old Man did.
Old Man...

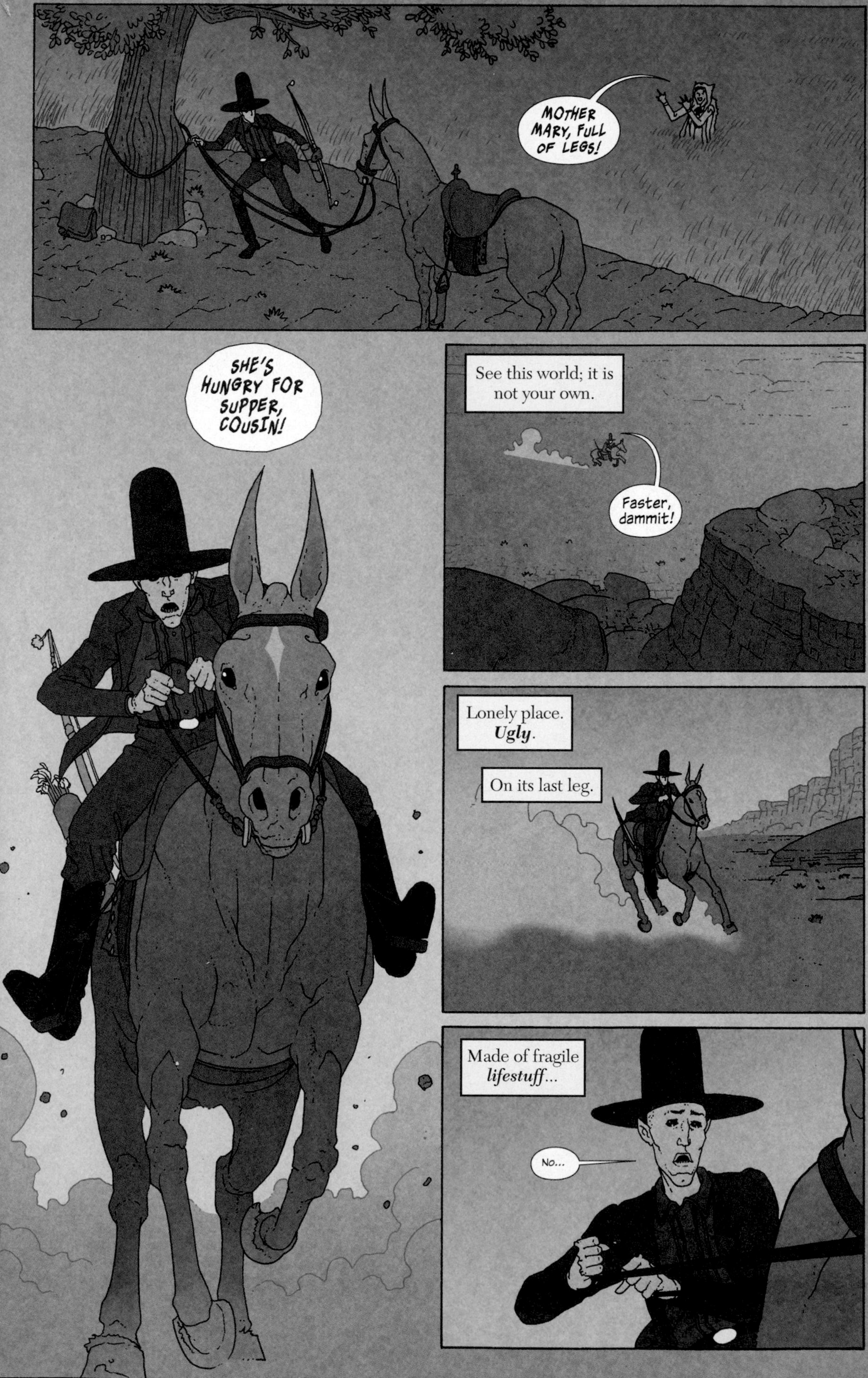
MOTHER MARY, FULL OF LEGS!
SHE'S HUNGRY FOR SUPPER, COUSIN!
See this world; it is not your own.
Faster, dammit!
Lonely place. *Ugly*.
On its last leg.
Made of fragile *lifestuff*...
No...

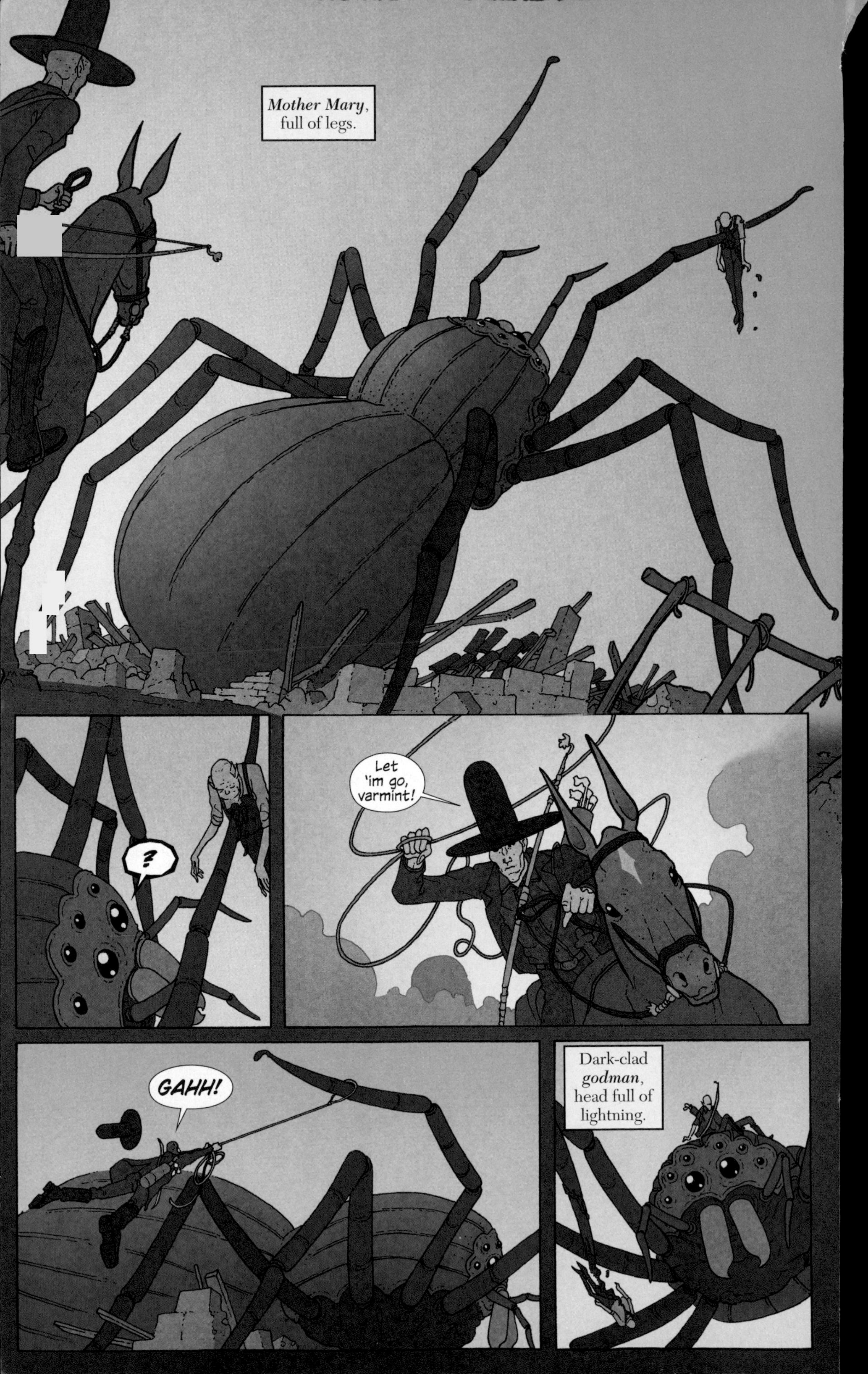

Mother Mary, full of legs.
?
Let 'im go, varmint!
GAHH!
Dark-clad *godman*, head full of lightning.

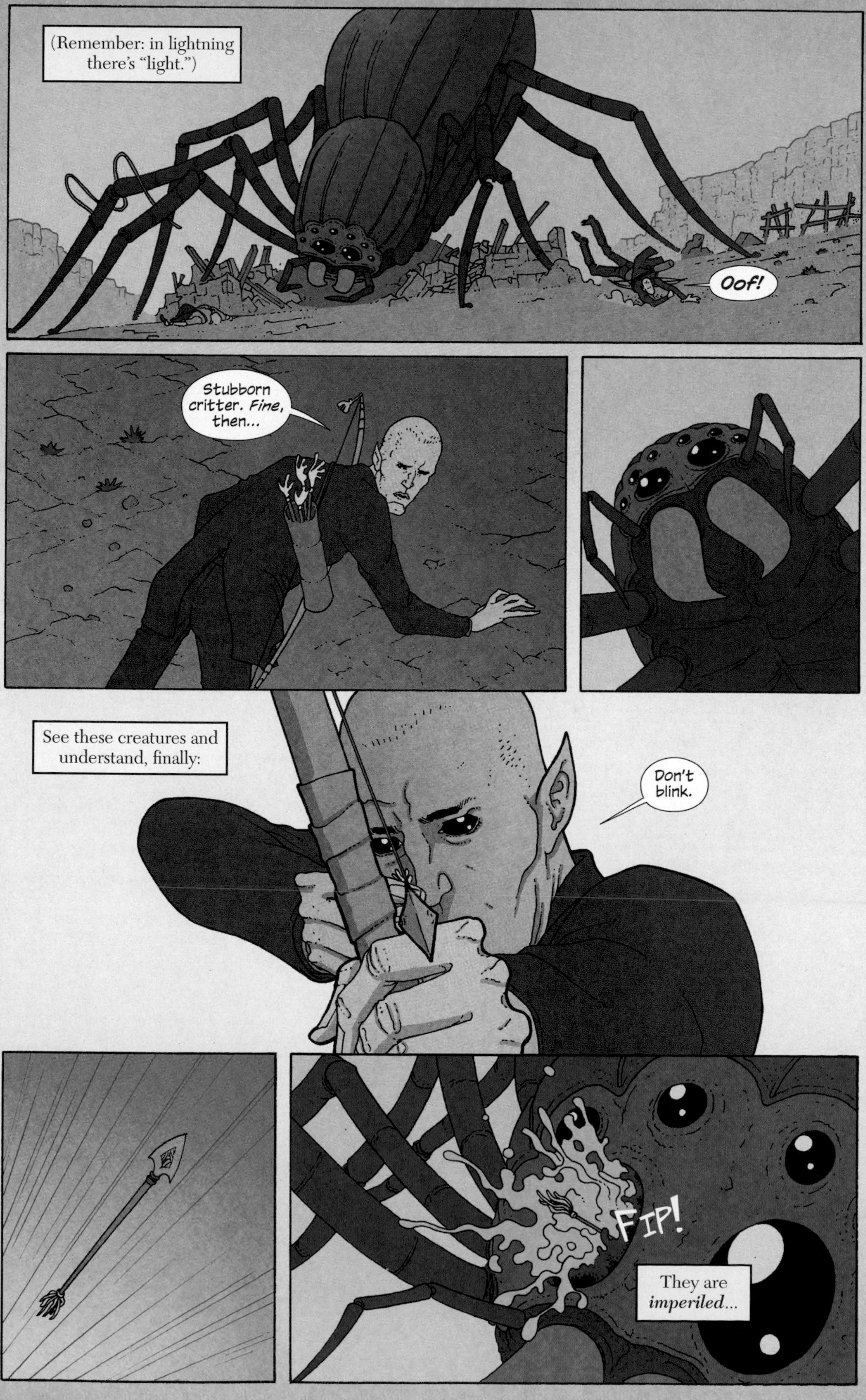
(Remember: in lightning there's "light.")
Oof!
Stubborn critter. *Fine,* then...
See these creatures and understand, finally:
Don't blink.
FIP!
They are *imperiled*...

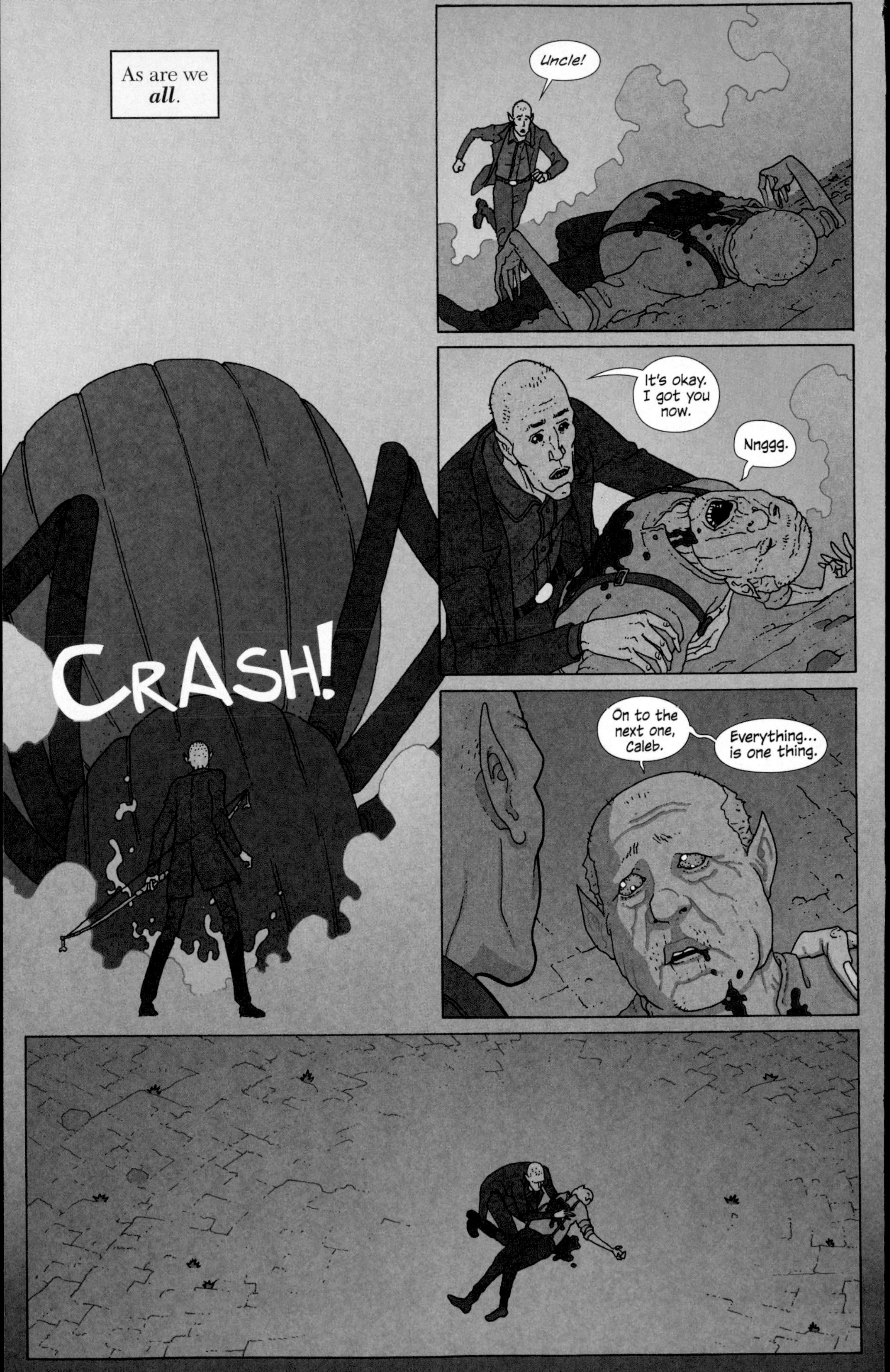
As are we *all*.
Uncle!
CRASH!
It's okay. I got you now.
Nnggg.
On to the next one, Caleb.
Everything... is one thing.

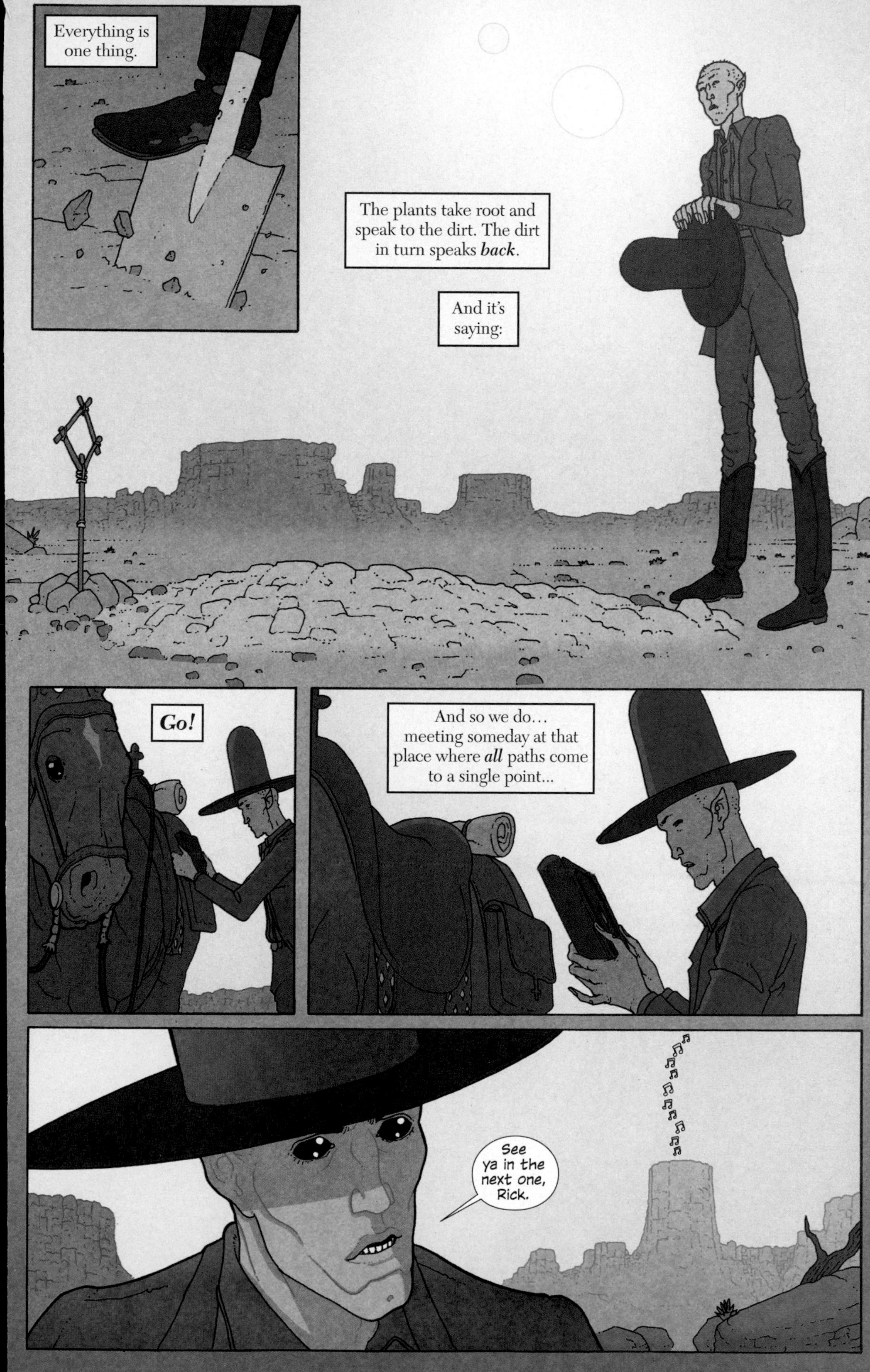
Everything is one thing.
The plants take root and speak to the dirt. The dirt in turn speaks *back*.
And it's saying:
Go!
And so we do… meeting someday at that place where *all* paths come to a single point…
See ya in the next one, Rick.

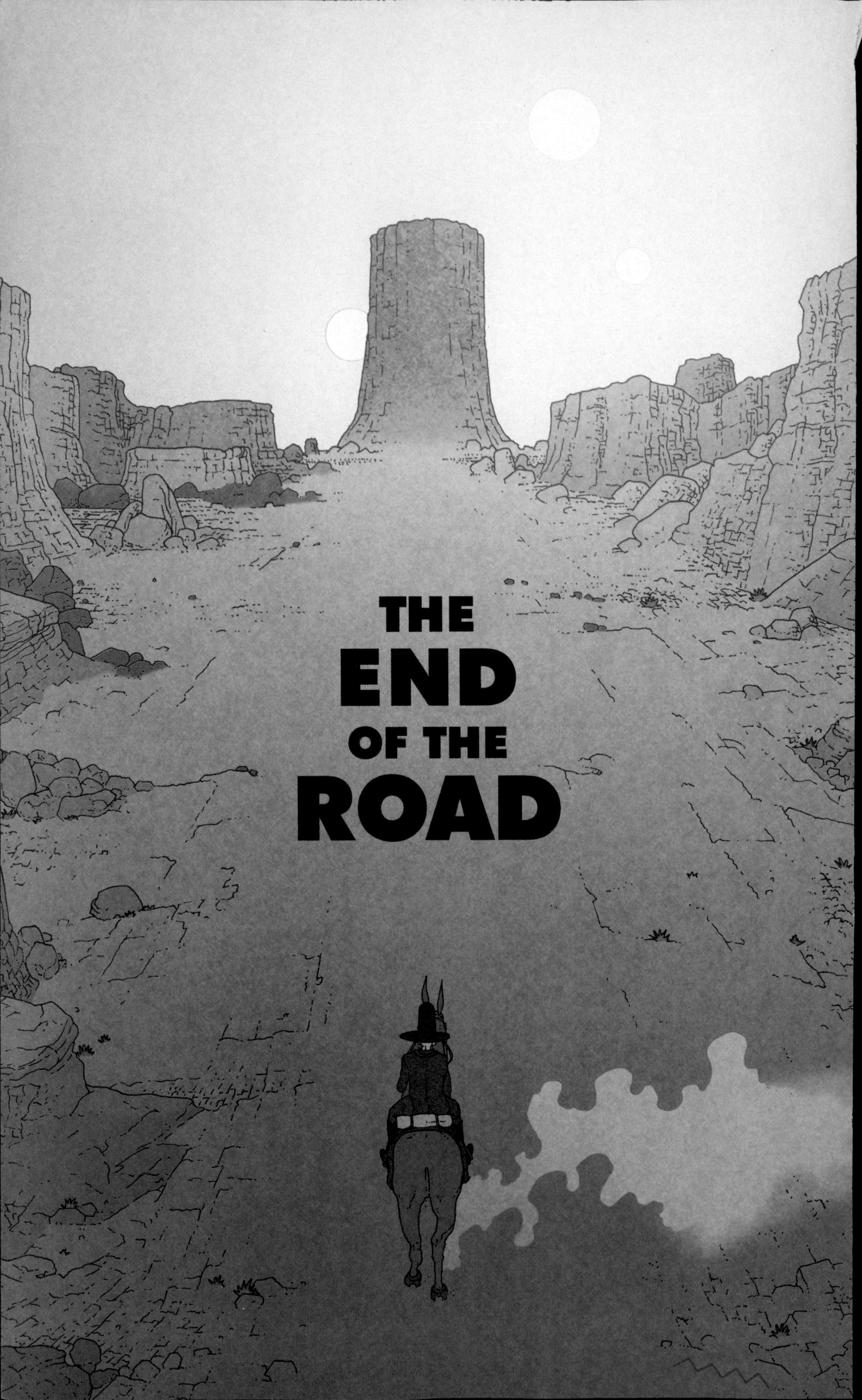
THE END OF THE ROAD

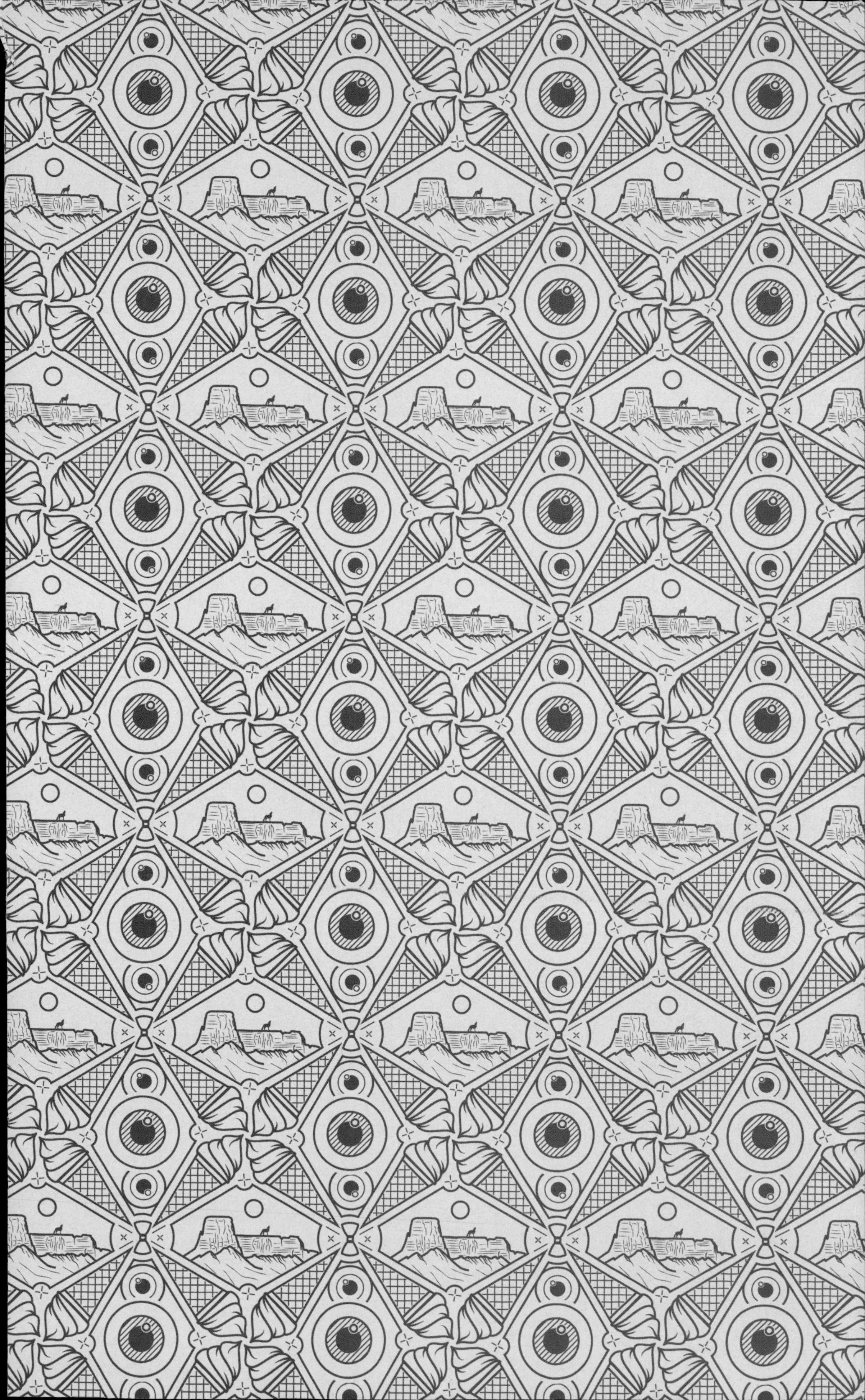

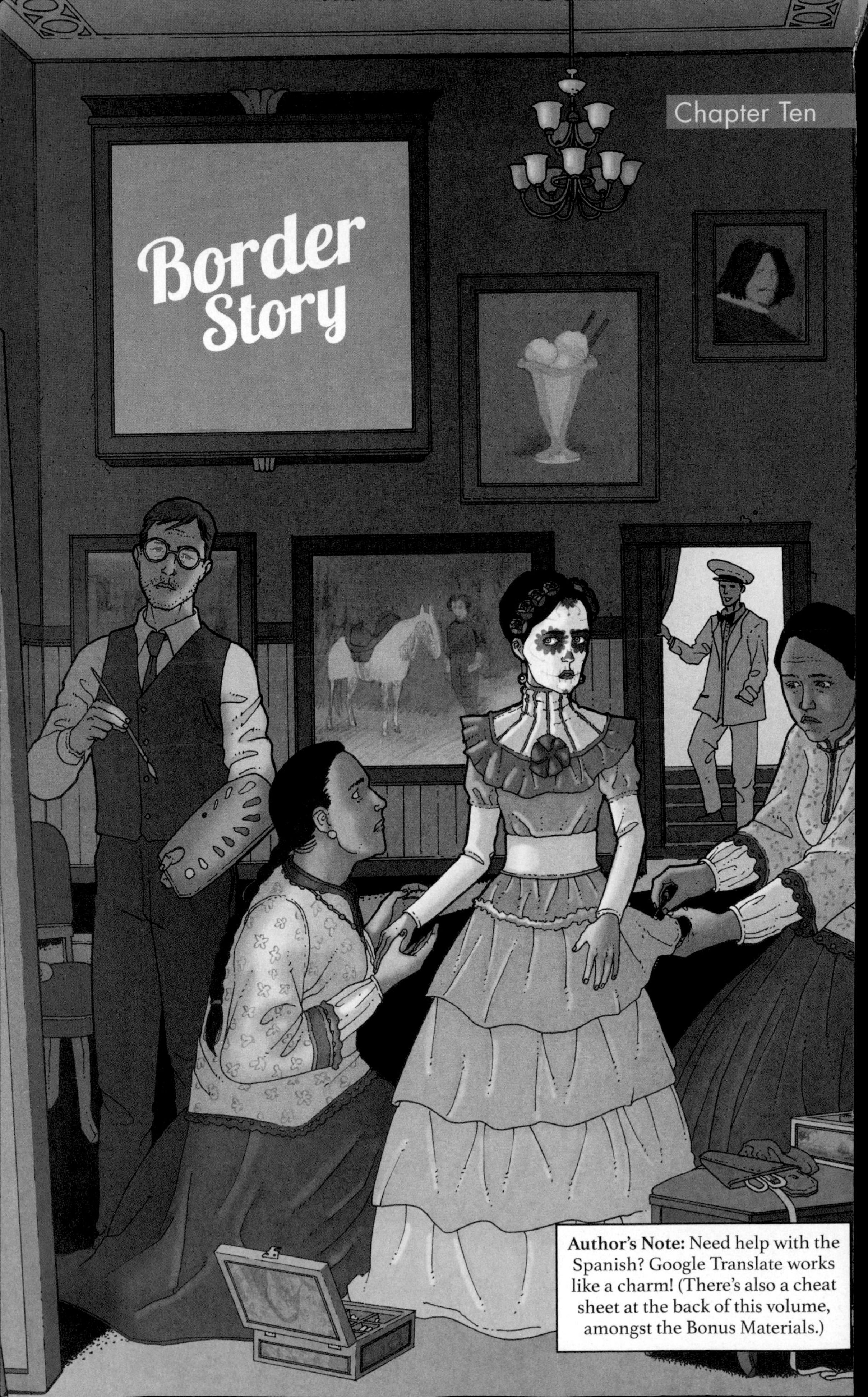
Chapter Ten
Border Story
Author's Note: Need help with the Spanish? Google Translate works like a charm! (There's also a cheat sheet at the back of this volume, amongst the Bonus Materials.)

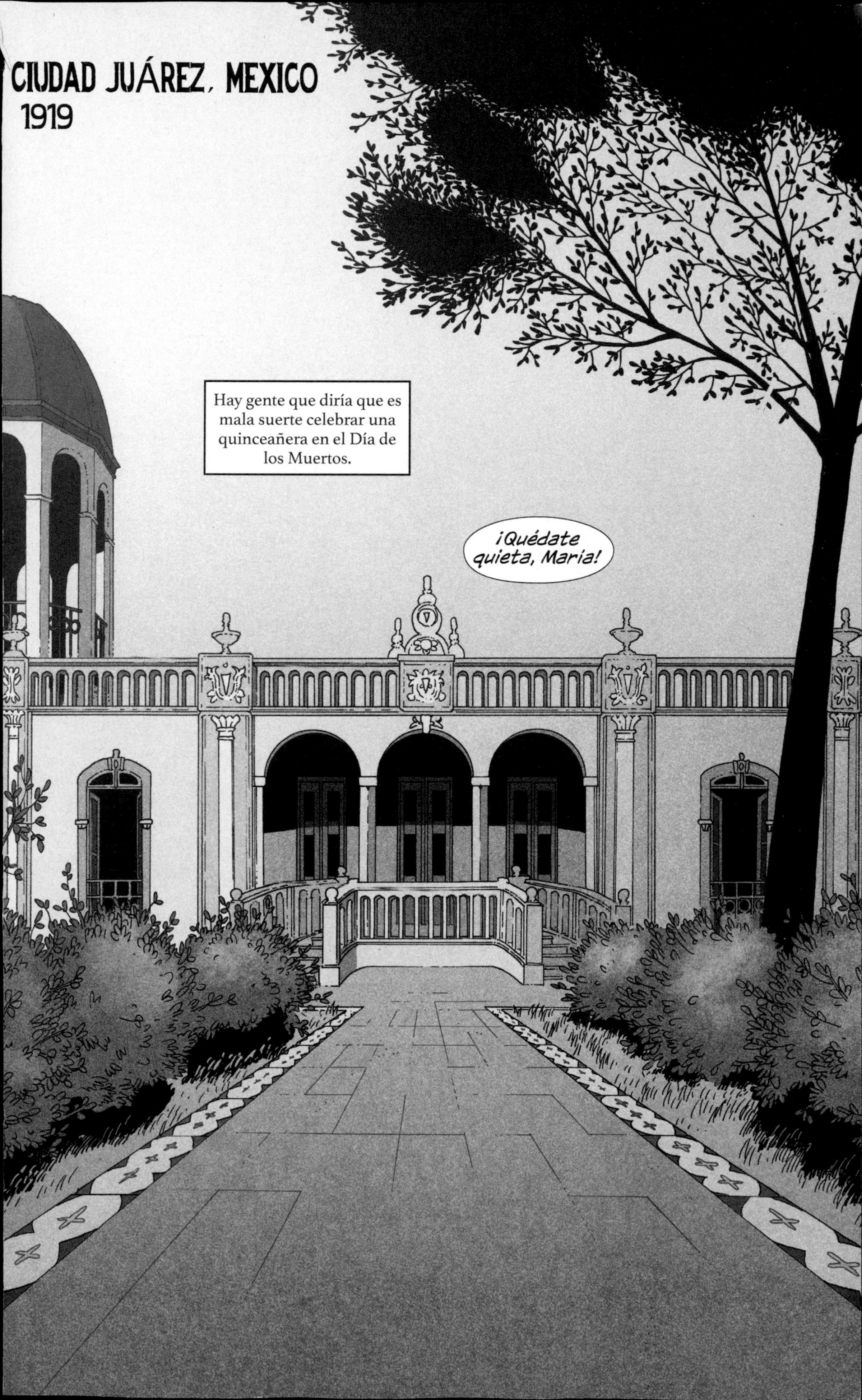
CIUDAD JUÁREZ, MEXICO
1919
Hay gente que diría que es mala suerte celebrar una quinceañera en el Día de los Muertos.
¡Quédate quieta, Maria!

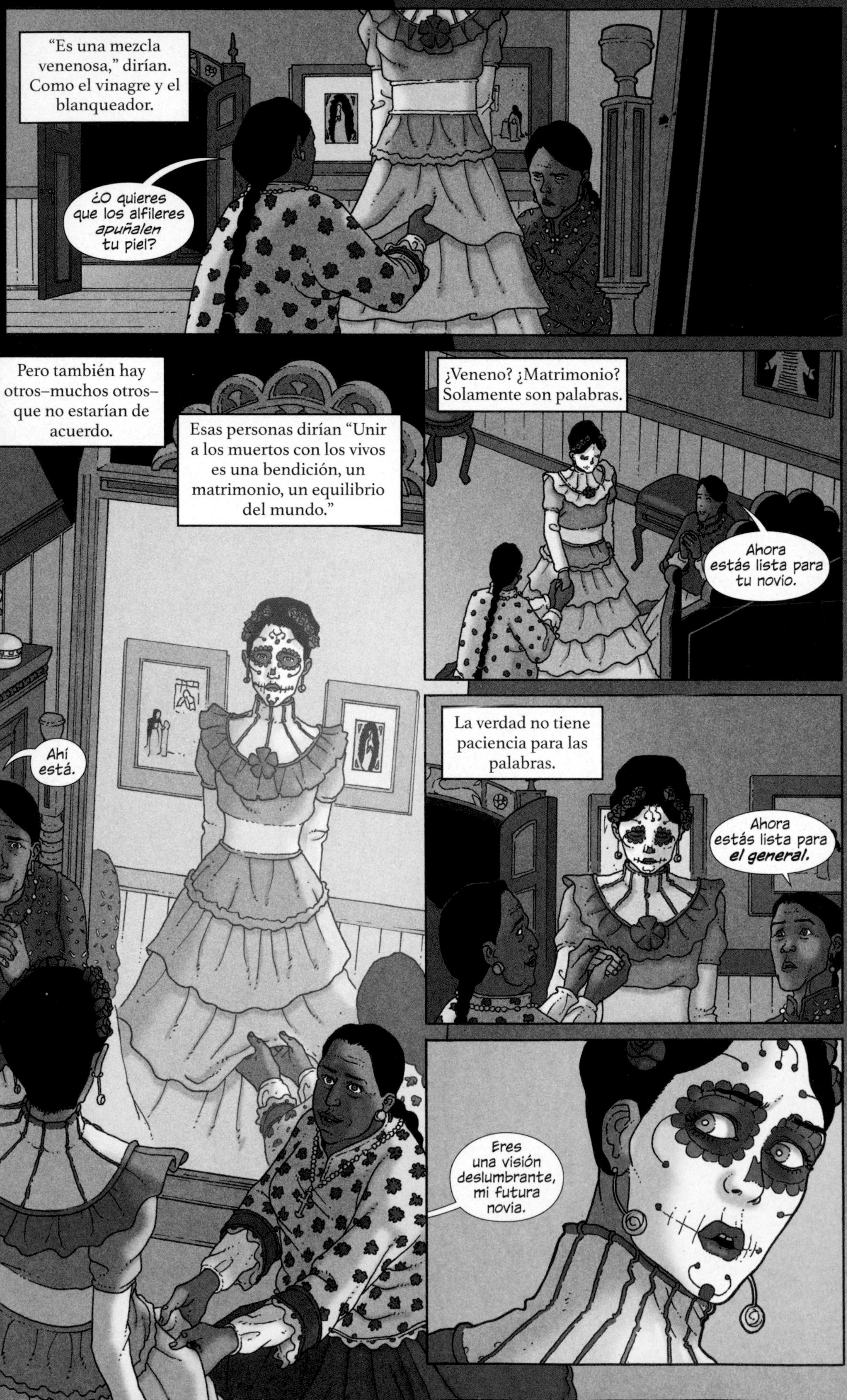
"Es una mezcla venenosa," dirían. Como el vinagre y el blanqueador.
¿O quieres que los alfileres *apuñalen* tu piel?
Pero también hay otros–muchos otros–que no estarían de acuerdo.
Esas personas dirían "Unir a los muertos con los vivos es una bendición, un matrimonio, un equilibrio del mundo."
Ahí está.
¿Veneno? ¿Matrimonio? Solamente son palabras.
Ahora estás lista para tu novio.
La verdad no tiene paciencia para las palabras.
Ahora estás lista para **el general.**
Eres una visión deslumbrante, mi futura novia.

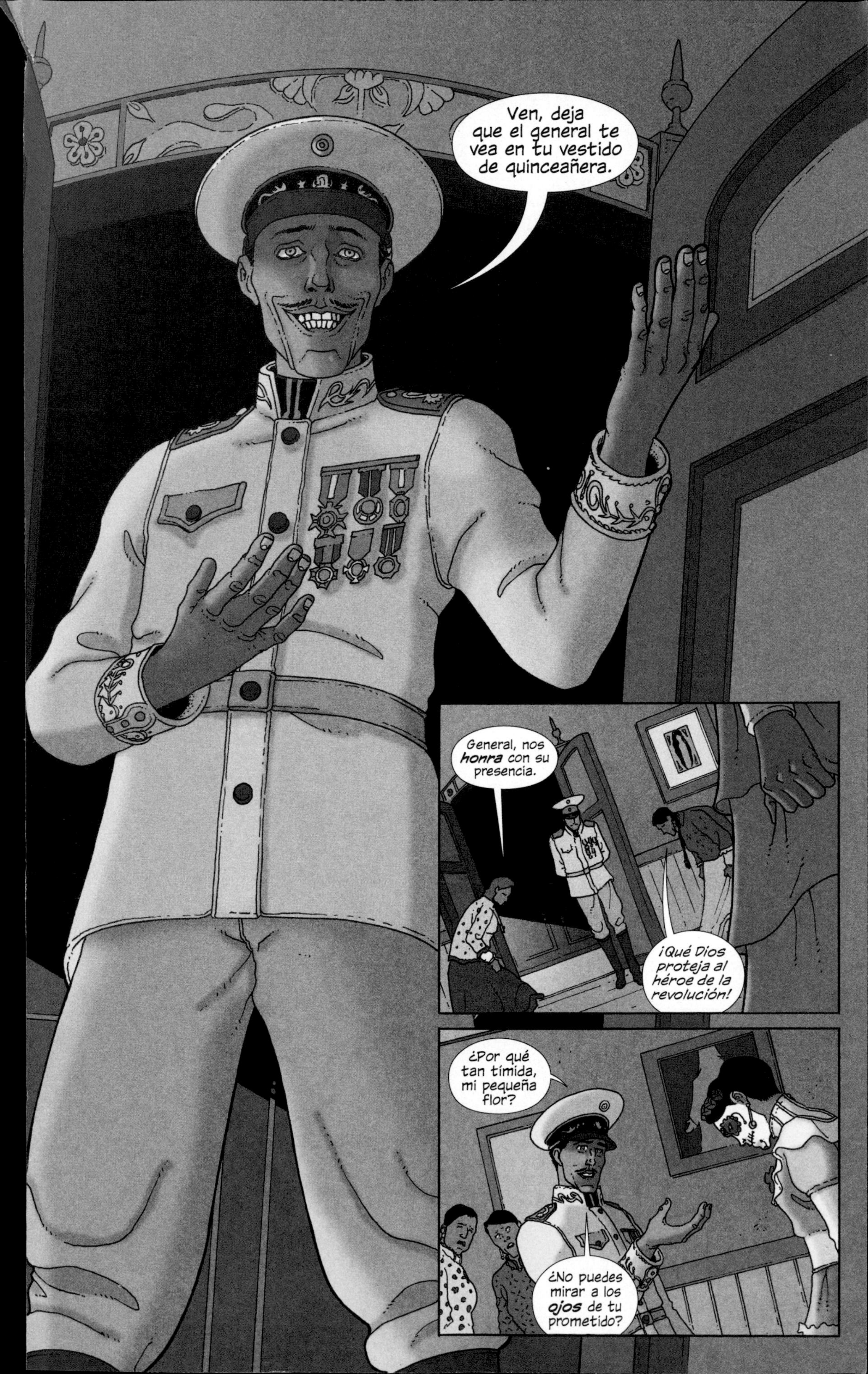
Ven, deja que el general te vea en tu vestido de quinceañera.
General, nos *honra* con su presencia.
¡Qué Dios proteja al héroe de la revolución!
¿Por qué tan tímida, mi pequeña flor?
¿No puedes mirar a los *ojos* de tu prometido?

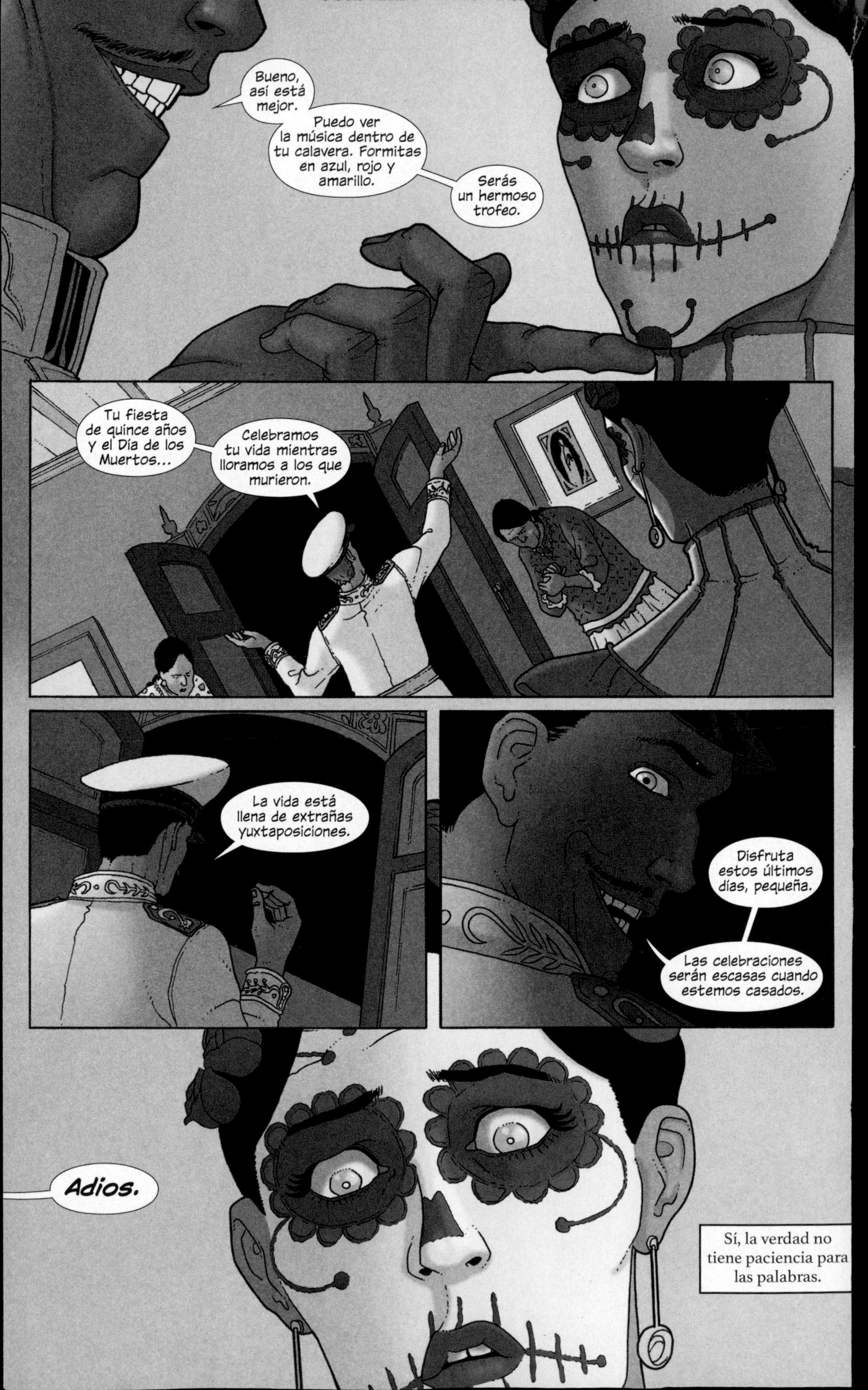
Bueno, así está mejor.
Puedo ver la música dentro de tu calavera. Formitas en azul, rojo y amarillo.
Serás un hermoso trofeo.
Tu fiesta de quince años y el Día de los Muertos...
Celebramos tu vida mientras lloramos a los que murieron.
La vida está llena de extrañas yuxtaposiciones.
Disfruta estos últimos días, pequeña.
Las celebraciones serán escasas cuando estemos casados.
Adios.
Sí, la verdad no tiene paciencia para las palabras.

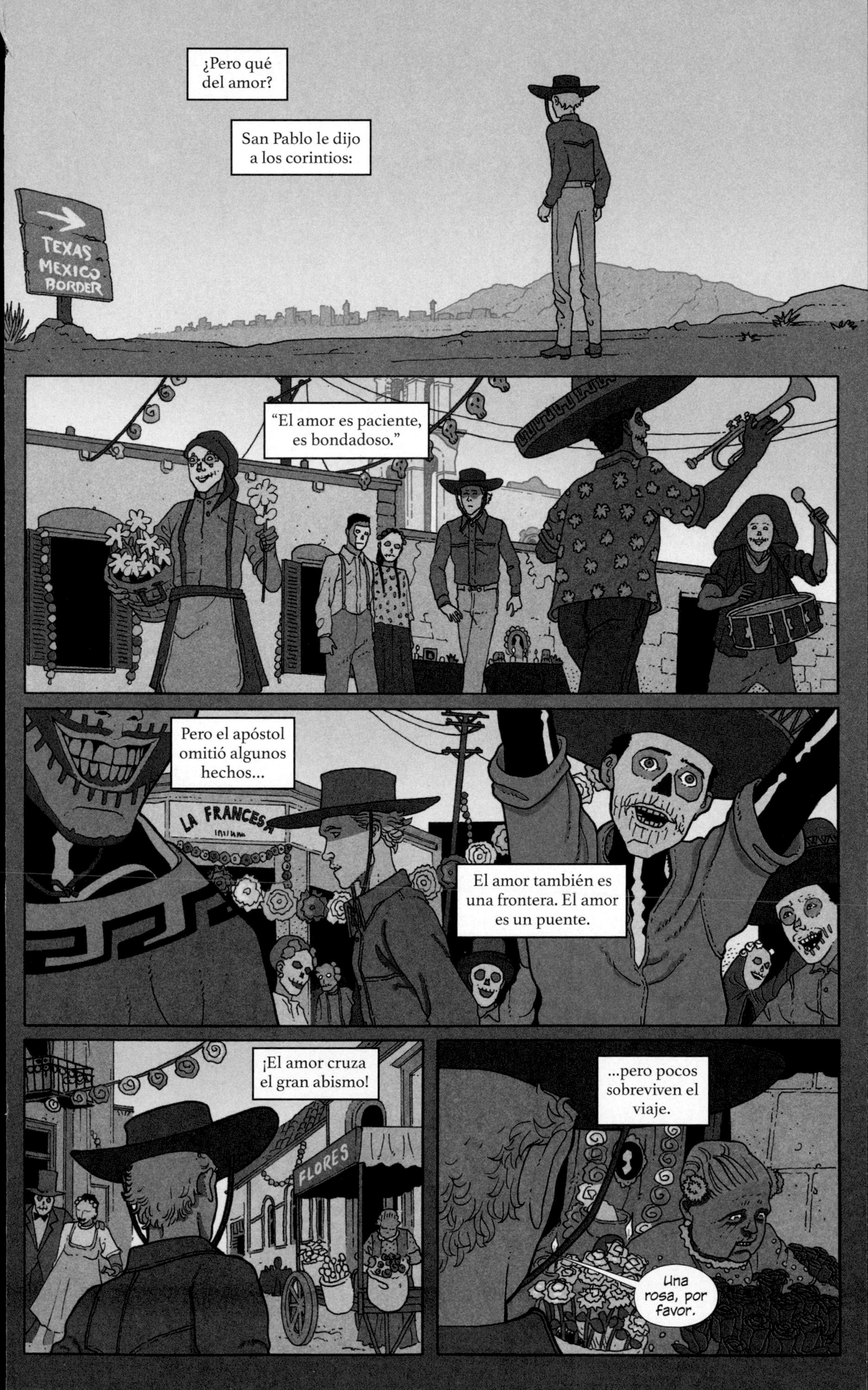
¿Pero qué del amor?
San Pablo le dijo a los corintios:
TEXAS MEXICO BORDER
"El amor es paciente, es bondadoso."
Pero el apóstol omitió algunos hechos...
LA FRANCESA
El amor también es una frontera. El amor es un puente.
¡El amor cruza el gran abismo!
FLORES
...pero pocos sobreviven el viaje.
Una rosa, por favor.

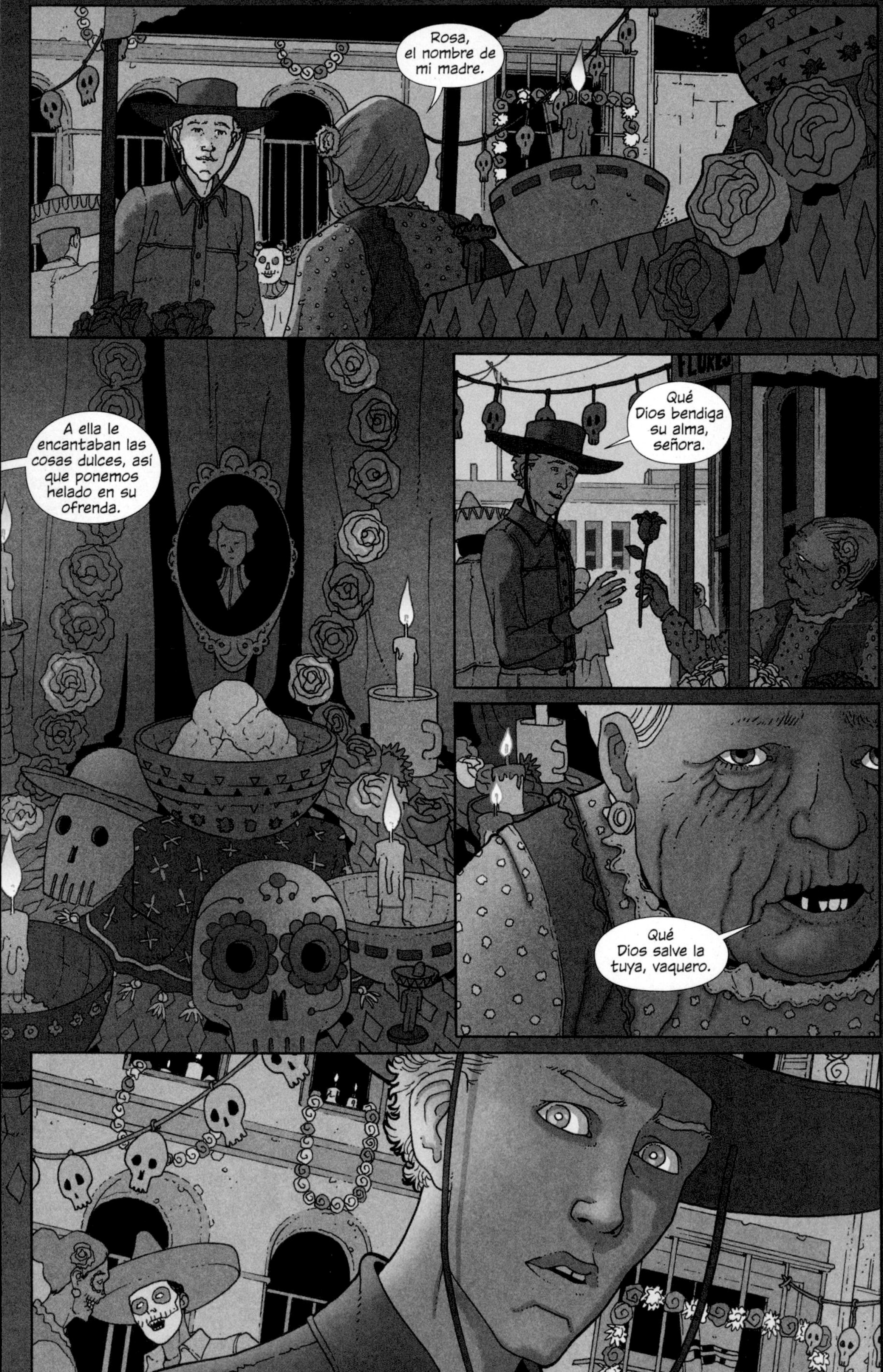
Rosa, el nombre de mi madre.
A ella le encantaban las cosas dulces, así que ponemos helado en su ofrenda.
Qué Dios bendiga su alma, señora.
Qué Dios salve la tuya, vaquero.

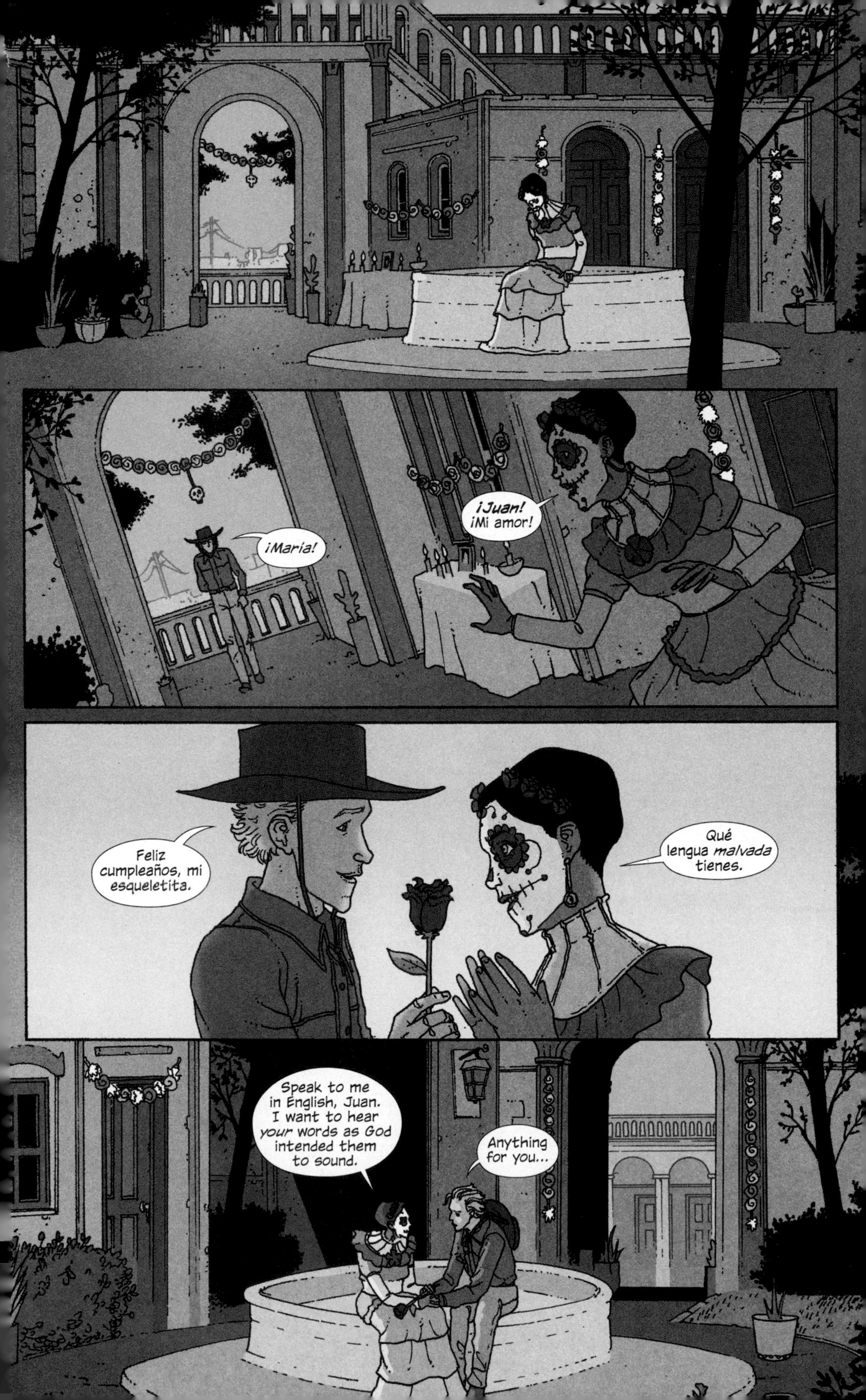
¡Maria!
¡Juan! ¡Mi amor!
Feliz cumpleaños, mi esqueletita.
Qué lengua *malvada* tienes.
Speak to me in English, Juan. I want to hear *your* words as God intended them to sound.
Anything for you...

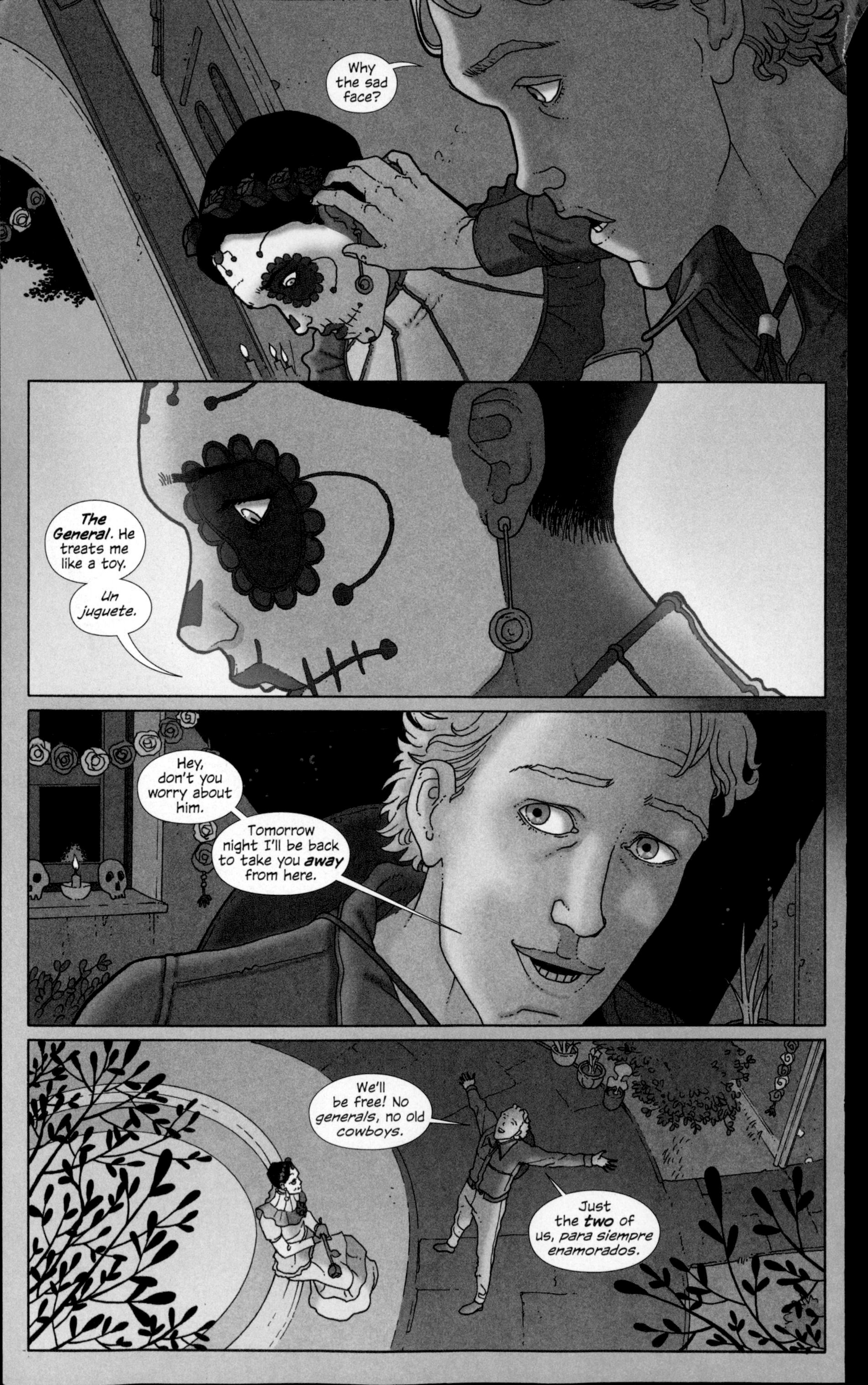
Why the sad face?
The General. He treats me like a toy.
Un juguete.
Hey, don't you worry about him.
Tomorrow night I'll be back to take you ***away*** from here.
We'll be free! No *generals*, no old cowboys.
Just the ***two*** of us, *para siempre enamorados.*

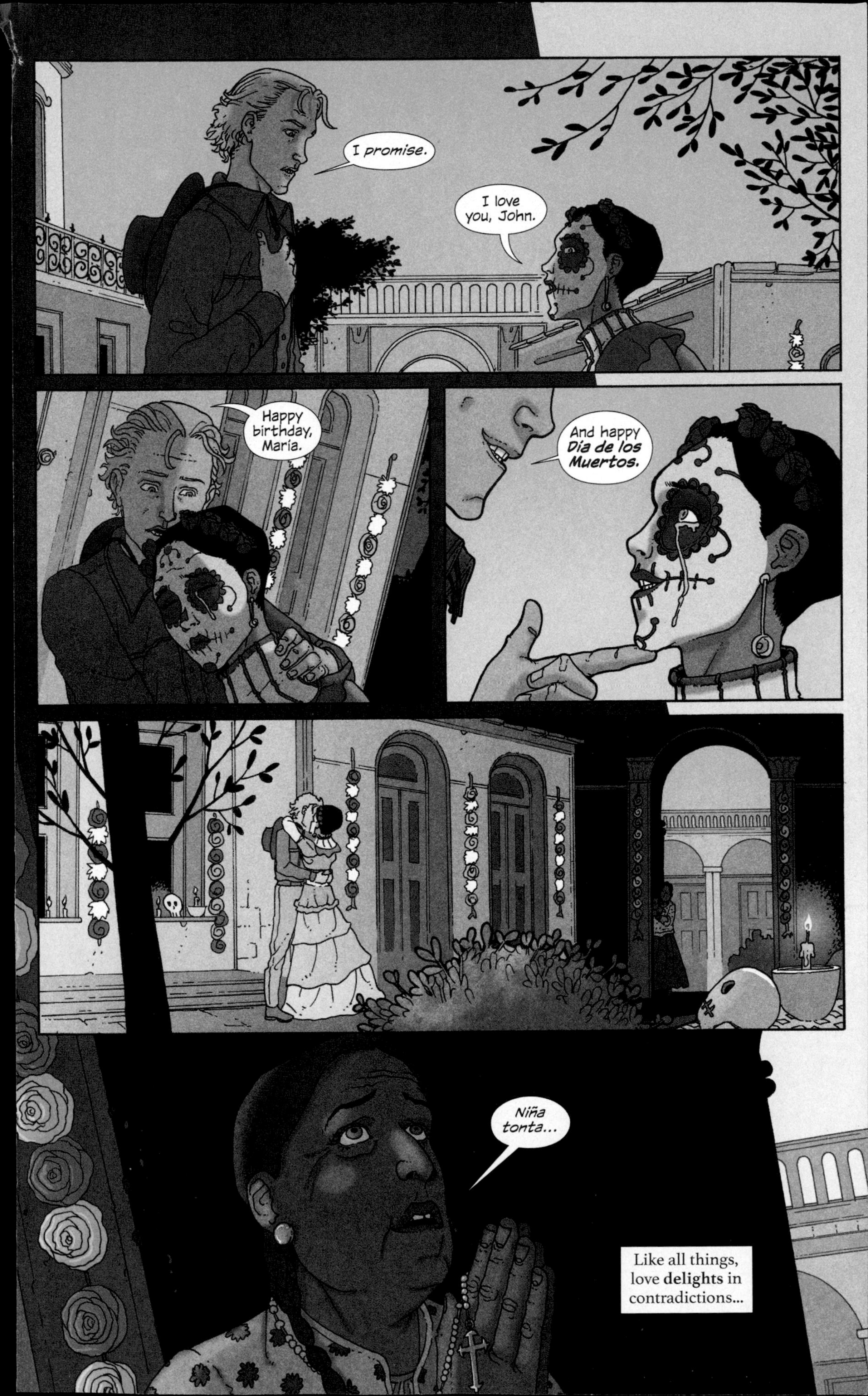
I promise.
I love you, John.
Happy birthday, Maria.
And happy *Dia de los Muertos.*
Niña tonta...
Like all things, love **delights** in contradictions...

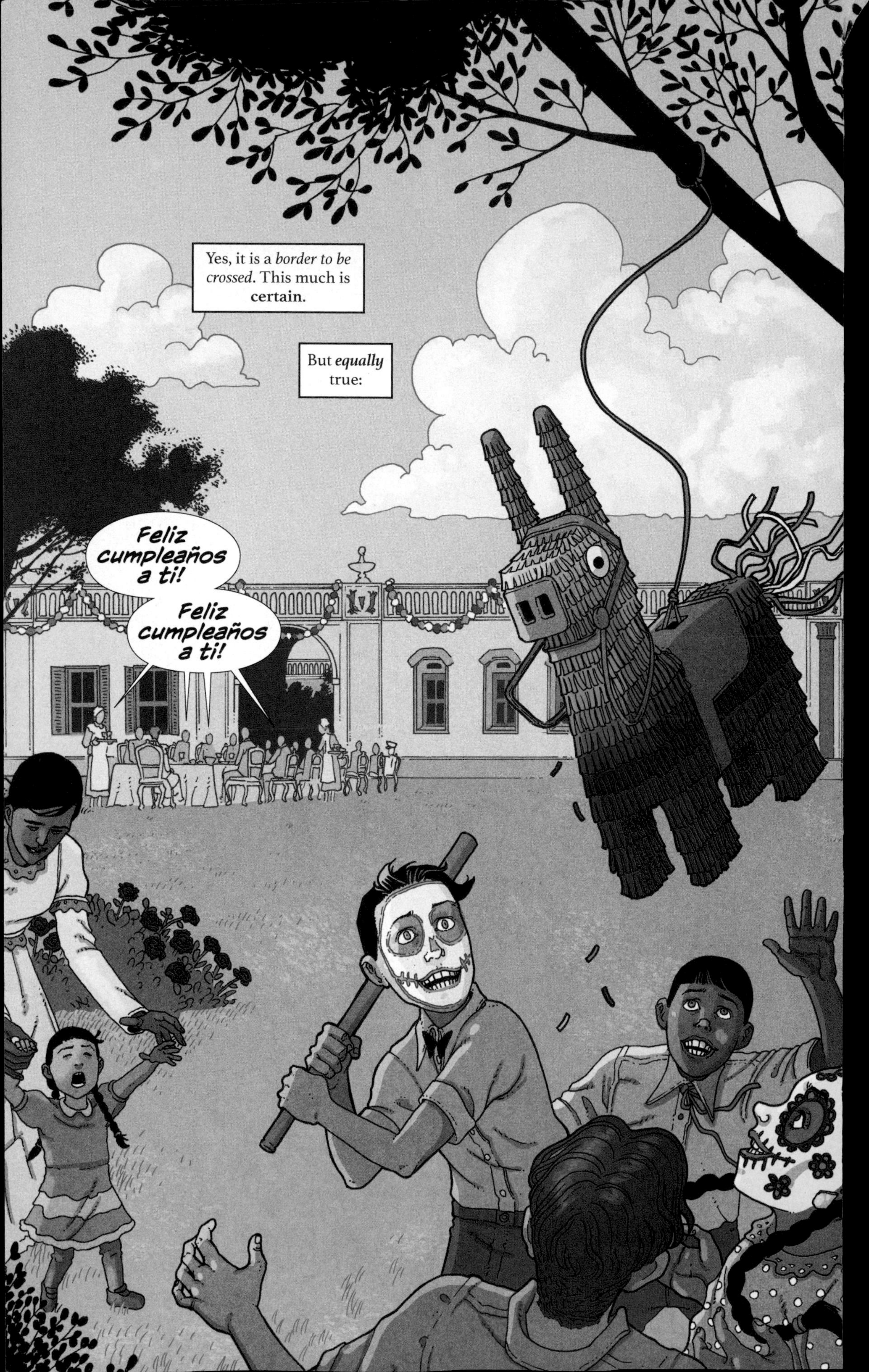
Yes, it is a *border to be crossed*. This much is **certain**.
But ***equally*** true:
Feliz cumpleaños a ti!
Feliz cumpleaños a ti!

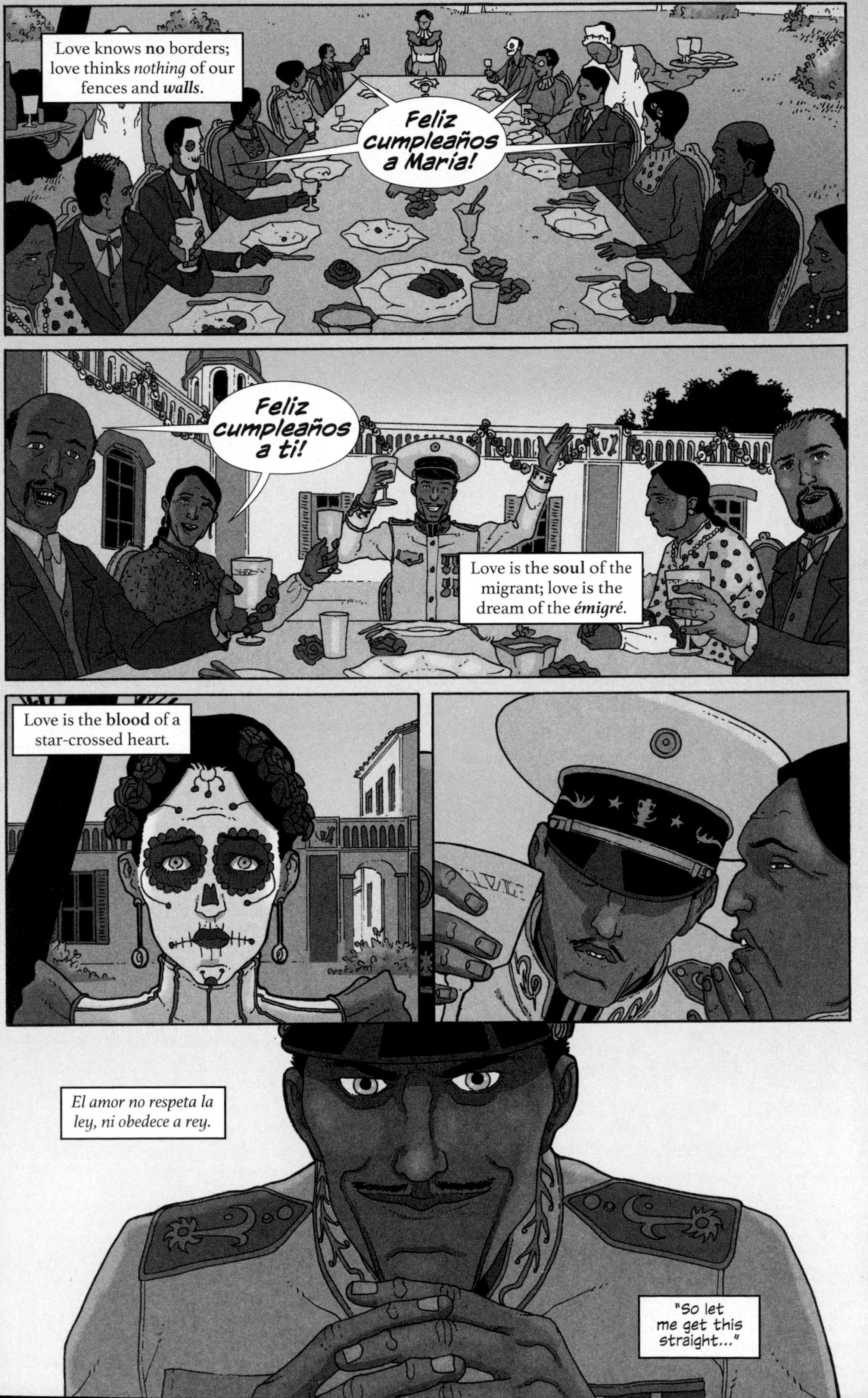
Love knows **no** borders; love thinks *nothing* of our fences and ***walls***.
Feliz cumpleaños a Maria!
Feliz cumpleaños a ti!
Love is the **soul** of the migrant; love is the dream of the ***émigré***.
Love is the **blood** of a star-crossed heart.
El amor no respeta la ley, ni obedece a rey.
"So let me get this straight..."

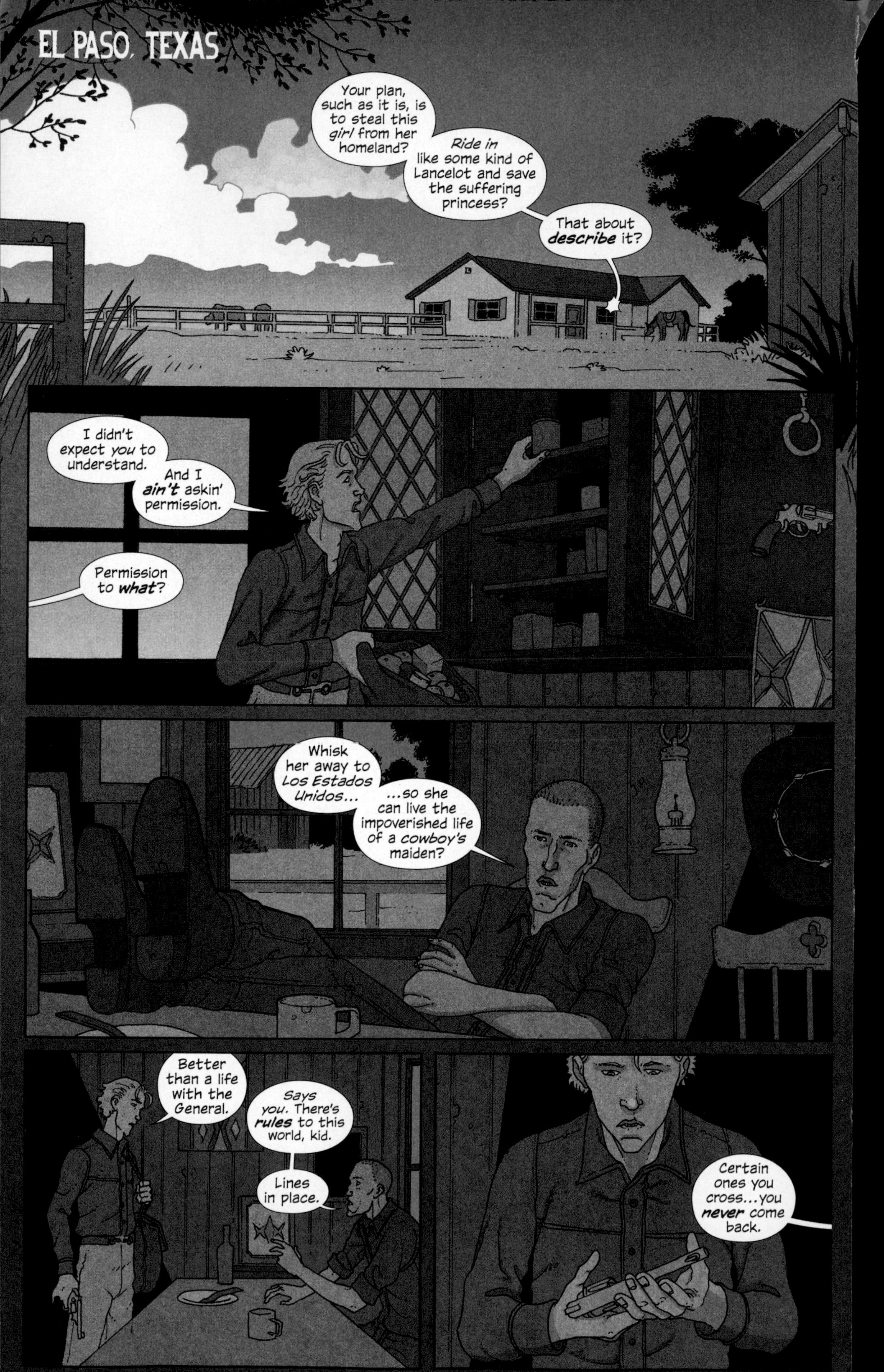
EL PASO, TEXAS
Your plan, such as it is, is to steal this *girl* from her homeland?
Ride in like some kind of Lancelot and save the suffering princess?
That about ***describe*** it?
I didn't expect *you* to understand.
And I ***ain't*** askin' permission.
Permission to ***what***?
Whisk her away to *Los Estados Unidos...*
...so she can live the impoverished life of a *cowboy's* maiden?
Better than a life with the General.
Says you. There's ***rules*** to this world, kid.
Lines in place.
Certain ones you cross...you ***never*** come back.

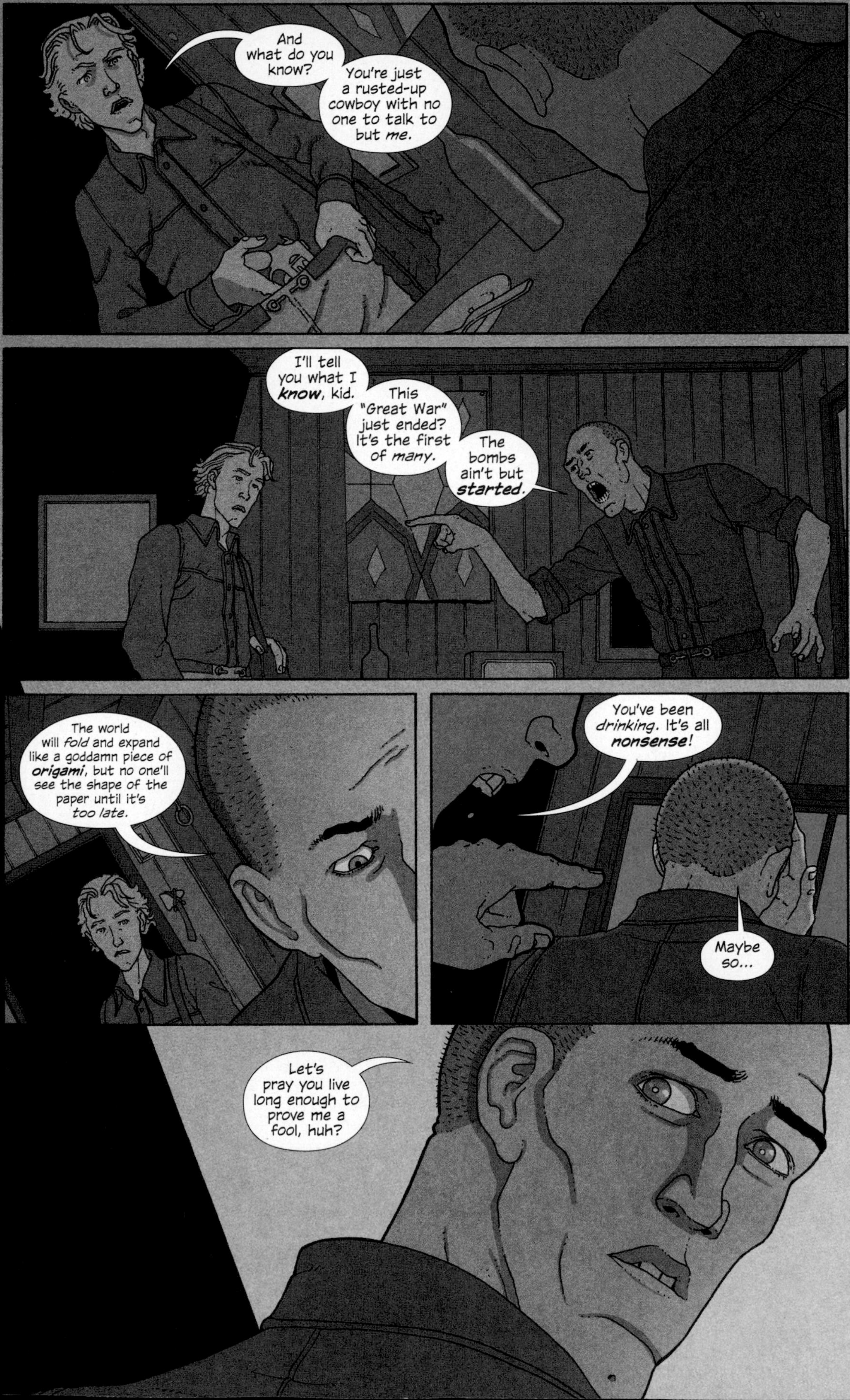
And what do you know?
You're just a rusted-up cowboy with no one to talk to but *me*.
I'll tell you what I ***know***, kid.
This "Great War" just ended? It's the first of *many*.
The bombs ain't but ***started***.
The world will *fold* and expand like a goddamn piece of ***origami***, but no one'll see the shape of the paper until it's *too late*.
You've been *drinking*. It's all ***nonsense***!
Maybe so...
Let's pray you live long enough to prove me a fool, huh?

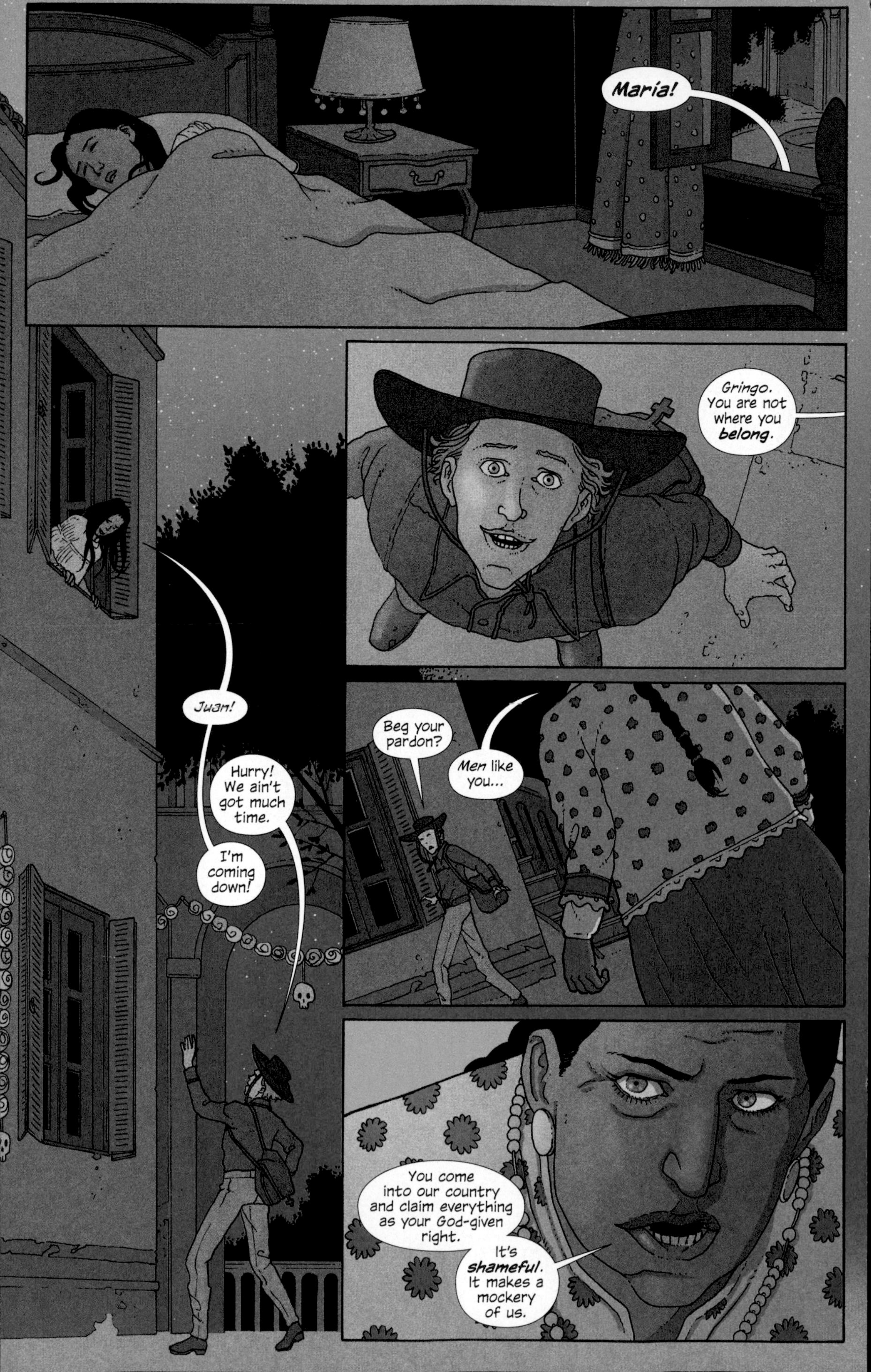
Maria!
Gringo. You are not where you belong.
Juan!
Hurry! We ain't got much time.
I'm coming down!
Beg your pardon?
Men like you...
You come into our country and claim everything as your God-given right.
It's shameful. It makes a mockery of us.

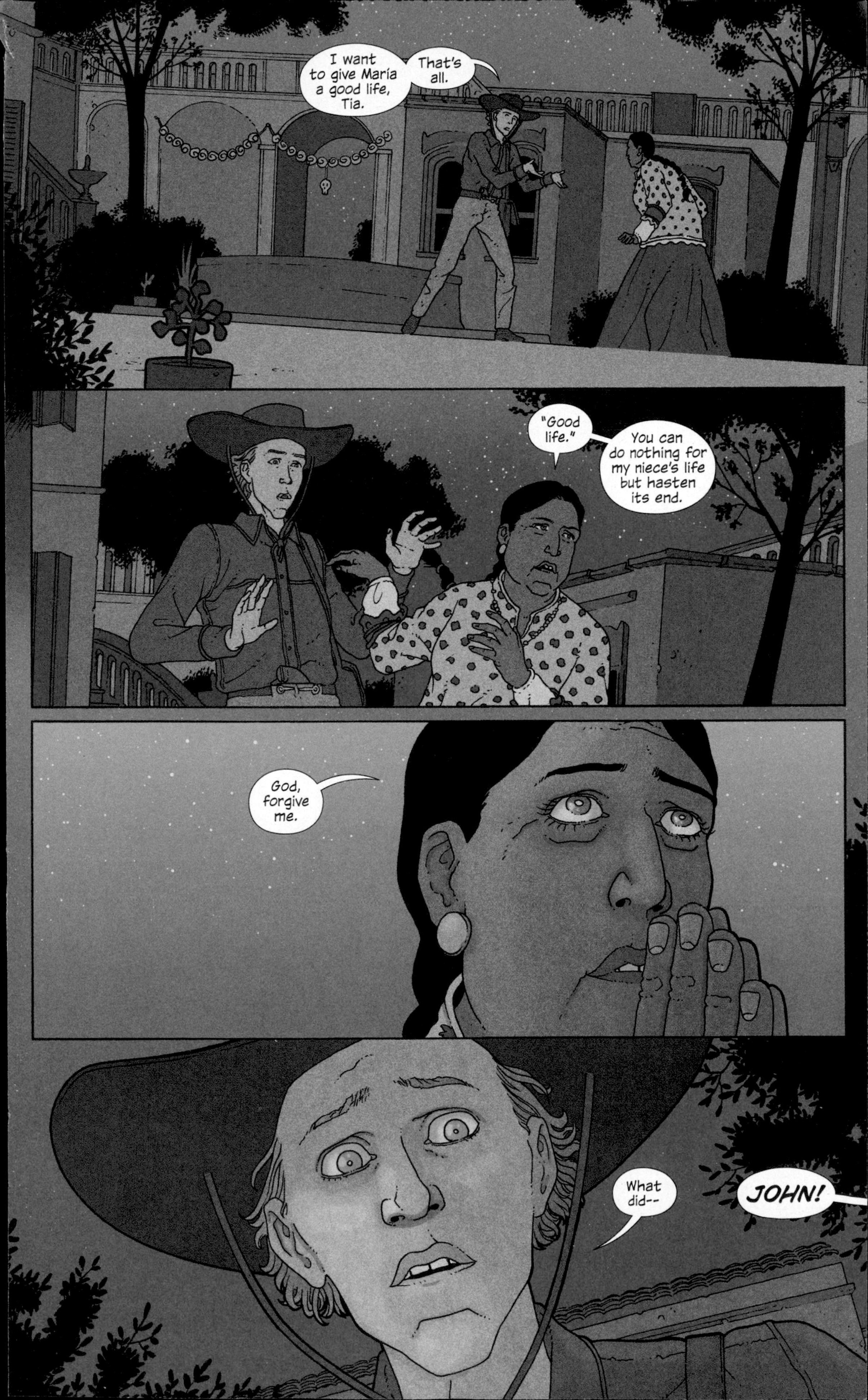

I want to give María a good life, Tia.
That's all.
"Good life."
You can do nothing for my niece's life but hasten its end.
God, forgive me.
What did--
JOHN!

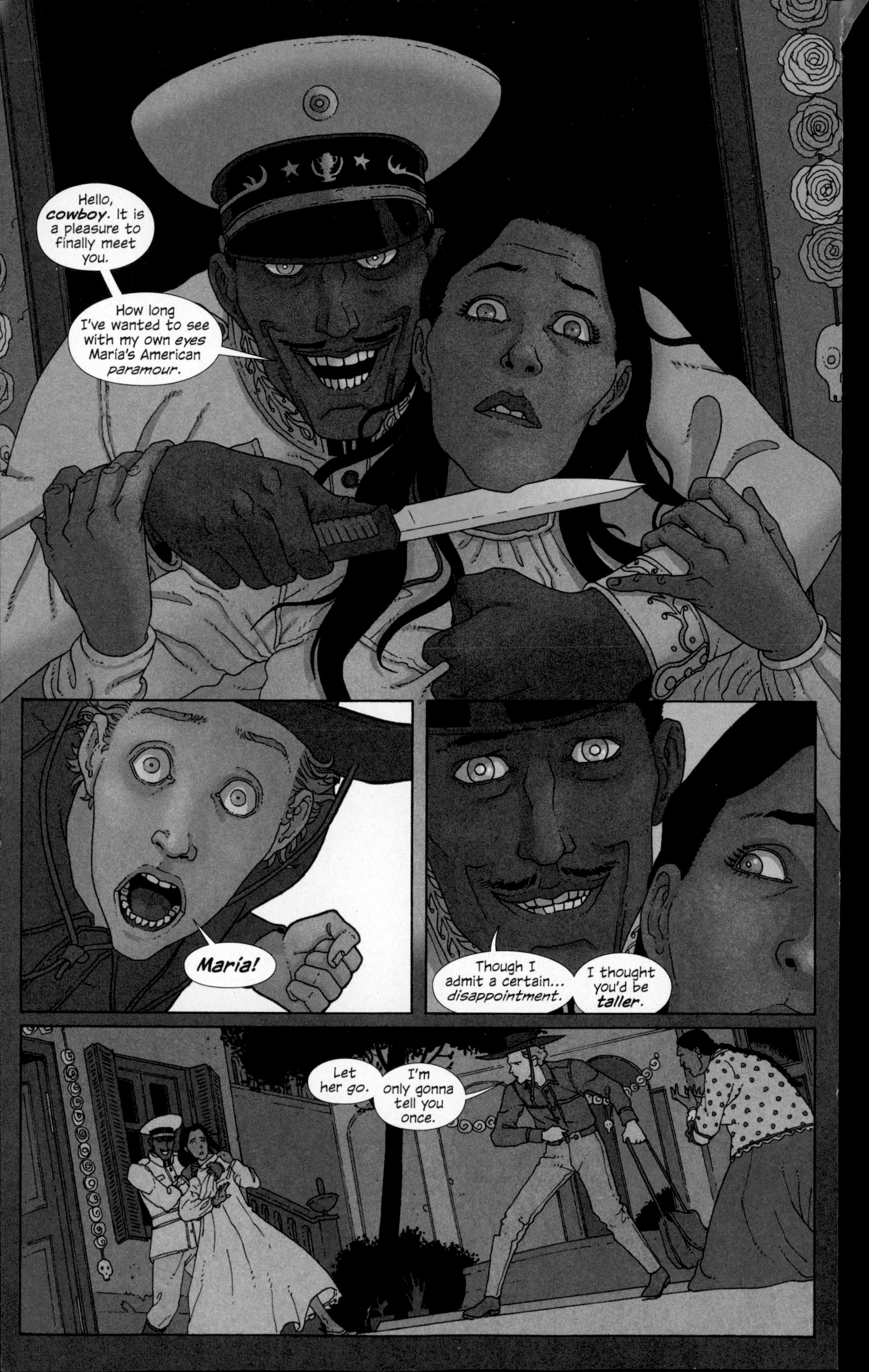
Hello, **cowboy**. It is a pleasure to finally meet you.
How long I've wanted to see with my own *eyes* Maria's American *paramour*.
Maria!
Though I admit a certain... *disappointment*.
I thought you'd be ***taller***.
Let her go.
I'm only gonna tell you once.

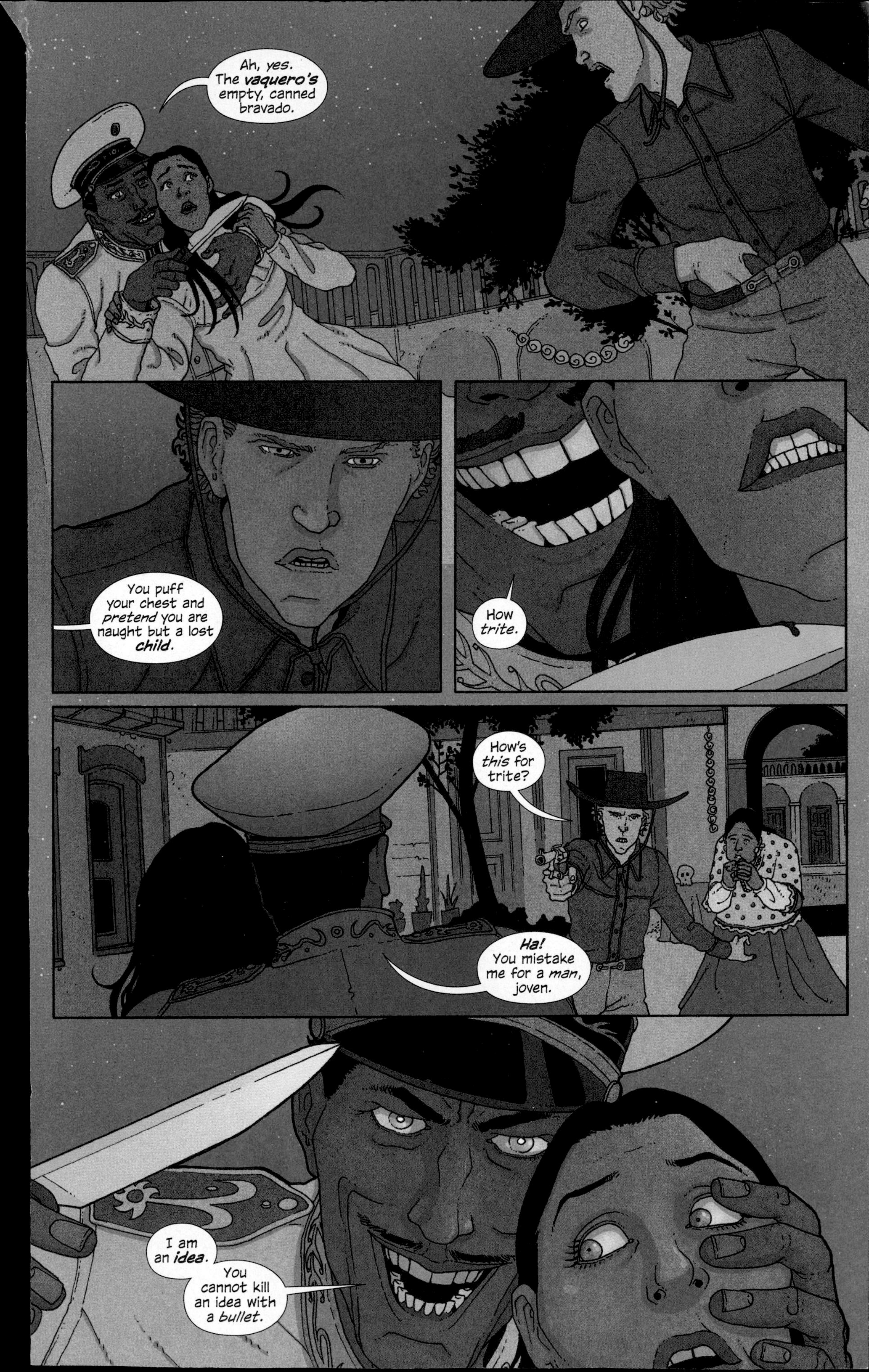
Ah, yes. The *vaquero's* empty, canned bravado.
You puff your chest and *pretend* you are naught but a lost **child**.
How *trite*.
How's *this* for trite?
Ha! You mistake me for a *man*, joven.
I am an *idea*.
You cannot kill an idea with a *bullet*.

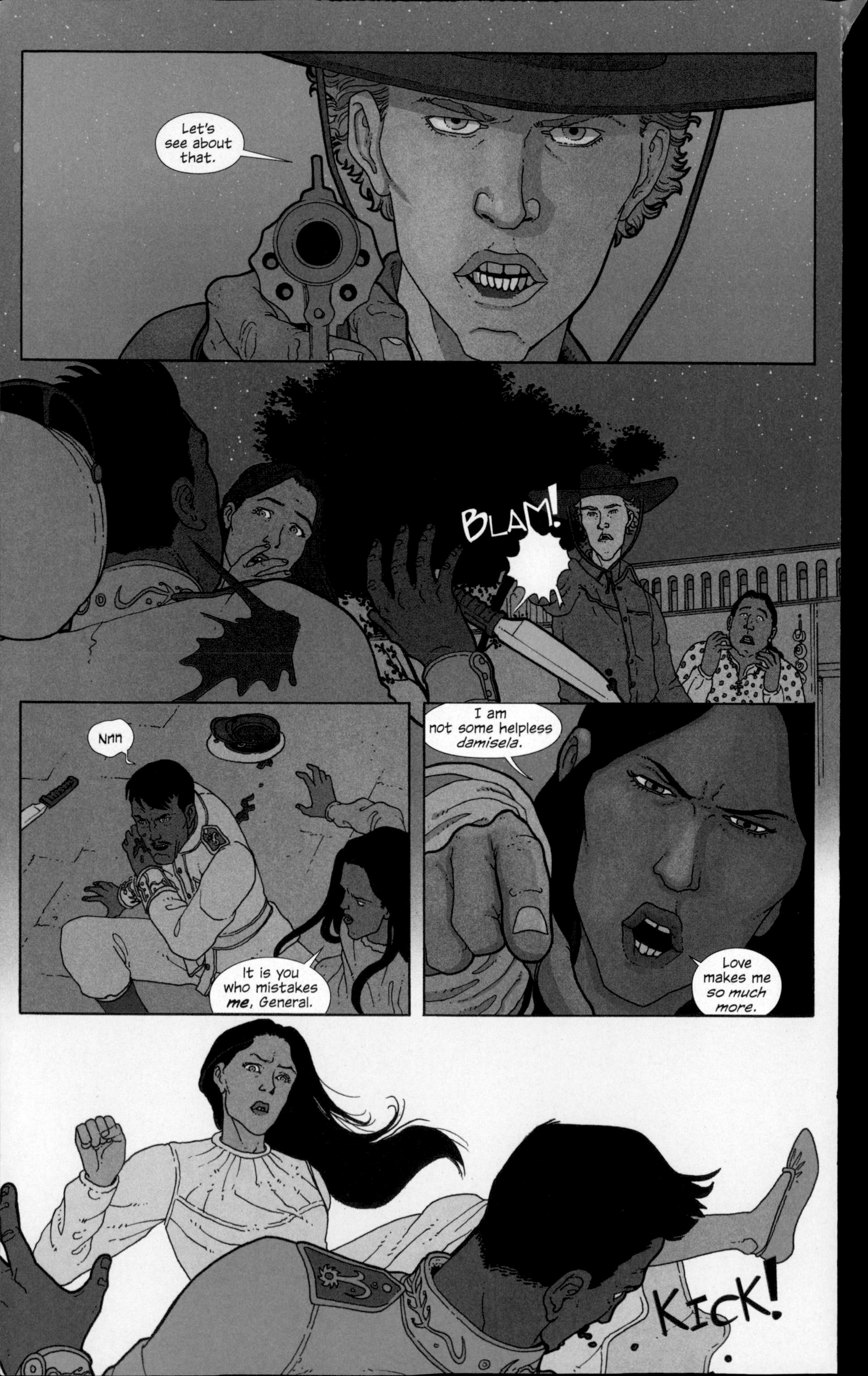
Let's see about that.
BLAM!
Nnn
It is you who mistakes *me*, General.
I am not some helpless *damisela*.
Love makes me so *much* more.
KICK!

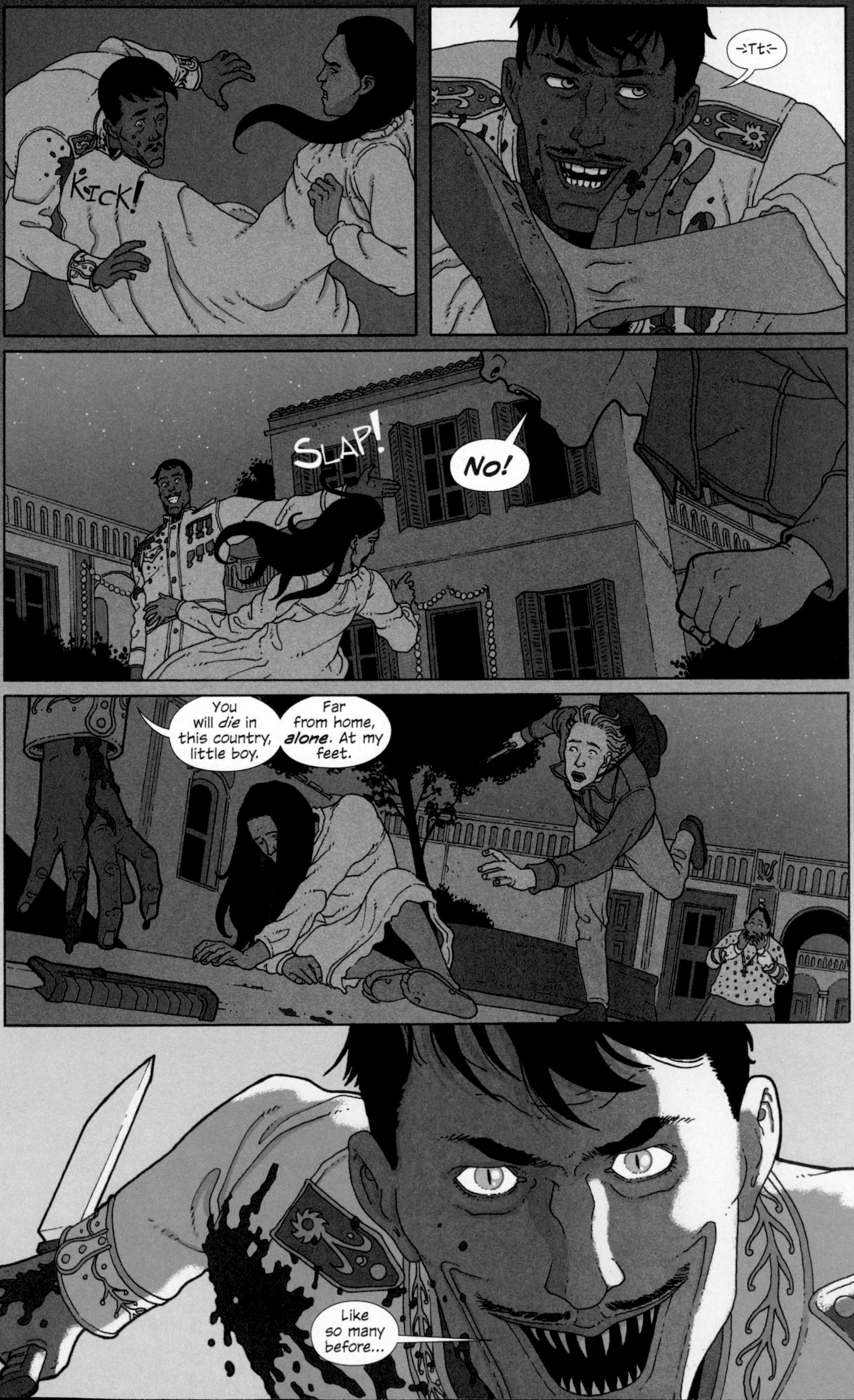
KICK!
-Tt-
SLAP!
NO!
You will *die* in this country, little boy.
Far from home, ***alone***. At my feet.
Like so many before...

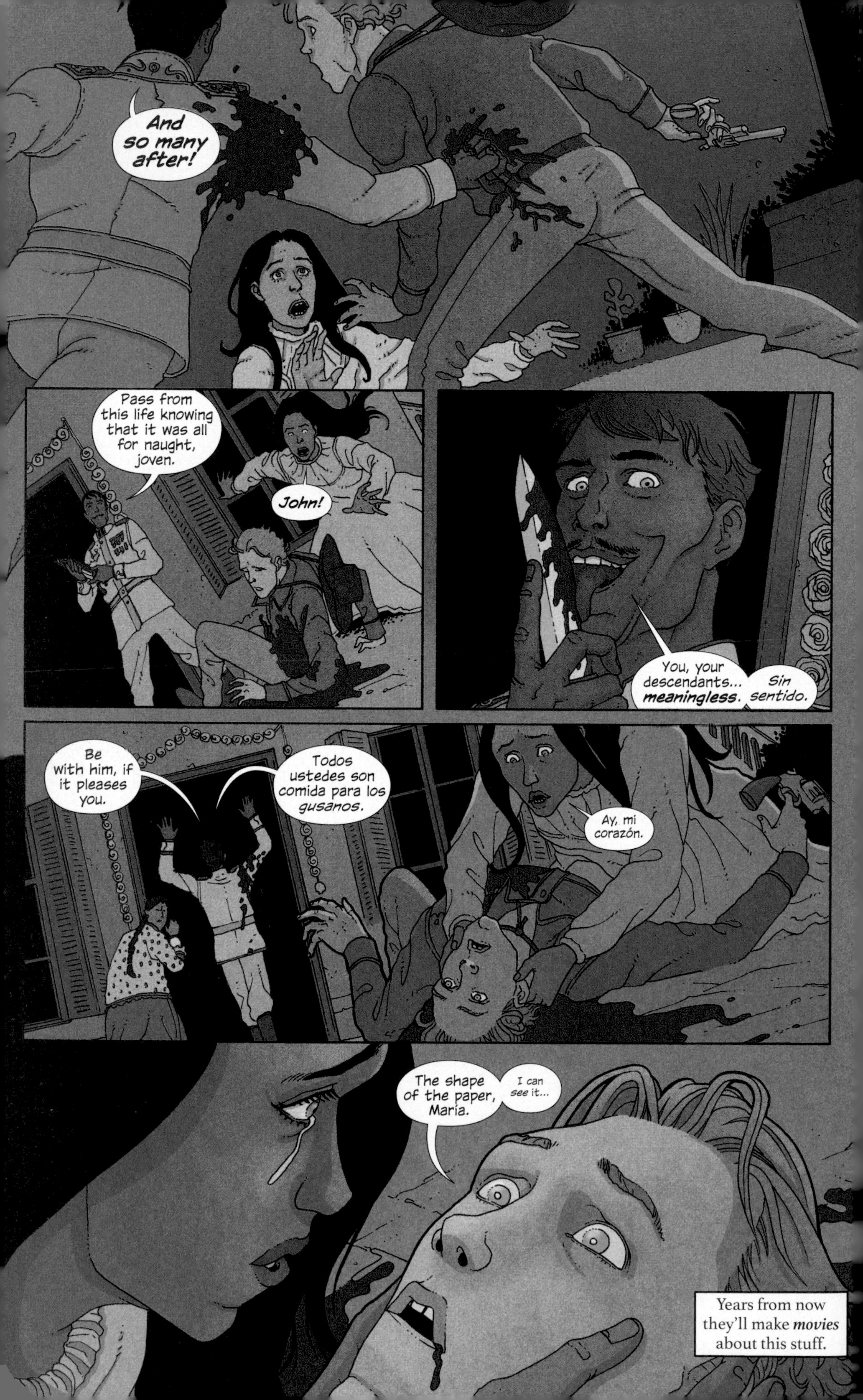
And so many after!
Pass from this life knowing that it was all for naught, joven.
John!
You, your descendants... **meaningless**.
Sin sentido.
Be with him, if it pleases you.
Todos ustedes son comida para los *gusanos*.
Ay, mi corazón.
The shape of the paper, María.
I can see it...
Years from now they'll make *movies* about this stuff.

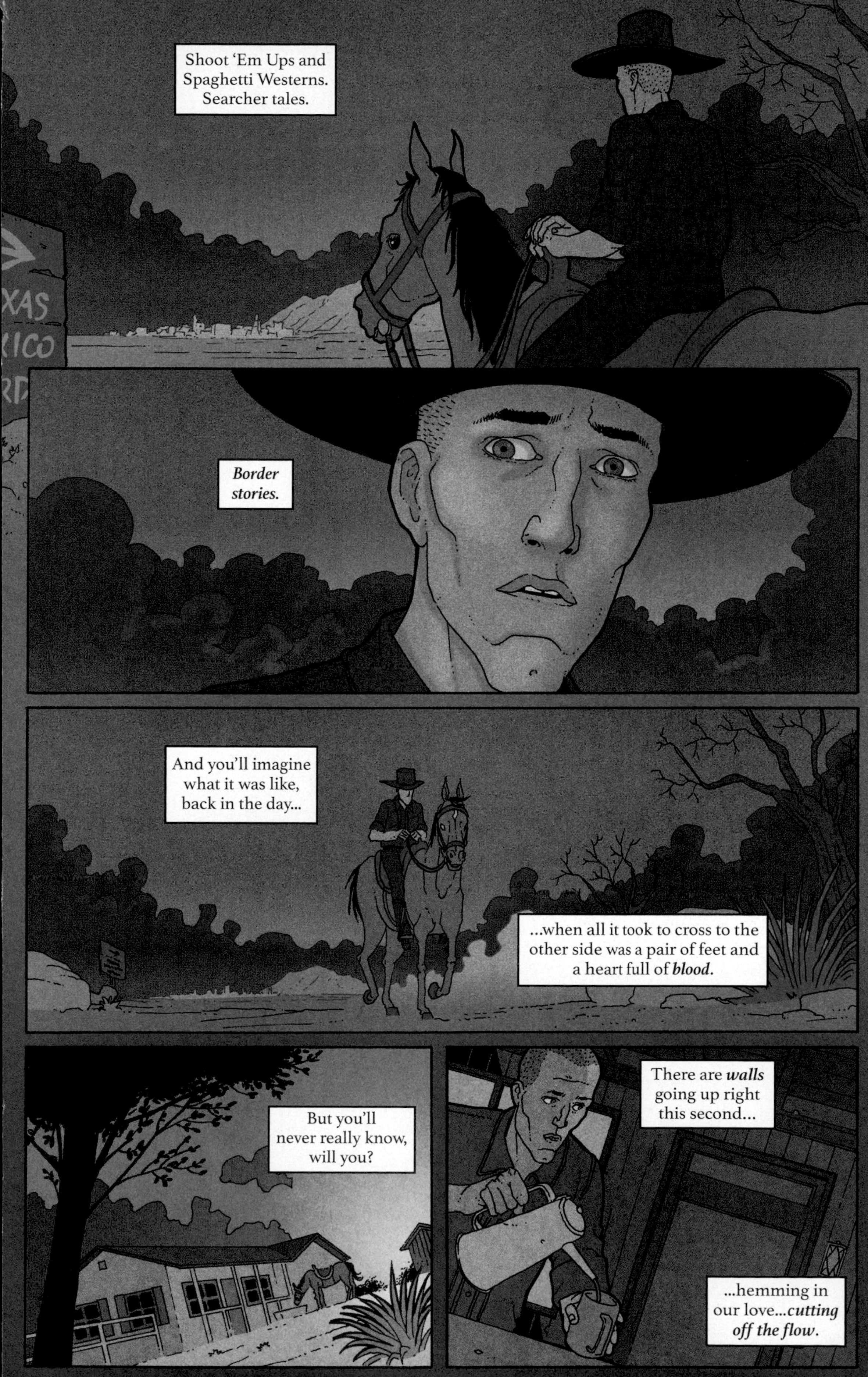
Shoot 'Em Ups and Spaghetti Westerns. Searcher tales.
Border stories.
And you'll imagine what it was like, back in the day...
...when all it took to cross to the other side was a pair of feet and a heart full of ***blood***.
But you'll never really know, will you?
There are ***walls*** going up right this second...
...hemming in our love...***cutting off the flow***.

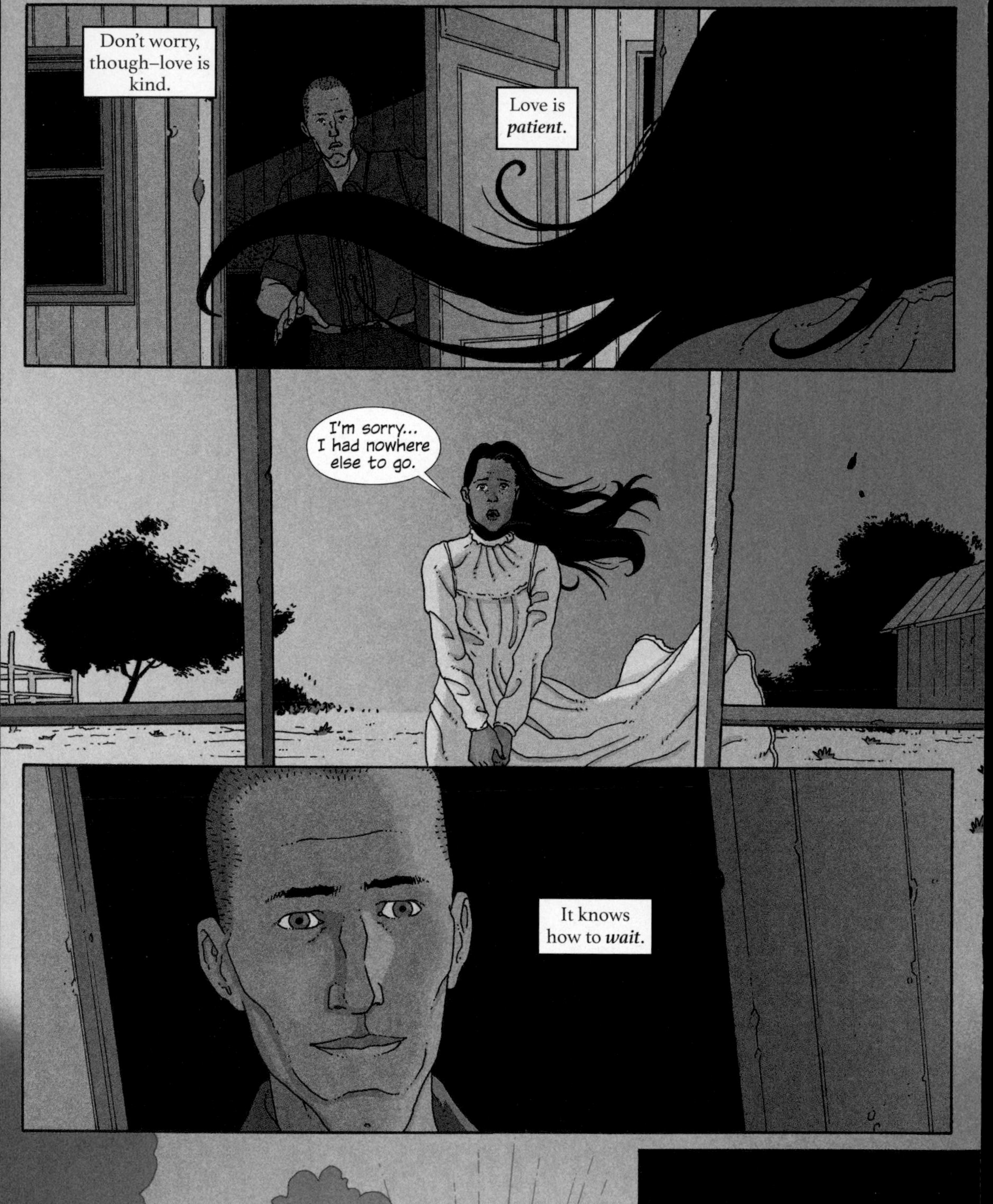
Don't worry, though–love is kind.
Love is *patient*.
I'm sorry... I had nowhere else to go.
It knows how to *wait*.

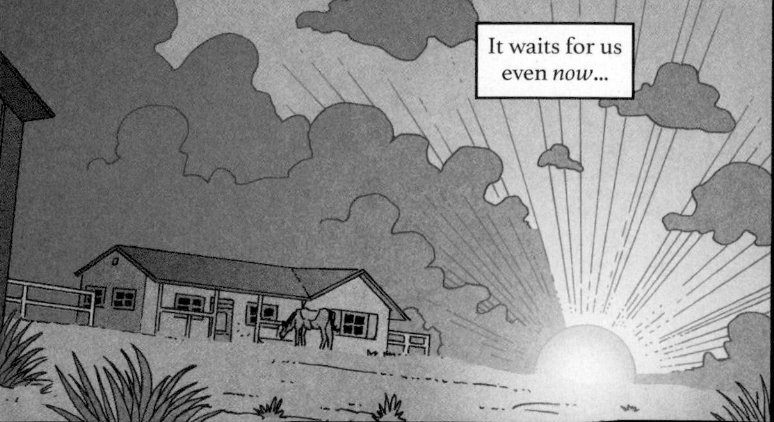
It waits for us even *now*...

Soy hombre: duro poco
y es enorme la noche.
Pero miro hacia arriba:
las estrellas escriben.
Sin entender comprendo:
también soy escritura
y en este mismo instante
alguien me deletrea.

–Octavio Paz, ***Hermandad***

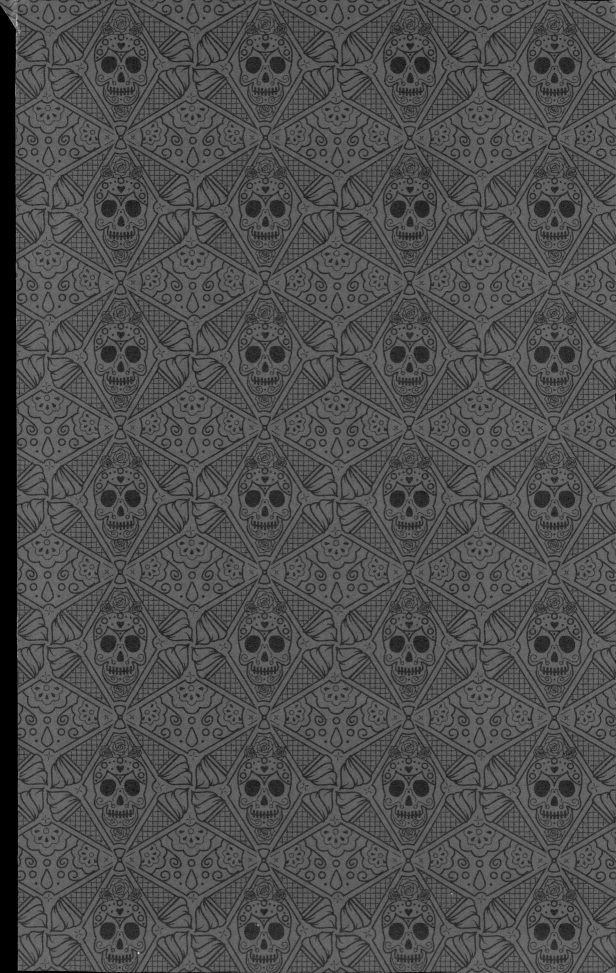

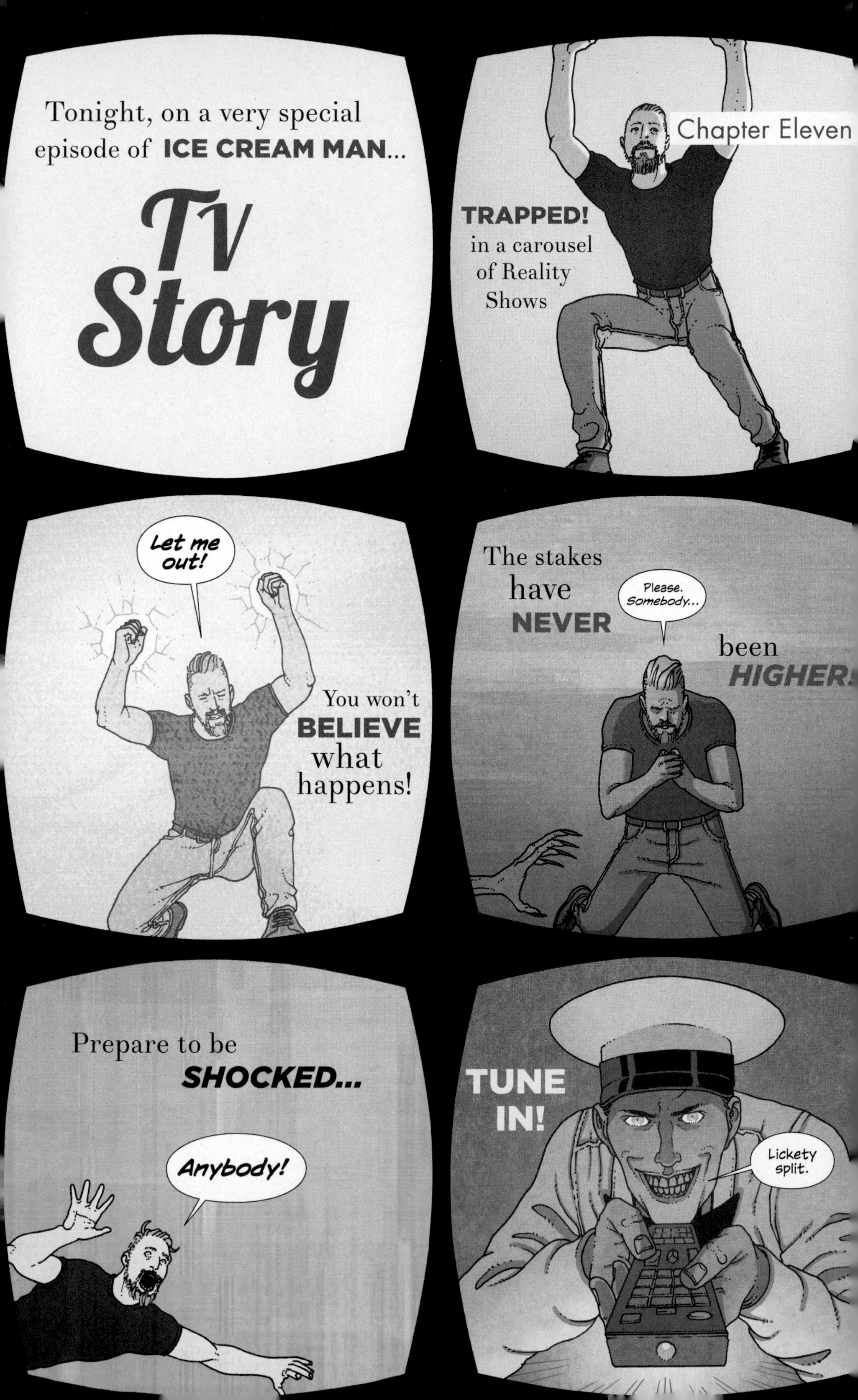
Tonight, on a very special episode of ICE CREAM MAN...
TV Story
Chapter Eleven
TRAPPED! in a carousel of Reality Shows
Let me out!
You won't BELIEVE what happens!
The stakes have NEVER
Please. Somebody...
been HIGHER!
Prepare to be SHOCKED...
Anybody!
TUNE IN!
Lickety split.

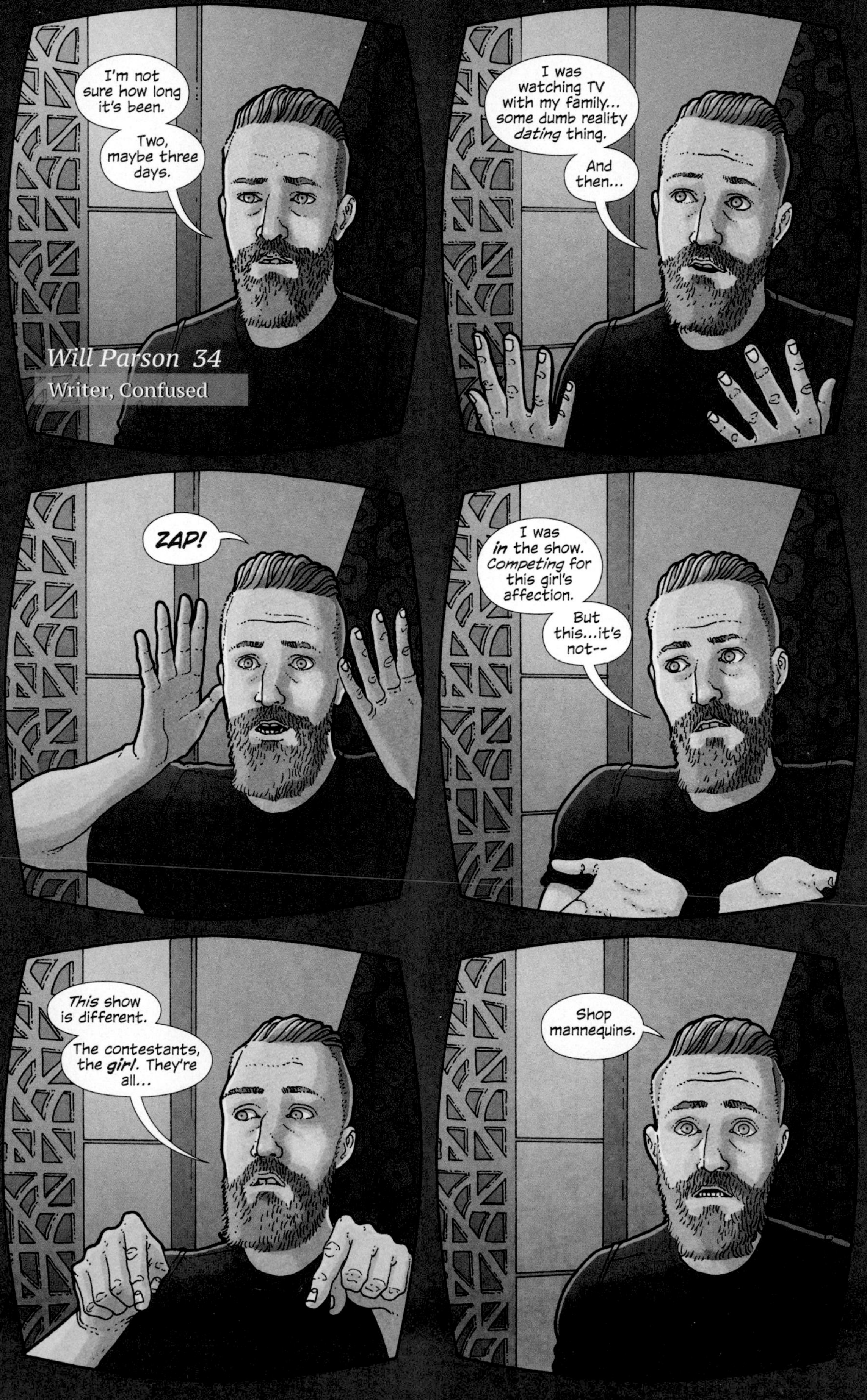
I'm not sure how long it's been.
Two, maybe three days.
Will Parson 34
Writer, Confused
I was watching TV with my family... some dumb reality *dating* thing.
And then...
ZAP!
I was *in* the show. *Competing* for this girl's affection.
But this...it's not--
This show is different.
The contestants, the *girl*. They're all...
Shop mannequins.

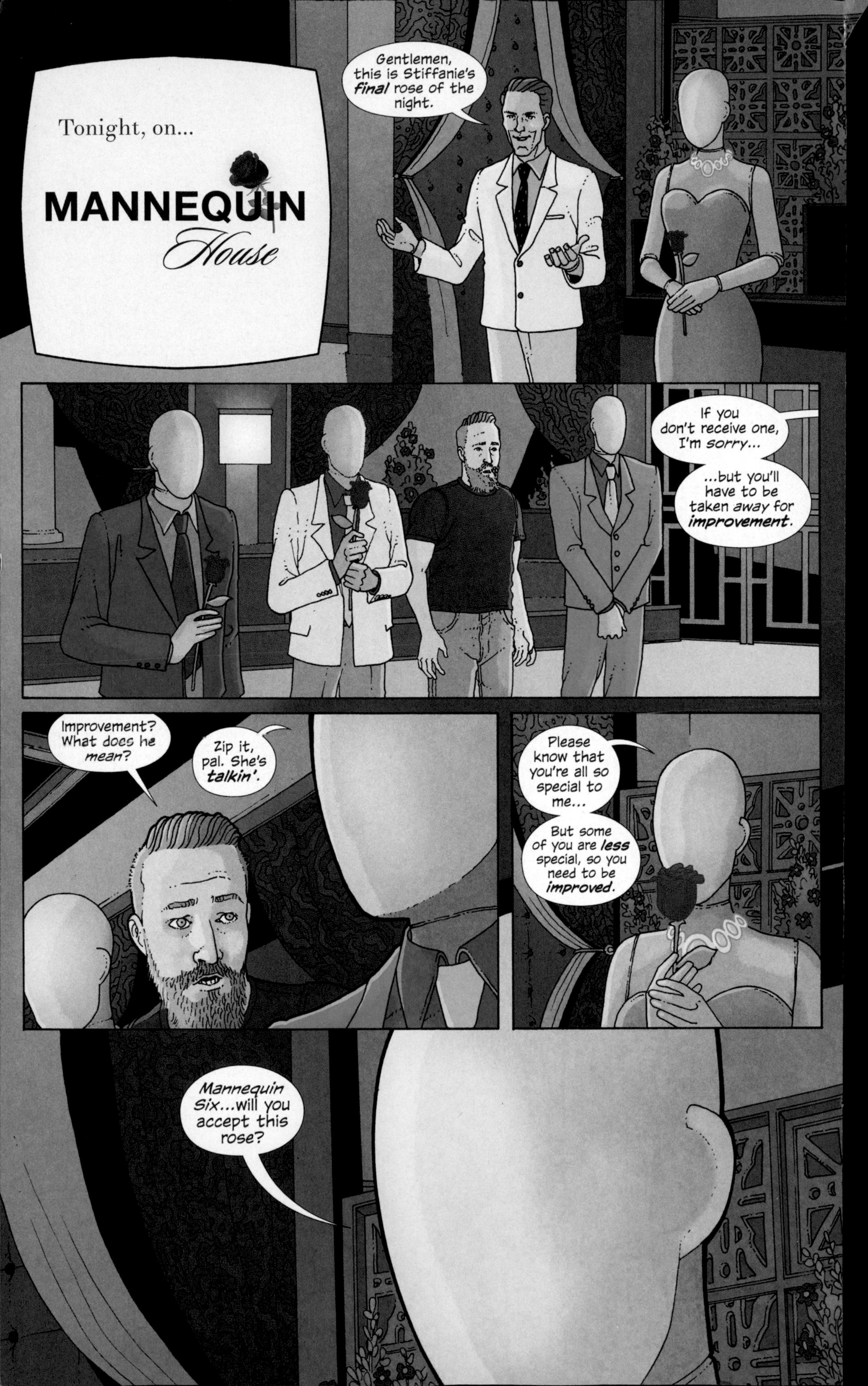
Tonight, on...
MANNEQUIN House
Gentlemen, this is Stiffanie's *final* rose of the night.
If you don't receive one, I'm *sorry*...
...but you'll have to be taken *away* for ***improvement***.
Improvement? What does he *mean*?
Zip it, pal. She's ***talkin'***.
Please know that you're all so special to me...
But some of you are ***less*** special, so you need to be ***improved***.
Mannequin Six...will you accept this rose?

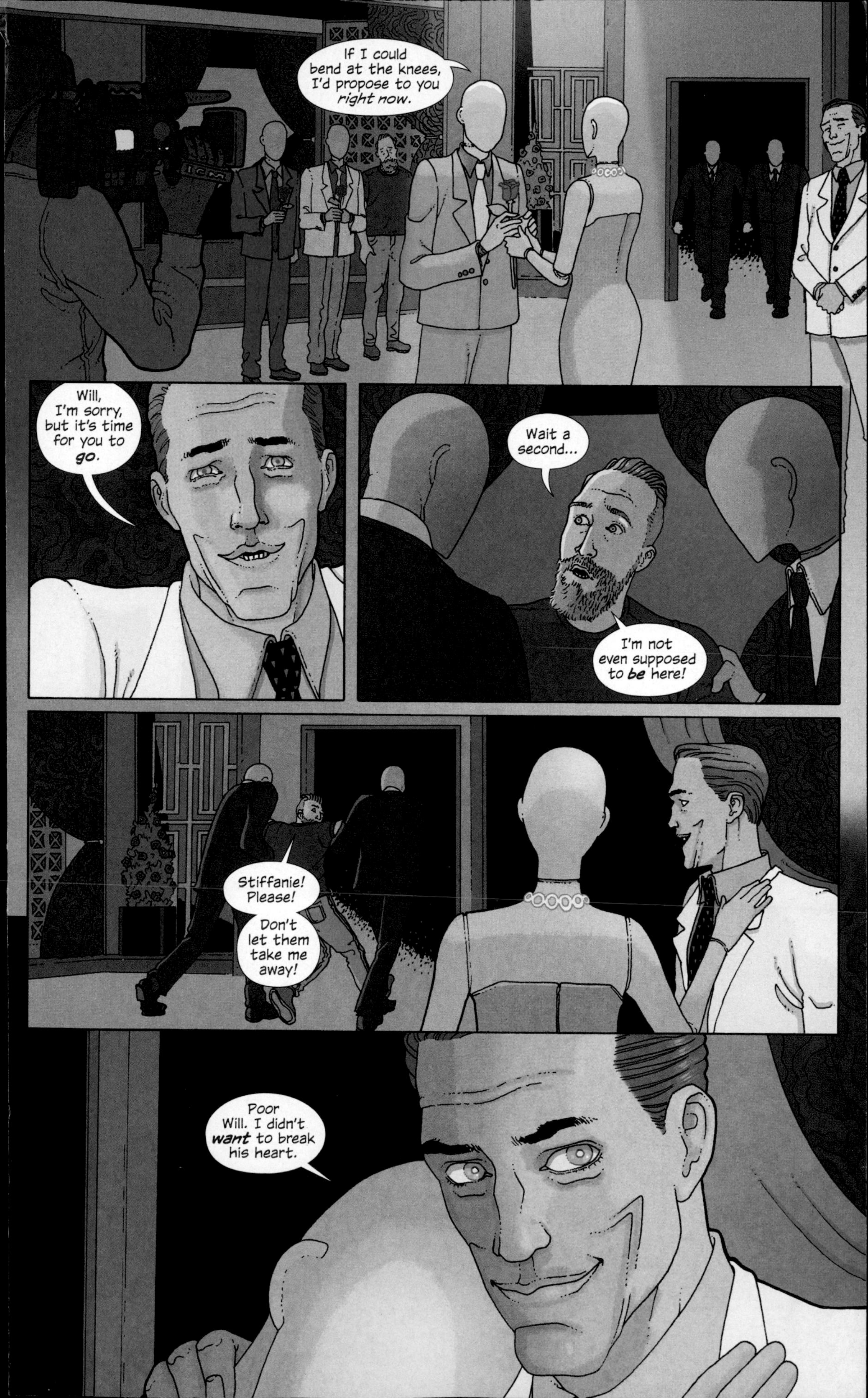

If I could bend at the knees, I'd propose to you *right now*.
Will, I'm sorry, but it's time for you to **go**.
Wait a second...
I'm not even supposed to **be** here!
Stiffanie! Please!
Don't let them take me away!
Poor Will. I didn't **want** to break his heart.

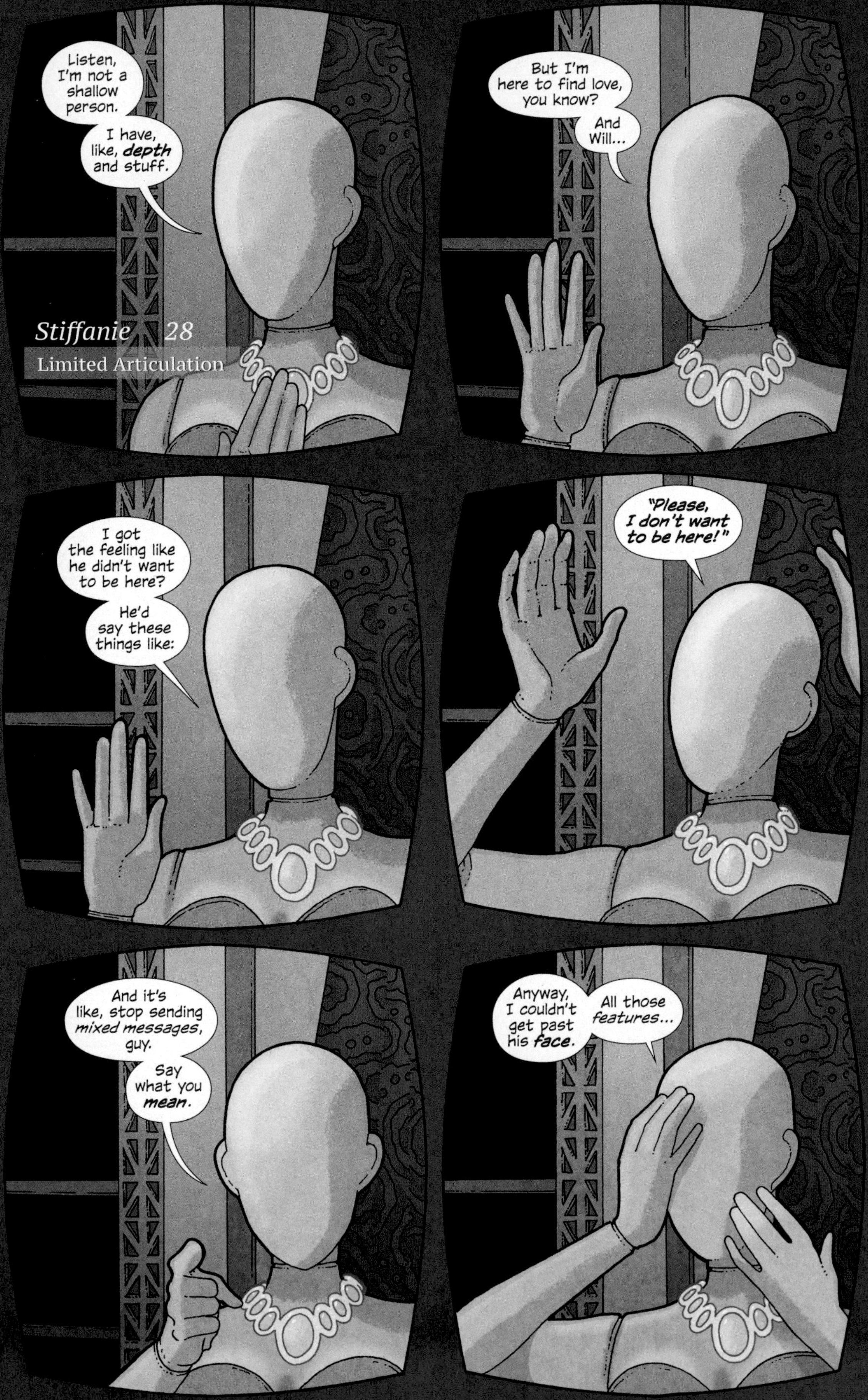
Listen, I'm not a shallow person.
I have, like, depth and stuff.
Stiffanie 28
Limited Articulation
But I'm here to find love, you know?
And Will...
I got the feeling like he didn't want to be here?
He'd say these things like:
"Please, I don't want to be here!"
And it's like, stop sending mixed messages, guy.
Say what you mean.
Anyway, I couldn't get past his face.
All those features...

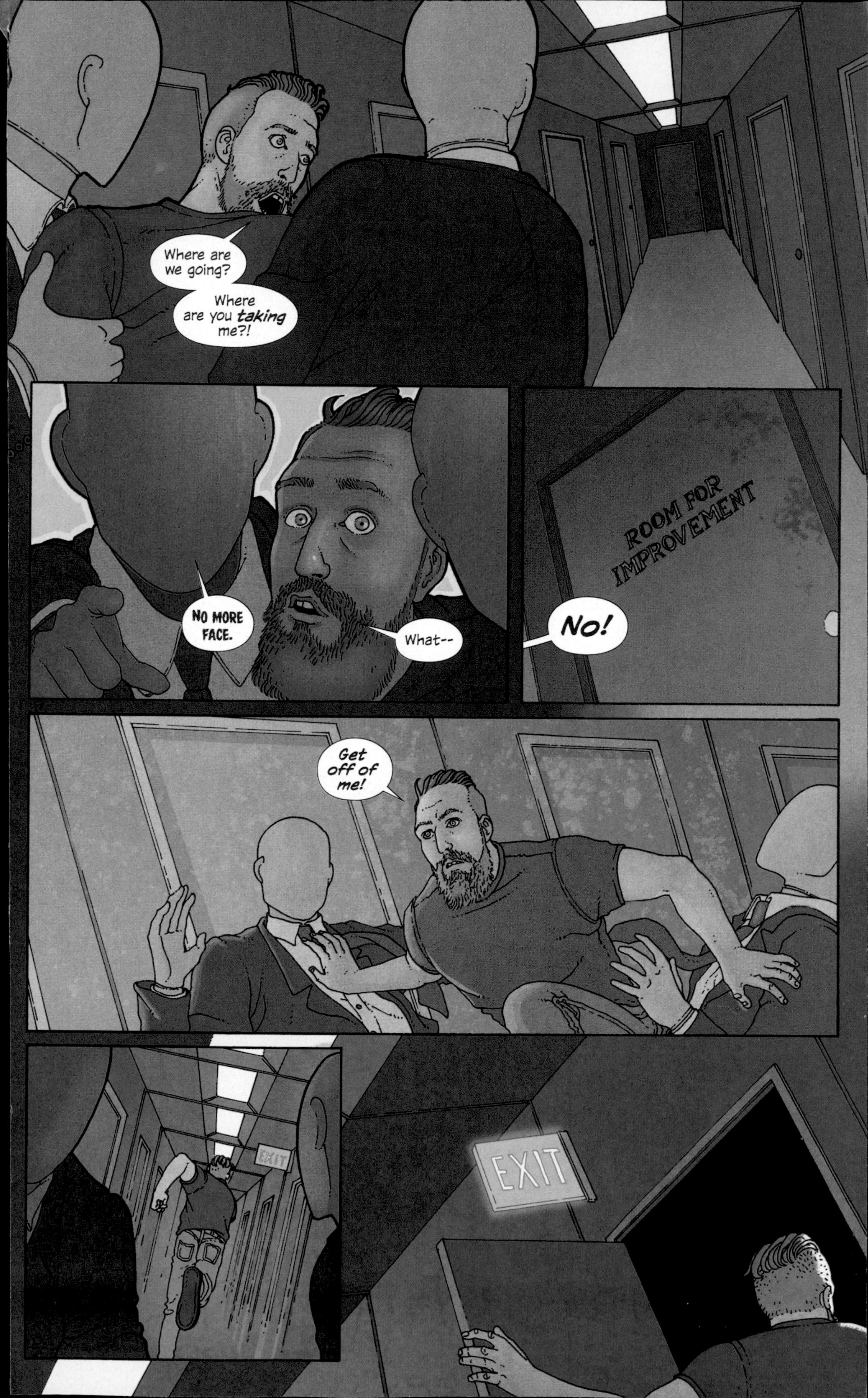
Where are we going?
Where are you *taking* me?!
NO MORE FACE.
What--
ROOM FOR IMPROVEMENT
No!
Get off of me!
EXIT
EXIT

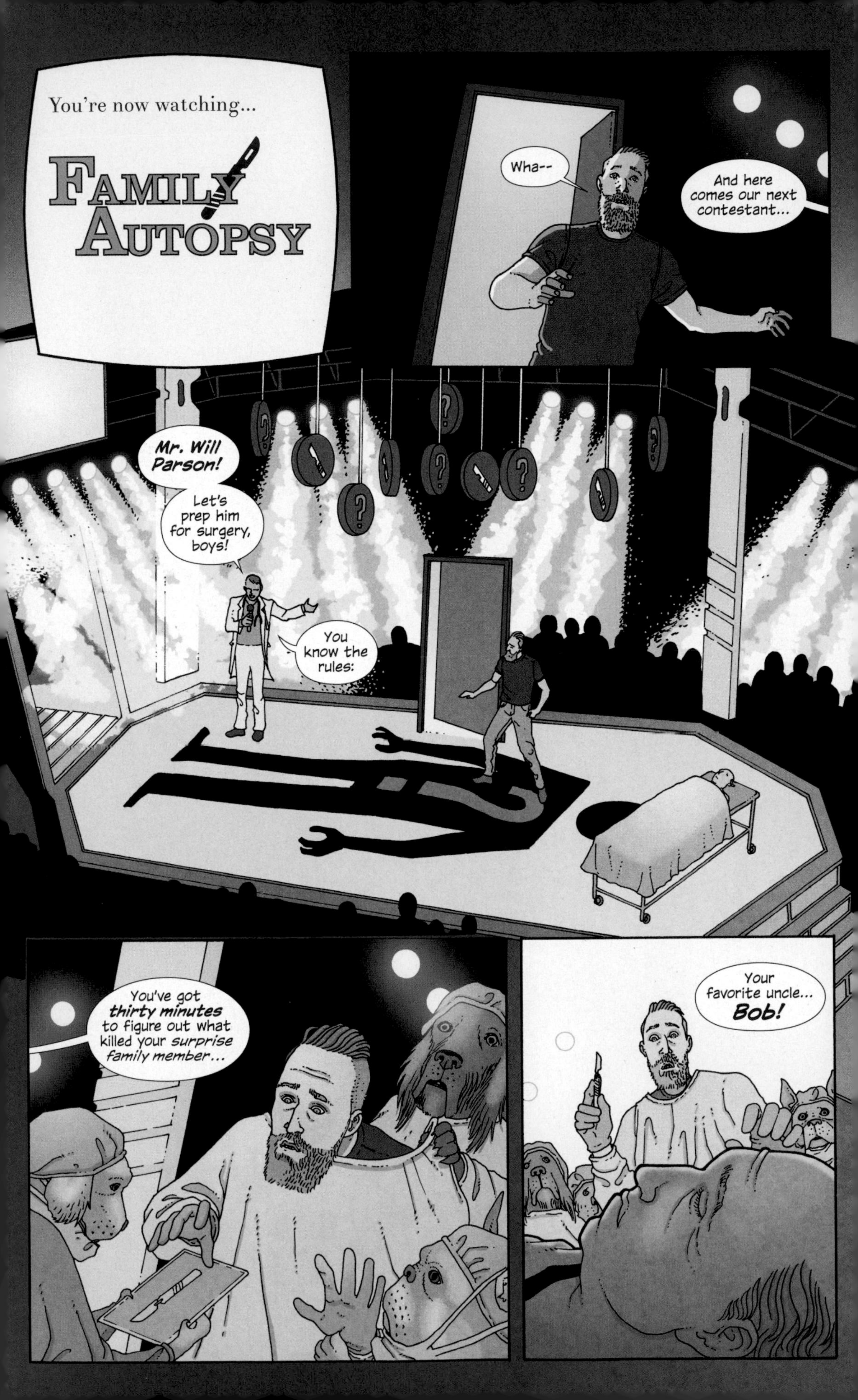
You're now watching...
FAMILY AUTOPSY
Wha--
And here comes our next contestant...
Mr. Will Parson!
Let's prep him for surgery, boys!
You know the rules:
You've got thirty minutes to figure out what killed your surprise family member...
Your favorite uncle... Bob!

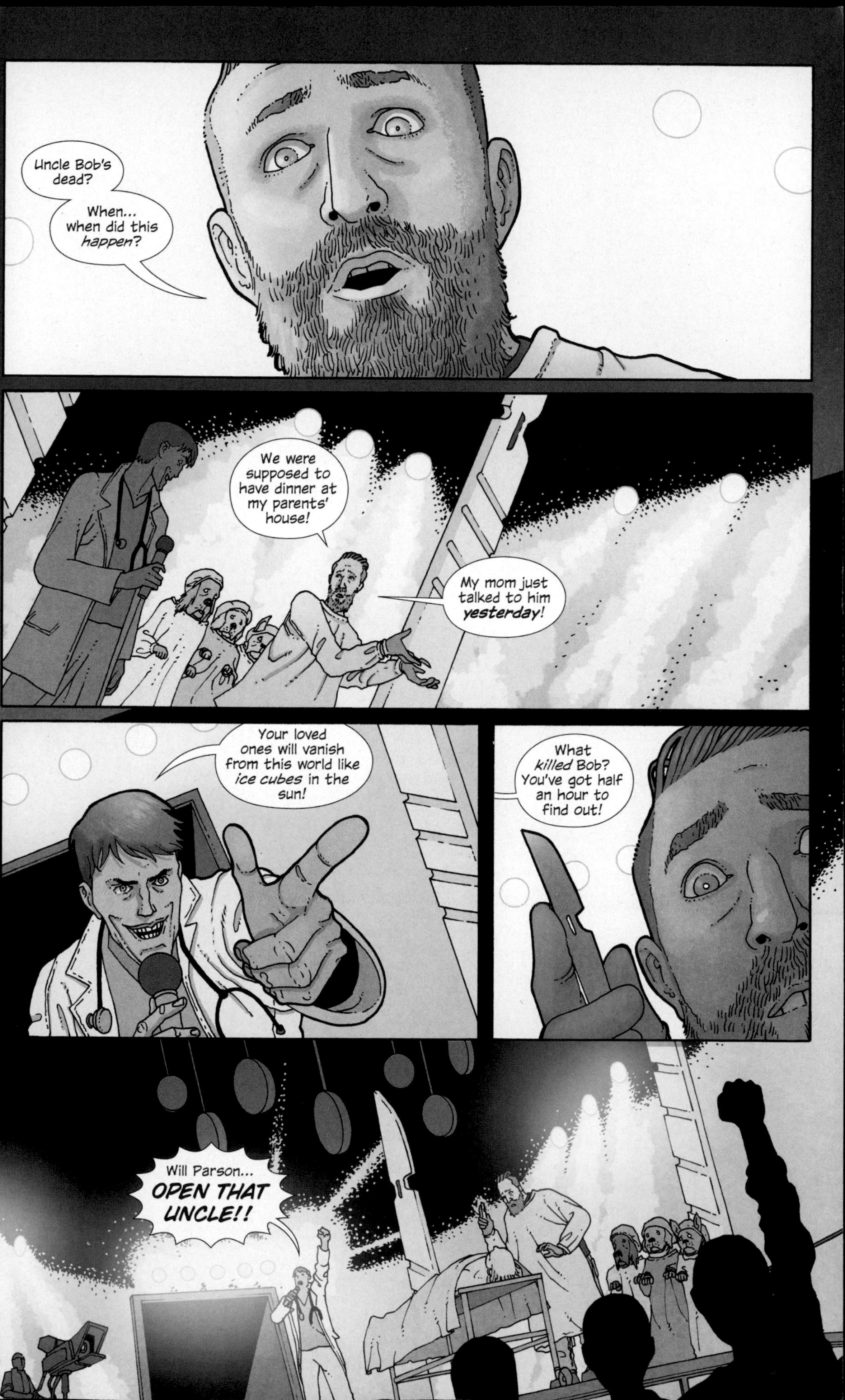
Uncle Bob's dead?
When... when did this *happen*?
We were supposed to have dinner at my parents' house!
My mom just talked to him ***yesterday***!
Your loved ones will vanish from this world like *ice cubes* in the sun!
What *killed* Bob? You've got half an hour to find out!
Will Parson... **OPEN THAT UNCLE!!**

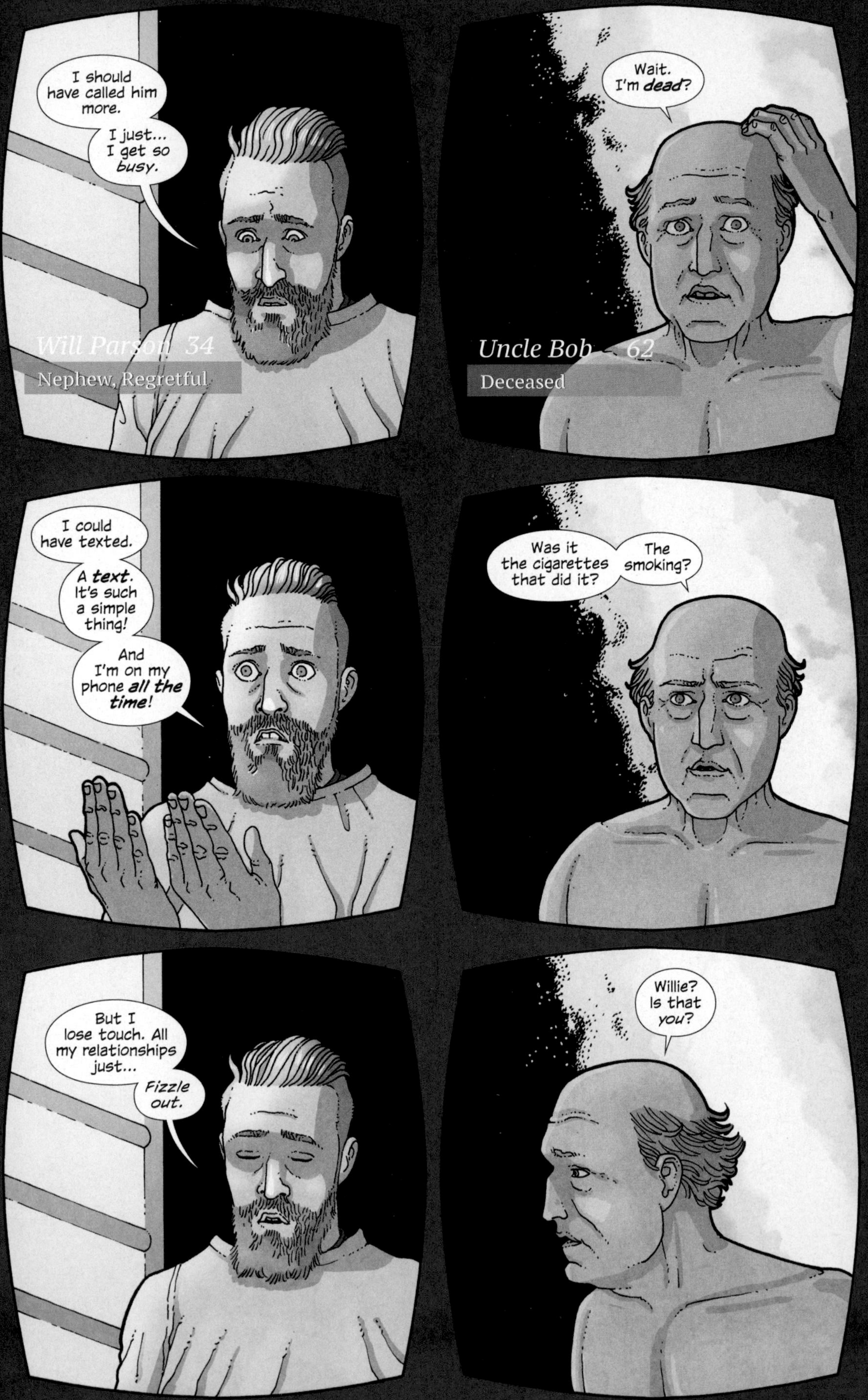
I should have called him more.
I just... I get so busy.
Will Parson 34
Nephew, Regretful
Wait. I'm dead?
Uncle Bob 62
Deceased
I could have texted.
A text. It's such a simple thing!
And I'm on my phone all the time!
Was it the cigarettes that did it?
The smoking?
But I lose touch. All my relationships just...
Fizzle out.
Willie? Is that you?

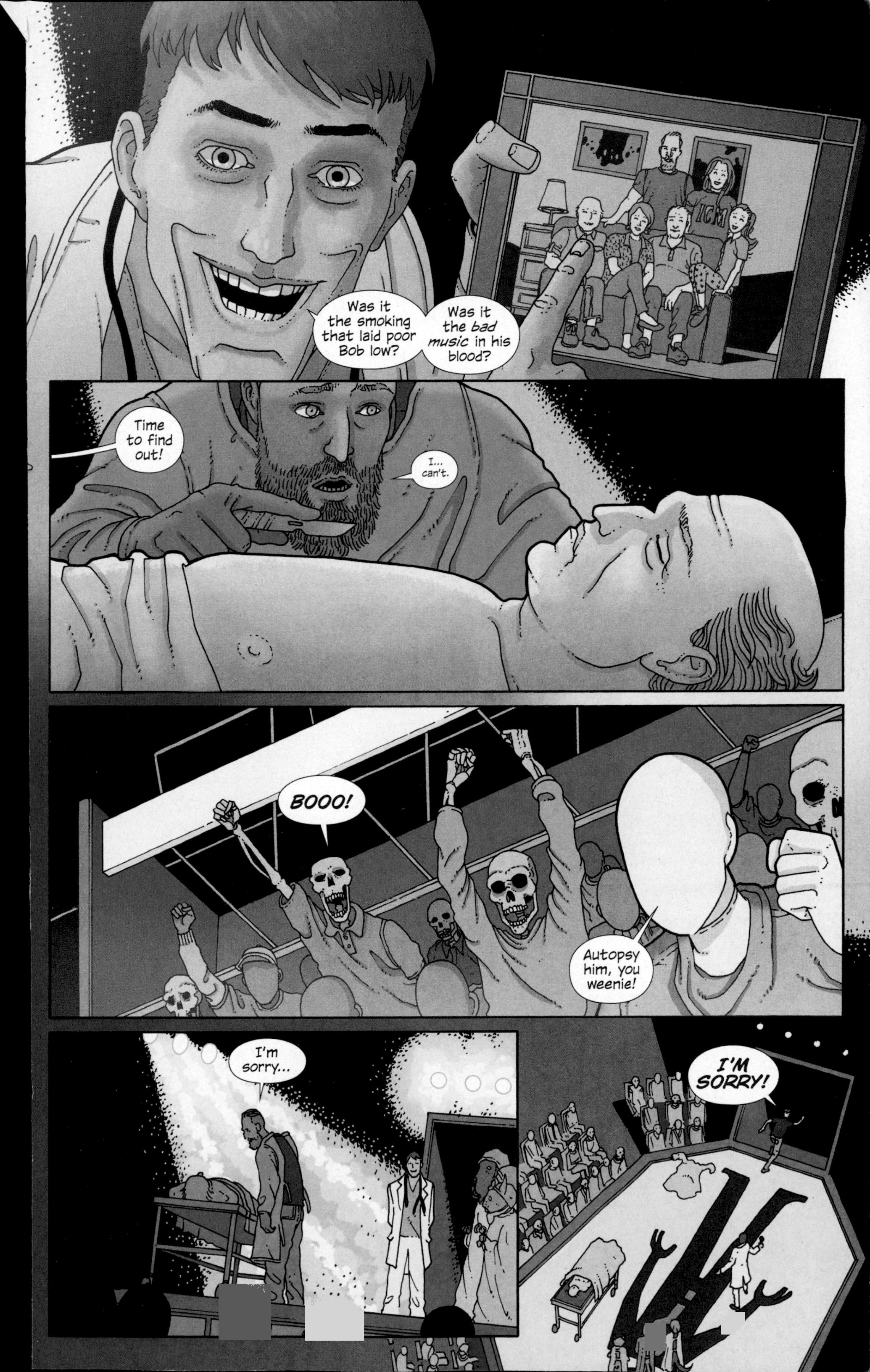
Was it the smoking that laid poor Bob low?
Was it the *bad music* in his blood?
Time to find out!
I... can't.
BOOO!
Autopsy him, you weenie!
I'm sorry...
I'M SORRY!

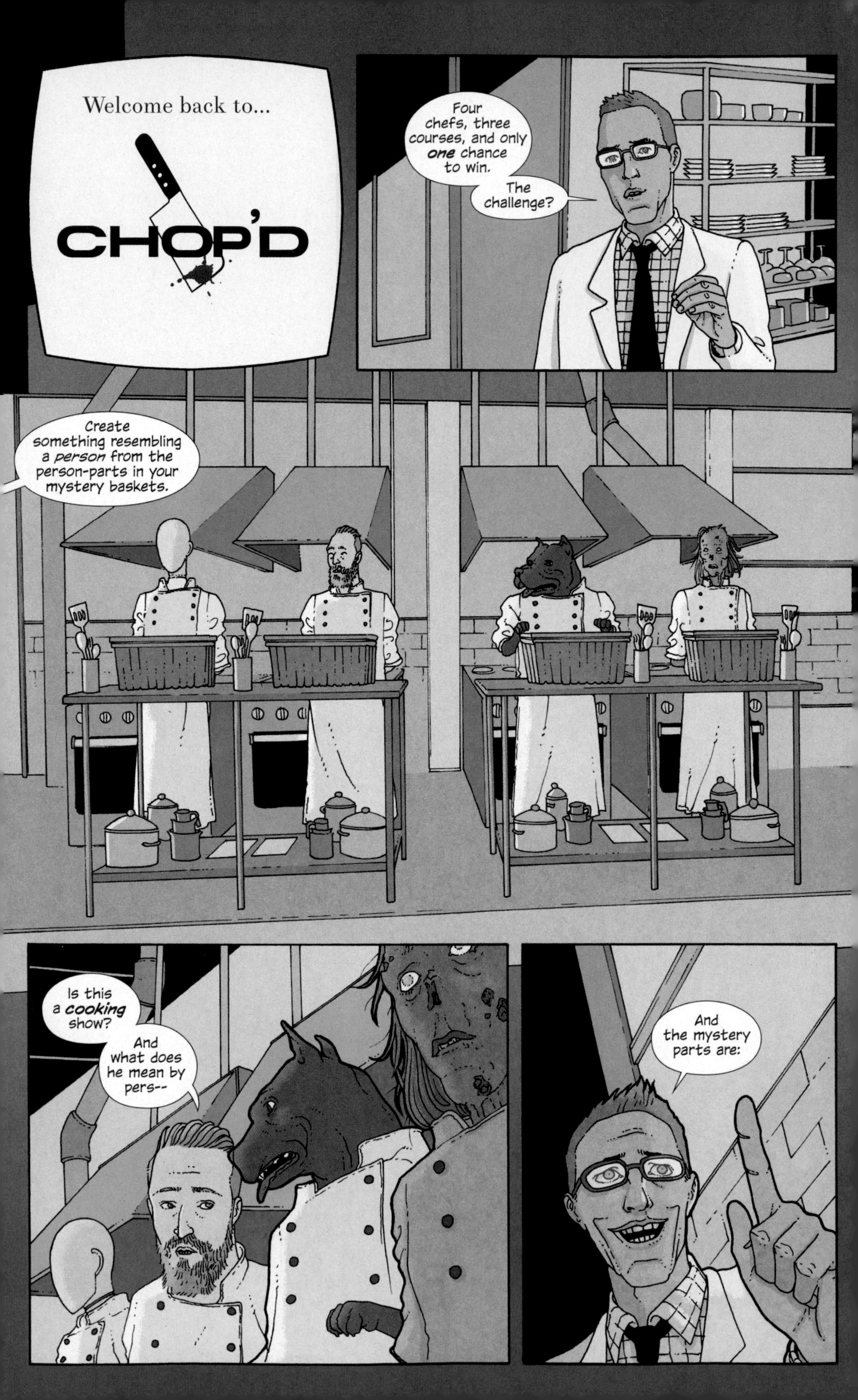
Welcome back to...
CHOP'D
Four chefs, three courses, and only one chance to win.
The challenge?
Create something resembling a person from the person-parts in your mystery baskets.
Is this a cooking show?
And what does he mean by pers--
And the mystery parts are:

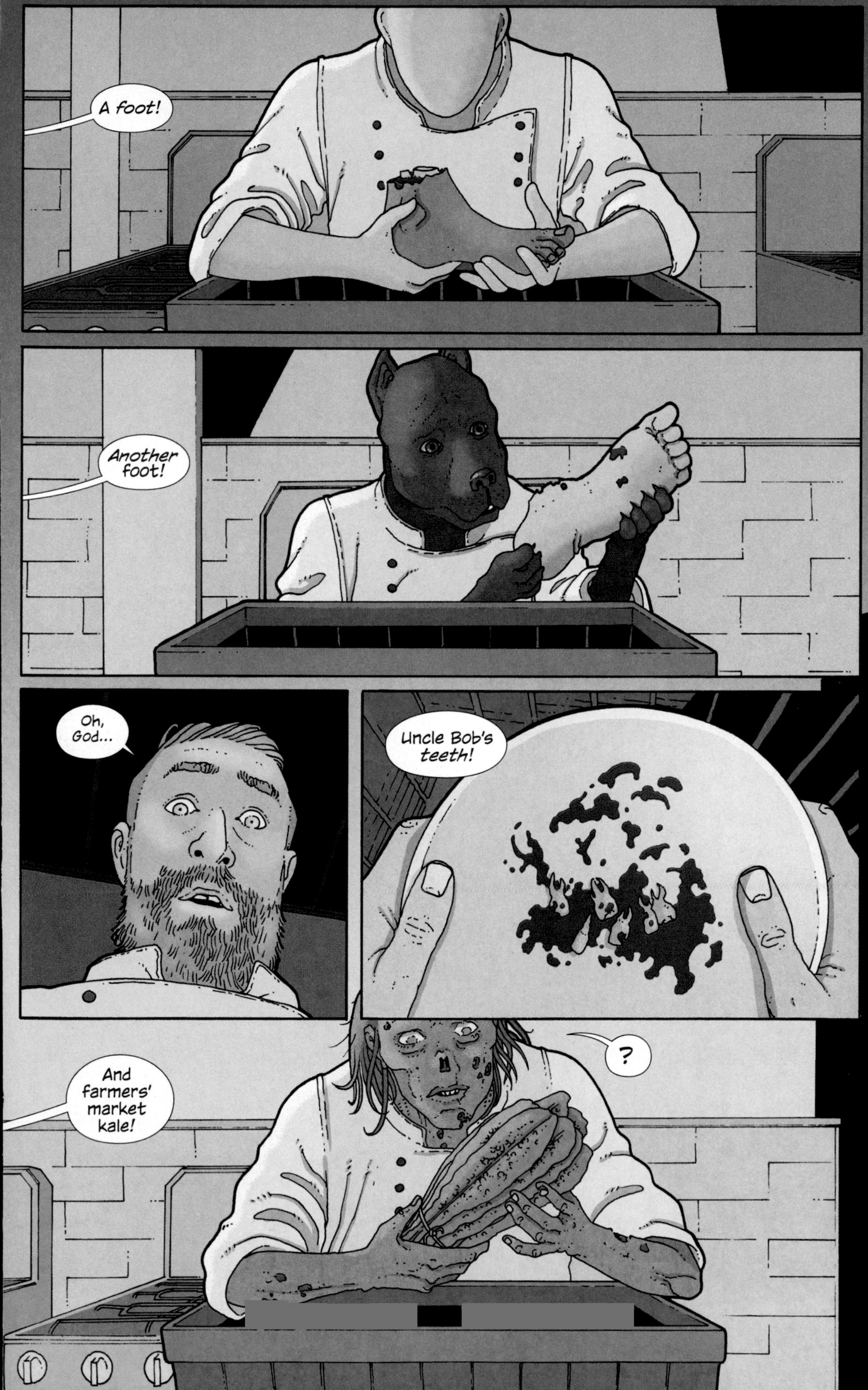
A foot!
Another foot!
Oh, God...
Uncle Bob's teeth!
And farmers' market kale!
?

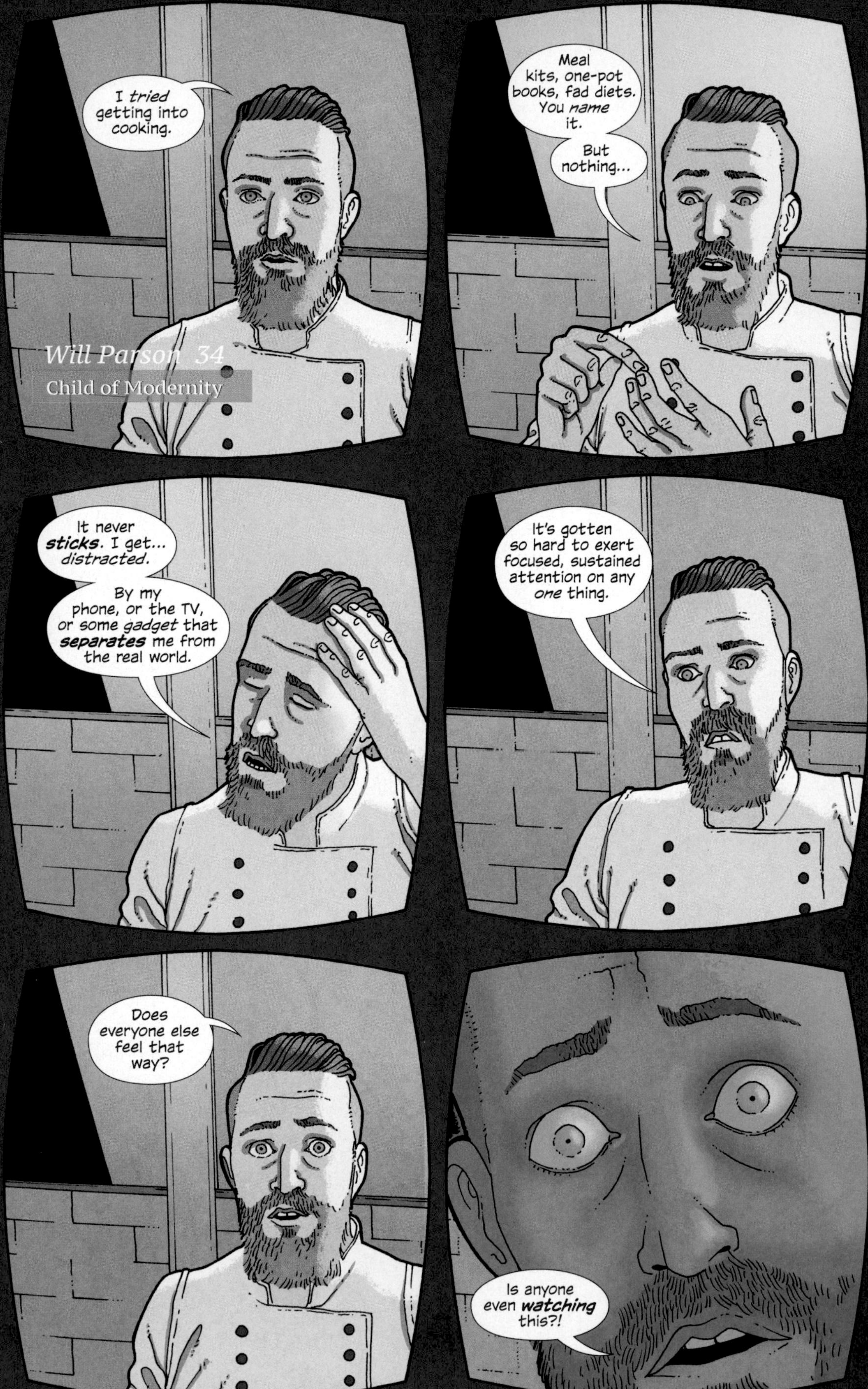

I *tried* getting into cooking.
Will Parson 34
Child of Modernity
Meal kits, one-pot books, fad diets. You *name* it.
But nothing...
It never **sticks**. I get... *distracted*.
By my phone, or the TV, or some *gadget* that **separates** me from the real world.
It's gotten so hard to exert focused, sustained attention on any *one* thing.
Does everyone else feel that way?
Is anyone even **watching** this?!

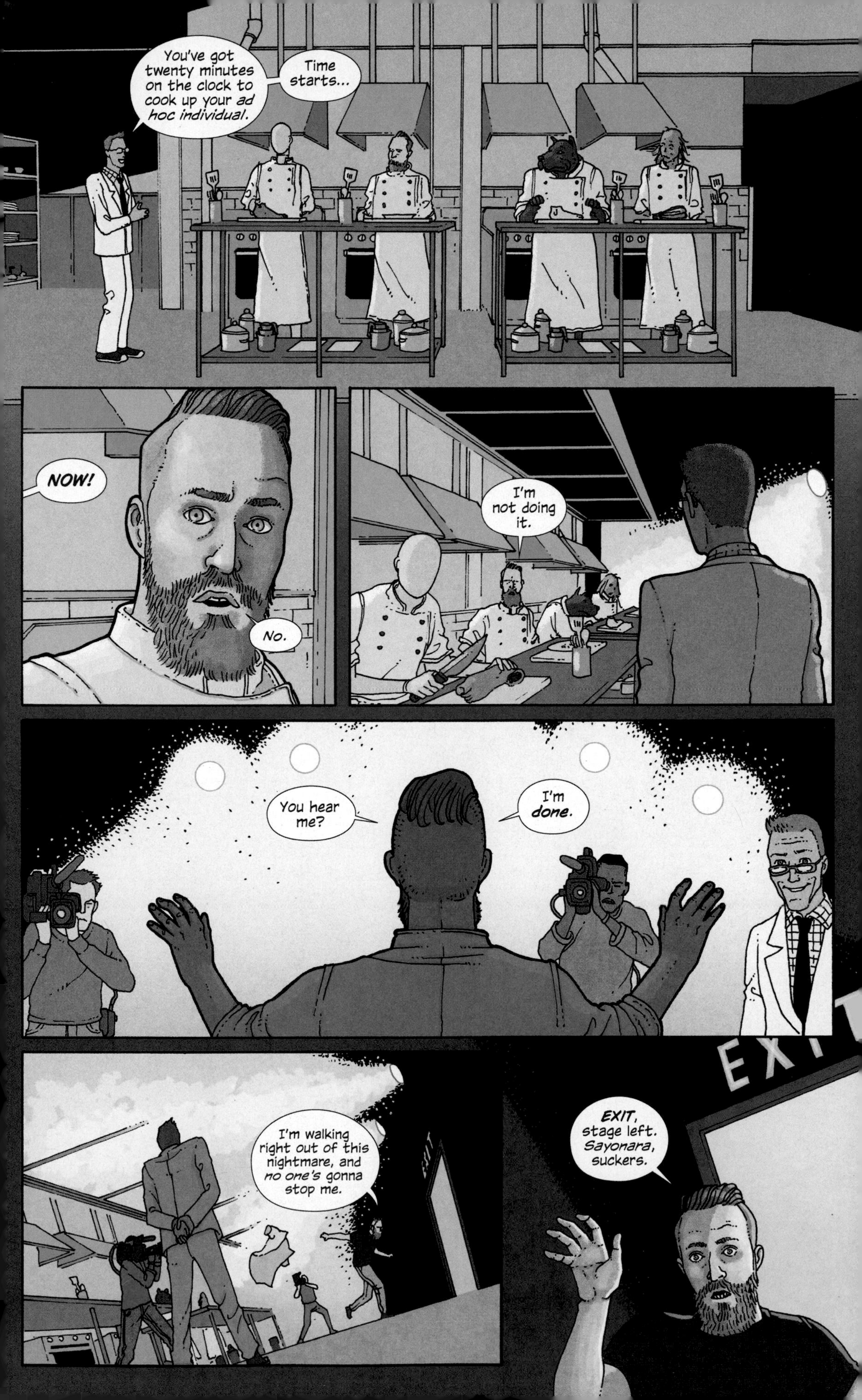
You've got twenty minutes on the clock to cook up your *ad hoc individual*.
Time starts...
NOW!
No.
I'm not doing it.
You hear me?
I'm *done*.
I'm walking right out of this nightmare, and *no one's* gonna stop me.
EXIT
EXIT, stage left. *Sayonara*, suckers.

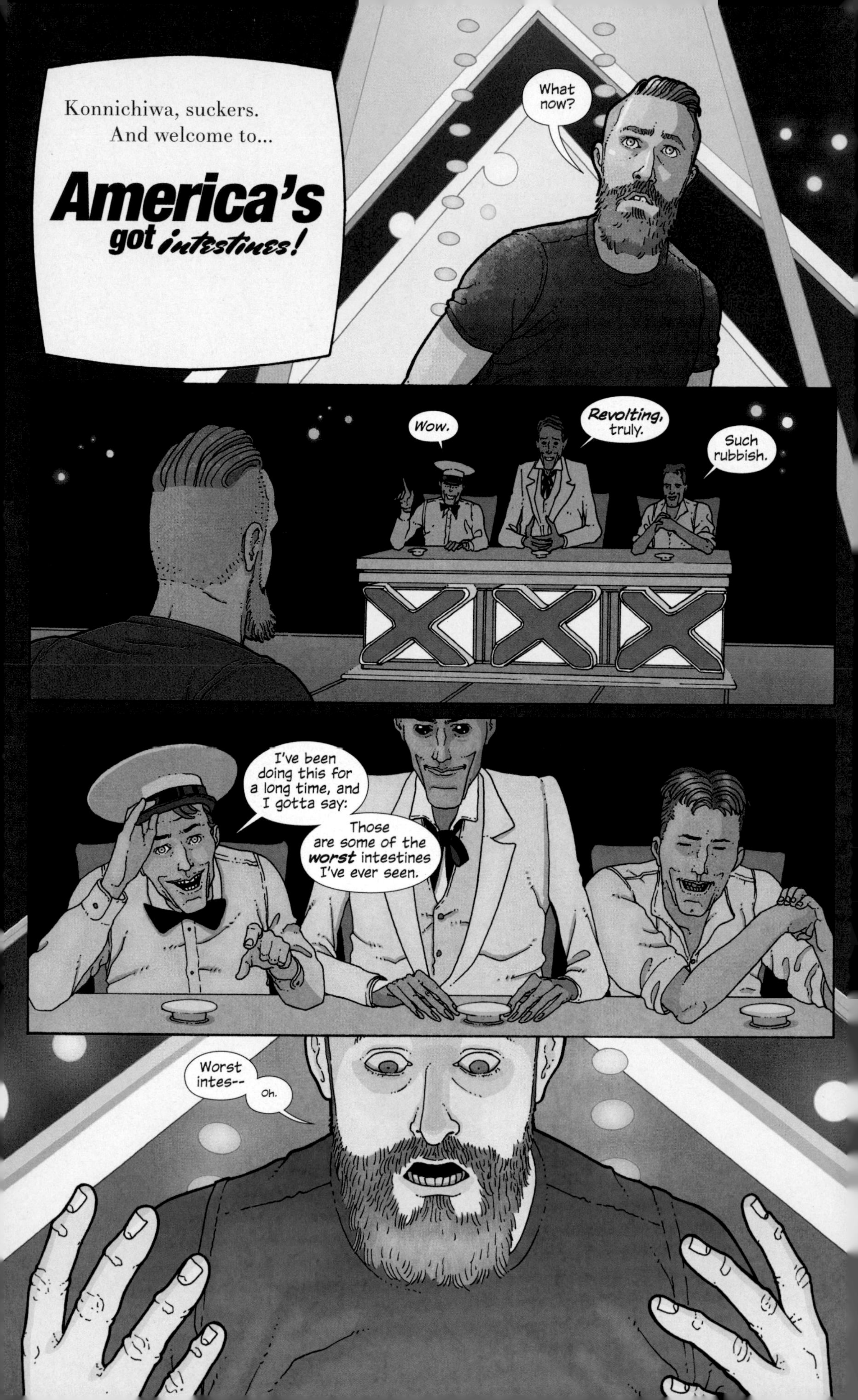
Konnichiwa, suckers.
And welcome to...
America's
got intestines!
What now?
Wow.
Revolting, truly.
Such rubbish.
I've been doing this for a long time, and I gotta say:
Those are some of the worst intestines I've ever seen.
Worst intes--
Oh.

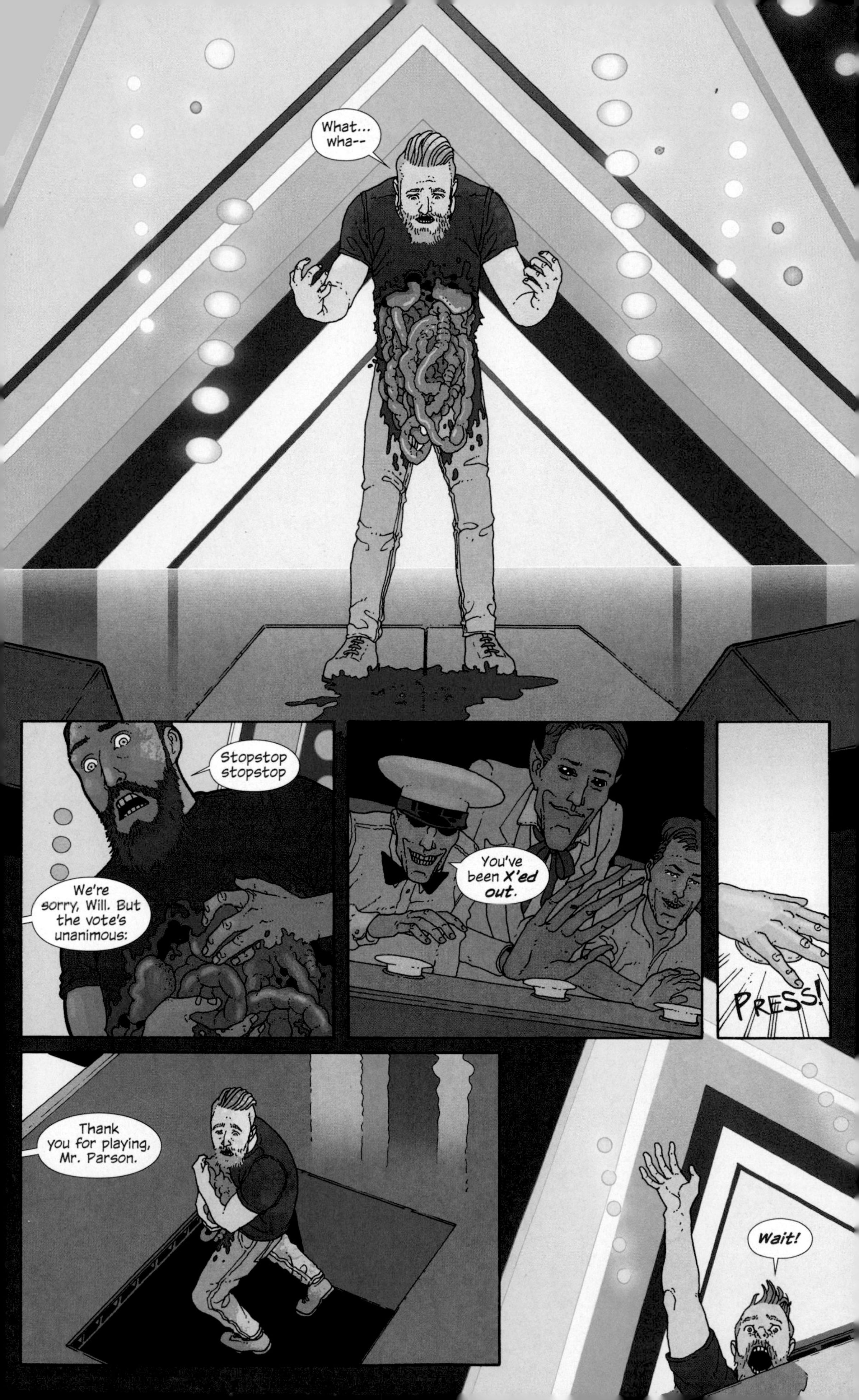
What... wha--
Stopstop stopstop
We're sorry, Will. But the vote's unanimous:
You've been X'ed out.
PRESS!
Thank you for playing, Mr. Parson.
Wait!

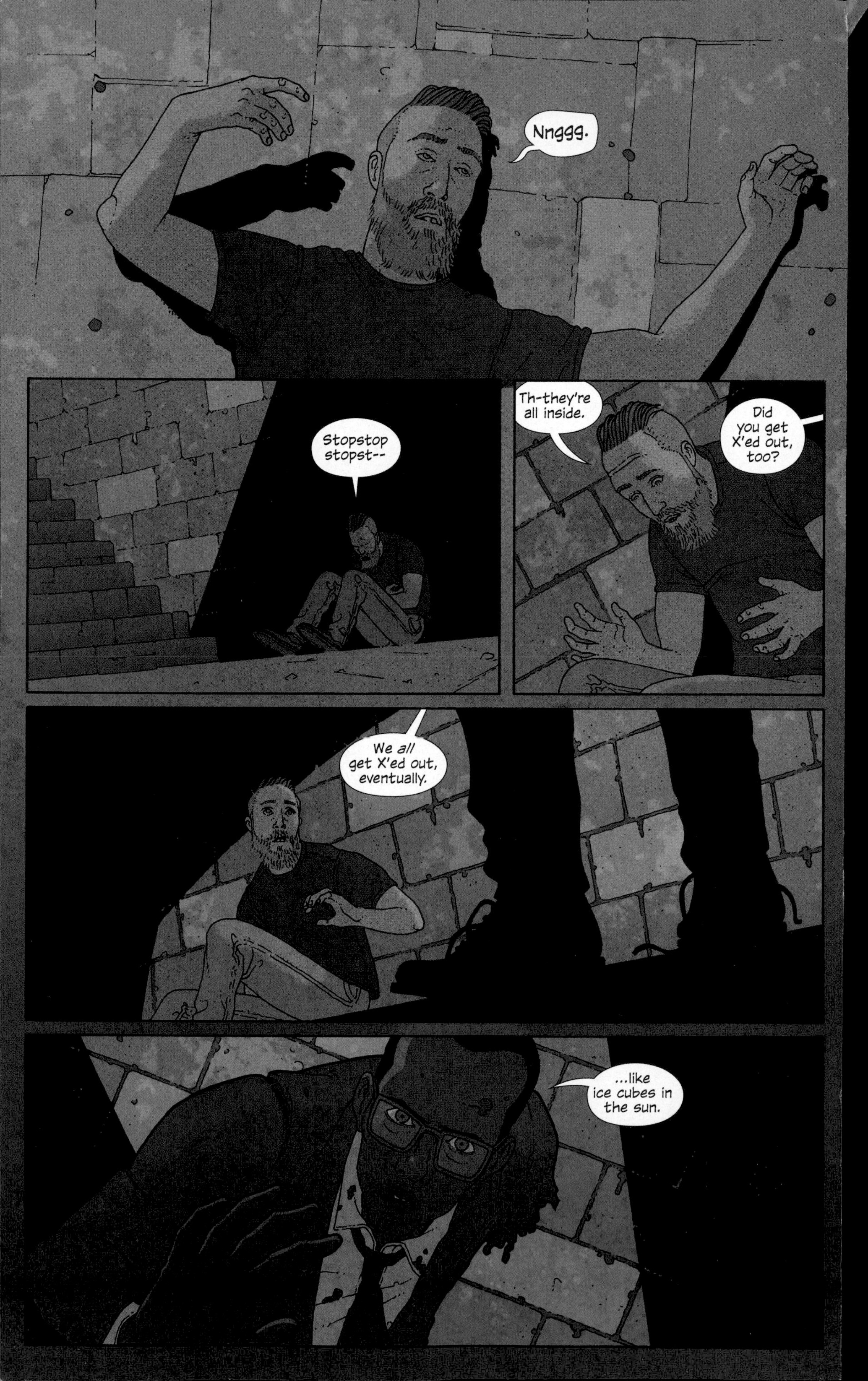
Nnggg.
Stopstop stopst--
Th-they're all inside.
Did you get X'ed out, too?
We *all* get X'ed out, eventually.
...like ice cubes in the sun.

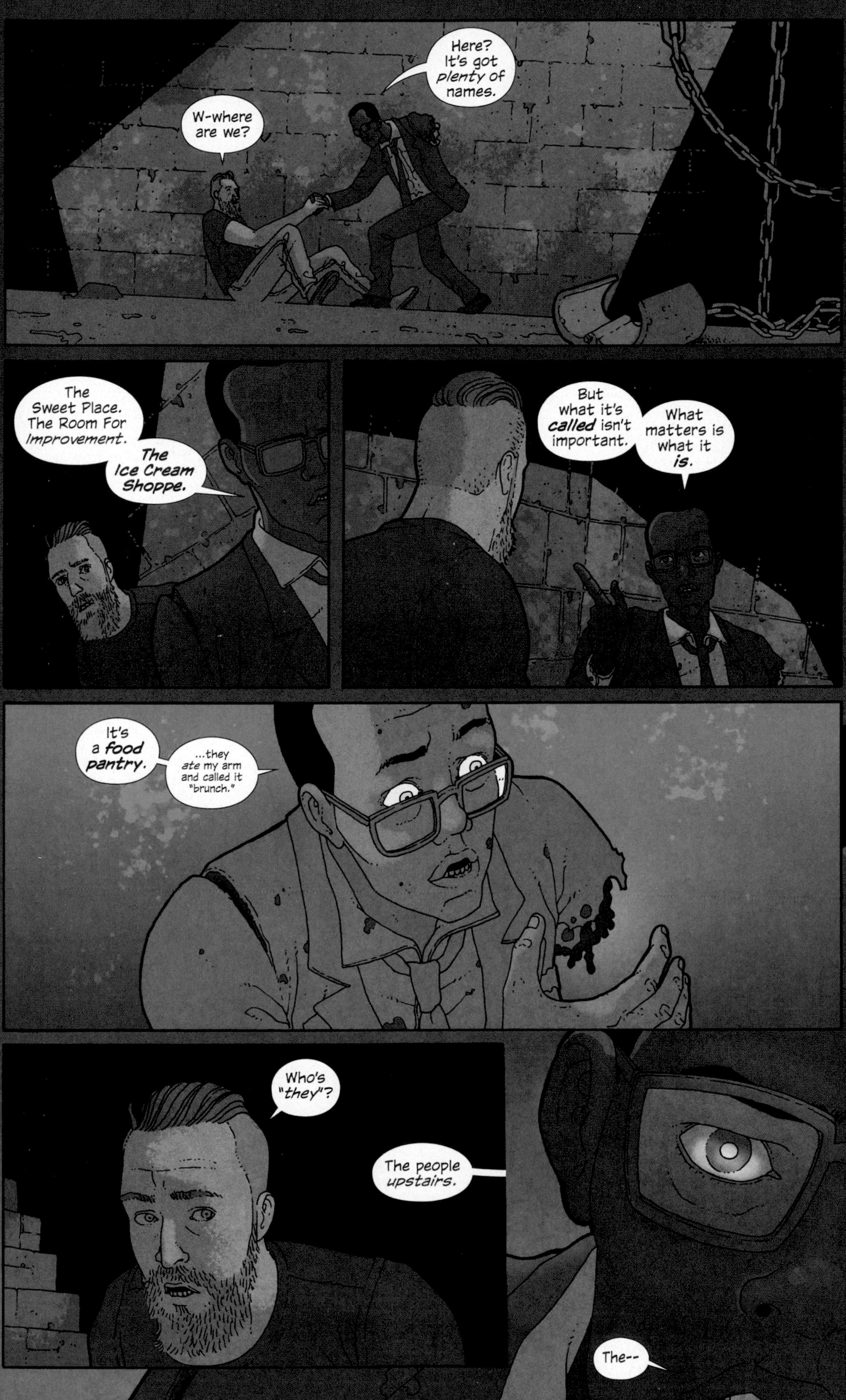
W-where are we?
Here? It's got *plenty* of names.
The Sweet Place. The Room For *Improvement*.
The Ice Cream Shoppe.
But what it's **called** isn't important.
What matters is what it **is**.
It's a **food pantry**.
...they *ate* my arm and called it "brunch."
Who's "*they*"?
The people *upstairs*.
The--

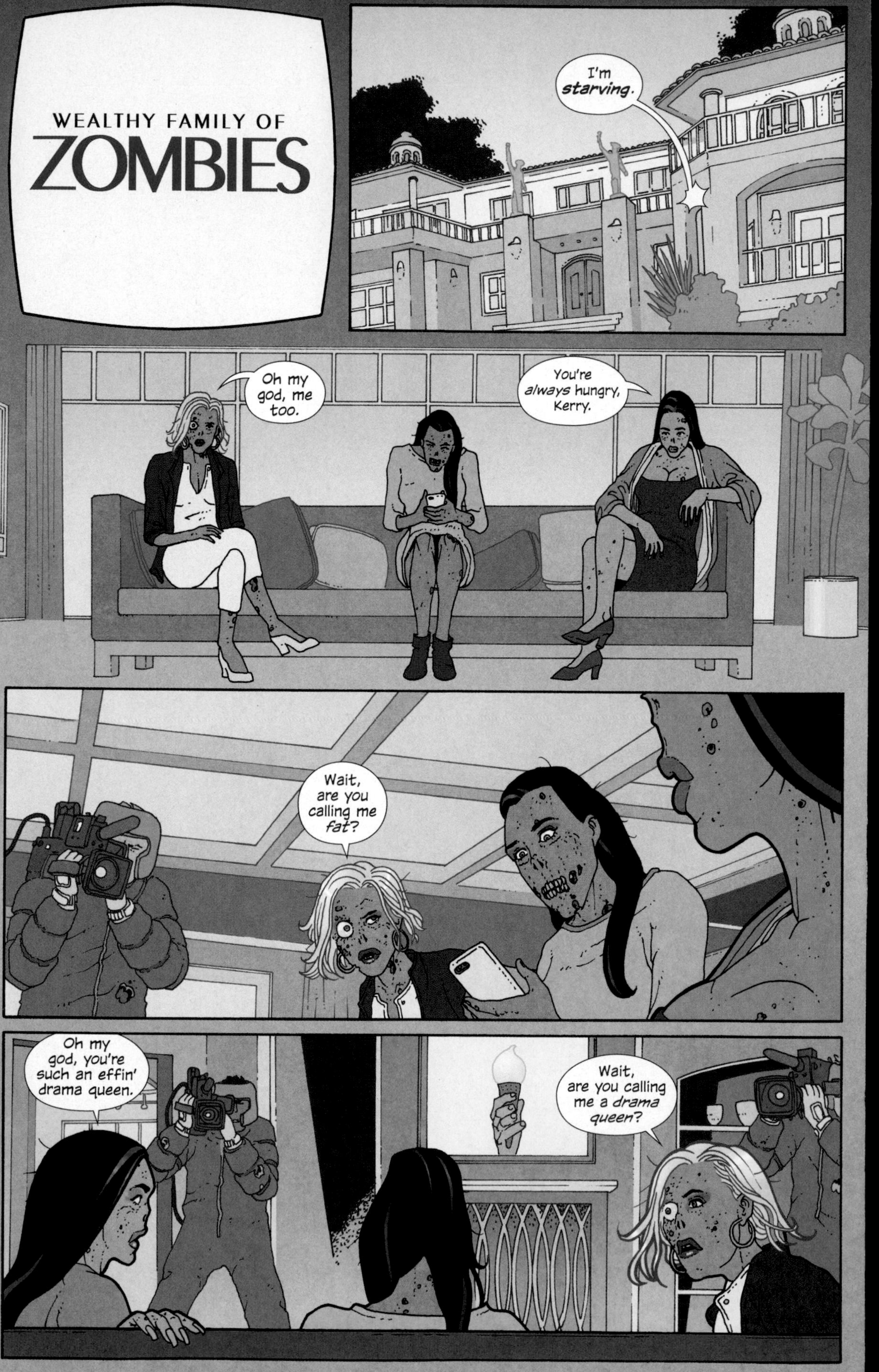
WEALTHY FAMILY OF
ZOMBIES
I'm starving.
Oh my god, me too.
You're always hungry, Kerry.
Wait, are you calling me fat?
Oh my god, you're such an effin' drama queen.
Wait, are you calling me a drama queen?

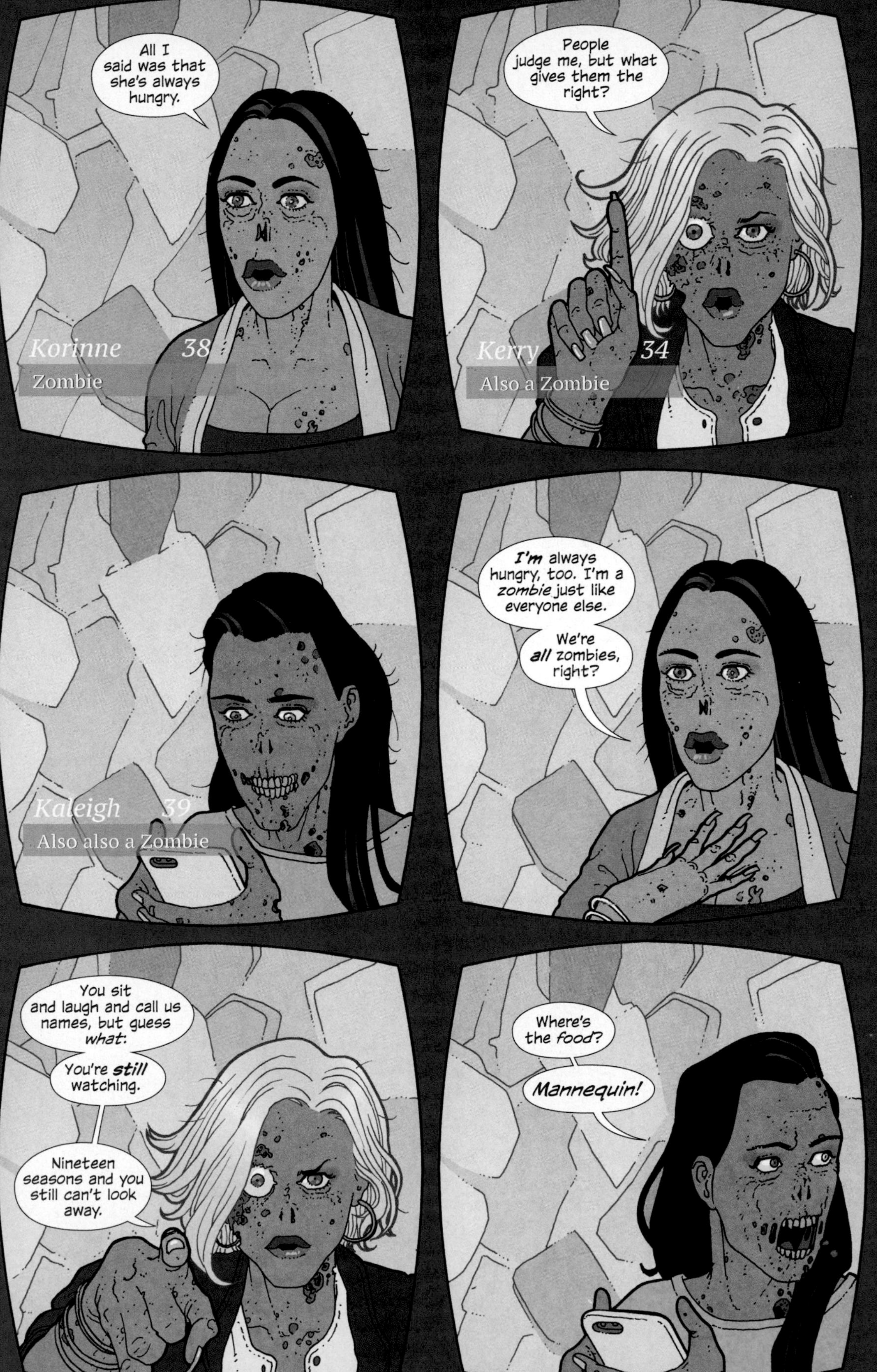
All I said was that she's always hungry.
Korinne 38
Zombie
People judge me, but what gives them the right?
Kerry 34
Also a Zombie
Kaleigh 39
Also also a Zombie
I'm always hungry, too. I'm a *zombie* just like everyone else.
We're *all* zombies, right?
You sit and laugh and call us names, but guess *what*:
You're *still* watching.
Nineteen seasons and you still can't look away.
Where's the *food*?
Mannequin!

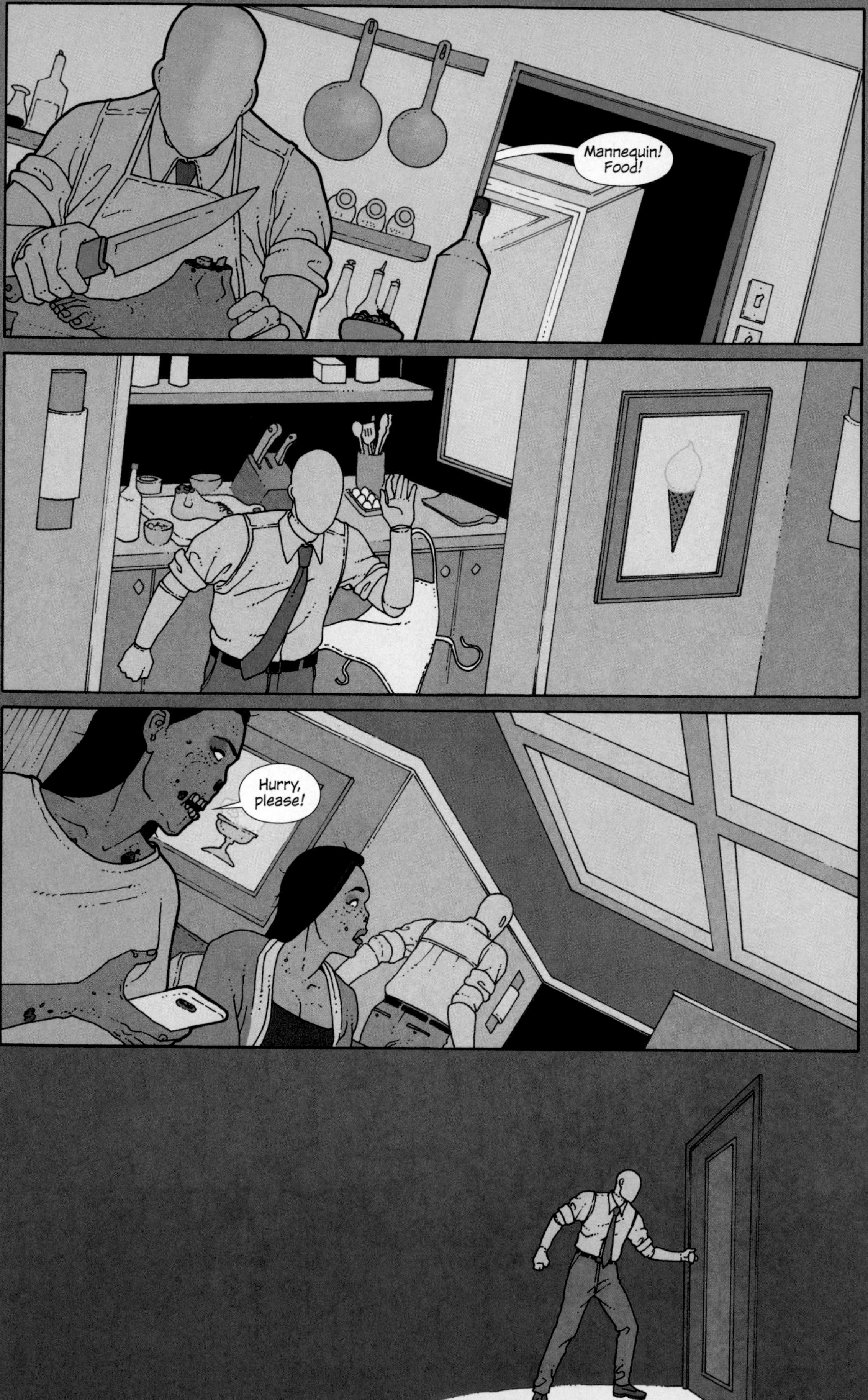
Mannequin! Food!
Hurry, please!

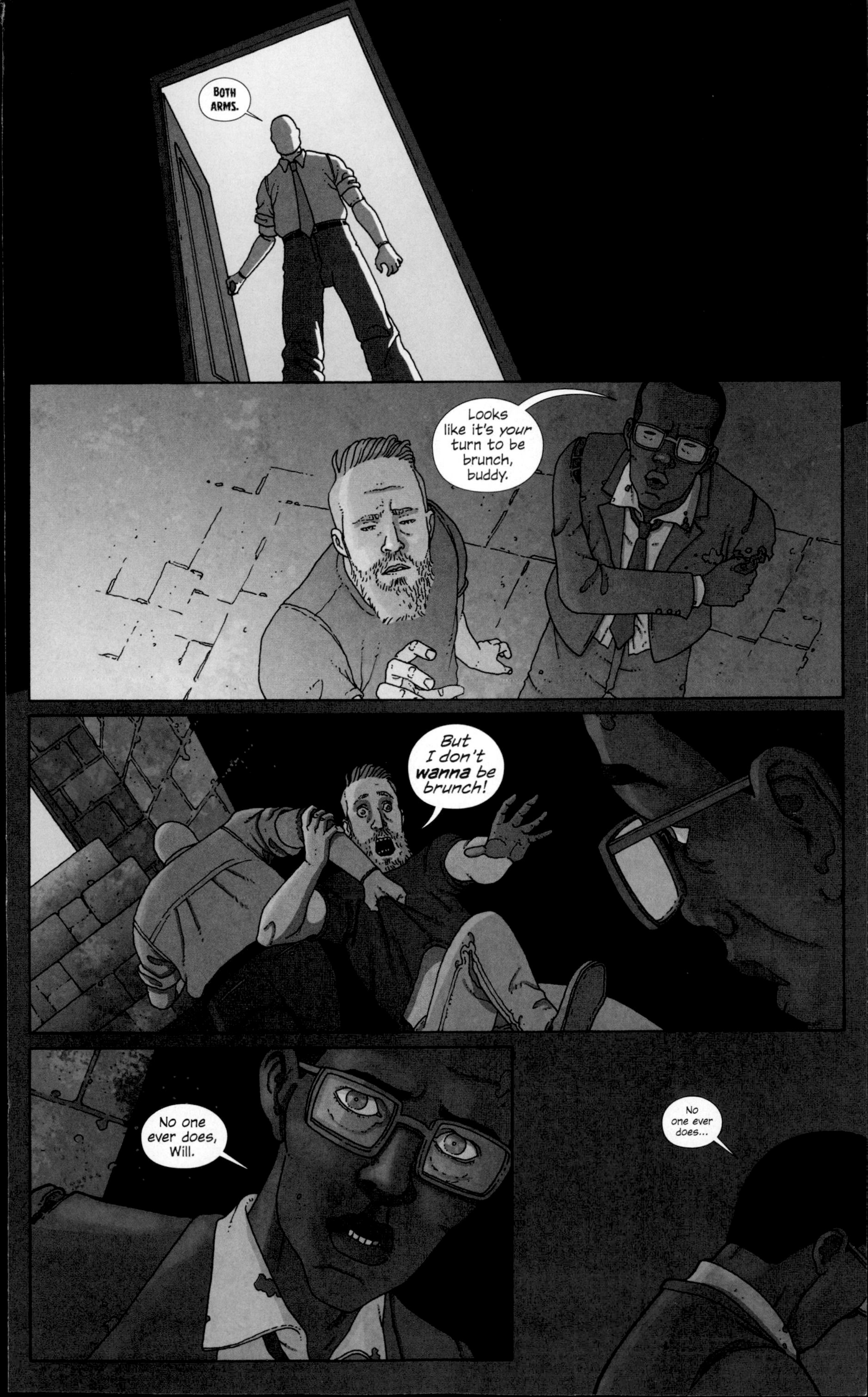
BOTH ARMS.
Looks like it's *your* turn to be brunch, buddy.
*But I don't **wanna** be brunch!*
No one ever does, Will.
No one ever does...

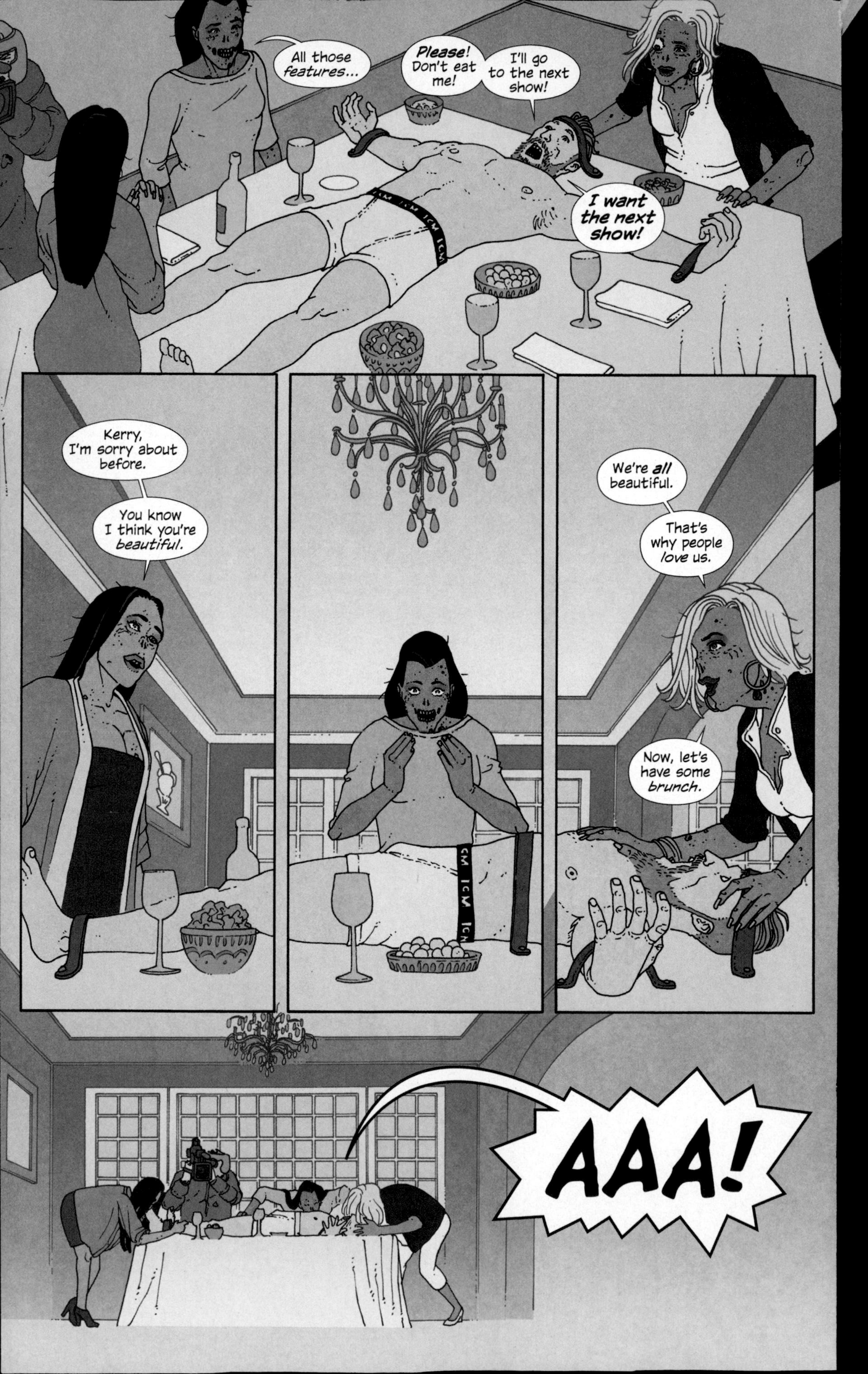
All those *features*...
Please! Don't eat me!
I'll go to the next show!
I want the next show!
Kerry, I'm sorry about before.
You know I think you're *beautiful*.
We're *all* beautiful.
That's why people *love* us.
Now, let's have some *brunch*.
AAA!

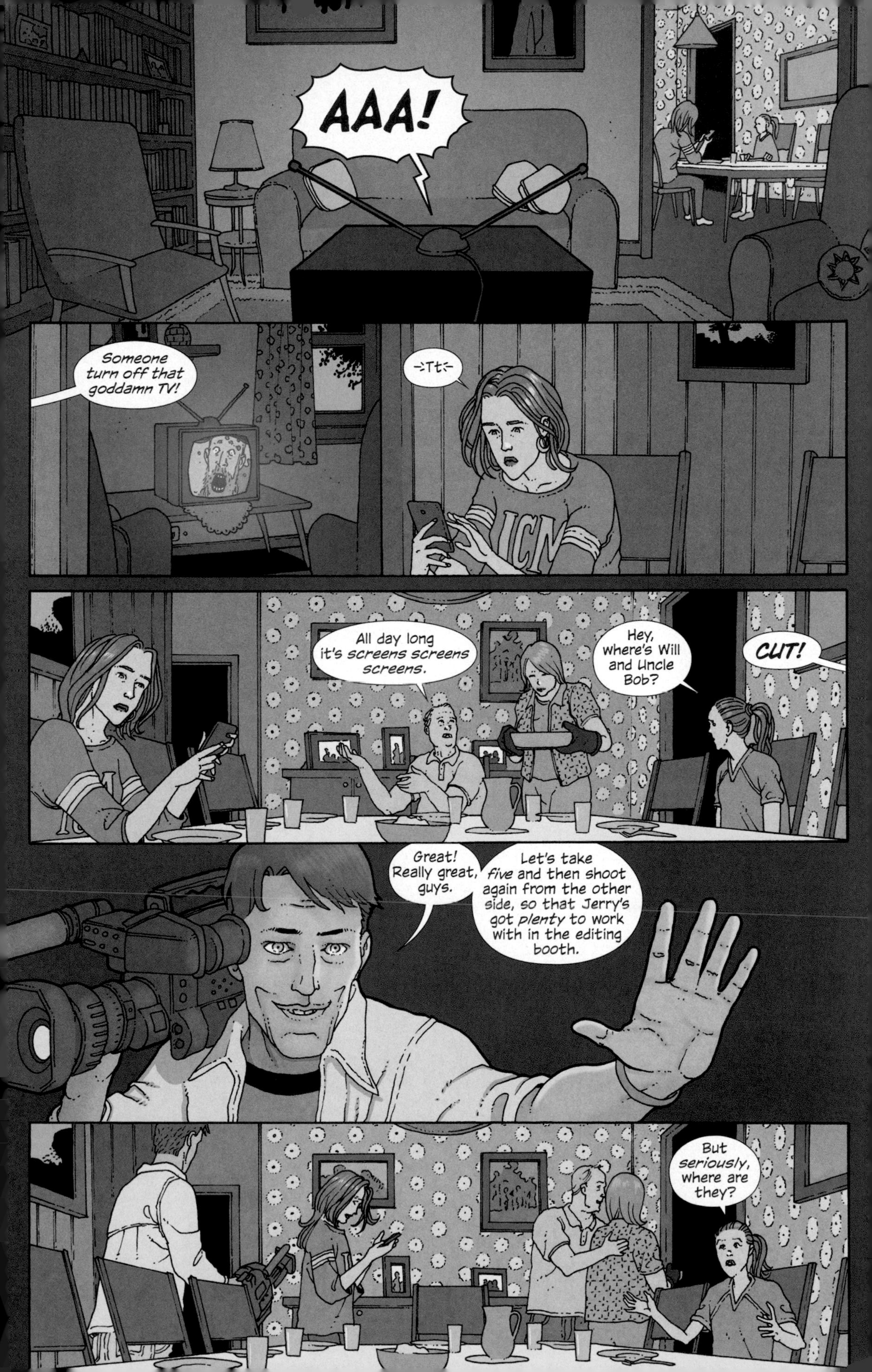
AAA!
Someone turn off that goddamn TV!
-Tt-
All day long it's *screens screens screens.*
Hey, where's Will and Uncle Bob?
CUT!
Great! Really great, guys.
Let's take *five* and then shoot again from the other side, so that Jerry's got *plenty* to work with in the editing booth.
But *seriously,* where are they?

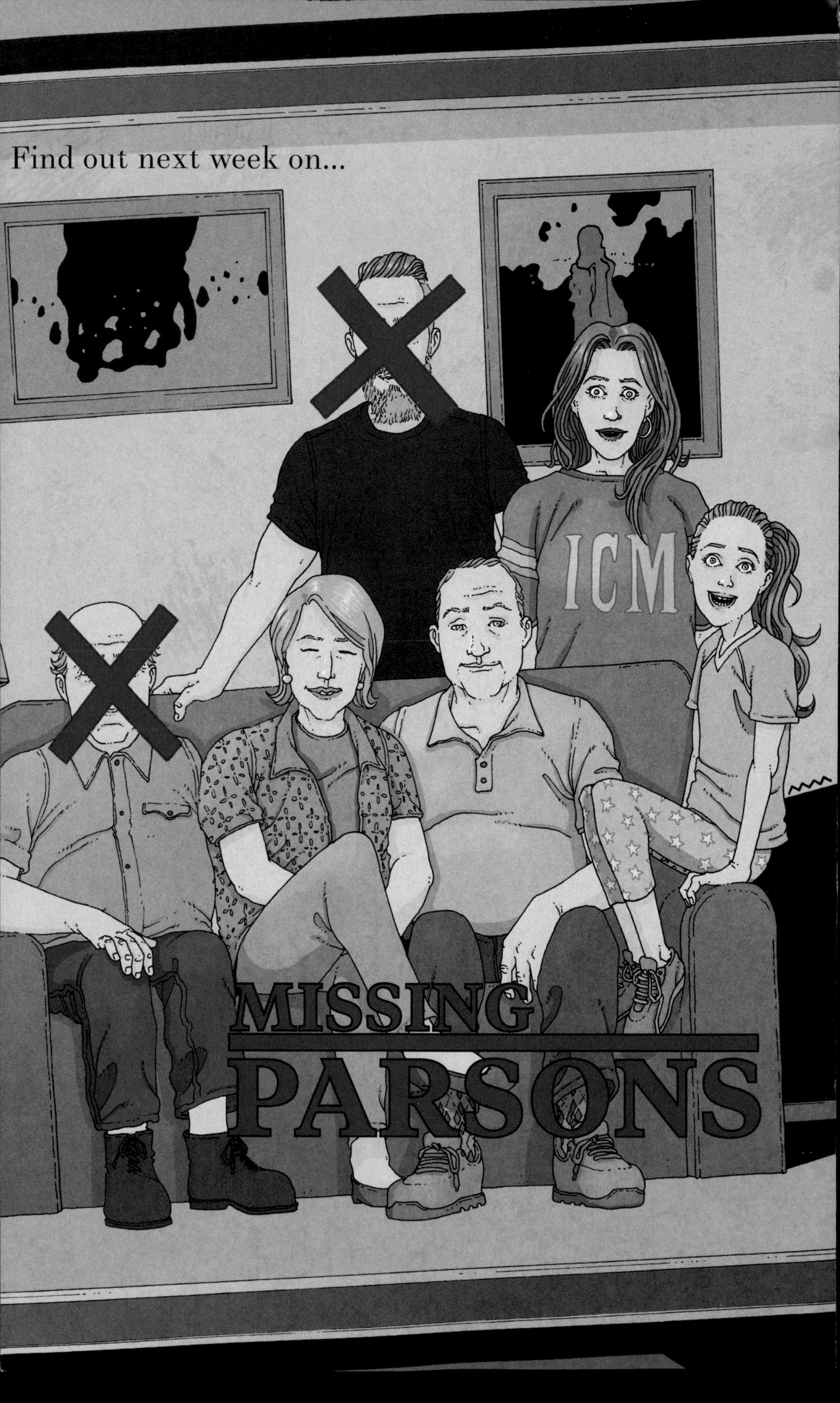

Find out next week on...
ICM
MISSING
PARSONS

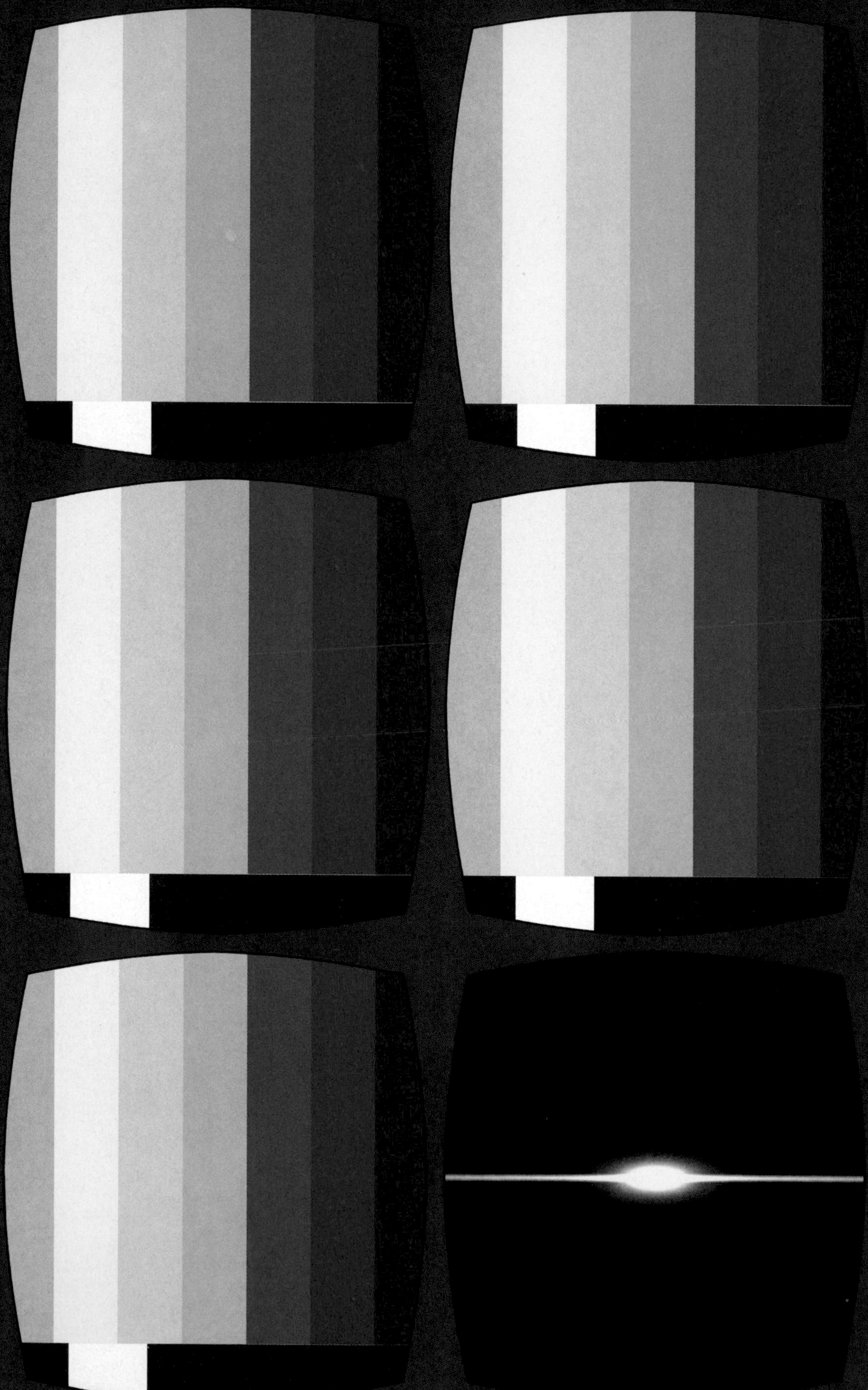

Chapter Twelve

Space Story

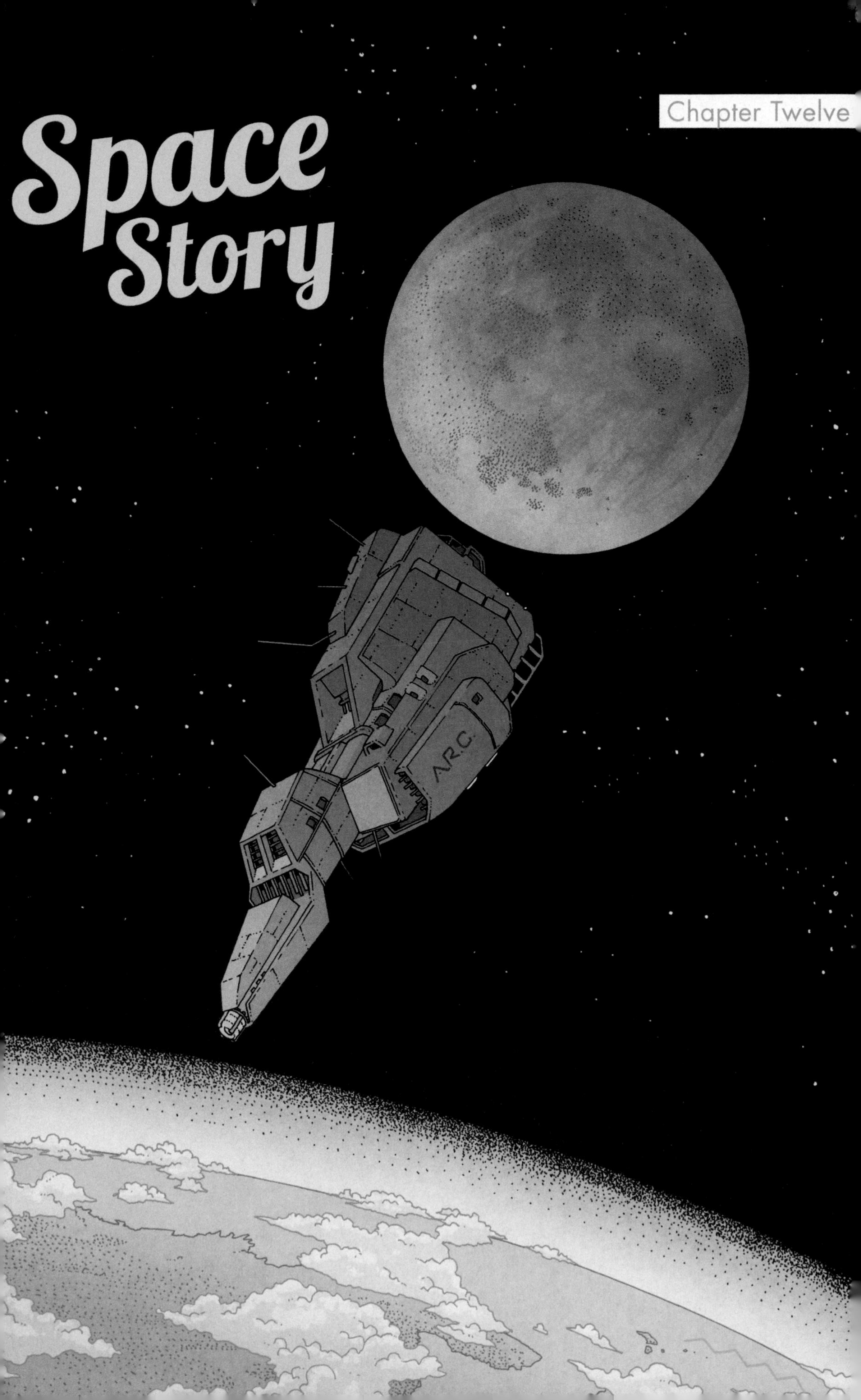
A.R.C.

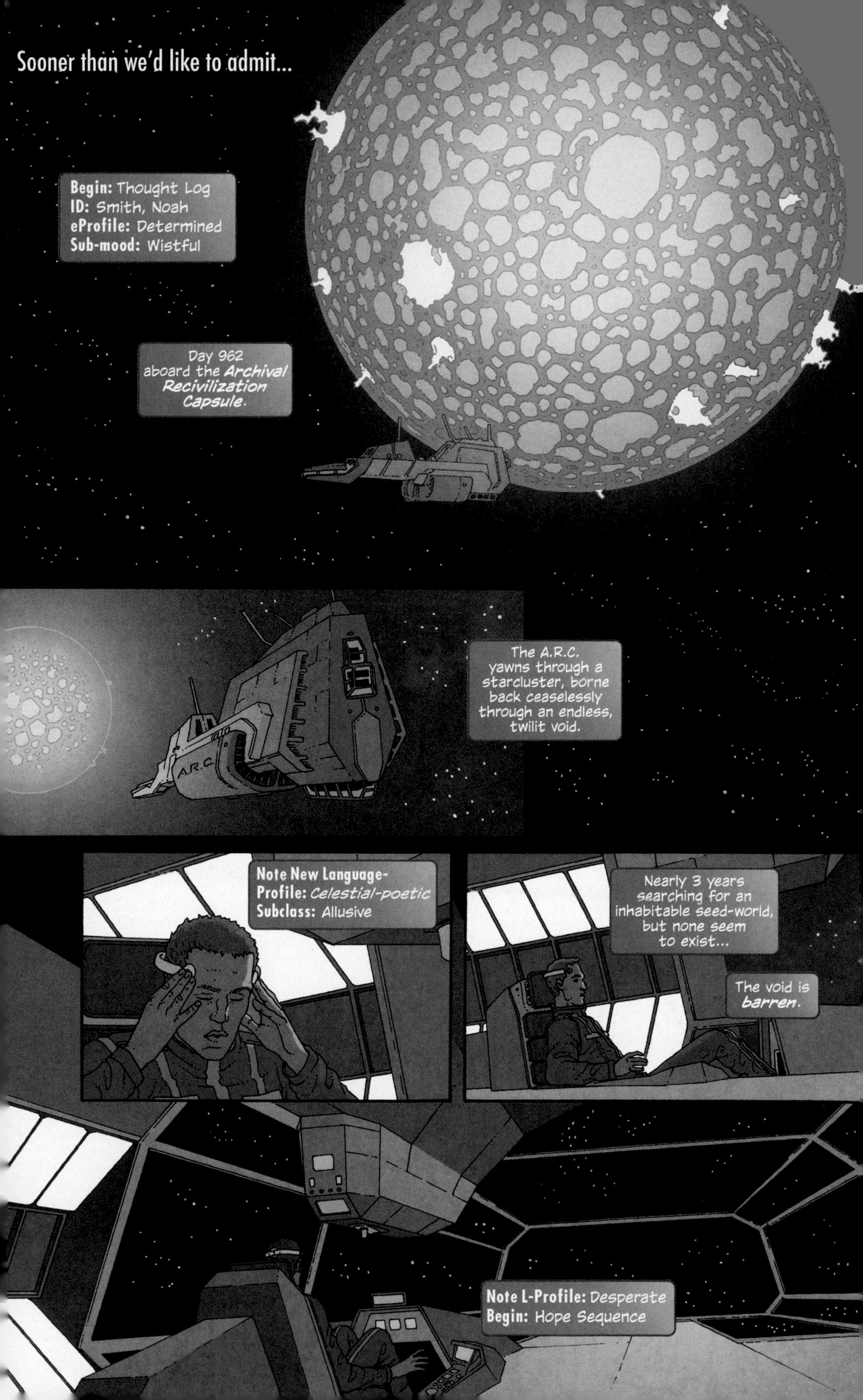

Sooner than we'd like to admit...
Begin: Thought Log
ID: Smith, Noah
eProfile: Determined
Sub-mood: Wistful
Day 962 aboard the Archival Recivilization Capsule.
A.R.C.
The A.R.C. yawns through a starcluster, borne back ceaselessly through an endless, twilit void.
Note New Language-Profile: Celestial-poetic
Subclass: Allusive
Nearly 3 years searching for an inhabitable seed-world, but none seem to exist...
The void is barren.
Note L-Profile: Desperate
Begin: Hope Sequence

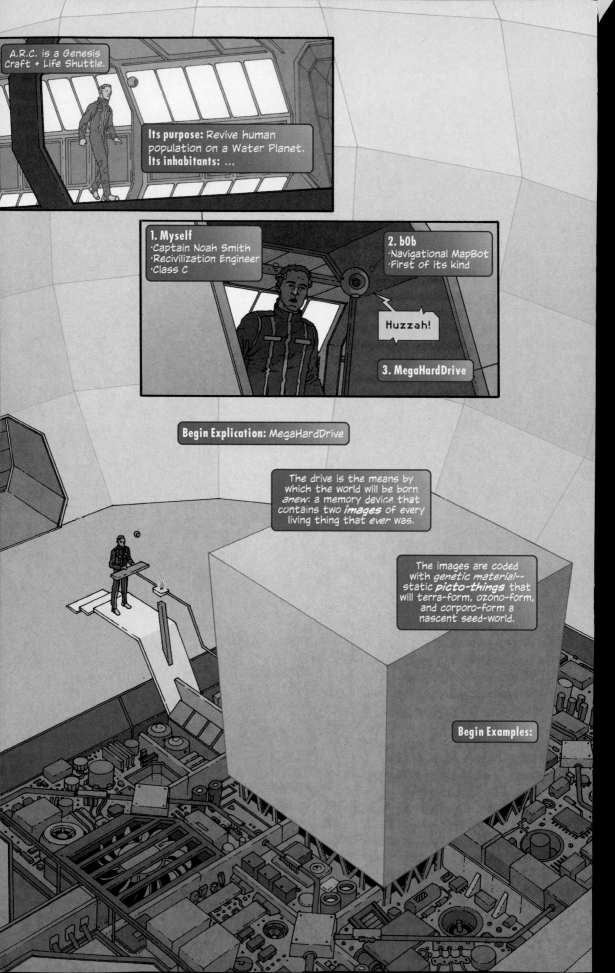

A.R.C. is a Genesis Craft + Life Shuttle.

Its purpose: Revive human population on a Water Planet.
Its inhabitants: ...

1. Myself
·Captain Noah Smith
·Recivilization Engineer
·Class C

2. b0b
·Navigational MapBot
·First of its kind

Huzzah!

3. MegaHardDrive

Begin Explication: MegaHardDrive

The drive is the means by which the world will be born *anew*: a memory device that contains two *images* of every living thing that *ever* was.

The images are coded with *genetic material*-- static *picto-things* that will terra-form, ozono-form, and corporo-form a nascent seed-world.

Begin Examples:

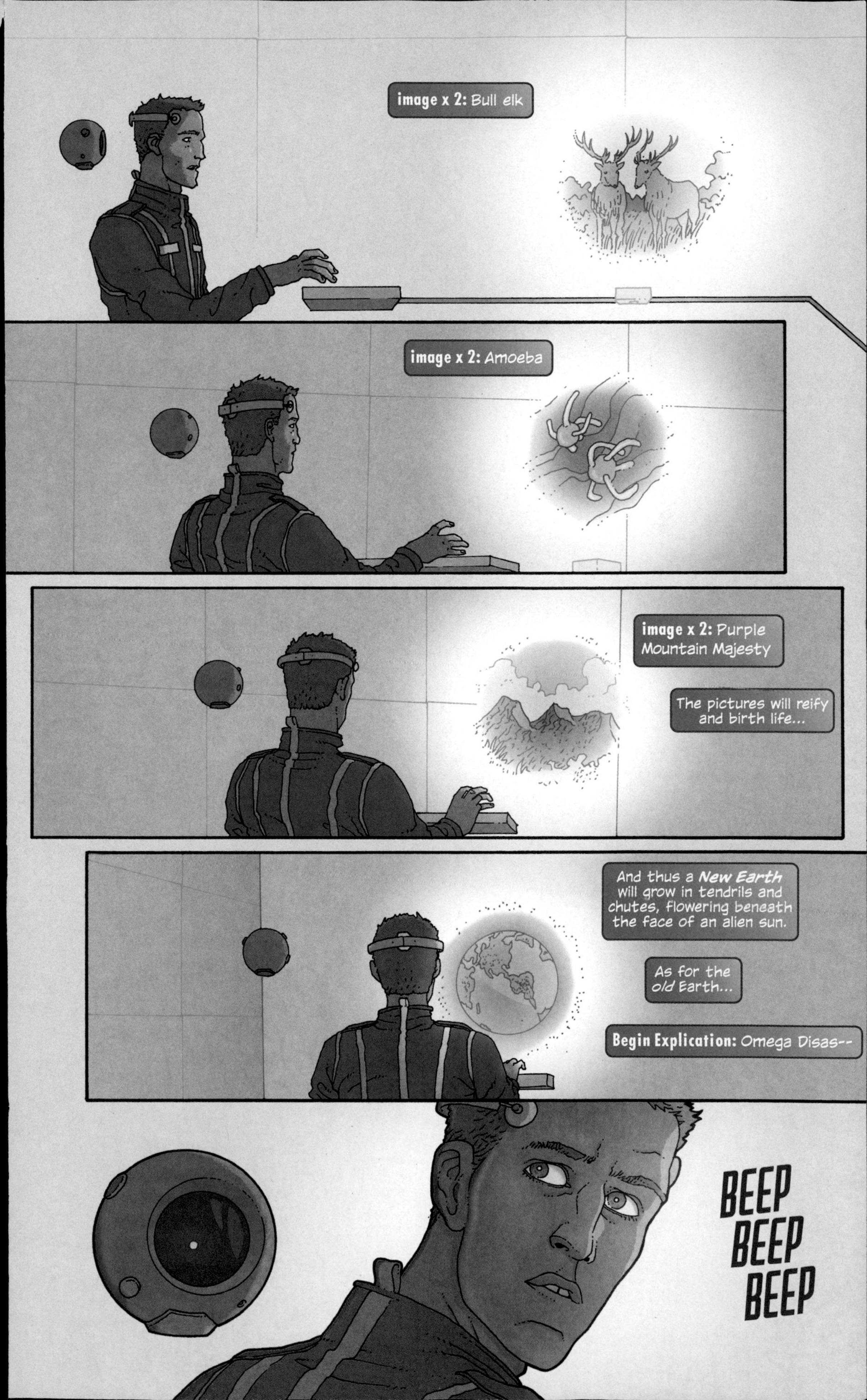
image x 2: Bull elk
image x 2: Amoeba
image x 2: Purple Mountain Majesty
The pictures will reify and birth life...
And thus a *New Earth* will grow in tendrils and chutes, flowering beneath the face of an alien sun.
As for the *old* Earth...
Begin Explication: Omega Disas--
BEEP
BEEP
BEEP

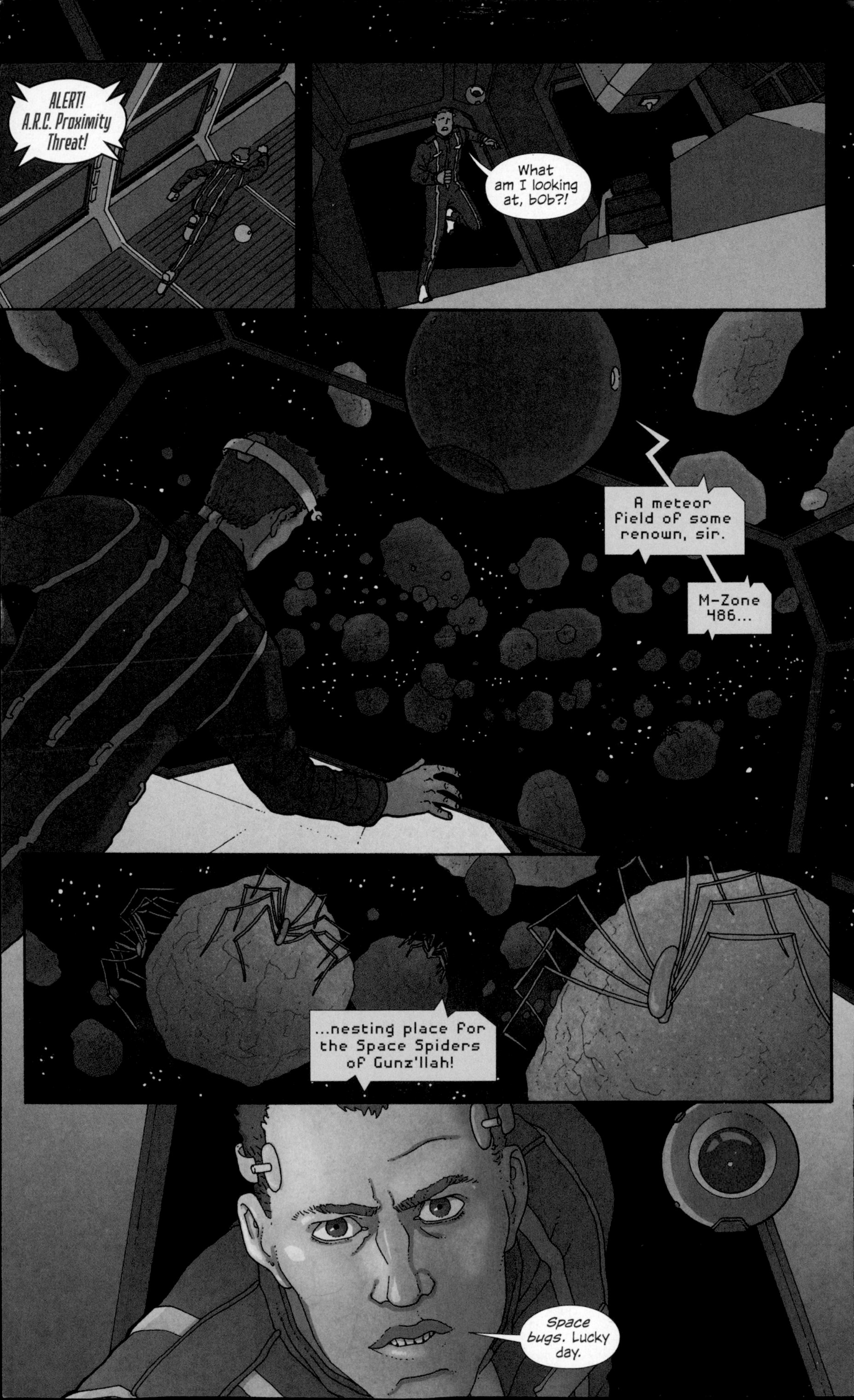
ALERT! A.R.C. Proximity Threat!
What am I looking at, bOb?!
A meteor field of some renown, sir.
M-Zone 486...
...nesting place for the Space Spiders of Gunz'llah!
Space bugs. Lucky day.

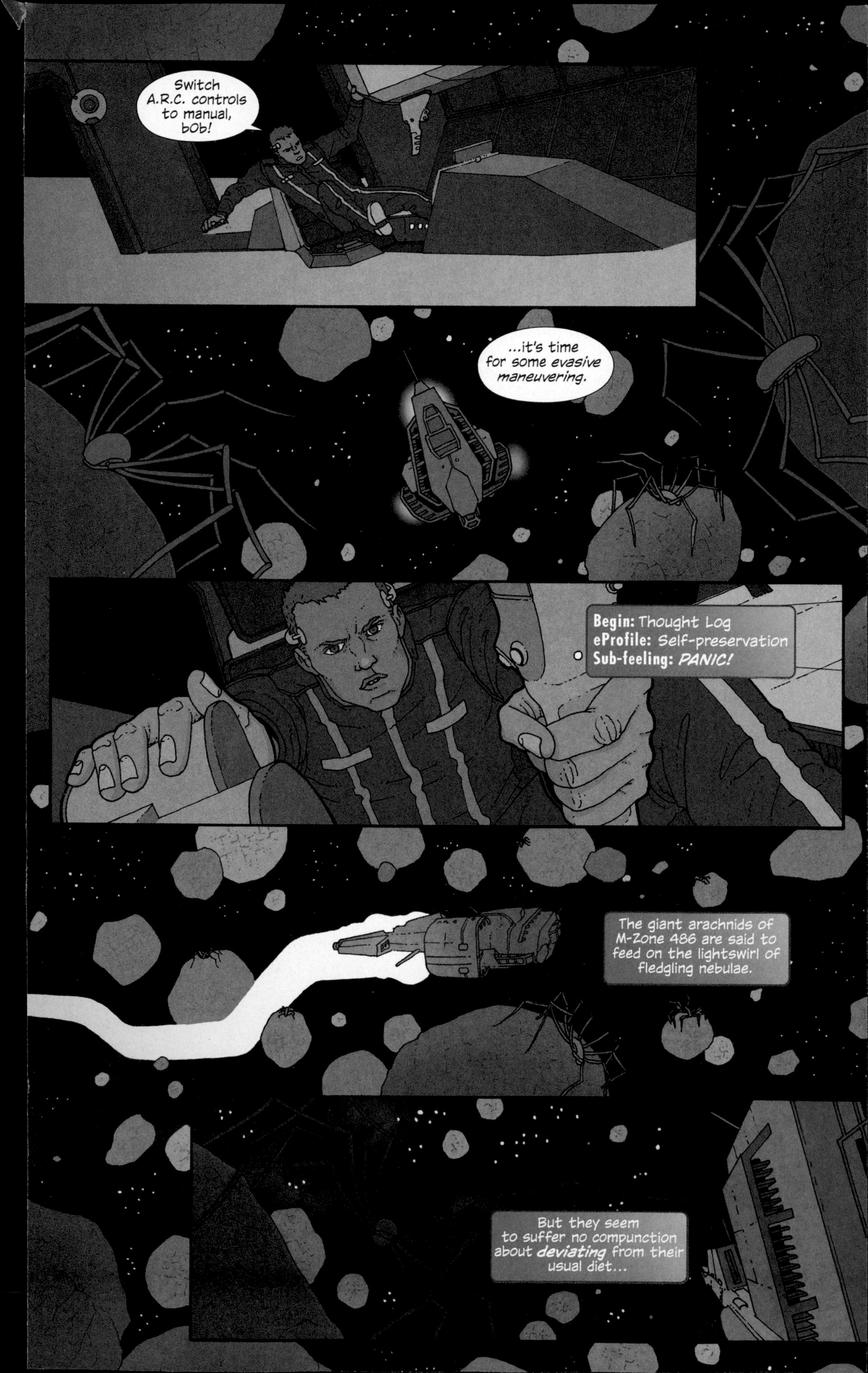
Switch A.R.C. controls to manual, bOb!
...it's time for some *evasive maneuvering.*
Begin: Thought Log
eProfile: Self-preservation
Sub-feeling: *PANIC!*
The giant arachnids of M-Zone 486 are said to feed on the lightswirl of fledgling nebulae.
But they seem to suffer no compunction about ***deviating*** from their usual diet...

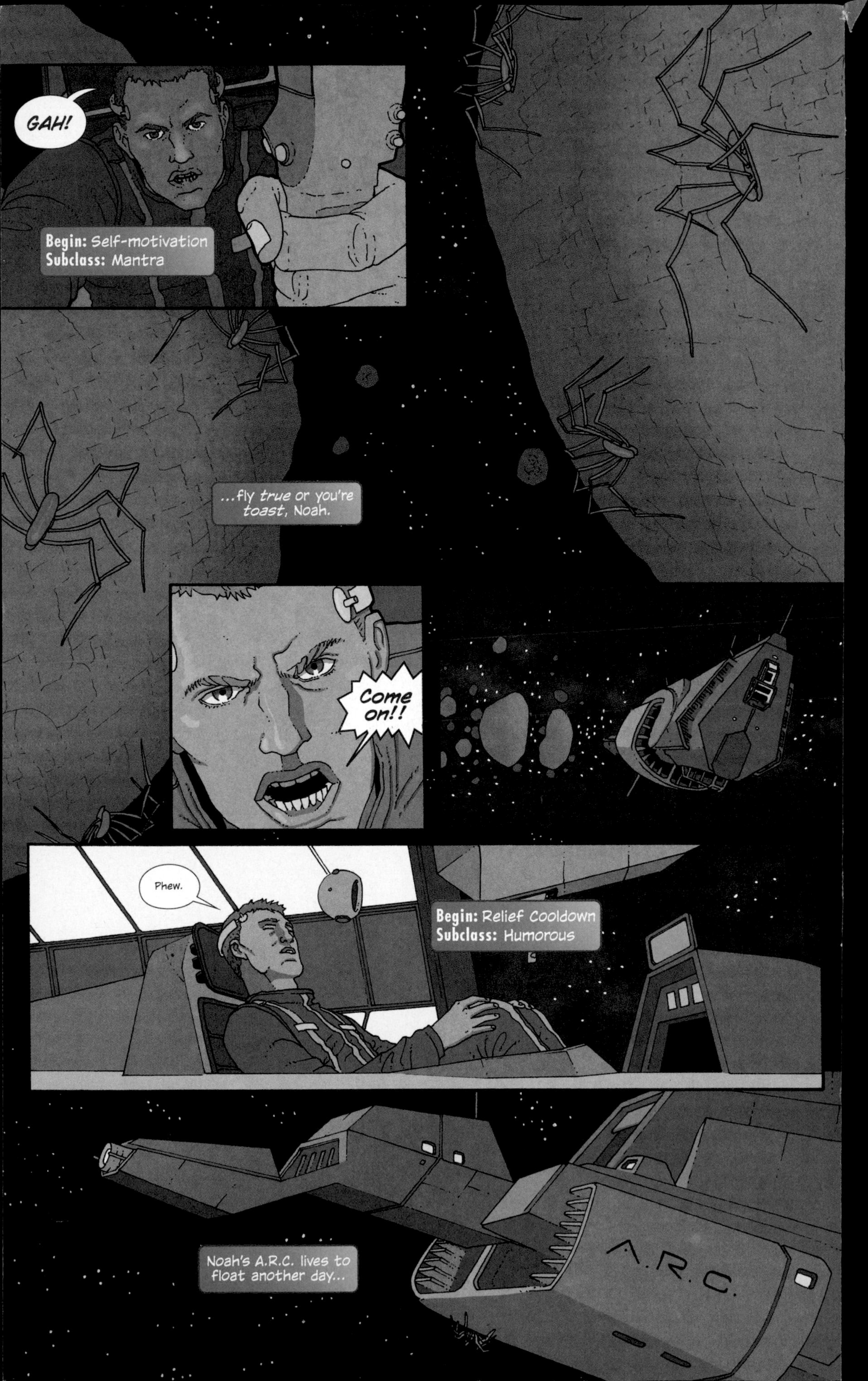
GAH!
Begin: Self-motivation
Subclass: Mantra
...fly true or you're toast, Noah.
Come on!!
Phew.
Begin: Relief Cooldown
Subclass: Humorous
A.R.C.
Noah's A.R.C. lives to float another day...

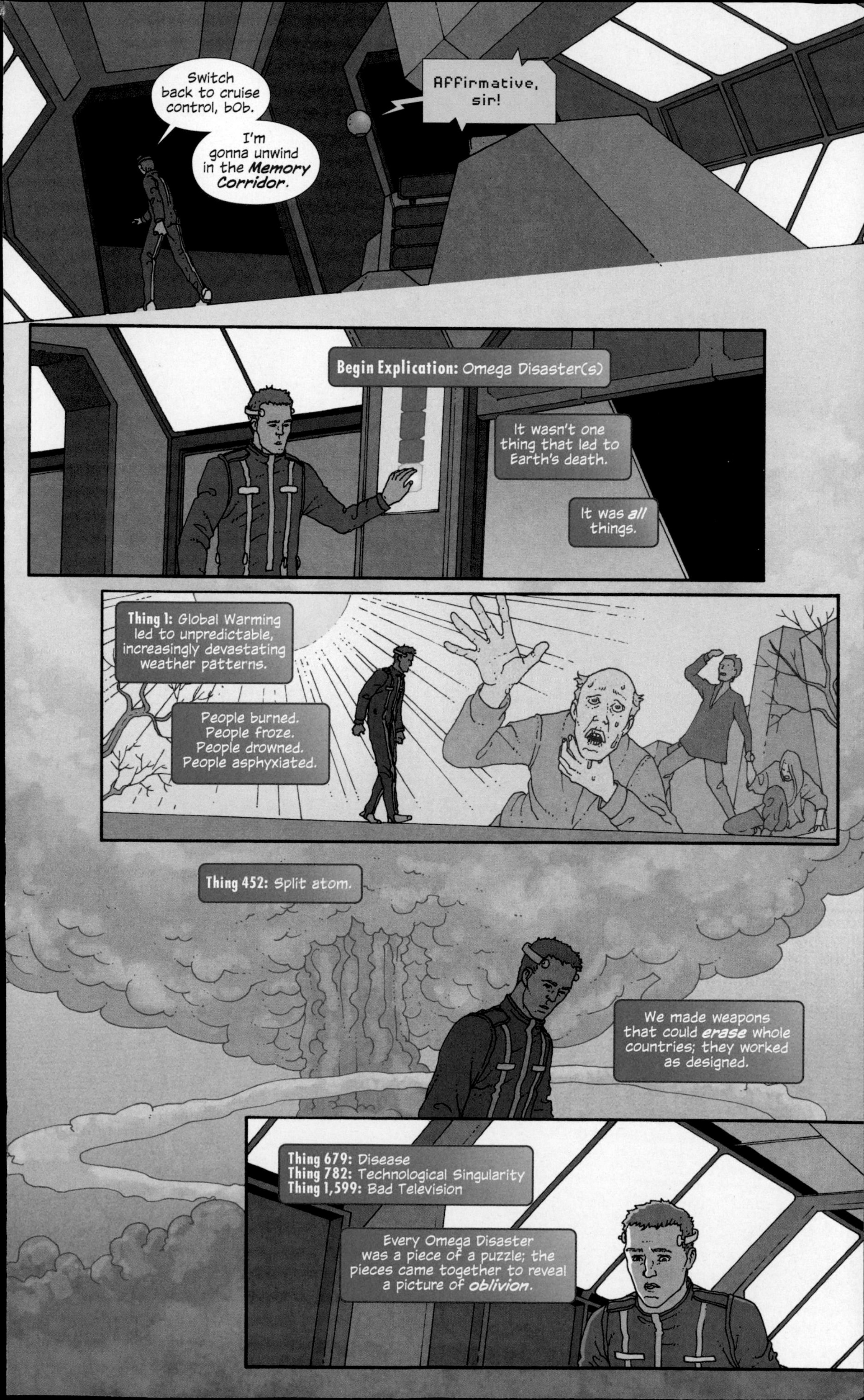

Switch back to cruise control, bOb.
I'm gonna unwind in the **Memory Corridor**.
Affirmative, sir!
Begin Explication: Omega Disaster(s)
It wasn't one thing that led to Earth's death.
It was *all* things.
Thing 1: Global Warming led to unpredictable, increasingly devastating weather patterns.
People burned. People froze. People drowned. People asphyxiated.
Thing 452: Split atom.
We made weapons that could *erase* whole countries; they worked as designed.
Thing 679: Disease
Thing 782: Technological Singularity
Thing 1,599: Bad Television
Every Omega Disaster was a piece of a puzzle; the pieces came together to reveal a picture of *oblivion*.

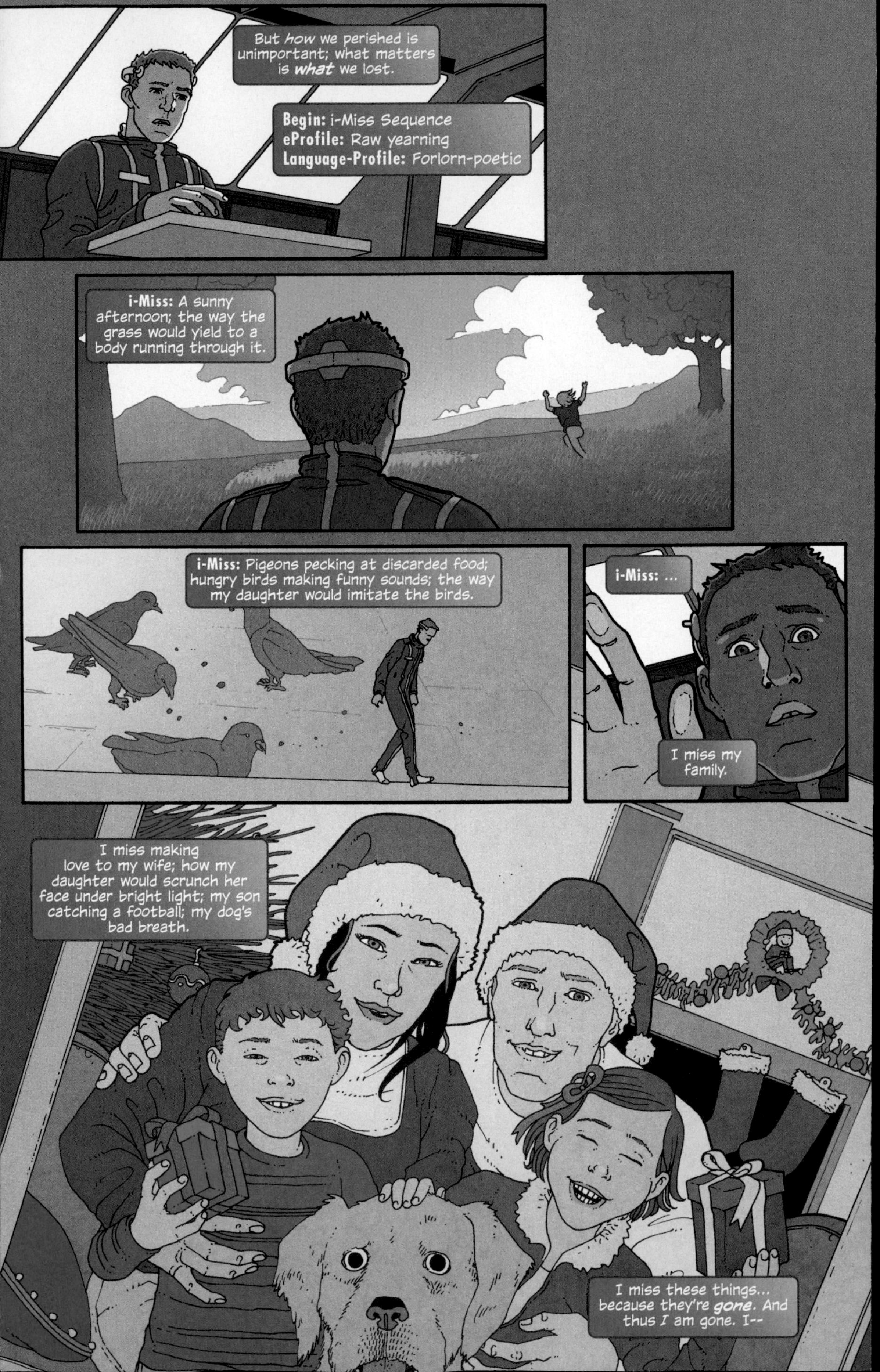
But *how* we perished is unimportant; what matters is ***what*** we lost.
Begin: i-Miss Sequence
eProfile: Raw yearning
Language-Profile: Forlorn-poetic
i-Miss: A sunny afternoon; the way the grass would yield to a body running through it.
i-Miss: Pigeons pecking at discarded food; hungry birds making funny sounds; the way my daughter would imitate the birds.
i-Miss: ...
I miss my family.
I miss making love to my wife; how my daughter would scrunch her face under bright light; my son catching a football; my dog's bad breath.
I miss these things... because they're *gone*. And thus *I* am gone. I--

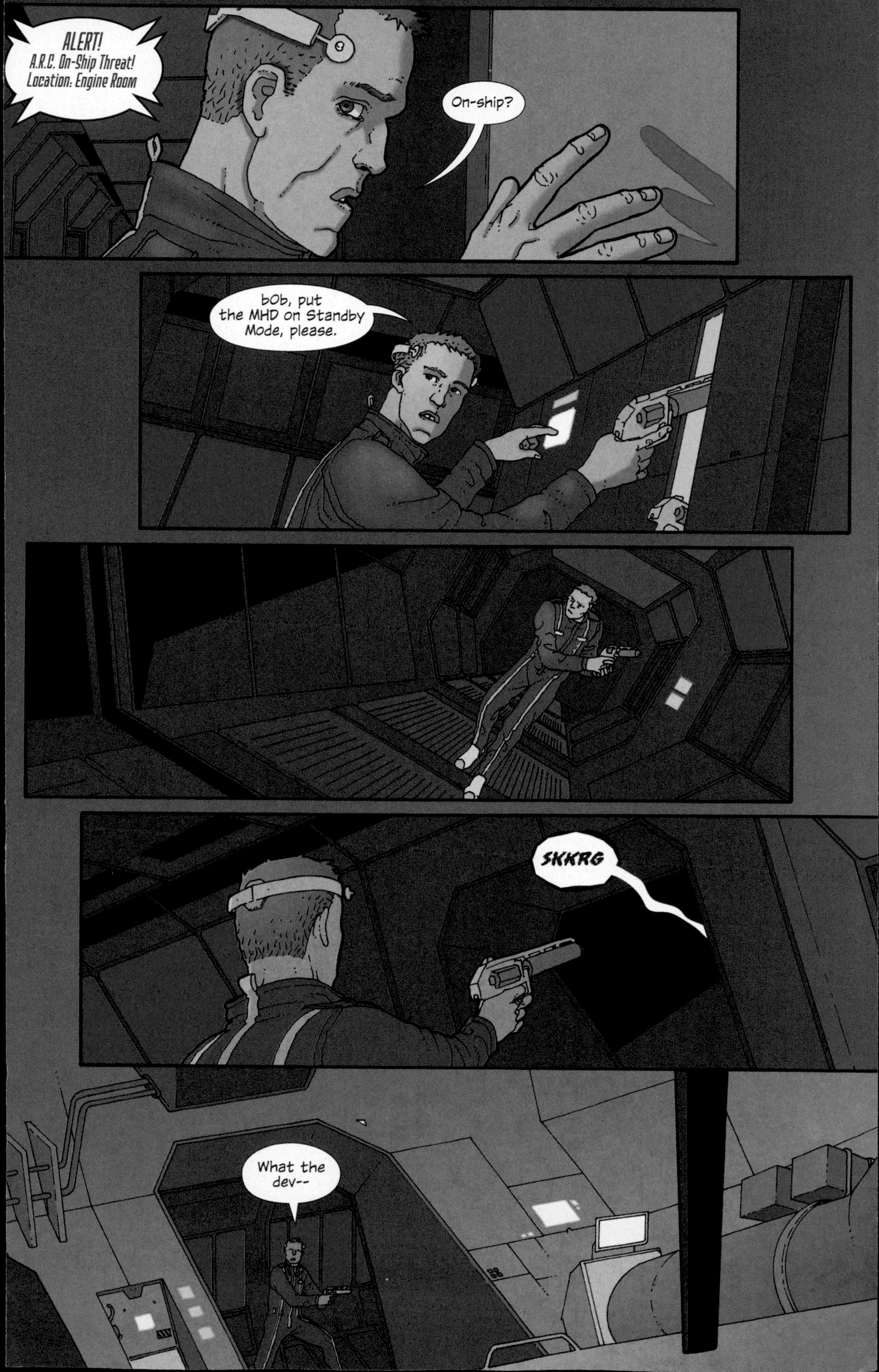
ALERT! A.R.C. On-Ship Threat! Location: Engine Room
On-ship?
bOb, put the MHD on Standby Mode, please.
SKKRG
What the dev--

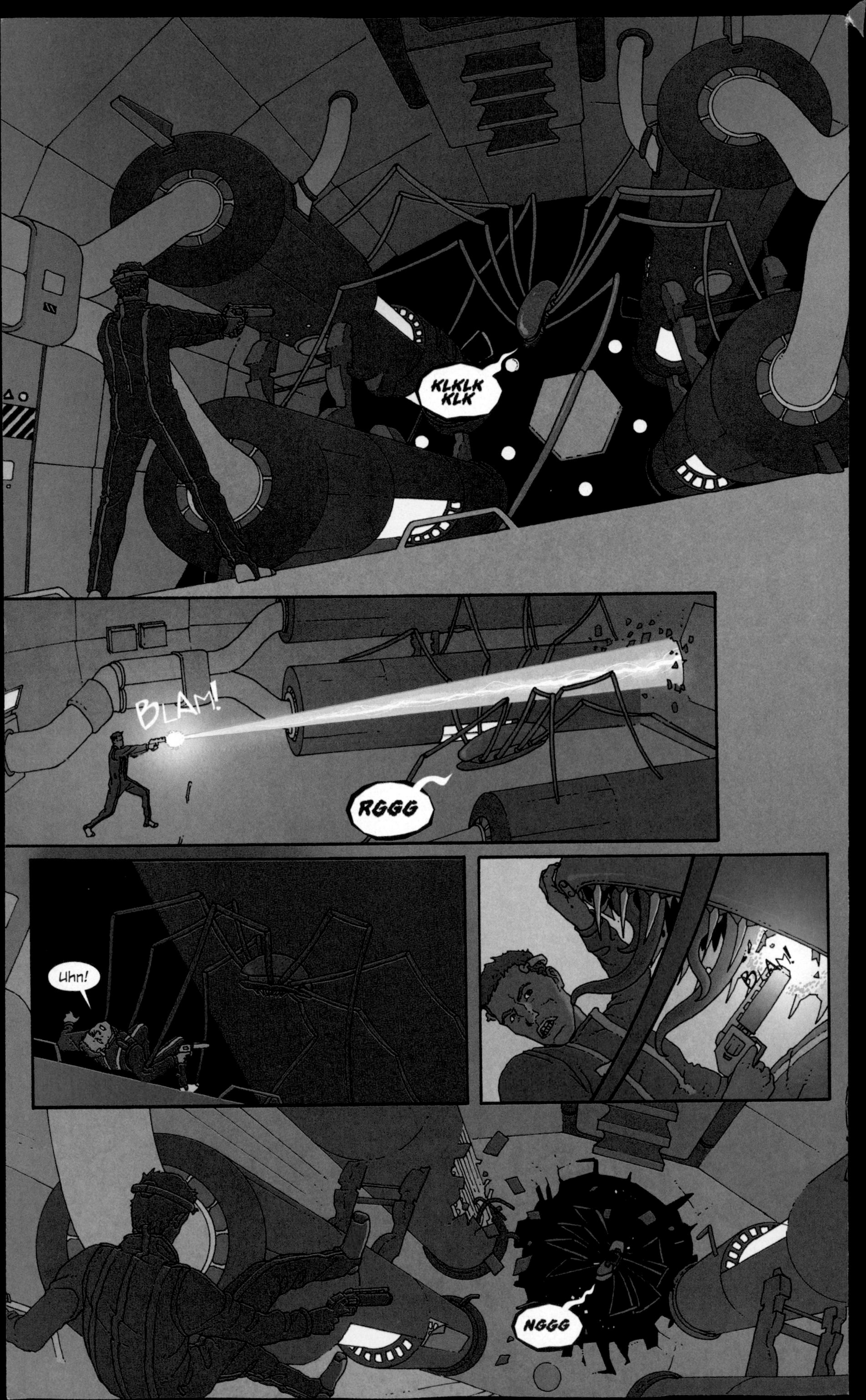
KLKLK
KLK
BLAM!
RGGG
Uhn!
BLAM!
NGGG

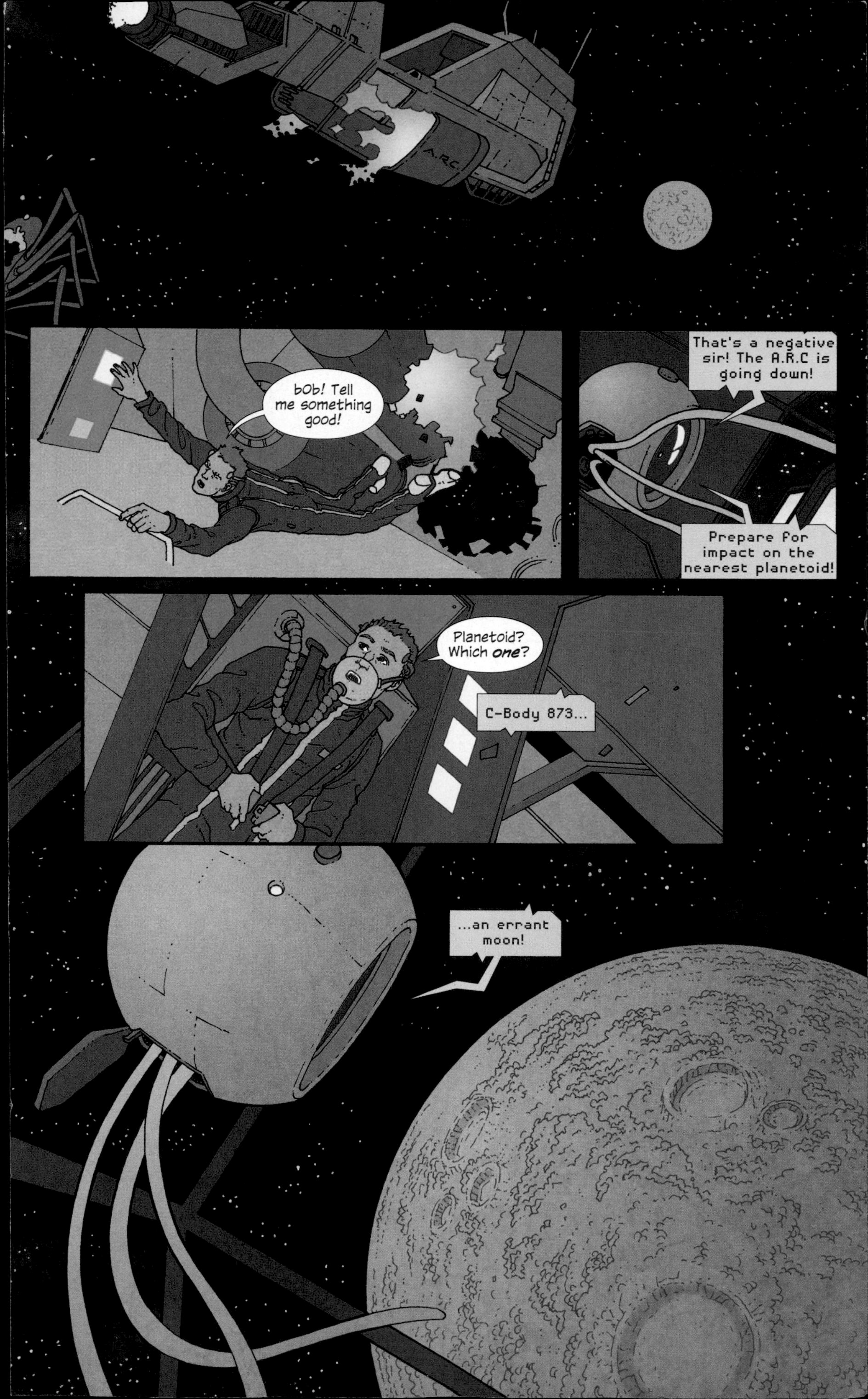
bOb! Tell me something good!
That's a negative sir! The A.R.C is going down!
Prepare for impact on the nearest planetoid!
Planetoid? Which *one*?
C-Body 873...
...an errant moon!

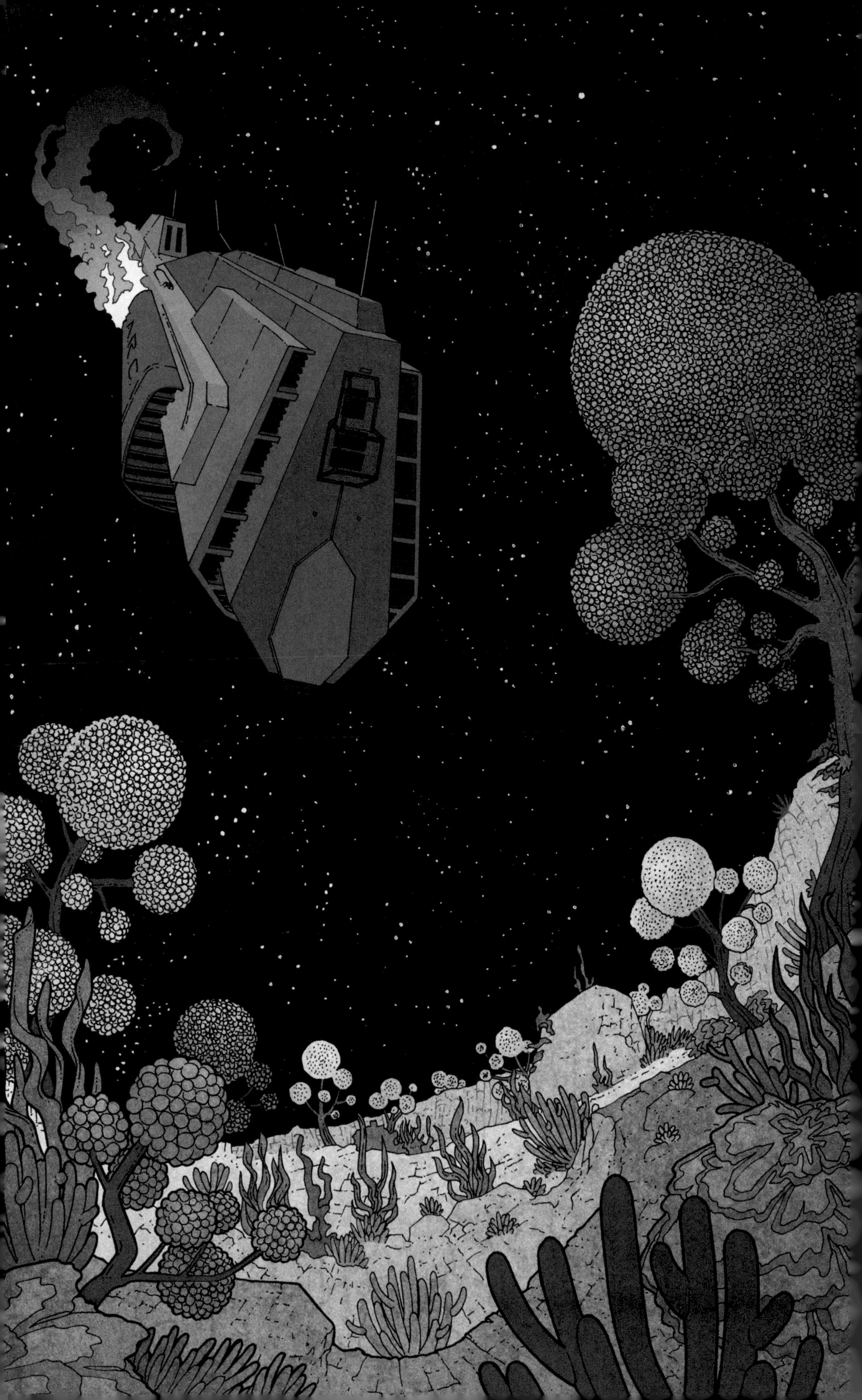
ARC

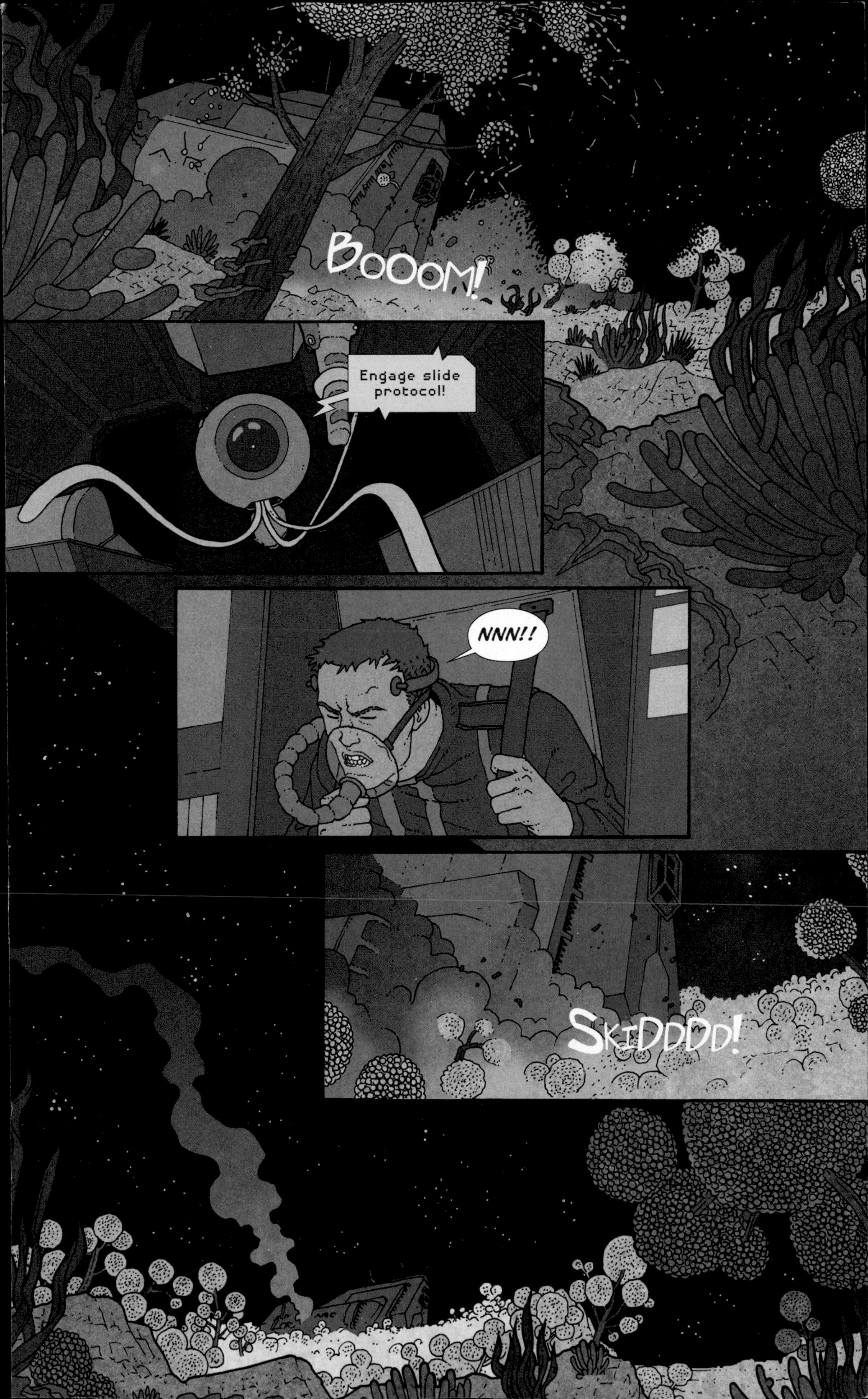
BOOOM!
Engage slide protocol!
NNN!!
SKIDDDD!

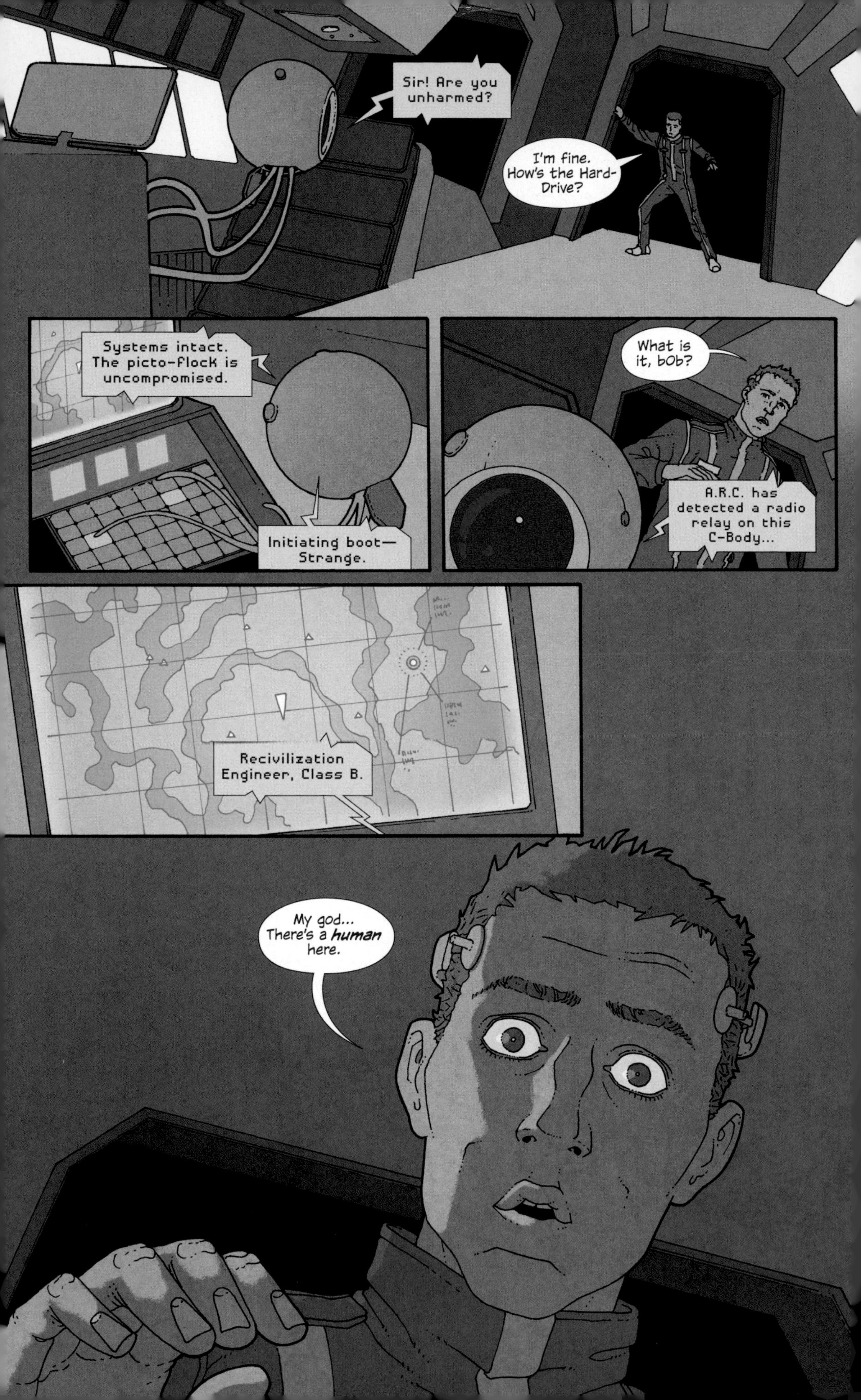
Sir! Are you unharmed?
I'm fine. How's the Hard-Drive?
Systems intact. The picto-flock is uncompromised.
Initiating boot—Strange.
What is it, bOb?
A.R.C. has detected a radio relay on this C-Body...
Recivilization Engineer, Class B.
My god... There's a *human* here.

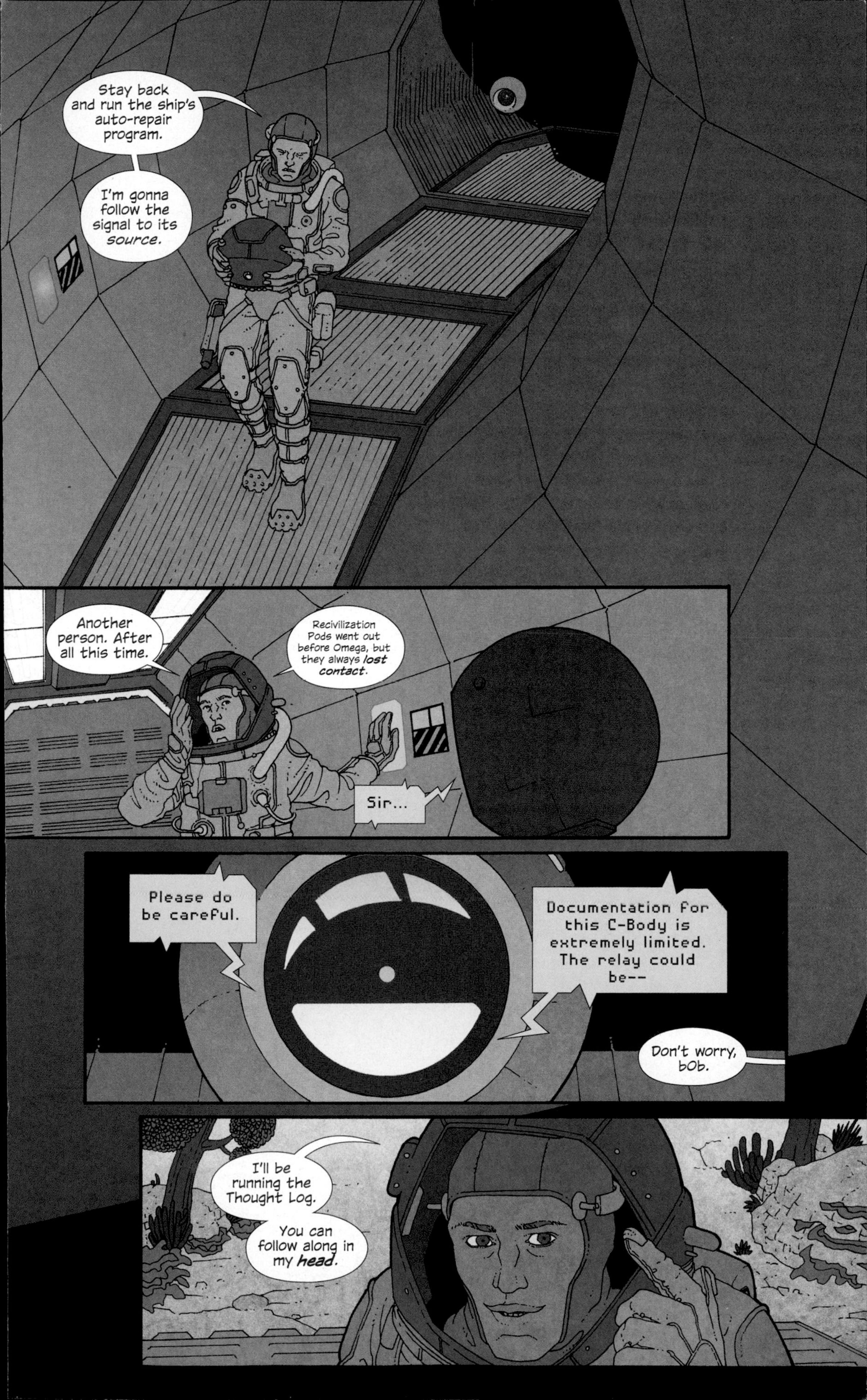

Stay back and run the ship's auto-repair program.
I'm gonna follow the signal to its *source*.
Another person. After all this time.
Recivilization Pods went out before Omega, but they always ***lost contact***.
Sir...
Please do be careful.
Documentation for this C-Body is extremely limited. The relay could be--
Don't worry, bOb.
I'll be running the Thought Log.
You can follow along in my ***head***.

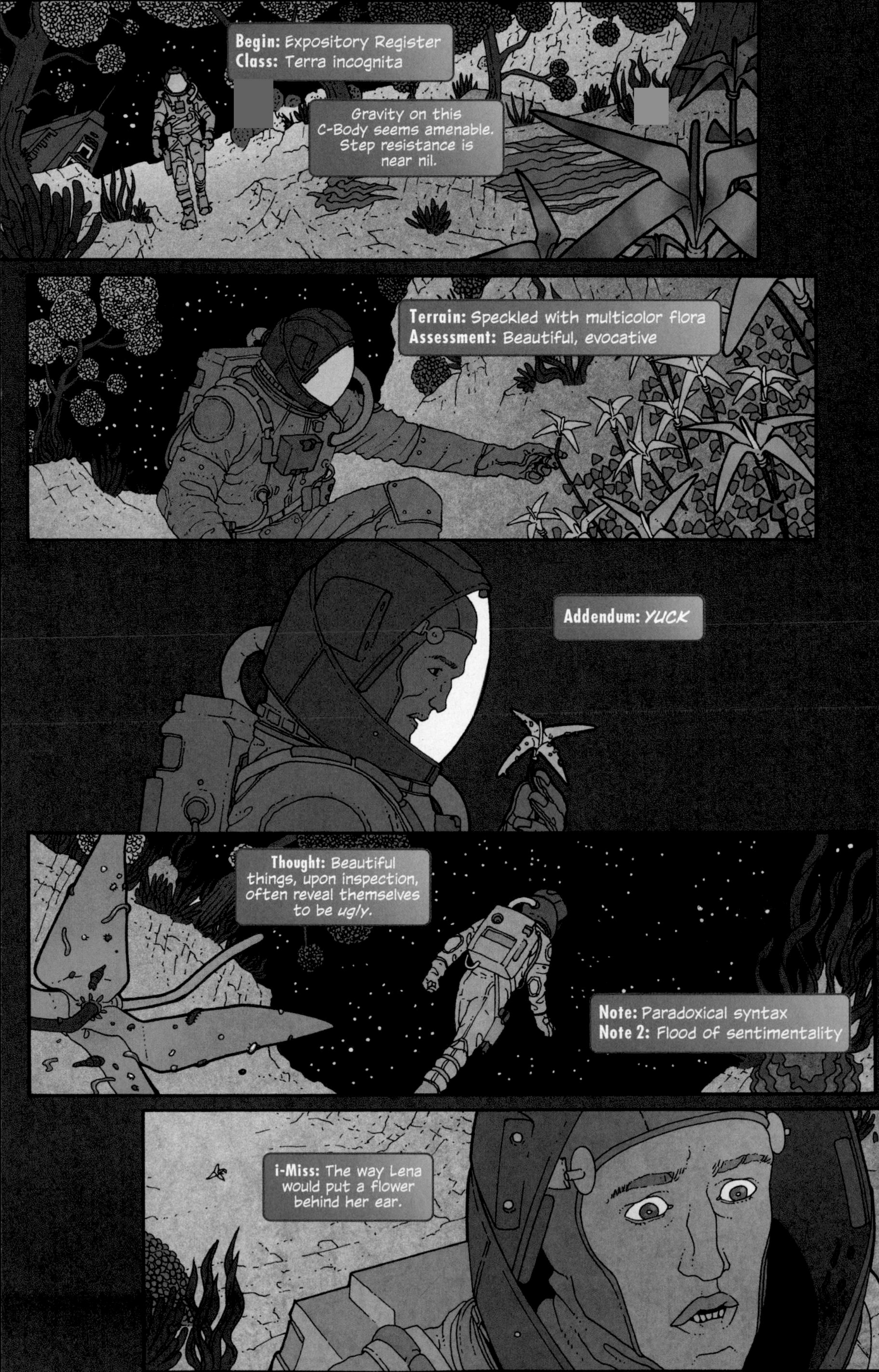
Begin: Expository Register
Class: Terra incognita
Gravity on this C-Body seems amenable. Step resistance is near nil.
Terrain: Speckled with multicolor flora
Assessment: Beautiful, evocative
Addendum: YUCK
Thought: Beautiful things, upon inspection, often reveal themselves to be ugly.
Note: Paradoxical syntax
Note 2: Flood of sentimentality
i-Miss: The way Lena would put a flower behind her ear.

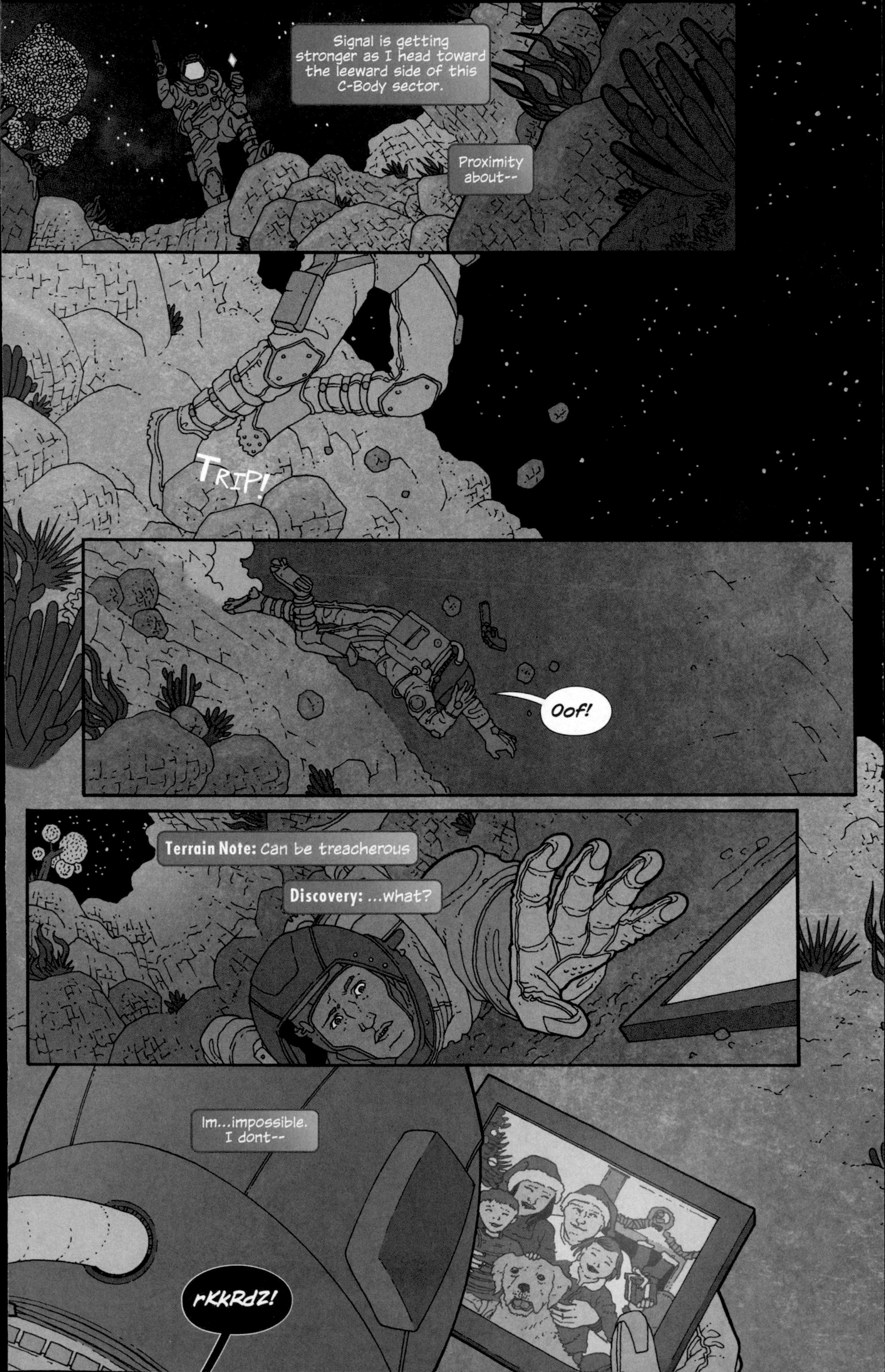
Signal is getting stronger as I head toward the leeward side of this C-Body sector.
Proximity about--
TRIP!
Oof!
Terrain Note: Can be treacherous
Discovery: ...what?
Im...impossible. I dont--
rKkRdZ!

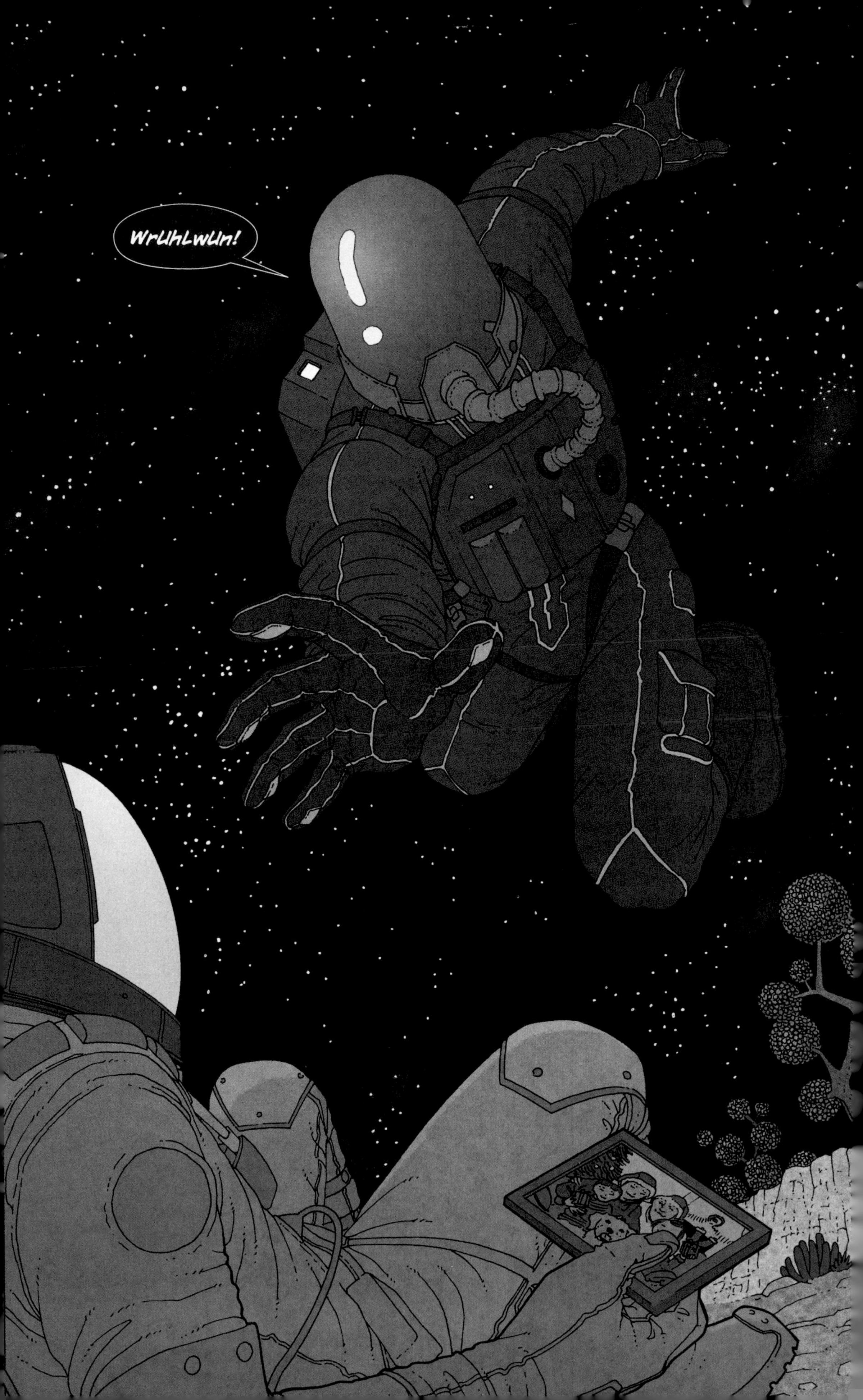
WrUhLwUn!

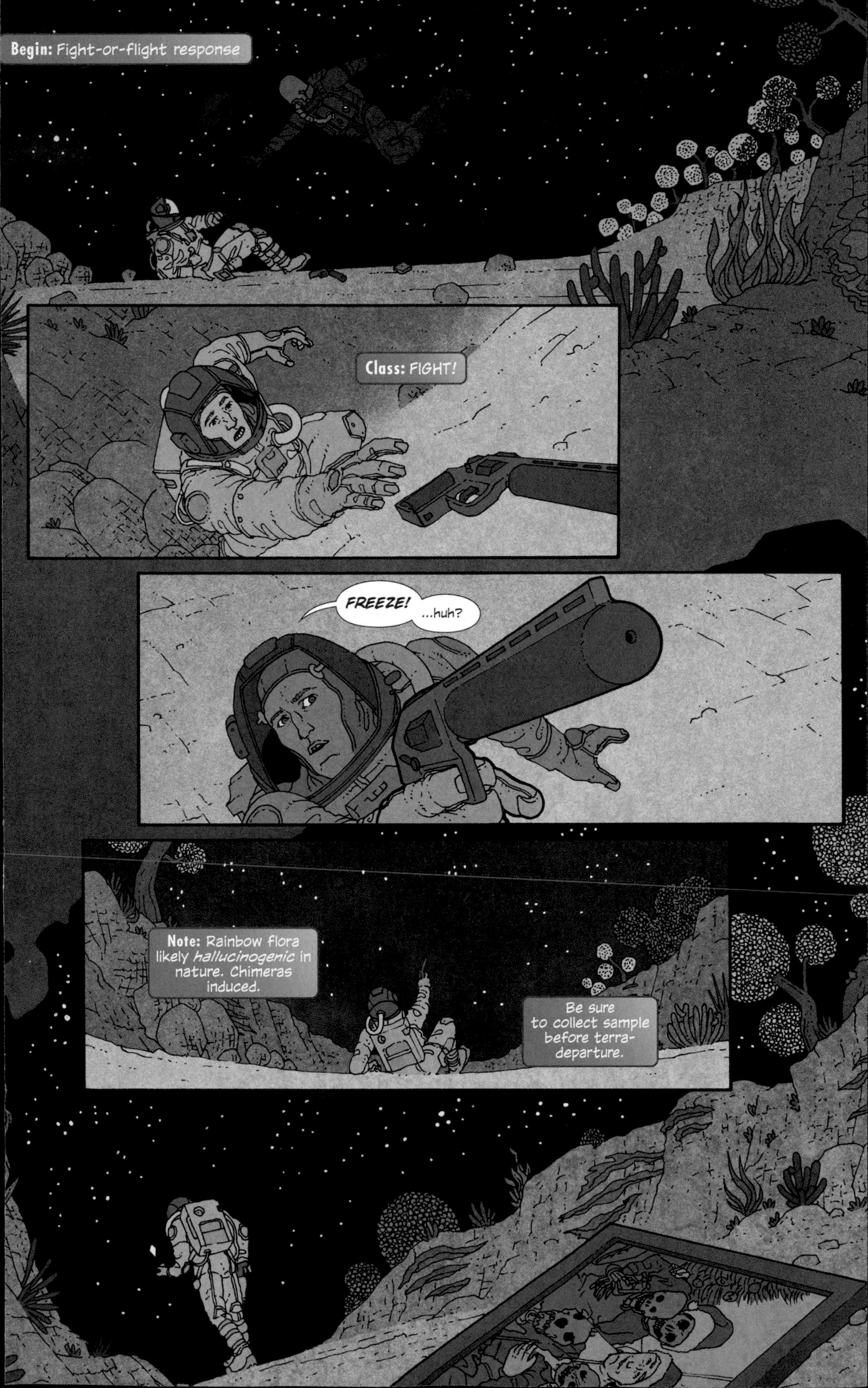
Begin: Fight-or-flight response
Class: FIGHT!
FREEZE!
...huh?
Note: Rainbow flora likely *hallucinogenic* in nature. Chimeras induced.
Be sure to collect sample before terra-departure.

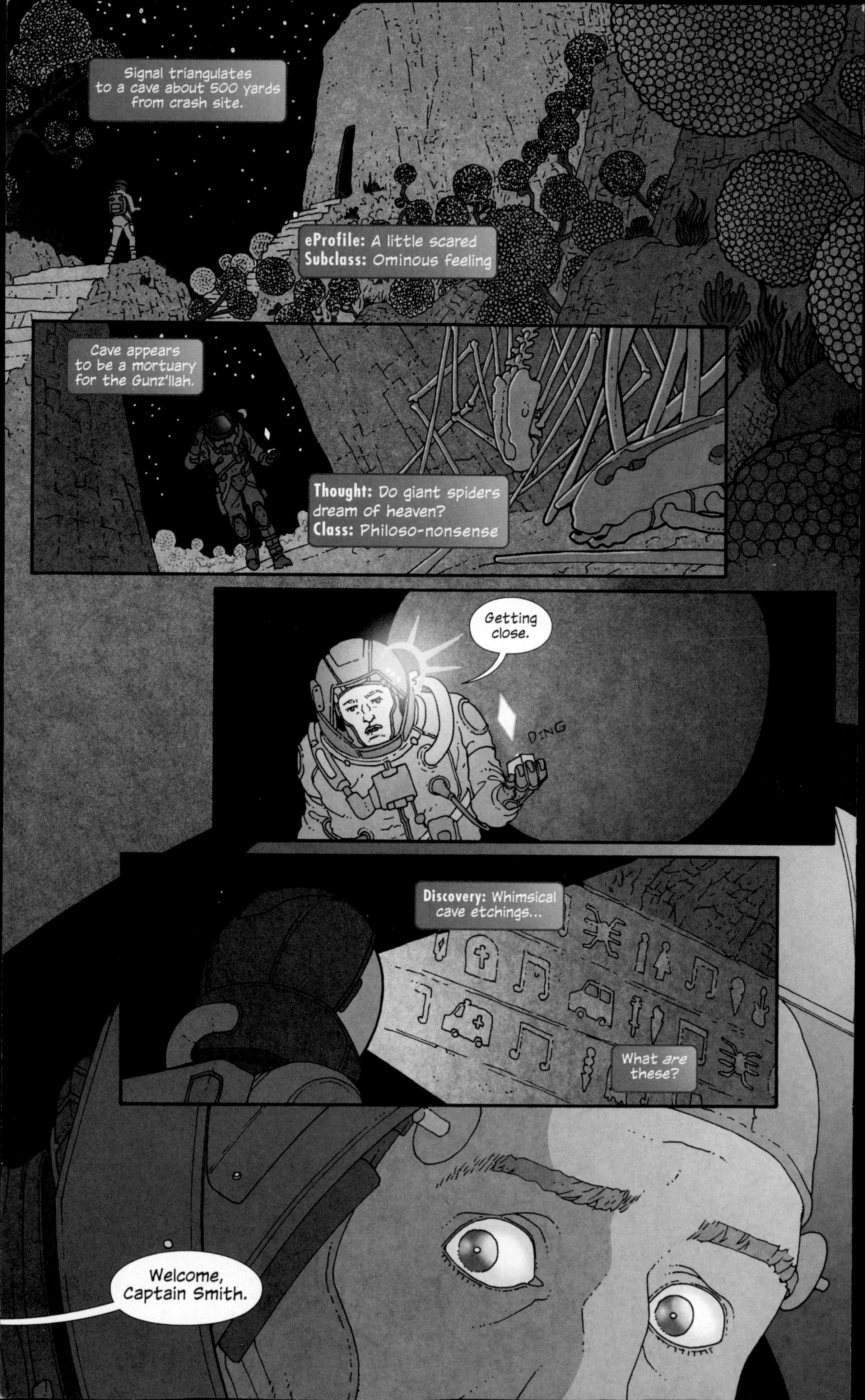

Signal triangulates to a cave about 500 yards from crash site.
eProfile: A little scared
Subclass: Ominous feeling
Cave appears to be a mortuary for the Gunz'llah.
Thought: Do giant spiders dream of heaven?
Class: Philoso-nonsense
Getting close.
DING
Discovery: Whimsical cave etchings...
What are these?
Welcome, Captain Smith.

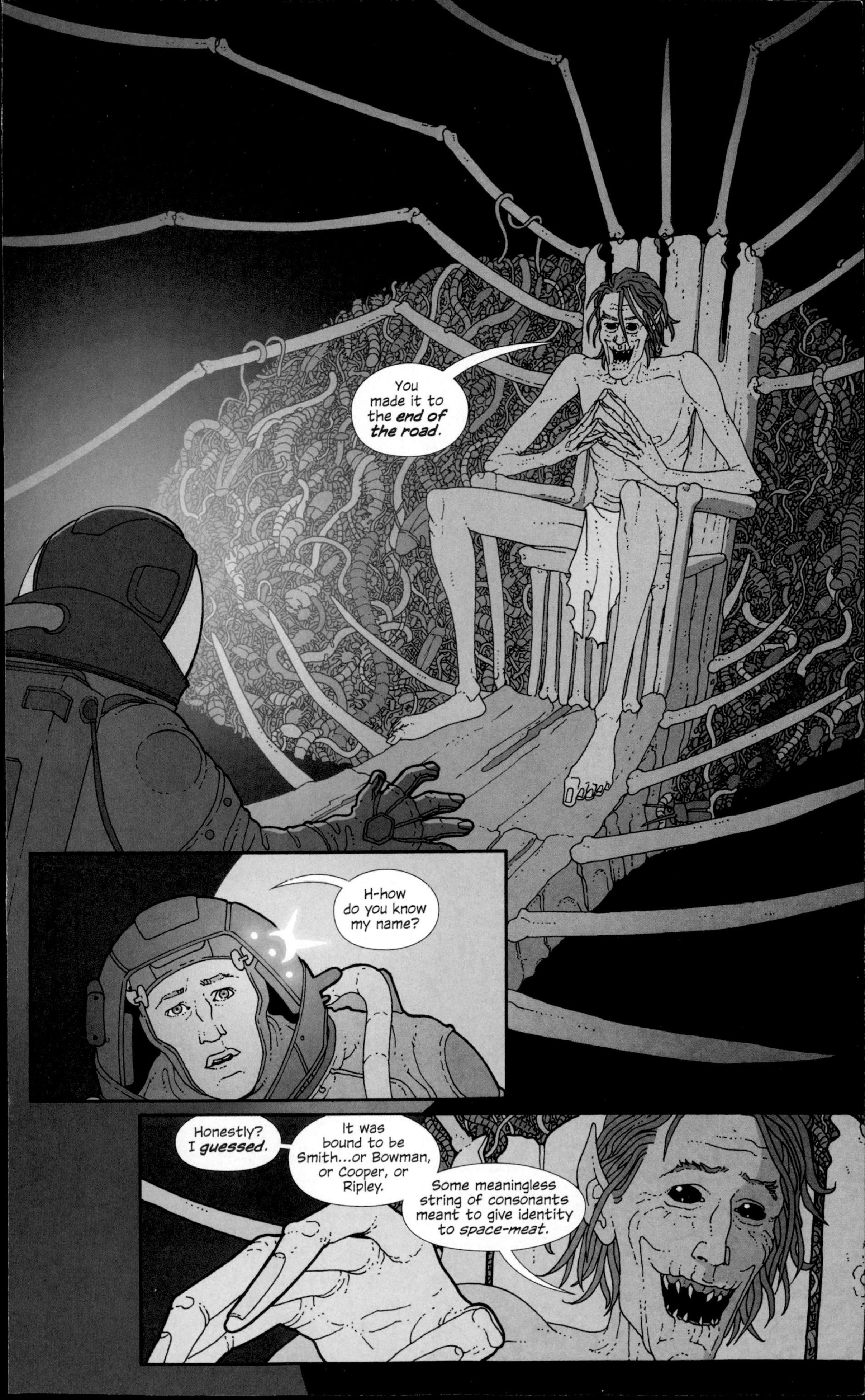
You made it to the *end of the road*.
H-how do you know my name?
Honestly? I *guessed*.
It was bound to be Smith...or Bowman, or Cooper, or Ripley.
Some meaningless string of consonants meant to give identity to *space-meat*.

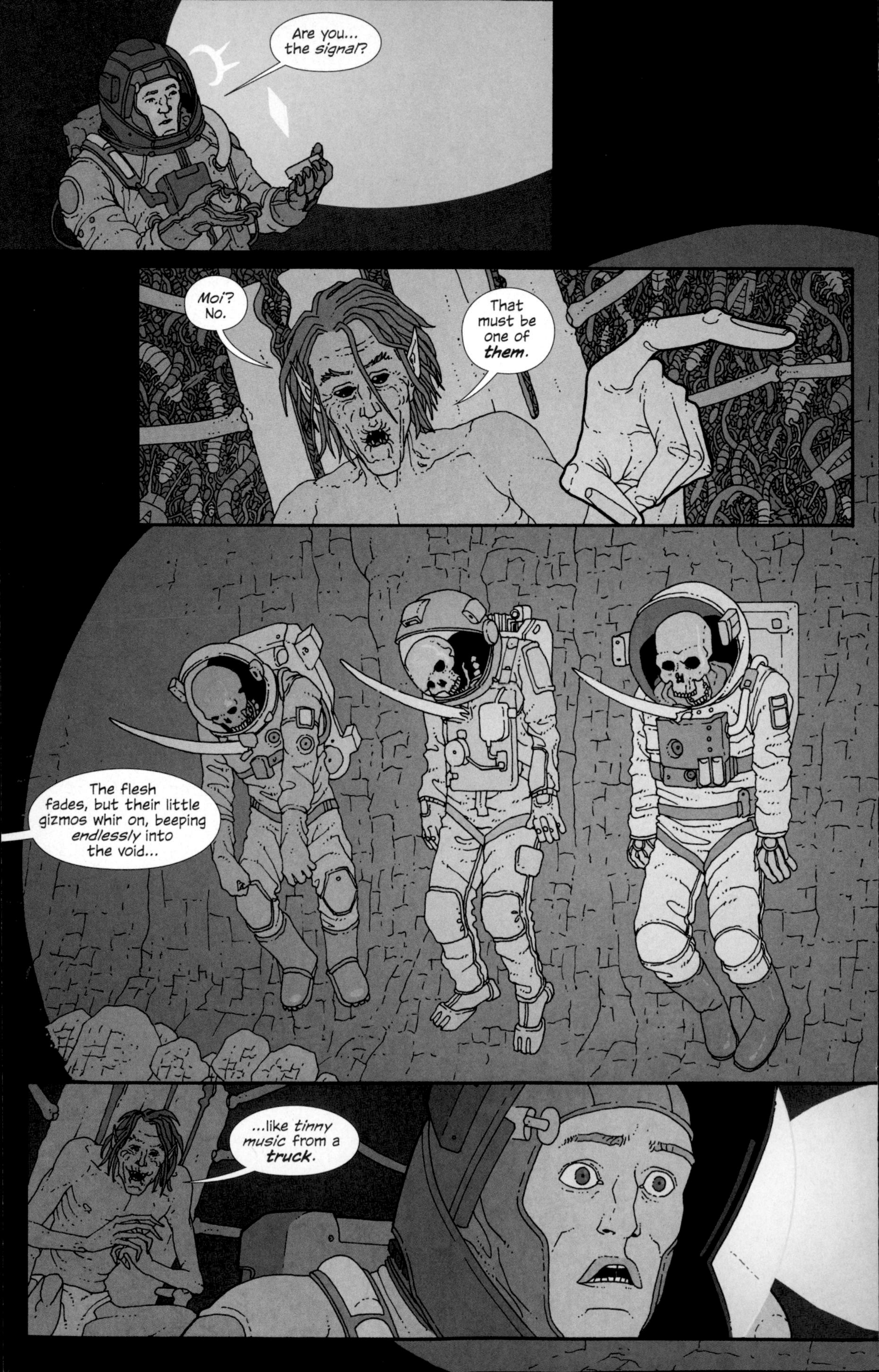
Are you... the *signal*?
Moi? No.
That must be one of ***them***.
The flesh fades, but their little gizmos whir on, beeping *endlessly* into the void...
...like *tinny music* from a ***truck***.

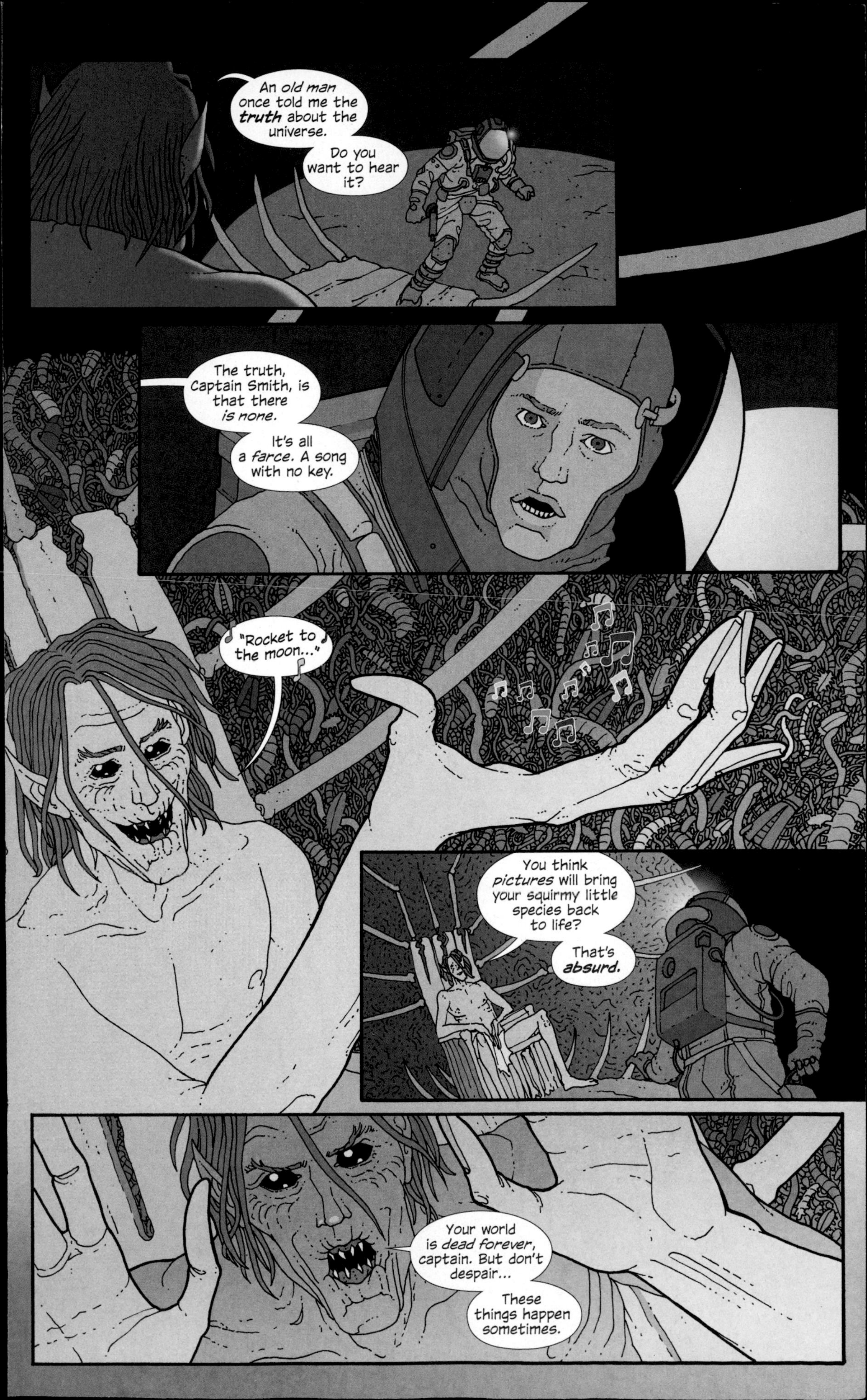
An *old man* once told me the ***truth*** about the universe.
Do you want to hear it?
The truth, Captain Smith, is that there *is none*.
It's all a *farce*. A song with no key.
"Rocket to the moon..."
You think *pictures* will bring your squirmy little species back to life?
That's ***absurd.***
Your world is *dead forever*, captain. But don't despair...
These things happen sometimes.

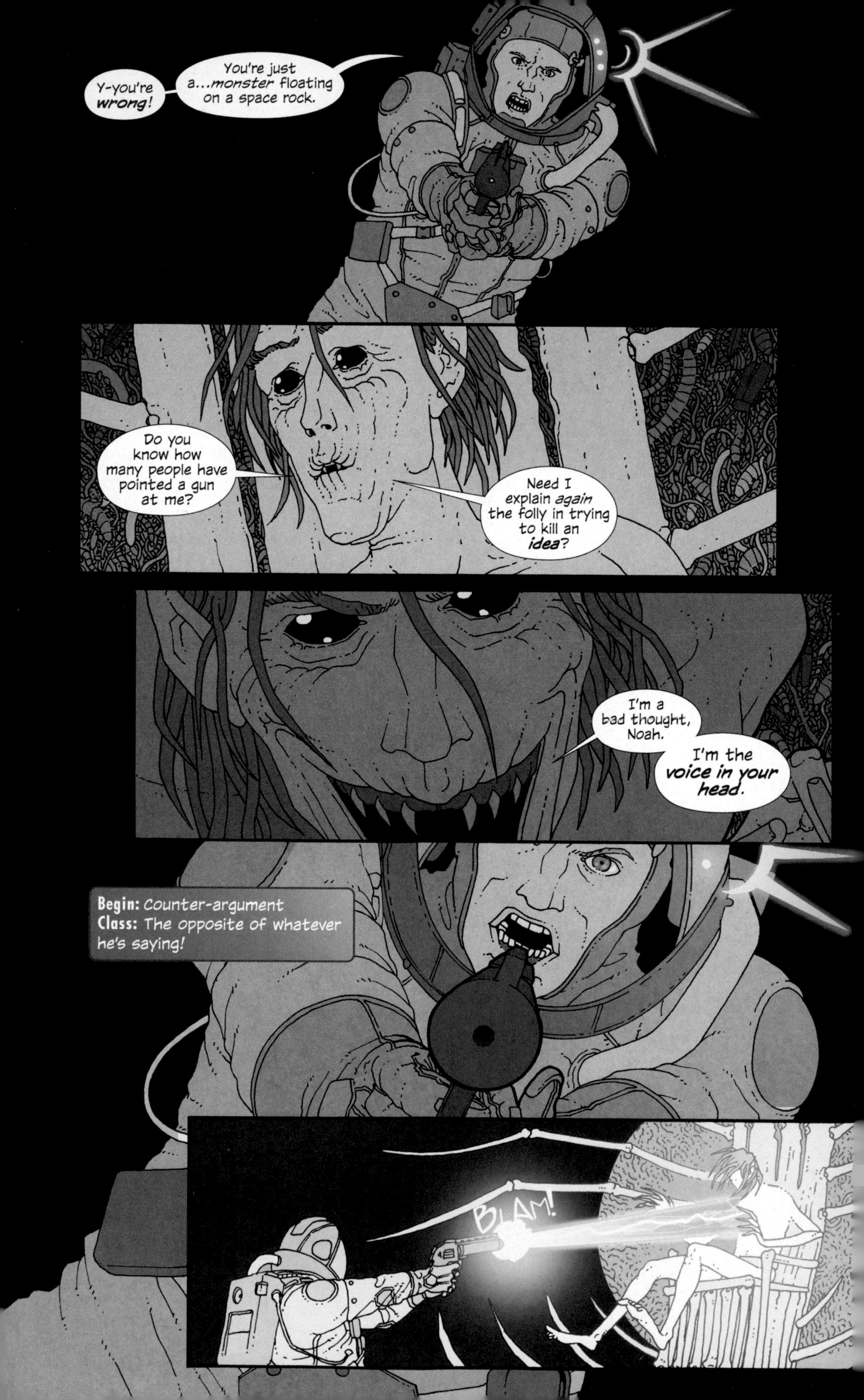
Y-you're *wrong*!
You're just a...*monster* floating on a space rock.
Do you know how many people have pointed a gun at me?
Need I explain *again* the folly in trying to kill an *idea*?
I'm a bad thought, Noah.
I'm the *voice in your head*.
Begin: Counter-argument
Class: The opposite of whatever he's saying!
BLAM!

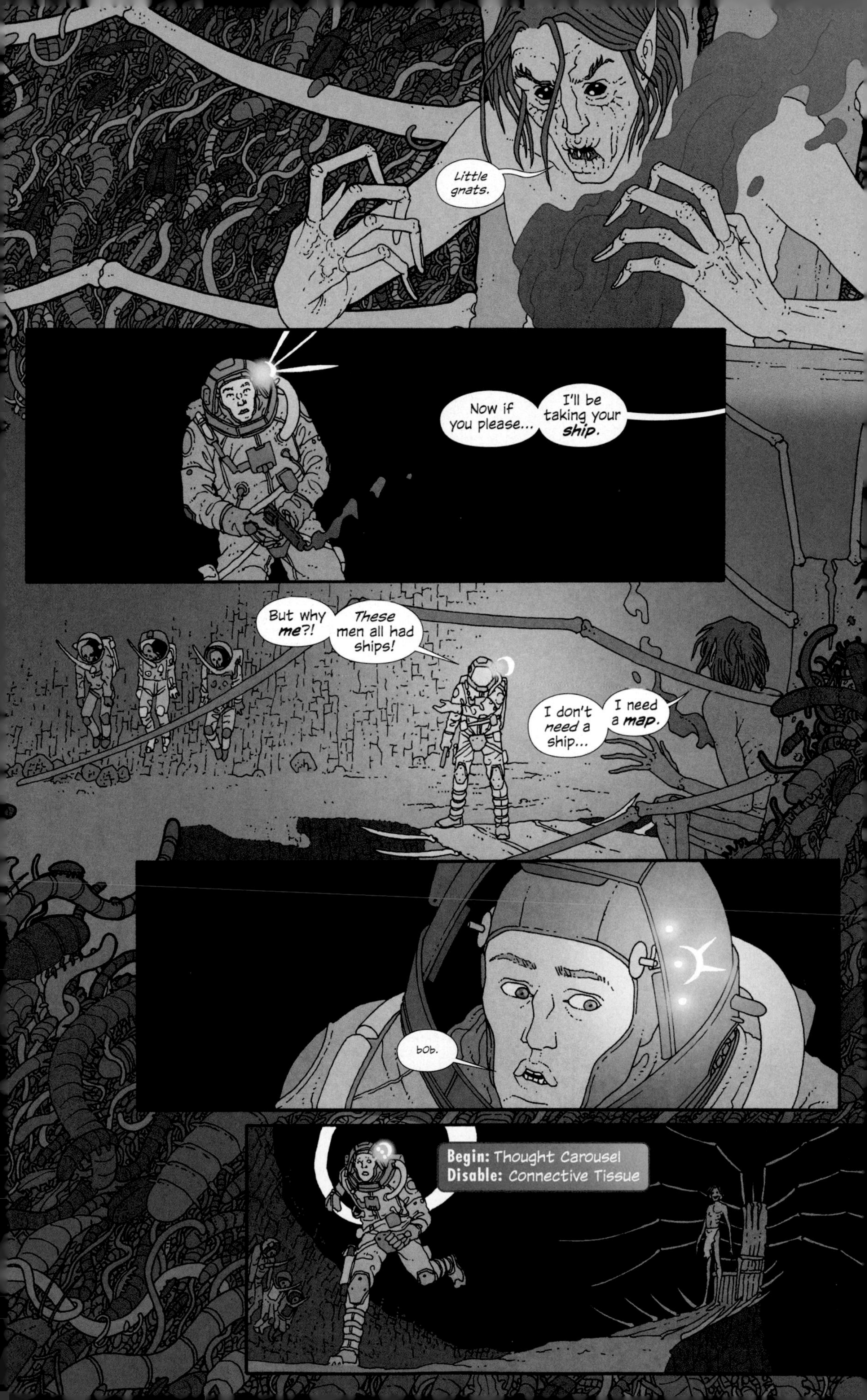
Little gnats.
Now if you please...
I'll be taking your ***ship***.
But why ***me***?!
These men all had ships!
I don't need a ship...
I need a ***map***.
bOb.
Begin: Thought Carousel
Disable: Connective Tissue

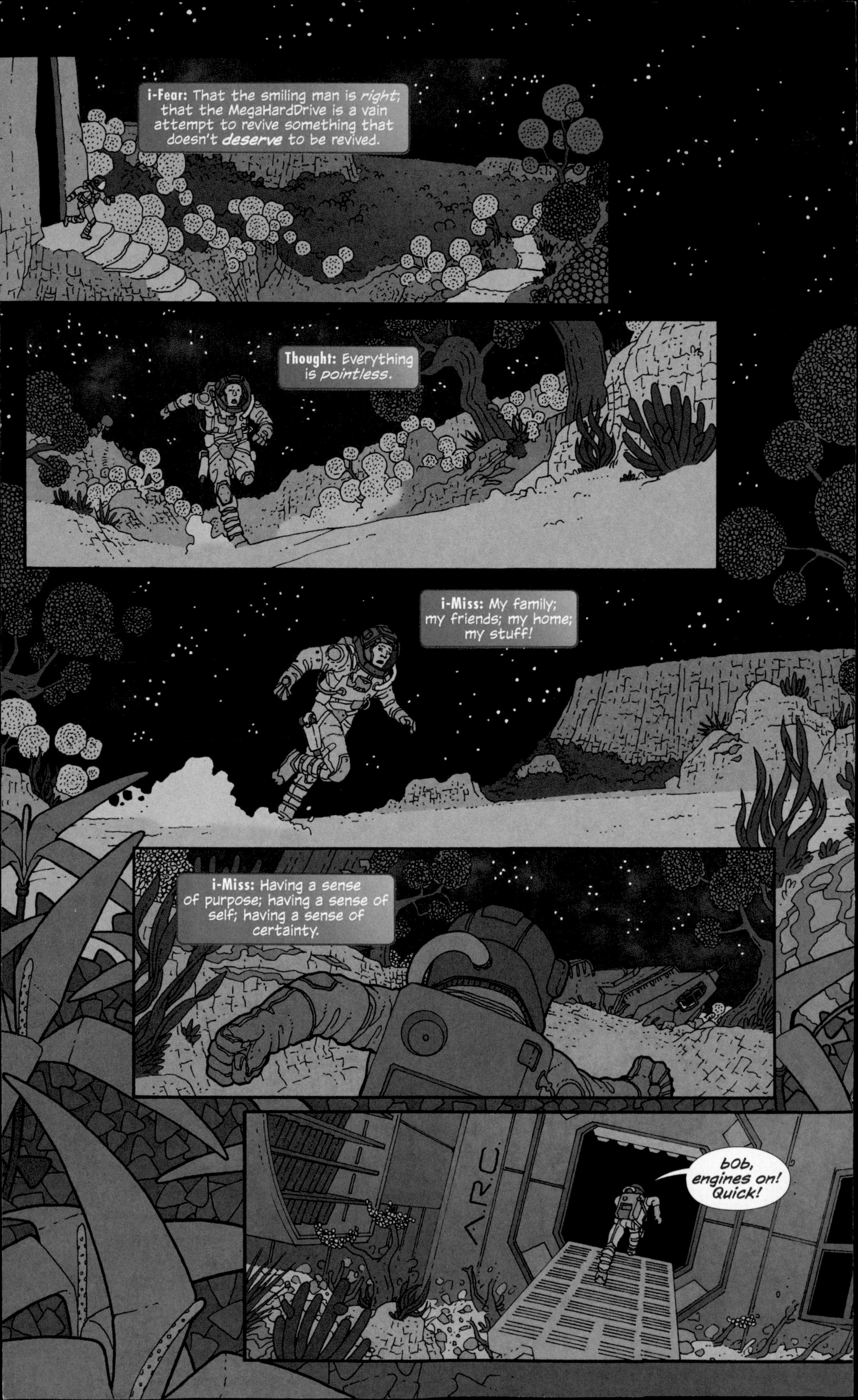
i-Fear: That the smiling man is right; that the MegaHardDrive is a vain attempt to revive something that doesn't deserve to be revived.
Thought: Everything is pointless.
i-Miss: My family; my friends; my home; my stuff!
i-Miss: Having a sense of purpose; having a sense of self; having a sense of certainty.
A.R.C.
bOb, engines on! Quick!

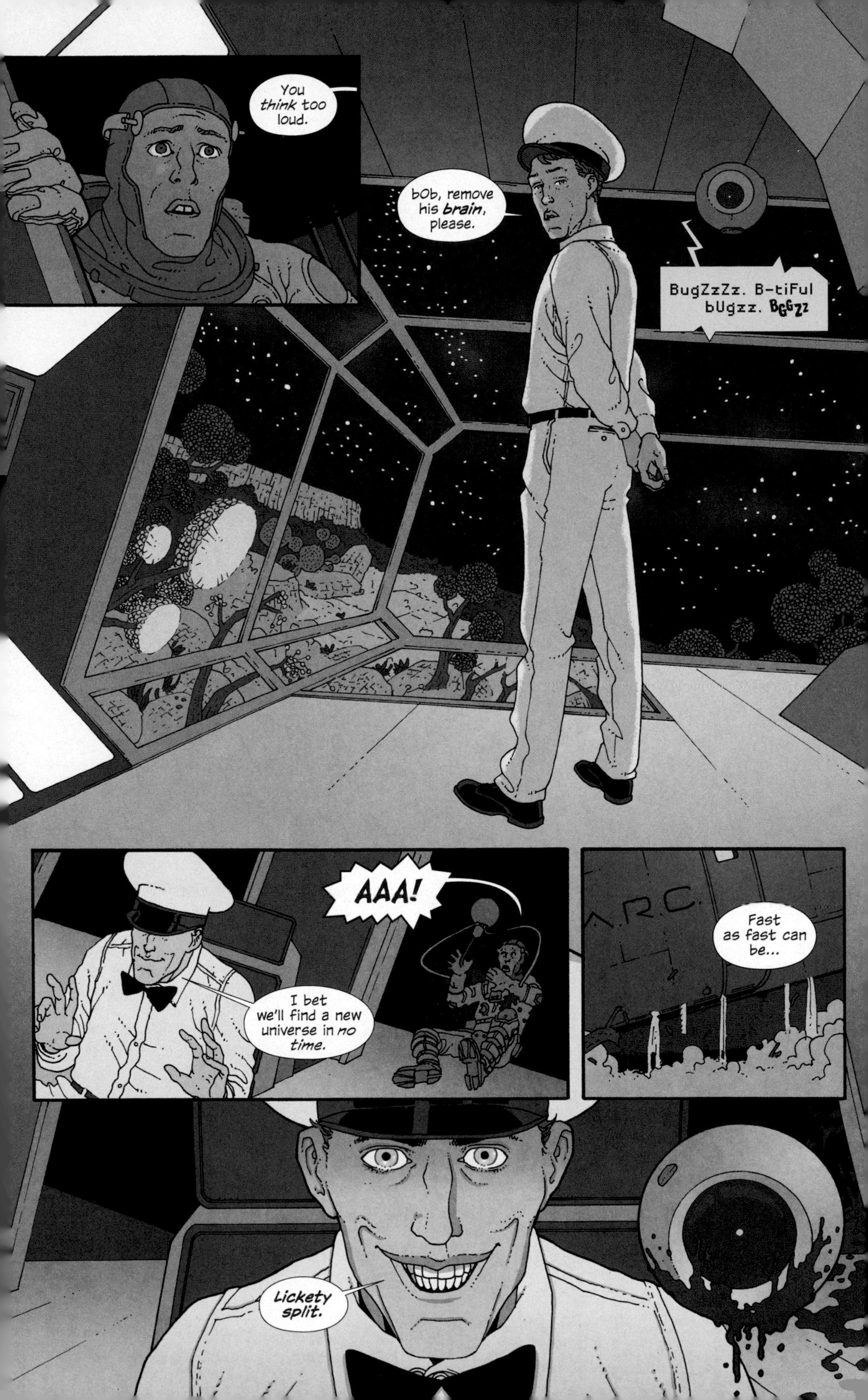
You think too loud.
bOb, remove his brain, please.
BugZzZz. B-tiFul bUgzz. BGGZZ
AAA!
I bet we'll find a new universe in no time.
A.R.C.
Fast as fast can be...
Lickety split.

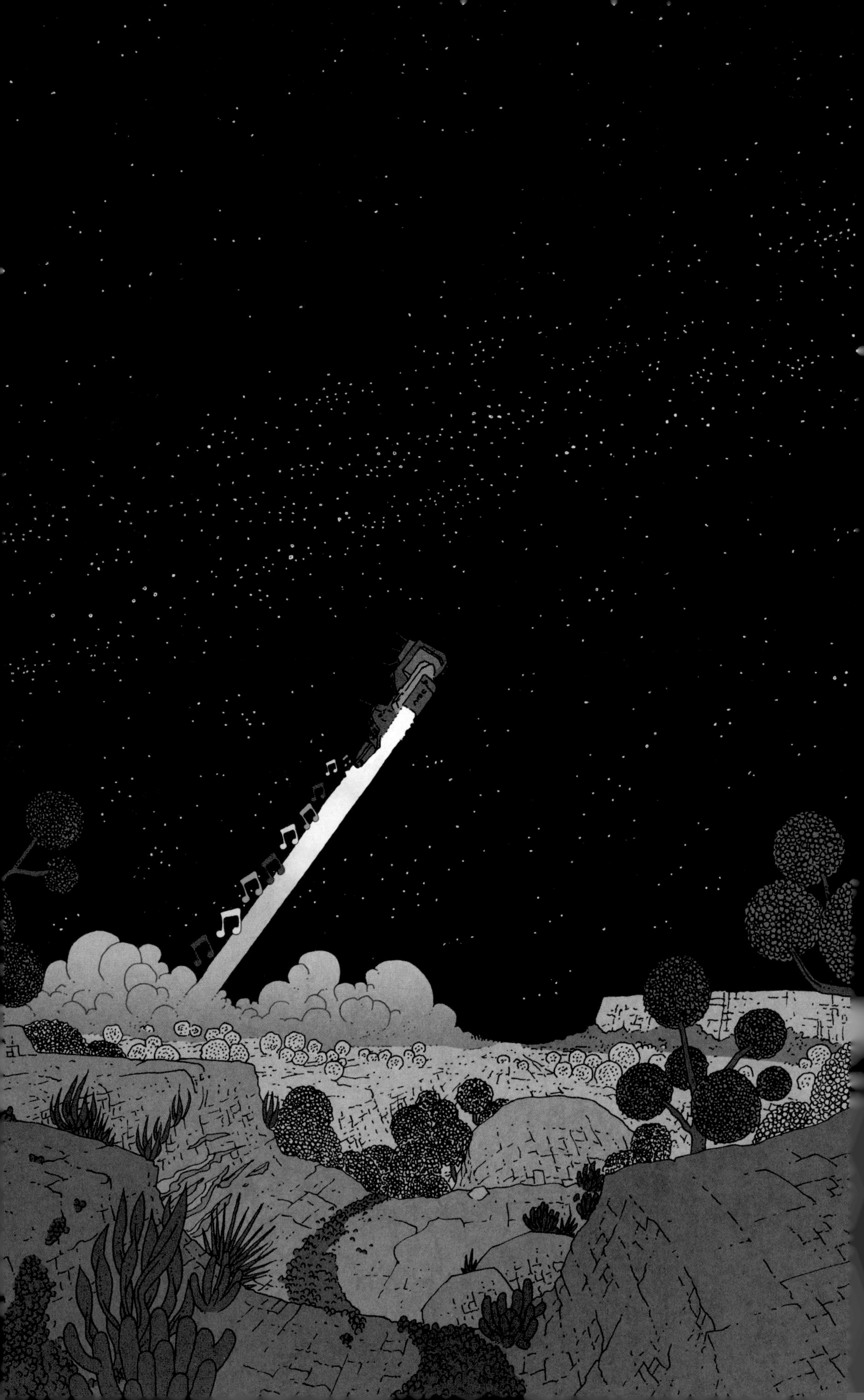

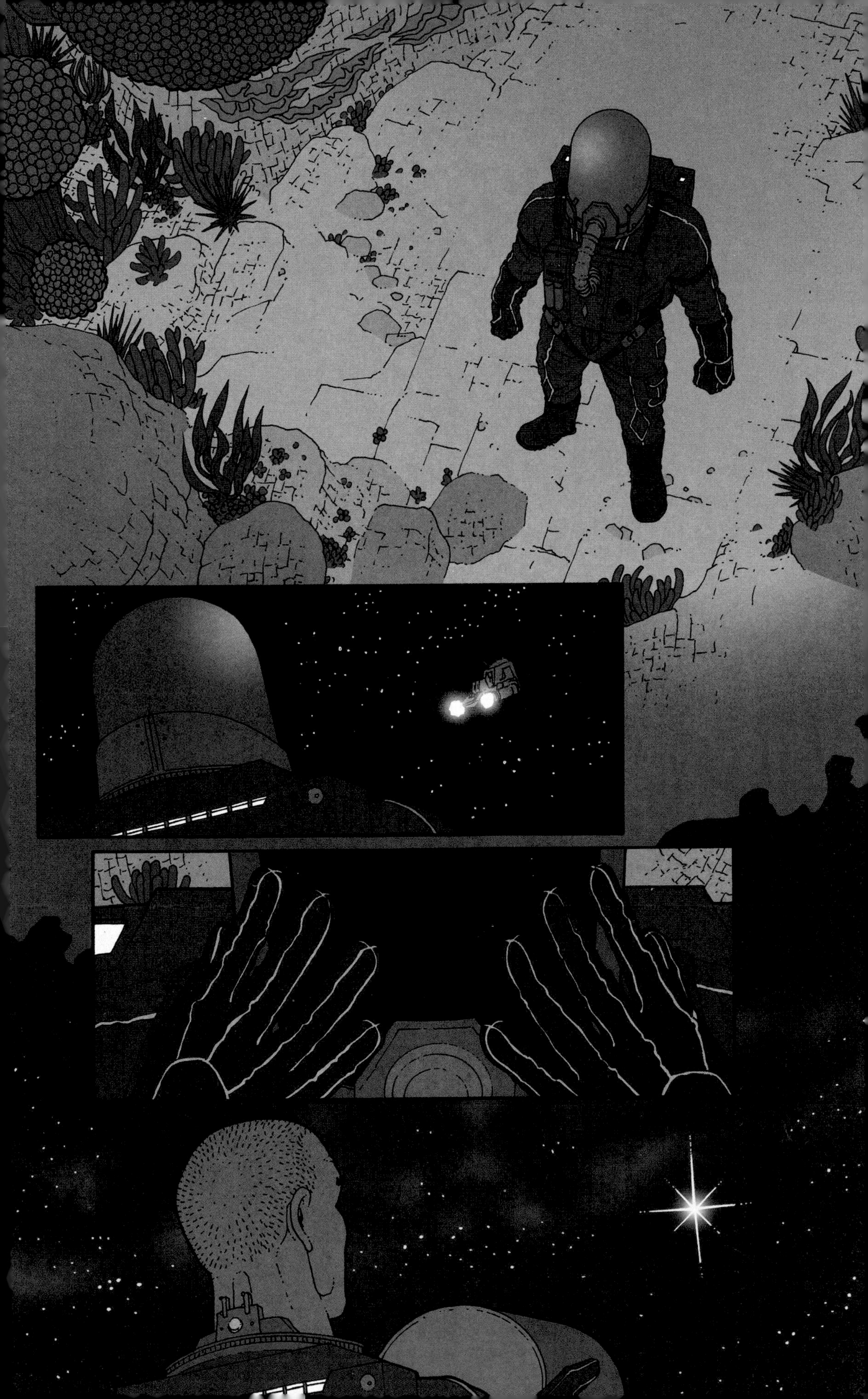

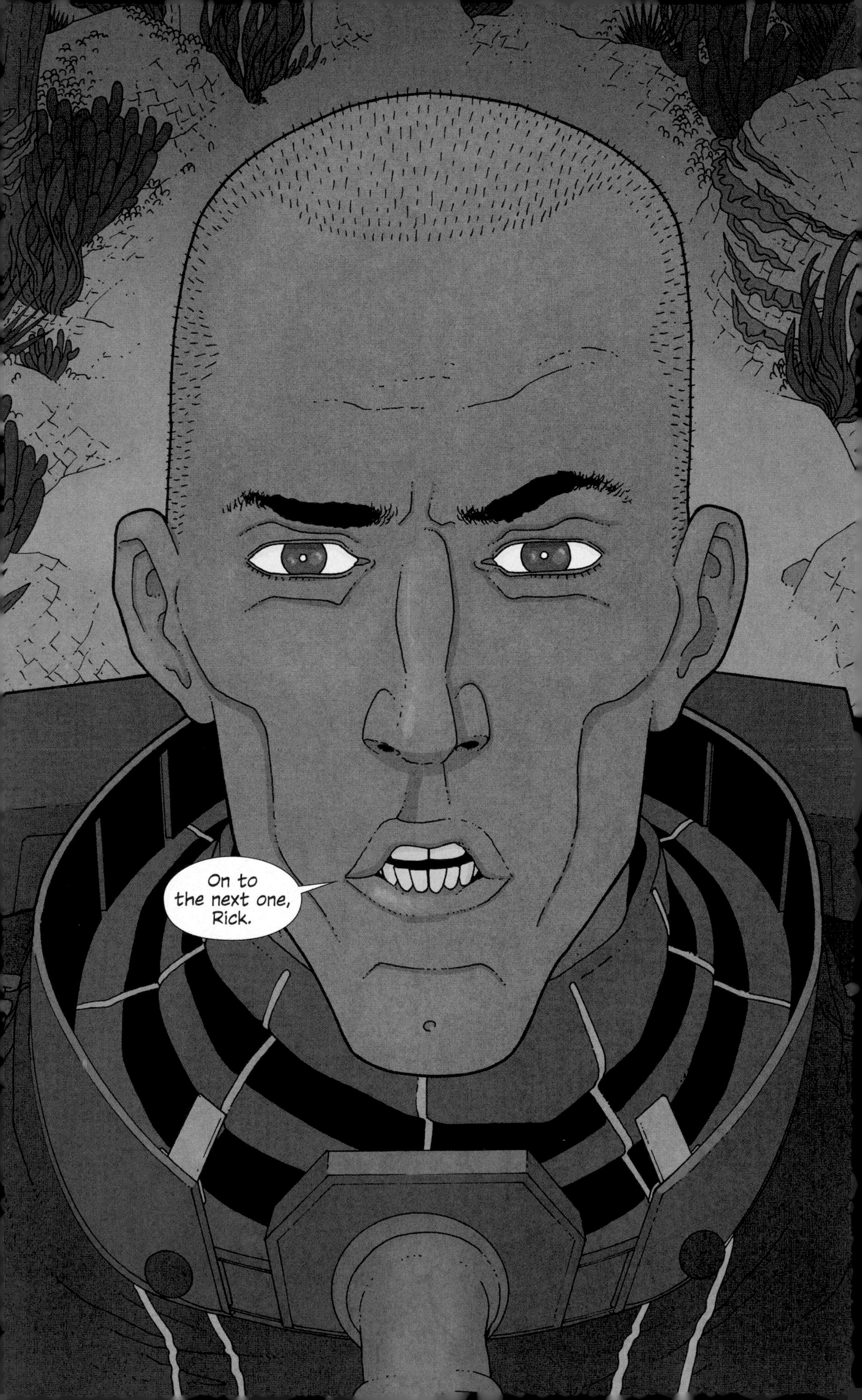
On to the next one, Rick.

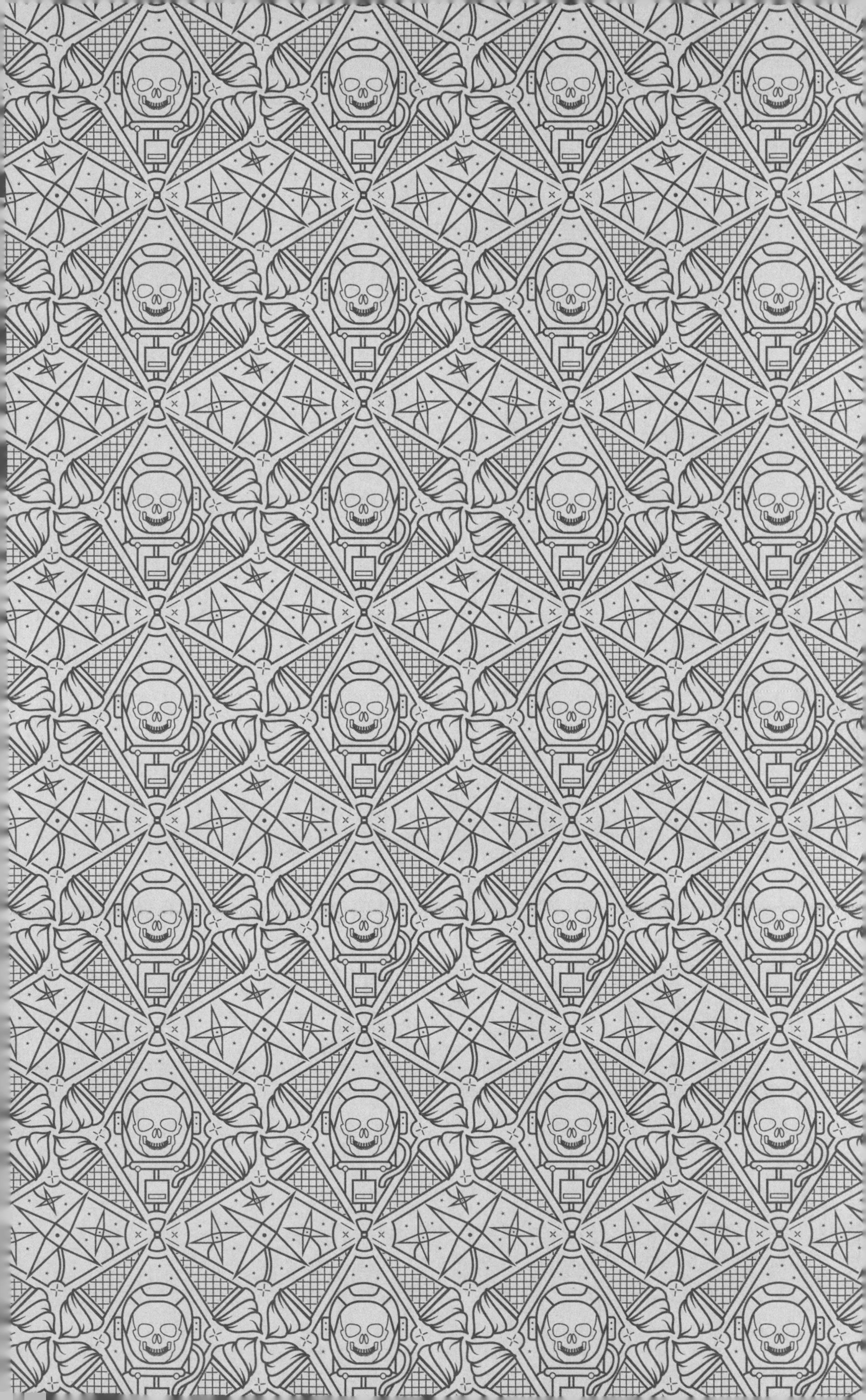

THE CHERRY ON TOP

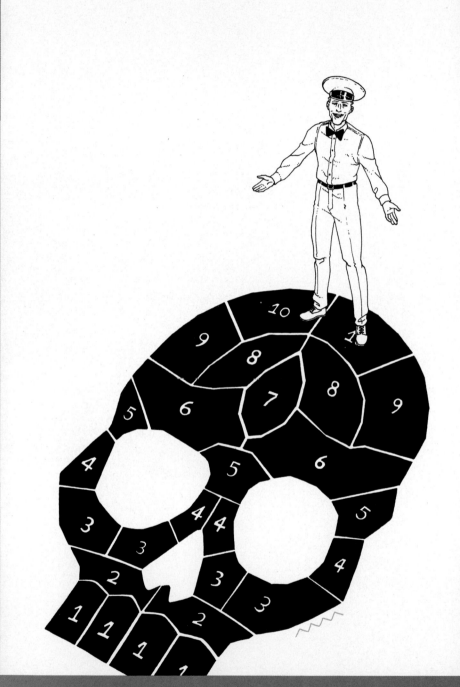

What follows are variant covers, sketches, and a
translation guide from the third volume of
ICE CREAM MAN.

Everything is one thing…

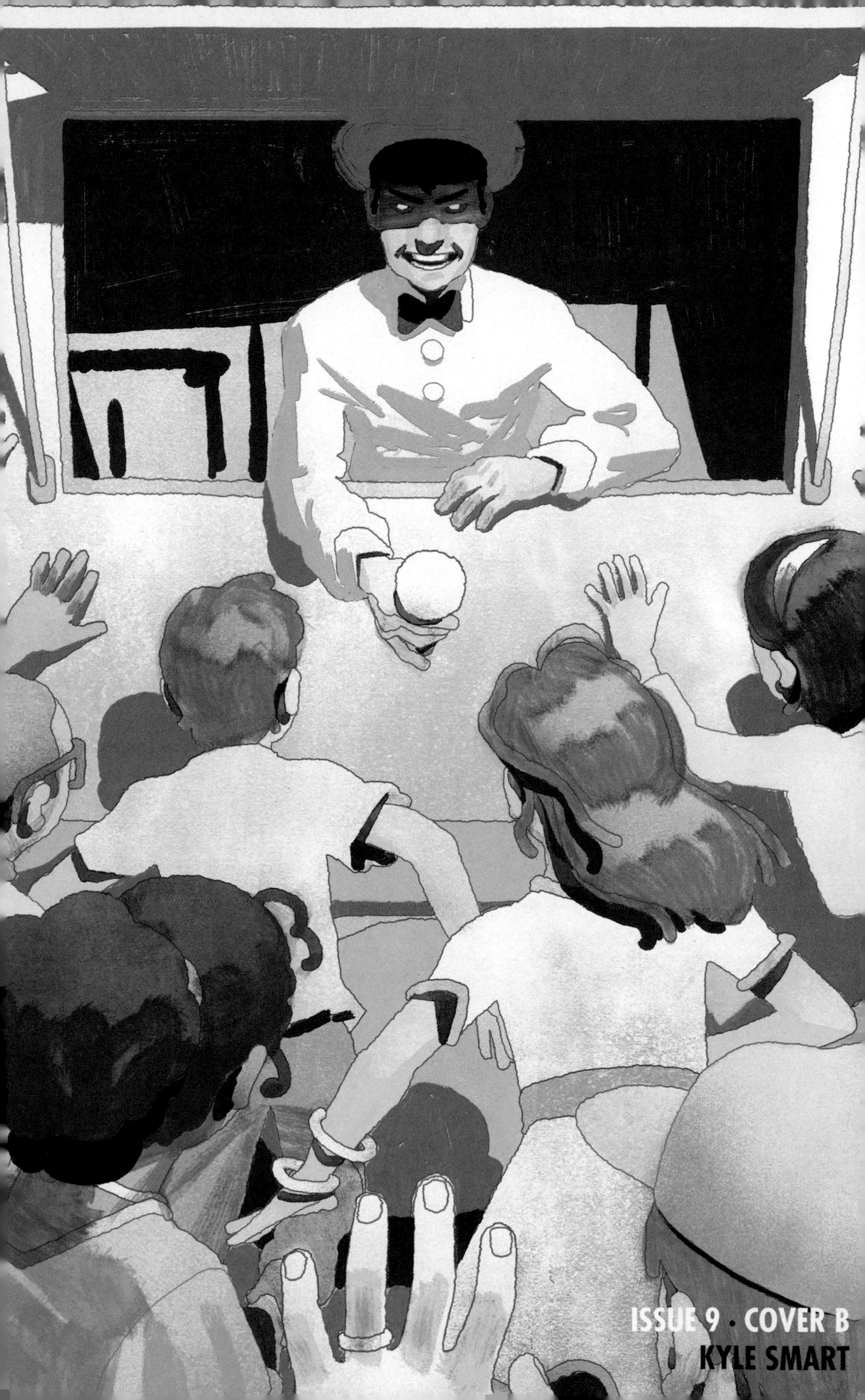
ISSUE 9 · COVER B
KYLE SMART

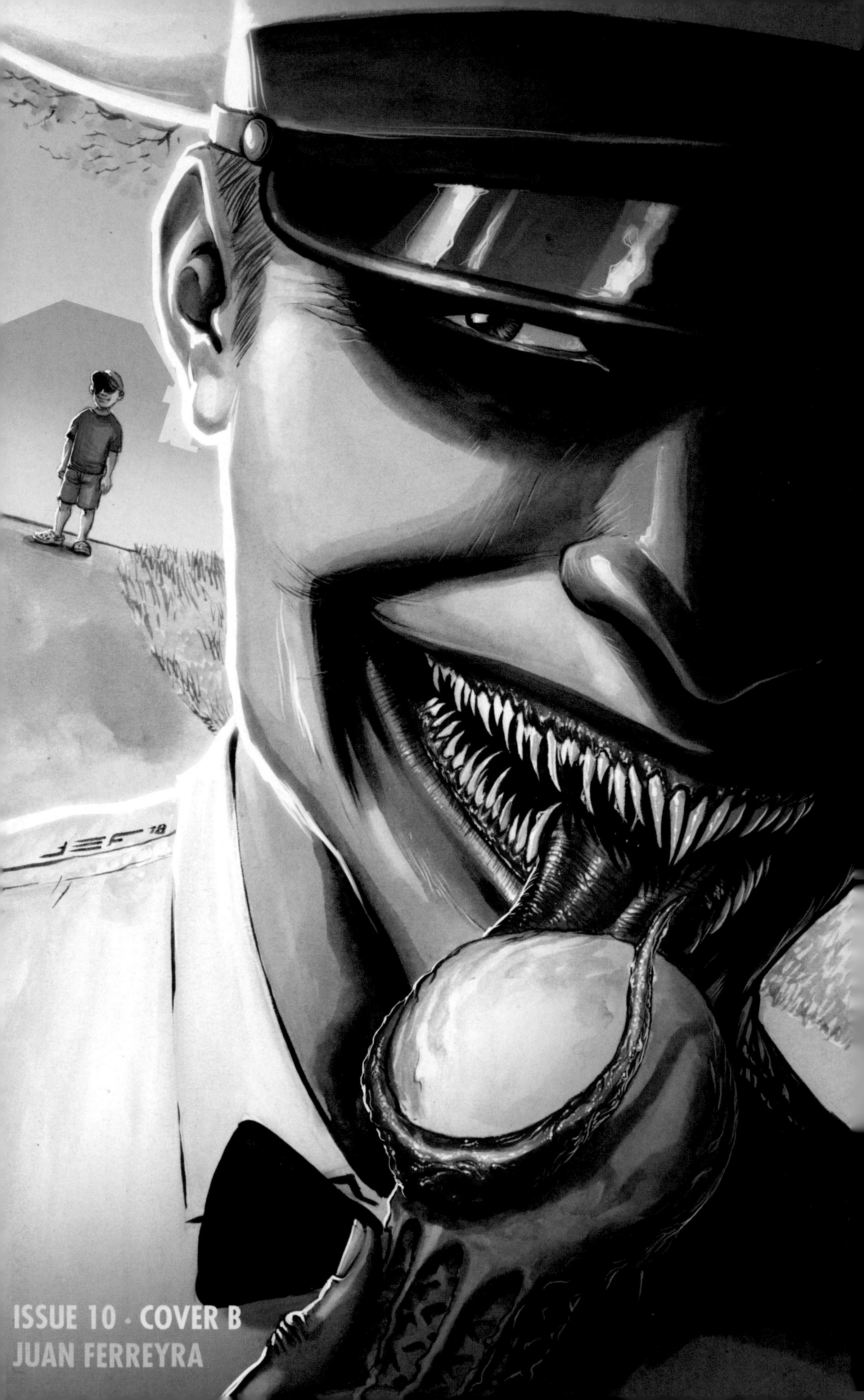

ISSUE 10 · COVER B
JUAN FERREYRA

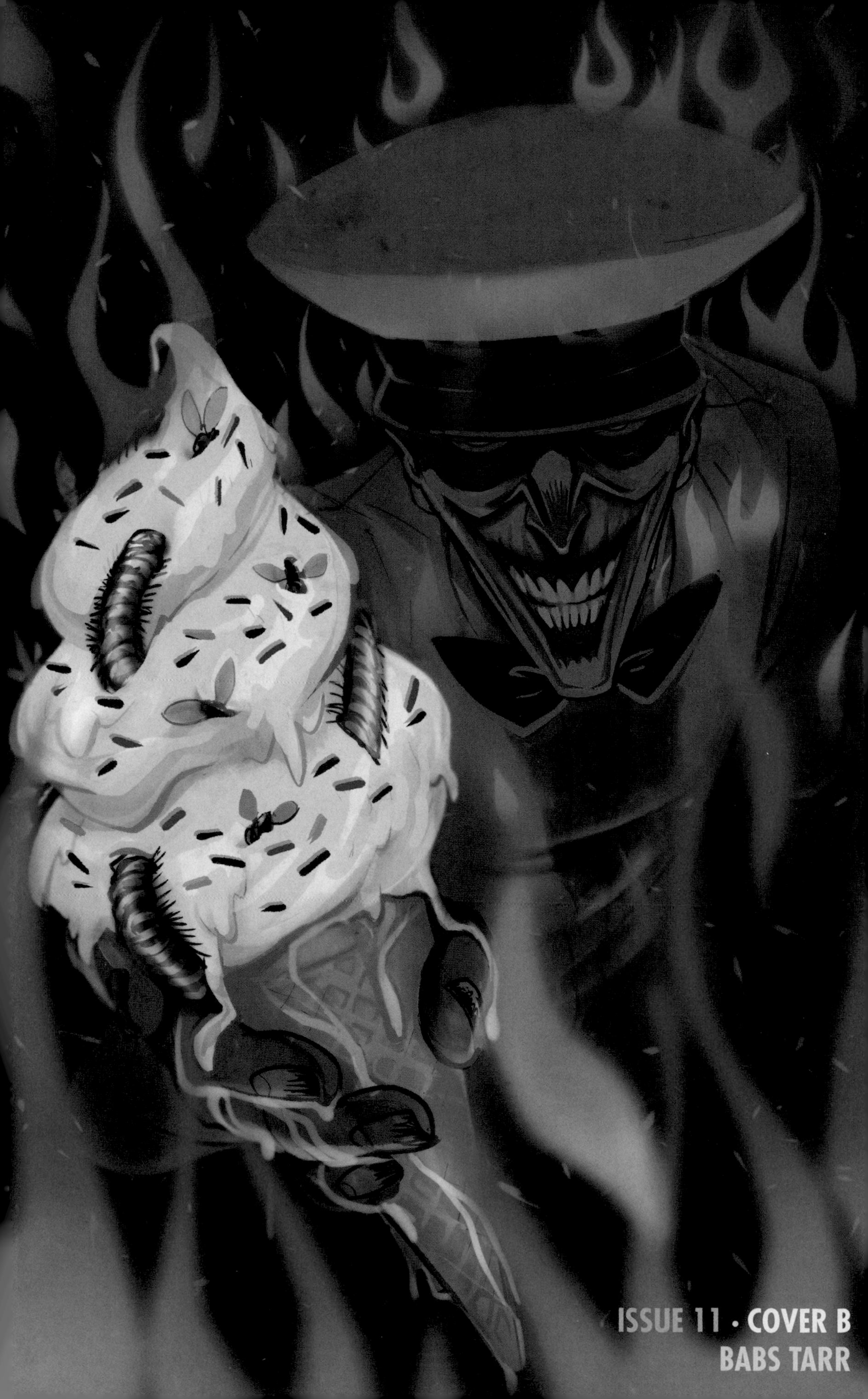
ISSUE 11 · COVER B
BABS TARR

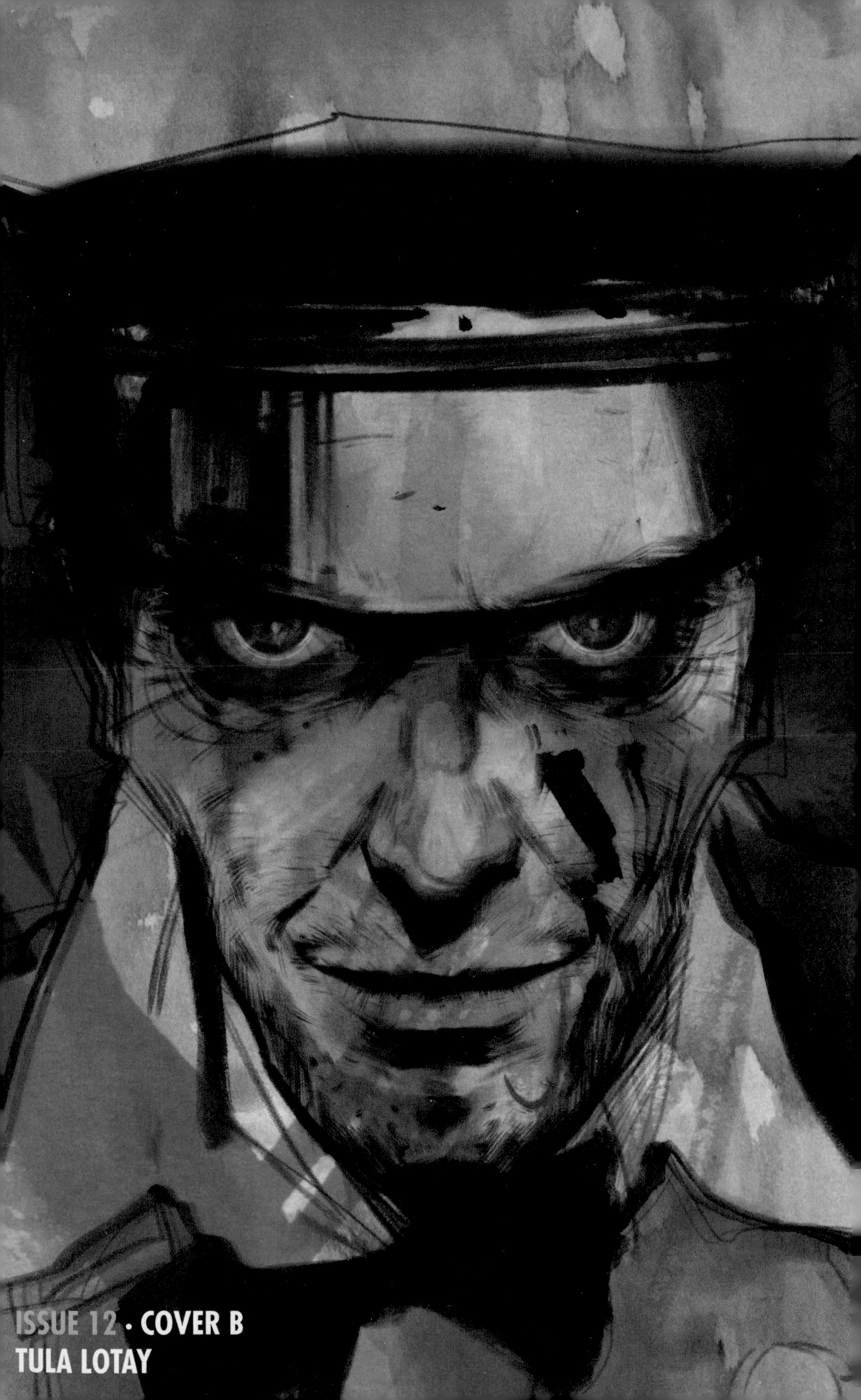
ISSUE 12 · COVER B
TULA LOTAY

EERIE VISAGES

ICE CREAM MAN #9
Sketches

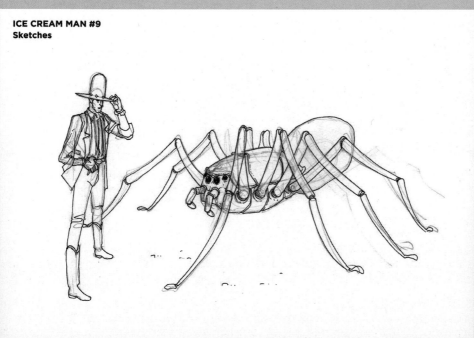

ICE CREAM MAN #9
Sketches

In what has now become standard operating procedure,
Martín provided character sketches with every issue's
sequential layouts. Each one teems with a buzzing kind
of *life*—an electricity operating beneath the ink that begs
to be pulled out and teased in some direction or another.

CREEPY COUNTENANCES

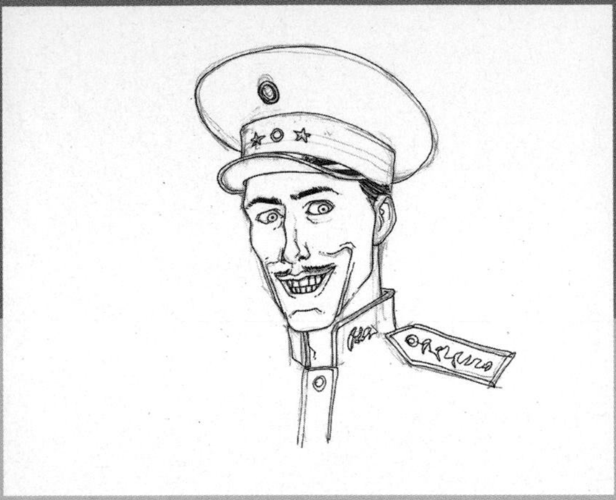

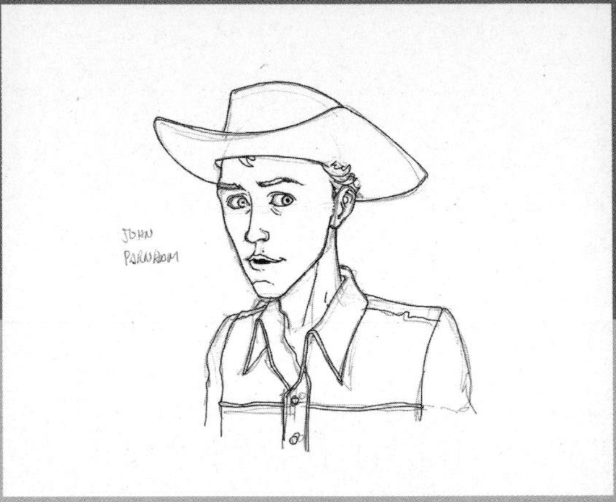
JOHN
PARNHAM

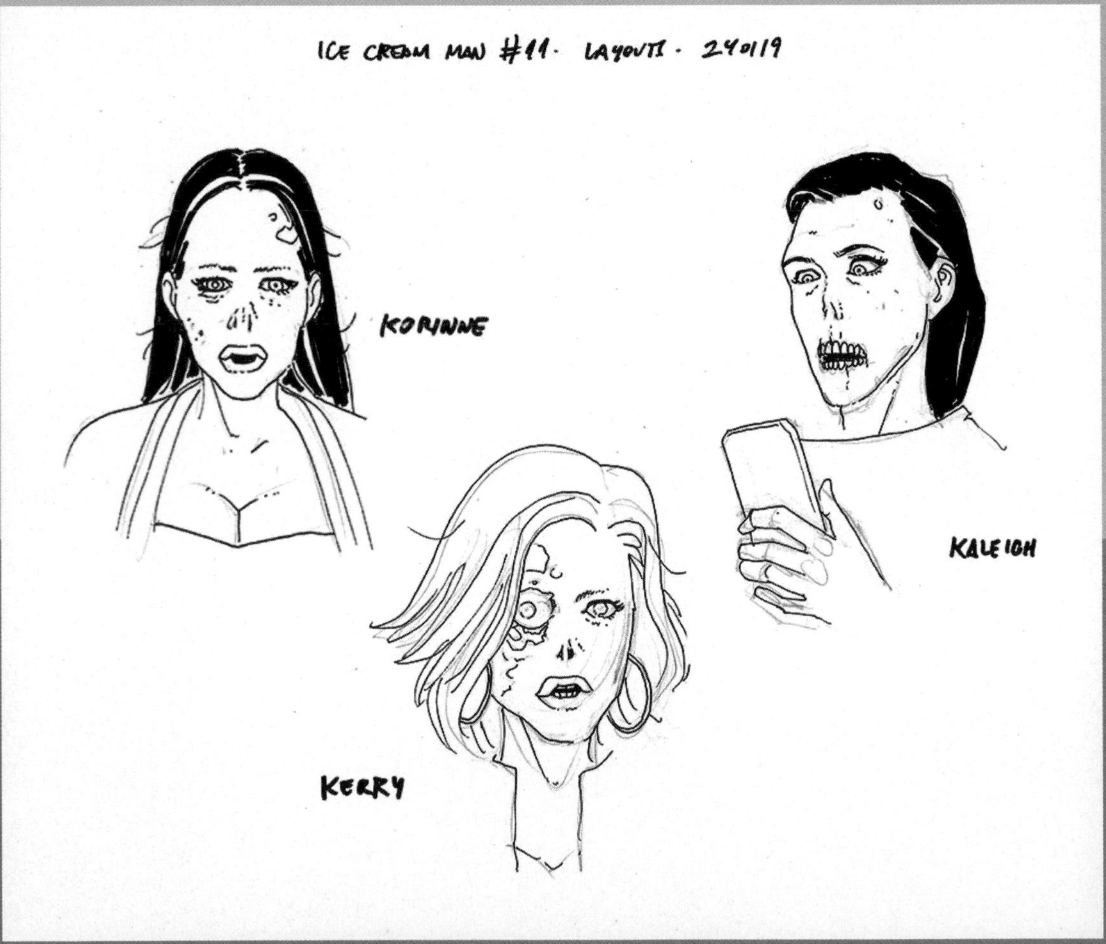
ICE CREAM MAN #11 · LAYOUTS · 240119
KORINNE
KALEIGH
KERRY

Of special note are his designs for the zombie send-ups of the three main Kardashian sisters—they're so *alive*, and yet also so *dead*.

GOING LUNAR

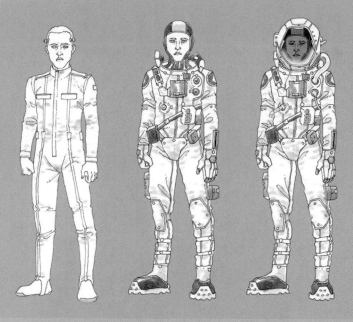

ICE CREAM MAN #12
NOAH SMITH

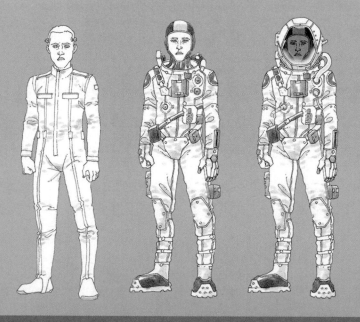

ICE CREAM MAN #12
NOAH SMITH

Wowza.

EL VENDEDOR DE HELADOS

Herewith the English script for the first pages of Chapter 10, "Border Story," before it was translated to Spanish by our pal Sam Stone. (*Gracias, Sam!*)

ICE CREAM MAN
Issue 10 · English Pre-Translation

PAGE ONE

NARRATION: There are people who would tell you that it is bad luck to celebrate a girl's quinceañera on The Day of the Dead.

Tia: Hold still, María!

PAGE TWO

Panel 1

NARRATION: "It is a poisonous mixture," they'd say. Like vinegar and bleach.

Tia: Or do you want the pins pressed into your flesh?

Panel 2

NARRATION: But there are others—many others—who would disagree.

NARRATION: Those people would say: "To join the dead with the living is a blessing, a marriage, a balancing of the world."

Tia : There.

Panel 3

NARRATION: Poison? Marriage? These are just words.

Tia: Now you are ready for your groom.

Panel 4

NARRATION: The truth has no patience for words.

Tia: Now you are ready for the General.

Panel 5

General (offscreen): You are a stunning vision, my bride to be.

PAGE THREE

Panel 1

General: Come, let the General see you in your quinceañera dress.

Panel 2

Tia 1: General, you grace us with your presence.

Tia 2: God protect the hero of the Revolution!

Panel 3

General: Why so shy, little flower?

General: Can you not look into the eyes of your betrothed?

PAGE FOUR

Panel 1

General: Ah, there, that's better.

General: I can see the music in your skull. Little shapes of blue, red, and yellow.

General: You will make a lovely trophy.

Panel 2

General: Your fifteenth birthday and the Day of the Dead…

General: We celebrate your life while we mourn those that have passed.

Panel 3

General: Life is full of these funny juxtapositions.

Panel 4

General: Enjoy these last few days, little one.

General: Celebrations will be scarce one we're wed.

Panel 5

General (offscreen): Adios.

NARRATION: Yes, the truth has no patience for words.

PAGE FIVE

Panel 1

NARRATION: But what about love?

NARRATION: Saint Paul said to the Corinthians:

Panel 2

NARRATION: "Love is patient. Love is kind."

Panel 3

NARRATION: But the apostle omitted certain facts...

NARRATION: Love is also a border. Love is a crossing.

Panel 4

NARRATION: Love is the bridging of a great void!

Panel 5

NARRATION: ...but few survive the journey

John: One rose, please.

PAGE SIX

Panel 1

Woman: Rose, the name of my mother.

Panel 2

Woman: She loved sweet things, and so we put ice cream on the ofrenda.

Panel 3

John: God bless her soul, ma'am.

Panel 4

Woman: God save yours, cowboy.

Panel 5

NO TEXT

PAGE SEVEN

Panel 1

NO TEXT

Panel 2

John: María!

Maria: Juan! My love!

Panel 3

John: Happy birthday, my little skeleton.

Maria: You have a wicked tongue.

(the rest of the page/issue proceeds in English, more or less.)

PAGE EIGHT

Panel 5

John: …, forever in love.

PAGE NINE

Panel 5

Tia: Foolish girl…

PAGE ELEVEN

Panel 5

NARRATION: Love does not respect law, nor obeys king. *(this is a Spanish saying)*

PAGE TWENTY

Panel 3

General: Without meaning.

Panel 4

General: You are all food for the bugs.

Panel 5

Maria: Oh, my heart.

PAGE TWENTY-TWO

Panel 5

I am a man: little do I last
and the night is enormous.
But I look up:
the stars write.
Unknowing I understand:
I too am written,
and at this very moment
someone spells me out.

(This is the Poetry Society's translation of my favorite Octavio Paz poem)

Thanks for reading. And remember:

In **"lightning,"** there's *light*.

—WMP, March 2019